THE WRight Story

Charleston, SC
www.PalmettoPublishing.com

The WRight Story

Second Edition

Paperback ISBN: 978-1-64990-956-5
Hardcover ISBN: 978-1-64990-589-5
eBook ISBN: 978-1-64990-591-8

THE
WRight Story

THE TRUE STORY
of the Wright Brothers'
Contribution to Early Aviation

Joe Bullmer

To My Father,

An Aviator

How He Would Have Loved
To Have Read This Book

Table of Contents

Illustrations

Preface

Most people throughout the developed world take pride in their national identity. Much of that pride is derived from the accomplishments of native sons and daughters throughout history. These accomplishments are usually from the arts, sports, sciences, politics, or warfare. As years go by the feats are recounted in ever more glorious fashion, positive aspects embellished and negative aspects downplayed or forgotten. Many historians, media outlets, and even governments eagerly participate in this enrichment of the images of national heroes. No doubt they believe this is a good thing since it makes people feel proud of the nation of which they are a part, and it gives them ideals to shoot for in their own endeavors.

America has always taken a great deal of pride in the accomplishments of the Wright brothers, Wilbur and Orville. Seemingly from out of nowhere, and against all odds and advice, these two bicycle builders with modest educations from Dayton, Ohio were the first to realize a dream that men had entertained for millennia, to soar through the air like birds, swooping whenever and wherever they pleased. And they accomplished this in a relatively short time with modest means, exhibiting a combination of inspiration, ingenuity, and determination that many Americans like to believe is uniquely American.

As the centennial anniversary of their first powered flight approached near the end of 2003, there were numerous events celebrating the accomplishments of the Wright brothers. Newspaper and magazine articles gave detailed accounts of their work. Television programs enlisted the aid of various experts to explain exactly why and how the Wrights did what they did and what they accomplished. A few groups with widely varying capabilities attempted to duplicate the Wright brother's accomplishment, actually intending to build and fly replicas of their gliders and the 1903 aircraft. Of course, all this created a surge in sales and library checkouts of books on the subject.

But for those truly seeking to gain accurate knowledge of what the Wrights did and why, unfortunately the story recounted in various media had undergone the enrichment process just described. Many of the details recounted simply were not true, and interesting parts of the story had been lost. Authors and spokespersons had bought into the popular legends and were simply wrong.

How could so many supposed experts be wrong? Isn't the true information recorded out there? If they dug deeply enough and really understood what they found, then couldn't they get it right? And then wouldn't they report it? Well yes, of course the information is there. It's not always easy to properly understand, but it is there. One problem is that many "experts" have taken the easy way out and just restated the same old legends. It seems a lot like a form of mob psychology. If all these other "experts" had been saying it, it must be true. Why stick your neck out and contradict them? After all, there's much to be gained by being part of the gang. Information that supports the groupthink is used, and that which doesn't is either misinterpreted to be compatible or ignored completely. And all involved remain comfortable and successful, relying on the innocent naïveté of an unaware audience.

Another problem is that many of these "experts" are not really scientific or engineering experts at all, but rather, they are "aviation historians". As such, they don't have the technical education and experience in aircraft design needed to understand and properly interpret the Wrights' technical material even if they went to it. Their interpretation of a result is mistaken, and therefore they ascribe incorrect reasons or steps leading up to it.

Some authors of books on the Wright brothers have actually taken pride in their total ignorance of the subject of aircraft design. The author of one of the most widely renowned books on the Wrights' work states in his preface that "such professional knowledge [as that of an aeronautical engineer] would tend to be a handicap, even a severe one, in any attempt to evoke the bright simplicity of the brothers' work." Bright simplicity indeed. He goes on to take pride in approaching the story "armed only with a deep interest and a willingness to learn" and a desire to "actually learn with them [the Wright brothers]." Can you imagine trying to accurately describe, in detail, the work of who were, in their time, two of the world's most significant engineers, and taking pride in your total ignorance of the subject? The fact is that only by having a complete understanding of the science involved can one realize what was and wasn't known about flight at the time the Wrights began their work. Only then can one clearly see how and why they were led to their conclusions, right and wrong. And no amount of enthusiasm, superficial qualifications, or previous publications can make up for that.

A few well-qualified true experts have gone to good sources and have done competent reporting on the Wrights. Good examples of this are contained in *A History of Aerodynamics* (reference 41), and *The Airplane, A History of its Technology* (reference 42), both by John D. Anderson Jr., Chair of Aeronautics at the University of Maryland and more recently Curator of Aerodynamics at the Smithsonian. I had not consulted these works when this book was first written, but was pleased to find later that his conclusions regarding the Wrights' wind tunnel results were the same as mine. Another example of extensive technical reporting is reference 3, *The Wright Flyer, An Engineering Perspective*. Unfortunately these works were constrained by the traditional story of the Wrights' work.

It is my objective here to provide, to the best of my ability, an accurate description and thorough analysis of all aspects of the Wrights' records of their work leading to the development of a controllable, powered aircraft. But beyond that, I have tried to place their work within the context of the efforts of the many other aviation researchers who preceded and succeeded them, thereby properly evaluating the significance of their achievements within the perspective of the entire story of the early development of the airplane.

Part of the true story is that the airplane wasn't really "invented" by anyone. More accurately, as with many complicated things, it evolved. True, the Wrights did their work largely in isolation from previous and concurrent developments. And they were the first to achieve a minimal combination of the essential elements comprising an airplane. In the process, they provided key steppingstones on the pathway to manned flight. So if we are to plant a milestone proclaiming the invention of the airplane, it is better that we put it on their work than on anyone else's. We will see, however, that it would be much more accurate to plant it in October 1905 rather than December 1903. We should also realize that almost nothing that the Wrights did was unprecedented. Moreover, some of the aircraft that preceded the Wrights' were superior in certain ways, and those that followed soon used none of the designs the Wrights originated.

There is very little in this book about what people's parents, childhoods, homes, working environments, etc. were like. I prefer to leave such detail for other authors, most of whom are no doubt better than I at verbally painting such landscapes. My purpose here is to set the record straight on the Wrights' work and its influence upon subsequent aviation. Hopefully this book will be considered useful within that limited scope.

Having criticized the qualifications of some previous authors, I had better say something about my own. I have a Master's Degree in Aeronautical Engineering from the University of Michigan along with additional graduate studies in the subject. I subsequently worked in this field for thirty-one years for the U.S. Air Force. A substantial portion of this time was spent as an aircraft performance engineer at Wright-Patterson Air Force Base. During that time I had the rare opportunity to work with some of the top designers at Boeing, North American, General Dynamics, Lockheed, and McDonnell Corporations. I also collaborated with some of the best aircraft performance engineers on the Air Force payroll. The technical areas of greatest interest to me have always been airplane aerodynamics, and stability and control. These areas are the keys to understanding the thoughts and testing of the Wright brothers.

Much of my work has been associated with the field of technical intelligence. In this, I was often examining someone else's airplane designs and trying to determine what they did, why, and what the resulting performance would be. That turned out to be excellent preparation for this book since it is precisely what I had to do with the Wright brothers' designs. Intelligence work is also valuable in developing general investigative and deductive skills, again useful tools for any historical investigation. Fortunately, now being retired from my engineering and technical intelligence career, I finally had the time to do the research necessary for this book, as well as writing and publishing it.

Finally, I'd like to say a few more words about my motivations for writing this book. First, I have no axe to grind with the Wright brothers. I have the utmost respect for their intellects and accomplishments. No matter his or her subject, every undergraduate engineer should study the Wrights' methodical and relentless engineering approach. But I also believe that we have a responsibility to record history accurately. We certainly have no right to expect the Wrights to have done everything perfectly. But we have no obligation to portray everything they did as being perfect either.

It is important that the unvarnished truth be passed on to future genera-
tions. It seems that failure to learn from history often impedes progress, and if
history is incorrectly recorded, progress is even more difficult. In this case, the
story as it is often told gives the impression that, before Wilbur and Orville,
the rest of the world had been sitting around accomplishing little or nothing
in aviation. Then the Wright brothers came along and showed everyone the
right way to do it, saving the world many years, if not decades, without flight.
As this book makes clear, nothing could be further from the truth.

To some readers this may seem like just another revisionist history book.
And revisionist history has sometimes met with scorn in recent years, occasionally well-deserved. But in this case there are a few crucial differences. First,
for conclusions pertaining to the Wrights' work, I have relied heavily upon an
extensive and literal interpretation of the primary subjects' own words. Many
hundreds of direct quotes from the Wright brothers and specific references
to the Wrights' words appear throughout this work. Second, the key conclusions presented concerning their work typically follow from the laws of physics and aerodynamics, as well as mathematics. In these cases there is very little
room for alternative interpretations. And finally, the conclusions presented
are compatible with the photographic record, where there is one. This is important since much of the conventional wisdom is in direct contradiction to
the Wrights' photos. In this author's opinion the record of the Wright brothers' work has been "revised" for a century. This book merely returns to the
original truths.

The Wright brothers built upon the work of highly qualified experimenters whose efforts spanned more than a century preceding them. Indeed, many
of the mistakes the Wrights made can be attributed to their not having paid
more attention to this available body of knowledge. So although the idea of a
grand achievement being the result of isolated inspiration is dramatic, it sets a
goal very rarely achieved. Such accomplishments are more often the culmination of the efforts of many. Each contribution, even each failure, is important
to the accumulation of knowledge. On this scale most of us are capable of
making worthwhile contributions.

Introduction

Most Americans are generally familiar with the accomplishments of the Wright brothers, when and where things happened and basically what occurred. Some can recite many of the widely known details of the Wrights' work leading up to their powered flights. Many had their memories refreshed or learned new information from the numerous programs and articles accompanying the centennial anniversary of the first powered flight. These programs and articles, as well as many long-established books on the subject, contain such facts as the following:

1. At the time the Wrights began their work the general consensus of knowledgeable experts was that manned flight was not possible.

2. The Wrights derived little of value from Professor Langley's experiments at the Smithsonian.

3. The Wrights were the first to make substantial tests with a wind tunnel that was totally of their own design.

4. The Wrights were the first to study wing camber shapes, wing planform shapes, and lift-to-drag ratios.

5. Octave Chanute gave the Wrights very little in the way of ideas or technical support.

6.   With their wind tunnel, the Wrights found major errors in Otto Lilienthal's data, then used their own results to solve their lifting problem caused by his data.

7.   The Wrights were the first to understand the principles of flight.

8.   The Wrights soon found out that airfoils produce lift by creating lowered air pressures above the wing.

9.   They originated the concepts of first testing gliders with tethering lines from the ground and mastering balance and control before adding power.

10. The Wrights were the first to make a thousand glides.

11. From the very beginning the Wrights believed that an airplane would have to be inherently unstable and would require constant balancing by the pilot.

12. The Wrights used the forward-mounted pitch control, or canard, from the very start of their testing.

13. The Wrights retained the canard for better control of level flight.

14. The Wrights were the first to control sideways tilt, or roll, of an aircraft.

15. The Wrights originated the concept of wing warping for lateral control, which greatly facilitated their early success at flight control.

16. The Wrights devised the coordinated rudder in order to make turns.

17. The Wrights could make controlled turns with their 1902 and 1903 aircraft.

18. The Wrights' engine was one of the most powerful for its weight at the time.

19. The Wrights were the first to recognize that propeller blades should be curved like airfoils.

20. They used two propellers to cancel out torque reactions.

21. The Wrights were the first to come up with a mathematical technique for propeller design.

22. The Wrights were the first to take a manned, powered aircraft off from level ground.

23. The 1903 Flyer was capable of taking off from level ground using only its own power.

24. The Wrights were eager to demonstrate their aircraft after its early flights.

25. The Wrights were not preoccupied with huge financial gain and were willing to share their knowledge with others.

26. The U.S. Army thought Wright Flyers were good airplanes but could see no practical uses for them.

27. The Wrights only approached foreign governments for sales after being turned down by the U.S. Army.

28. Wright aircraft designs were copied for many years by builders worldwide.

29. The Wrights' design led the development of aircraft for the first ten years of powered flight.

30. The Wright airplane manufacturing company was the first successful one.

Over the past century, the Wrights have been credited with these accomplishments in countless publications and presentations. Most of these statements have become common knowledge, many being known even by those with only a passing interest in aviation history. Other statements are familiar only to those who have dug into the subject to some depth. But all of these thirty statements have one thing in common. They are all DEAD WRONG! Every one of them. That's right. Read them again. Not one of them is true.

How in the world could this be possible? How could so many things become common knowledge among "experts" as well as laymen and not be correct? In fact, how could the Wrights have managed to fly a powered aircraft in 1903 without at least some of these things having been true? This book answers these questions.

My resolve to do the necessary research and write this book emerged over the course of decades. During my years at Dayton, Ohio, I took advantage of the proximity of the Air Force museum and other sources to occasionally study the development of manned flight, including the work of Dayton's native sons, the Wright brothers. Eventually, a curious realization began to emerge. The more I looked at the writings, sketches, and hardware of the Wrights, the less what I had heard in my earlier years made sense. Things simply couldn't have been the way I had learned in my youth. So I studied the subject over a couple of years until the Wrights' words, logic, procedures, tests, and the science itself all merged together into a consistent logical story. In the process, I developed a whole new appreciation for what the Wrights did right and what the Wrights did wrong. It turns out the true story is not as mellifluous as the traditional one, but in many ways it is much more interesting.

This book does not attempt to give an exhaustive account of aviation events before 1900 or after 1905. Events during these periods are discussed only to the extent that they reveal many of the misconceptions that are prevalent regarding the Wrights' original contributions to the science of early flight. In the first two chapters, we begin in the later part of the eighteenth century at the time when the colonies in America were struggling to become a union. We will see that an amazing amount was known about aerodynamics and the proper configuration of a stable, controllable aircraft by the time the United States had its third president. And we will see that a surprising number of highly qualified people did a great deal of serious work and experiments in the century before the Wrights began their aviation efforts.

Chapters III and IV, which discuss the Wright brothers' work from 1899 through 1905, rely almost exclusively on the Wrights' own words. This was greatly facilitated by Marvin W. McFarland's compilation of *The Papers of Wilbur and Orville Wright* (Reference One). In Chapter III we ride along with the Wrights, generally following the traditional account of the problems they encountered and their thought processes to achieve solutions. But in Chapter IV, we take a more detailed and critical look at their work. Here information that was determined before the Wrights began, information they had available, reveals that in some ways they went or were led astray causing them problems that took years to resolve. Unfortunately, certain attitudes prolonged their difficulties.

Chapter V traces the evolution of aircraft design from the only example at the start of 1906, the Wright Flyer, to the combat-capable, 100+ mile per-hour machines available in many countries at the start of World War I in 1914. Here, the impact of the Wrights' bad design and business decisions become painfully evident. Within just a few years of their singular triumph in December of 1903, the Wrights' designs became obsolete, their own obstinacy and patent battles having stifled their progress. When they finally gave in and attempted to modernize their designs, it was too little, too late.

Next, Chapter VI takes a brief look at some of the major patent battles the Wrights entered into in their effort to cash in on all aspects of aviation throughout the world. The treatment here is merely an overview as there exists sufficient material on these protracted cases to fill volumes. Still, Chapter VI does reveal that, while in some cases the Wrights were certainly entitled to a significant degree of compensation, in most cases their claims of originality were false. Moreover, they attempted to extend their patent coverage to devices they had never even thought of much less tested or used.

Chapter VII has the unlikely title, at least for a book about the Wright brothers, "Secrets, Spies, and Enemies." It addresses the controversial subject of whether or not the Wright brothers were open or secretive about their work and testing. Next, a couple of examples of actual industrial espionage, both on the Wrights and by the Wrights, are presented. The chapter ends with an aspect of the Wrights that is seldom mentioned, their creation of numerous antagonists and enemies. These ran the gamut from former collaborators and those they sued, to family members.

A brief discussion of the birth of the aviation industry is presented in Chapter VIII. Here, we look primarily at the Wrights' efforts to sell their airplanes or licenses to build them, both in the United States and abroad. Next, we see an interesting review of the various designs they developed during the six years their company was in business. The chapter concludes with a brief but fascinating description of the genealogy of the U.S. aircraft industry. It turns out that most of the entire industry can be traced back to just a couple origins.

The final chapter, number IX, is a summary. We come back to the thirty "facts" presented earlier in this introduction and address each of them using the information revealed in previous chapters. Finally, an overview of the previous subject matter is given. A discussion of the strengths and weaknesses of the Wrights' work, decisions, and testing is followed by a summary of their problems with patent battles and design and production competition. The impact of all this on early United States aviation is also readdressed.

Many quotes, facts, and explanations are relevant to more than one subject and reappear from time to time. I believe this occasional redundancy is worthwhile for the completeness of each discussion. Anyone reviewing a particular section of interest will see all quotes, facts, and explanations pertinent to that subject.

In an attempt at full disclosure, I would like to point out that considerable effort has been made to insure that facts presented are accurate. However I have found disagreement among various sources, particularly regarding performance records, production numbers, costs, and dates associated with aviation experiments and events both preceding and succeeding the Wrights. In most cases I have used the data upon which there is most agreement or, alternatively, that which seems most credible within its context. Still, it is likely that one will see differences between some numbers presented here and those appearing in other sources.

References to sources in this book are given in the format (reference number/page number) within the text to which they pertain. The few exceptions to this format, for example citation of a whole chapter or document, are clearly called out. With nearly eight hundred of these, I believe this brief form is most useful yet least disruptive to a comfortable reading of the text.

Discussion of the flight and design of flying machines necessitates using special terms, some of which are peculiar to aviation. Often these terms are defined when they appear in the text. However this is not always done since it would distract from the basic point being made. Consequently I suggest the reader first review the list of terms presented in the Glossary before beginning Chapter I. It might even be a good idea to tab this Glossary for easy reference since the terms keep appearing throughout the text.

I hope you enjoy this unusual description of one of the most technically significant episodes in human history. This information is largely different from what you have seen on this subject in the past. But I can assure you it is true and, I believe, far more interesting.

CHAPTER I
Aviation's First 150 Years: 1740 to 1890

In the Beginning

As stated in the Preface, the purposes of this book are to correct many of the common misconceptions concerning the Wright brothers' work and to properly evaluate its significance within the context of the work that preceded and succeeded theirs. To achieve this I don't believe it is necessary to slog through ancient Greek myths, Chinese kites, da Vinci sketches, or one hundred years of balloon flights. But there are a couple things worth noting before starting. First, although hot air balloons were around for over a century before the Wrights' first airplane, serious productive recorded work on heavier-than-air flying machines actually began within a few years of the first balloon flights. In other words, the inventions of lighter-than-air and heavier-than-air flight were much more concurrent events than most people realize. It's just that the relative complexity and difficulty of airplane development kept it from yielding a usable result for over a century.

Another point worth remembering is the degree of apprehension, and indeed mysticism, associated with humans leaving the ground by any means during these times. Throughout most of the nineteenth century it was considered impossible or at least extremely dangerous. Some even considered it very much against the natural order of things. They felt that going into the sky would be trespassing on the domain of God and, in that sense, irreligious. Balloons often contributed to these fears with their hazards of fire, lack of control, and crash landings. Such was the awe of leaving the ground that many hailed the first balloon crossing of the English Channel in 1875 to be the "feat of the century." The first balloon flight in North America, at Philadelphia in 1793, was witnessed and certified by no less than President George Washington, a testament to the gravity of the undertaking.

It is within this atmosphere of fear, apprehension, skepticism, and ridicule that the development of the airplane had to occur. There were no government programs and, with only a couple exceptions, no government funding. Although a few experimenters found private sponsors, most had to provide their own funds. And few with that kind of money had the requisite skills and motivation. Of these, fewer still were willing to risk their lives for such a wild quest. So the pool of qualified experimenters was small indeed. Moreover, communication and sharing of information across distances and languages was nowhere near as easy as it is today. Considering all this, the amount of discovery and progress made during his period is nothing short of amazing.

The Marquis de Bacqueville is often cited to have made the first attempt at winged flight. However all he did was to strap four panels to his arms and legs and jump off of a balcony overlooking the Seine in Paris. He of course went nearly straight down, breaking his legs on a moored barge and contributed nothing to the science of flight. (41/80) Unfortunately other "jumpers" followed his example, also contributing nothing, but usually with even more grave results.

However something scientifically meaningful did indeed occur during the 1740s. An English ballistician named Benjamin Robins invented a device that was to become the primary laboratory tool of aviation researchers for over a century. It was descriptively named the whirling arm. It consisted of a vertical rotating shaft, around which was wrapped a cord for many turns. The chord was run horizontally to a pulley and then down to a weight. Across the top of the shaft was mounted a long, counterbalanced horizontal arm. When the weight was released, the chord was pulled, and thus the arm would whirl around and around. The item to be tested was fastened to the long end of the arm. Using various weights, counterbalances, and a timing system, the lift and drag of test surfaces could be measured.(7/37)

The device had a few inherent weaknesses. One had to take great care to achieve anything near steady state measurements. But even more troubling, since the test section traveled fairly rapidly in a circular path, it was always passing through its own wake of disturbed air. Still, at least first order comparative measurements could be made in a somewhat controlled environment. This device was used for aviation research by many experimenters until late in the nineteenth century when steam, and later gas engines and electric motors, made the wind tunnel possible. Being a ballistician, Robins also made open range tests of projectiles, varying their shapes, weights, and firing loads. By 1746 he had correctly calculated the speed of sound to be 1100 feet per second.(7/37) But he found something even more interesting about the speed of sound. By firing projectiles of known weight into a suspended target of known weight, he was able, through simple momentum calculations, to accurately determine the velocity of the projectile at impact. Varying the distance of the target from the muzzle yielded a velocity, and thus deceleration, profile for the projectile. This indicated that no matter what the projectile's size, weight, or shape, above the same certain speed the rate of deceleration was dramatically higher. And what's more, this certain speed coincided exactly with the speed of sound. So Robins concluded that above the speed of sound the drag of air on moving projectiles increases greatly. This was the discovery of what was to become known as the "sound barrier." It was to be another two hundred years before a vehicle could be built that could carry a man through this speed barrier that was first described by Benjamin Robins in 1746.

Obviously, the whirling arm made no contribution to Robins' discovery of the sound barrier. But within a decade of its invention it led to what could be considered the most significant aerodynamic discovery ever made. During the 1750s John Smeaton and his associate, a Mr. Rouse, used a whirling arm to test the lift and drag of a number of different flat, curved, and angled sections. In this manner they determined that a cambered, or slightly arched, airfoil section gave much more lift and less drag (a better lift-to-drag ratio) than any kind of flat section. This data was formally presented to the Royal Society in 1759(7/39) It is not known whether Smeaton and Rouse noticed that the cambered section was also easier to control in pitch than were flat sections. And it is also not known whether anyone present at that meeting of the Royal Society had any idea that they were learning about a concept, the cambered wing, which would still be key to efficient, controlled flight 250 years later.

The first well-documented creation of a heavier-than-air flying machine occurred in Paris in 1784. Mssrs. Launoy and Bienvenu demonstrated a mechanical helicopter of sorts to the French Academy of Sciences at their meeting on April 28th that year. The small device had two rotors, each consisting of four feathers stuck into a central cork. These were at opposite ends of a shaft. A springy bow had the shaft running through a hole in its center and was fastened to one of the corks. A string was fastened to one end of the bow, wound around the shaft, and then fastened to the other end of the bow. When the rotors were twisted repeatedly in opposite directions, the string was wound around the shaft bending the bow. When released, the bow would unwind the string, spinning the rotors in opposite directions. Thus, a lifting force was generated.(8/49,50)

Although the device worked, it was only capable of uncontrolled, vertical flight. Still, it was claimed to be able to reach a high ceiling. The inventors were said to have visions of building a large enough version of the device for them to fly in. Fortunately for them, there is no indication that this ever came to pass. Eleven years later, however, their invention would inspire an English gentleman who went on to become the most significant figure in the creation of heavier-than-air flight.

Sir George Cayley, the Father of Aviation

The first well-organized, documented, and protracted research and testing leading toward the advent of airplanes as we know them today was done by a well-born and well-educated English nobleman named George Cayley. His privately tutored education included a solid background in mathematics and what we would today call physics.(23/40) An extensive, detailed study of the man and his accomplishments can be found in *Sir George Cayley—Inventor of the Airplane* by Lawrence Pritchard.

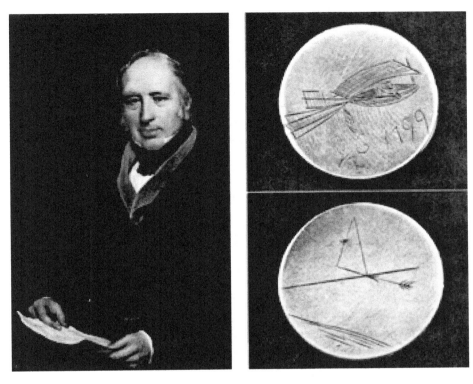

Figure 1: Sir George Cayley, His First Glider and Resolution of Forces

During his lifetime, Cayley accomplished significant research in a number of scientific disciplines. He knew well what he was doing, and he was amazingly persistent in his search for understanding. The knowledge he amassed about the science of aviation by the time Thomas Jefferson became President of the United States is nothing short of astounding.

Cayley became interested in the possibility of manned flight in his youth, and in 1795, when he was twenty-two, he built a replica of Launoy and Bienvenu's counter-rotating bird feather helicopter. This was, and remained for many years, the only man-made device capable of propelling itself into the air under its own power. Also, as had many before him, Cayley studied the flight of birds. But he was evidently the very first to apply the concept of balanced forces to their motion. He resolved these forces into lift, which counteracted gravity, as well as some form of propulsive force or thrust to overcome the drag of air on the body. This resolution of the forces involved represented quite a conceptual leap since birds, bats, and bugs all counteract both gravity and drag with what is apparently one motion. It is even more amazing when one realizes that at this time, 1799, it was not at all clear where any source of thrust would come from.

No doubt Cayley fully realized the significance of this concept. Rather than merely committing it to something as perishable as paper, he had a diagram of the force concept engraved onto a silver disk.(7/22) On the other side of the disk an engraving was made of something equally profound and unprecedented. It was a depiction of his first concept of a heavier-than-air flying machine. It had a low-aspect-ratio cambered wing, a separate boat-like fuselage, and both horizontal and vertical adjustable tail surfaces for stability and control that were to be positioned by the pilot or "aerial navigator." All this in 1799!

By 1804 Cayley had constructed a whirling-arm aerodynamic test apparatus.(6/Nov.1809 issue) He used this device and also glide tests of models to investigate the effects of various cambers, aspect ratios, speeds, and angles of attack.(23/41) He was even aware of the phenomenon of flow separation and some of its effects on the center of pressure (lift), although his concept of movement of the center of pressure was apparently somewhat limited. (7/237) During this time Cayley was experimenting with both tethered and free-flying glider models. His models had cambered wings and horizontal and vertical tail surfaces, some of which were adjustable between flights.(23/44) The largest of these models were 4 feet in length.

Sir George made one of his more important aerodynamic discoveries not with the whirling arm or his gliders, but with parachute-like devices with which he was also experimenting. These were simple paper cones with weights at their vertexes.(7/235) He quickly discovered that if the cones were dropped point (and weight) down, they would simply sink to the ground in a steady fashion. But if they were dropped with the point (or weight) above, they would quickly flip around to the point-down orientation and then float steadily down. He soon realized why this was so. If the point-down cone tilted toward one side, the lower side presented more surface to the airflow and thus was pushed back harder. Similarly, the other side had less drag and could be swung back forward into the airflow. Thus the cones dropped point-down were self-stabilizing. For similar reasons, those dropped point-up were unstable and would flip around to the stable position.

That was all simple enough. But Sir George Cayley's inspiration was to extend this concept to his gliders, thus becoming the inventor of wing dihedral. Dihedral is the shaping of a wing into a very shallow V as viewed from the front or back rather than having it flat or straight across from tip to tip. When a wing with dihedral is tilted toward one side or the other, the lower wing becomes more horizontal while the raised wing gets even more slanted. As a consequence, the lower wing develops more vertical lift than the higher one, rolling the wing, and thus the whole aircraft, back toward level. (See Figure 2A) In this fashion, a wing with dihedral stabilizes an aircraft in roll much like the downward pointing cones were stabilized

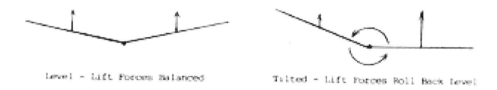

Level - Lift Forces Balanced   Tilted - Lift Forces Roll Back Level

Figure 2A: Dihedral Effect

Figure 2B: Skidding Turn with Dihedral

It turns out Cayley's dihedral has another valuable effect. It automatically banks an aircraft into a turn without any active roll control. If a vertical tail or rudder is deflected toward one side to turn the aircraft into a slide or skid toward the other side, the leading wing will have more air blowing on its bottom surface, while the trailing wing will have more air blowing on its top. (Actually, due to spanwise flows over the canted wings, the leading wing will have a higher effective angle of attack due to inward flow, while the trailing wing with outward flow will have its angle of attack reduced.) As a result, the wings, and thus the whole aircraft, will then roll away from the initial skid and enter into a banked turn. (See Figure 2B) Most all airplanes can be turned this way. In fact, some large gliding birds can be seen to turn this way. Throughout the nineteenth century these straight-line stabilizing and automatic turn banking properties of dihedral were considered by most aviation experiment-ers to be sufficient control of aircraft roll. That's why so few experimented with active aerodynamic control of aircraft roll during that period.

By 1804 Cayley had built and flown gliding models that were stable in all three axes of flight. They could be directionally controlled in pitch (nose up or down) and yaw (nose right or left), and they would stay level or bank into turns automatically. In fact, these models were far more stable and, in that sense, had better flying qualities than the Wright brothers' planes a century later. They had to be. There was nobody in them to make the constant correc-tions required to keep a Wright Flyer in the air.

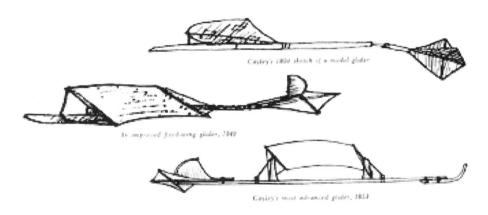

Cayley's 1804 sketch of a model glider

An improved free-wing glider, 1849

Cayley's most advanced glider, 1853

Figure 3: Some of Cayley's Model Gliders

His notes reveal that by 1804 Cayley had also built his first glider that was "large enough for aerial navigation," in other words, large enough to carry a man.(7/45, 237, 238) It had a wing area of 300 square feet, the same size later determined by both Lilienthal and the Wrights to be required for manned flight. Yet the machine itself weighed only 56 pounds. It also had tail-mounted stabilizers and control surfaces. Although of sufficient size, Cayley intended the aircraft to be flown unmanned, at least until stability and control were verified. There is no record that this machine was ever intentionally flown with a pilot onboard. However Cayley noted that on several occasions the young assistant launching it held on and was lifted up and carried along in the air for "several yards" thus possibly becoming the first person to leave the ground with a heavier-than-air device.

By 1809 Cayley had compiled an incredibly comprehensive body of knowledge concerning the aerodynamics of flight. But the problem of devising a mode of propulsion was still an enigma to him although he was well aware that some form of power would be necessary to maintain flight.(7/36)

Actually, this awareness was an example of Cayley's scientific approach putting his thinking nearly a century ahead of many that came after him. In the 1880s and 1890s, many experimenters were unaware of localized thermal updrafts, the upward flow of warmer lighter air. They thought that the commonly observed prolonged soaring of birds without flapping their wings proved that there was some mysterious general updraft of the atmosphere as a whole. Some believed that flight without power could be maintained indefinitely if only this updraft could be harnessed. Cayley knew better in 1809. He just couldn't find a source of the needed power.

Nonetheless, he had done so much work and amassed so much knowledge that he felt it was time to officially document his results by publishing them. So near the end of 1809 he wrote a series of articles that were published in three issues of *Nicholson's Journal of Natural Philosophy, Chemistry, and the Arts.* (6/all) (What was termed natural philosophy at that time we now call physics.) These three articles, particularly the first published in November of 1809, constitute by far the greatest single quantum leap in knowledge of the physics of flight that has ever been published.

In the first, Cayley said of flight, "The whole problem is confined within these limits—to make a surface support a given weight by the application of power to the resistance of air". This was, in effect, a verbal summary of the force diagram he had engraved into the silver disk a decade earlier, and is exactly the basis of flight today, two centuries later. Elsewhere he stated "I am apt to think that the more concave the wing, to a certain extent, the more it gives support, and that for slow flights a long thin wing is necessary, whereas for short quick flights a short broad wing is better adapted." He verified Sir Isaac Newton's discovery that drag varies with the square of airspeed, and added that lift also varies with the square of speed and directly with the angle of attack of the wing. Today, two centuries later, we can say that all these statements are absolutely correct.

Also in the first article he presented the concept of dihedral for maintaining lateral stability. He went on to declare that the use of both vertical and horizontal tail surfaces is absolutely essential to stable controlled flight. (7/48) As he put it, an aircraft needs an "up-and-down" rudder in addition to a "side-to-side" rudder. But even more amazing, he described the use of a forward center of gravity along with a negatively loaded horizontal tail surface for maintaining longitudinal stability. The center of gravity was to be placed ahead of the center of lift and drag (the center of pressure) in order to provide basic directional stability just as an arrow has. The horizontal tail must then be angled so as to push downward to balance out the weight with the lift acting between them. Then if the aircraft pointed slightly up, the tail would push down less and weight could pull the nose back down. Similarly, if the aircraft pointed slightly nose down, the more negatively angled tail would push down more, prying the nose back up. He was even aware of the additional penalty in drag associated with the use of this trim system.(7/47) This system of longitudinal stability is often called the Penaud system by those unaware that the scheme was discovered by Cayley seventy years earlier.

In the 1809 article, Cayley discussed the phenomena of flow separation and the existence of a downwash field behind the wing. But unfortunately, he misinterpreted the relationships of these to the production of lift by a cambered surface. He mentioned "a slight vacuity immediately behind the point of separation," but he was talking about the area "under the anterior edge of the surface." In other words, he was picturing a thin, cambered surface, concave side down, at a small positive angle to the airflow (positive angle of attack). He claimed the airflow under the front edge would continue straight back, leaving a region of trapped, or stagnated, air just behind and below the leading edge of the thin wing. He envisioned this trapped air being eventually pushed down by the aft portion of the wing's bottom surface, creating the lift observed on a cambered wing at a small angle of attack. It could be argued that a slight portion of the lift on a thin cambered wing may be generated this way, but certainly the vast majority of lift is generated by the lower pressure on the upper surface. And Cayley made no mention of the upper surface or the flow over it. Some have assumed that his use of the term "slight vacuity" referred to the flow above the wing, but it clearly did not.

It seems a shame that such a great mind could come so close to getting everything perfectly correct but miss the physical phenomenon that is the essence of flight. Still, considering the knowledge and equipment available at the time, it is remarkable that he was able to determine the effects of camber, aspect ratio, and such, much less their precise causes. And besides, we will find out that the Wright brothers, a century later, had no better understanding of how cambered wings generate lift.

George Cayley did extensive drag studies and evolved what he believed to be the ideal streamlined minimum drag shape, as he called it, the "teardrop" shape. He actually derived this shape by beginning with the shape of a dolphin's body.(7/66A) Astoundingly, Cayley's minimum drag shape is, along its entire length, within a couple percent in width of the ideal shape determined by the great aerodynamicist Theodore Von Karman 150 years later.(7/53,54)

Cayley also discussed the use of wheels on aircraft. This might not seem like such a conceptual triumph, but remember, it took the Wrights ten years to accept this feature, a delay that contributed significantly to their downfall as aircraft producers as we shall see. But the important point here is that Cayley invented a whole new kind of wheel for use on airplanes. He invented the cross-tension spoked wheel.(7/139-141) His studies of bird skeletons had impressed him with the need to optimize the strength-to-weight ratio of all parts of a successful aircraft's structure.(7/50-52) Solid disk or wooden-spoked wheels that would be up to the job seemed to be prohibitively heavy, so he came up with the idea of using wire spokes since the wires could support the load in tension and thus could be made quite thin and light. But the problem was lateral stability. What would keep such wheels from folding up sideways? Cayley found that by widening the hub and cross lacing the spokes back and forth slightly outside of the plane of the wheel, a great deal of lateral strength could be obtained with no increase in weight. (Later it was found that by somewhat leading and trailing these spokes around the hub, driving and braking forces could also be safely transmitted.) Not only were Cayley's cross-tension spoked wheels used on both aircraft and cars in their early decades, but their light weight and minimal gyroscopic effects made the invention of the bicycle possible.

In his second article, published in February 1810, he discussed the locations of the center of pressure on lifting surfaces. Here, he described the center of pressure as moving aft along the surface with increasing angle of attack (increasing inclination of the surface from the direction of motion). Considering the detail and accuracy of most of his other statements, this is somewhat perplexing. Within the normal operating angles of cambered wings, the center of pressure actually moves forward with increasing angle of attack due to earlier acceleration of the airflow and increasing separation on the aft upper surface. Perhaps Cayley was referring to a surface at very high angles or maybe to a flat plate as opposed to a cambered section. But again, it becomes apparent that his understanding of the relationships of flow to pressures around a cambered wing was just not sufficient to properly explain everything. Another example of this is in his third article, where he stated that a wing develops its lift "on the principle of the inclined plane."

It was also in the third article in *Nicholson's Journal* appearing in March 1810 that Cayley presented his calculations giving the values of reasonable wing loadings that one could expect to achieve. He showed that to lift an average man, an aircraft would have to have a wing area of at least 300 square feet. As with nearly all of his conclusions, this value generally holds good to this day.

Near the end of this third article Cayley provided a diagram and discussion of the twin rotor helicopter-like device previously mentioned. He suggested scaling up the device and replacing the feathers with much larger flat surfaces. He could certainly see that the feathers were cambered, as are all feathers involved in lifting. Considering this and the previous discussion, it becomes apparent that Cayley really did think that both the flat and cambered wing sections functioned simply by their lower surfaces being pushed up as they encountered air at a slight positive angle. The only difference would be that the positively cambered section (concave downward) would do so only over its aft portion. One wonders how he might have rationalized the cambered section producing more lift with less drag than a flat plate. Apparently, he never recorded his thoughts on this specific subject.

In all three articles, he addressed the problem of propulsion. In the first he presented his conclusion that steam engines were simply too heavy to power an airplane. Even after another century of refinement this was to prove essentially correct. He looked longingly at the possibilities of using some sort of internal gas combustion engine. But, as he pointed out, in 1809 experiments on exploding gasses in contained cylinders were just getting under way. A reliable internal combustion engine was a long way off.

The only other option, if man were to attempt powered flight in the early nineteenth century, was to supply the power himself. Cayley addressed this in all three articles in *Nicholson's Journal*, the second and third being mostly devoted to various schemes of flapping wings and calculating the forces involved. Even in the first article he compared man's upper body strength to

that of birds and found it to be woefully inadequate. Still, with no other alternative, he discussed various wing flapping schemes that could employ a
man's entire body strength. He obviously had little faith in these schemes and
was purposefully vague as to how well they might work. Most of the second
and third articles address the various forces required and generated by beating wings. He said nothing to indicate that he had confidence that any man-
powered scheme would be practical.

Looking back at all this, it is apparent that by 1809 Sir George Cayley had
everything he needed to make a manned, controlled aircraft except power.
Indeed, he asserted this himself.(7/48) He was aware of the need for cambered wings even though he didn't really understand how they worked. He
knew both horizontal and vertical tail surfaces were needed for stability, and
that the aircraft's motion in all three axes must be controlled, and how to do it.
He was also well aware of the need for lightness in all components, and how to
shape them for minimum drag. He even knew how to balance and trim the aircraft for natural stability. All this nearly one hundred years before the Wrights!

Most accounts of Caley's work skip ahead to the 1840s, leaving the impression that for thirty years he had abandoned thoughts and efforts concerning manned flight. It's true that he did diversify his efforts somewhat, working
on lighter-than-air flight and even entering into politics and being elected to
Parliament in 1832.(7/81) But his first love was still technology. He put some
of his effort into developing practical versions of and uses for the caterpil-
lar tread which he invented in 1810.(7/146) He went so far as to propose
mounting artillery on a treaded vehicle for use in warfare, thus presaging self-
propelled artillery. In fact, with some defensive armor against opposing artillery, which many artillery pieces already had, it can be said that this idea
constituted the first concept of a tank—yet another example of Cayley thinking one hundred years ahead of everyone else.

But Cayley did not abandon the dream of powered, manned flight during these thirty years. On the contrary, he knew that all he needed to have a
complete airplane was a source of rotary power. In *Nicholson's Journal* he had
predicted that an internal combustion engine, when developed, would probably be the source of that power.(7/69) So he devoted most of his technical
research during these years toward creating a successful internal gas engine
with which to power an aircraft, among other things.(7/87) During the nineteenth century the creation of a gas engine was actually considered the most
important engineering problem to be solved. Along with Cayley, this problem

consumed the efforts of Robert Sterling, W. J. M. Rankine, J. P. Joule, and Lord Kelvin himself. Indeed, some of Cayley's research proved to be valuable groundwork for the efforts of these men.(7/56,86,87)

Cayley realized that any successful early gas engine would have marginal power at best. It would therefore behoove him to have the capability to accurately determine the power that would be required of any such machine. He soon realized that by flying an unpowered machine of known weight using the wind while it was tied to the ground, the angles of the tethering lines could be used to determine the drag, and therefore the thrust required for the vehicle to maintain level flight.(7/44,45) Unfortunately, Cayley never came close enough to creating a successful gas engine to exploit this technique. However, it was used successfully by the Wright brothers to size their 1903 engine nearly a century later. But unfortunately for the Wrights, they did not allow for the extra power needed for takeoff and climb, a requirement of which Cayley was well aware.(7/49)

In the 1840s Sir George once again turned his attention to the creation of aircraft. By then, another Englishman, William Samuel Henson, was proposing a design for a steam- powered "Aerial Carriage" with a huge, externally-braced single wing. Henson presented this design in the April 1, 1843 issue of *Mechanics Magazine*. In the following issue Cayley pointed out that steam propulsion would not work out. He also expressed grave doubts that Henson's huge single wing would have sufficient strength. Instead, Cayley proposed a "three-decker" triplane as a solution to the structural problem he foresaw. (23/48-50) Such was Cayley's stature that Henson immediately requested both technical and financial help from him. Cayley declined, and there is no indication that Henson's machine was ever built.

A few years later Cayley did press ahead with the construction of a triplane. The vehicle was very much like his 1799 configuration but with three stacked, low aspect ratio wings. It was reported that a ten-year-old apprentice flew for "several yards" in the vehicle on at least one occasion. That same year, 1849, the year of the California gold rush, Cayley was again flying unmanned gliders. One of his sketches is of a 14-foot-long cambered wing monoplane glider with adjustable horizontal and vertical tails. The sketch shows the horizontal tail surface set at a negative angle of incidence allowing a center of gravity ahead of the aerodynamic center, his scheme for inherent longitudinal stability. (7/198-20)

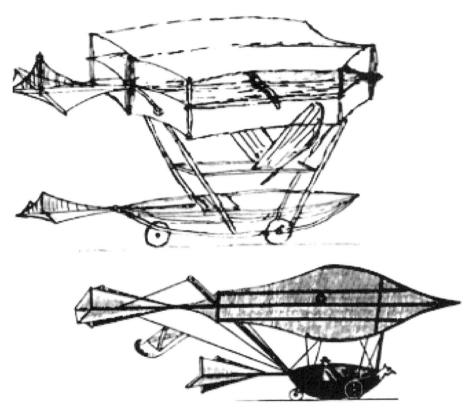

Figure 4: Cayley's 1849 and 1852 Manned Gliders

Within a few more years Cayley had completed construction of his largest aircraft. It was similar to his other "manned" designs, but this time he employed a single large low aspect ratio wing of 500 square feet. (7/203,204) The glider had an empty weight of 300 pounds. It again featured tail stabilizers and controls. It was recorded that a number of his assistants made "hops" of dozens of yards in the machine, gliding down a hill and across a small valley. The culmination of this test series seems to have been a flight by Sir George's coachman in 1853. Cayley's granddaughter was there and claimed that the horrified gentleman was airborne for "hundreds of yards." Perhaps Sir George was much more of a scientist than a psychologist and hadn't sufficiently prepared his coachman for the experience. After the flight the terrified man is said to have emphatically given notice to Sir George that he wanted nothing further to do with his aviation experiments.

This flight by his coachman appears to have been the pinnacle of Sir George Cayley's quest for manned flight. However, his greatest achievement was undoubtedly the breadth and depth of his self-taught understanding of the aerodynamics of flight. No one since has come close to equaling this body of original, accurate research. In 1912 Orville Wright wrote, "Sir George Cayley was a remarkable man. He knew more of the principles of aerodynamics than any of his predecessors and as much as any that followed him up to the end of the century. His published work is remarkably free of error."

In 1973 and again in 1985, an exact replica of Cayley's 1853 "man carrying" glider was successfully flown at the original site, Brompton Dale, for Television and I-Max films by Derek Piggott. Allan McWirter and Richard Branson of Virgin Atlantic Airways flew the replica again in 2003. So there is little doubt that with a suitable source of rotational power, Cayley would have invented the manned, controlled, powered airplane at least half a century before it actually happened. The implications of this upon the technological and geopolitical history of the world are beyond comprehension. But no doubt Cayley's incredible mind was even pondering these implications. He wrote that, with enough power, as many as "500 men" could be carried by a "vessel in aerial navigation." Once more it took over a century, but eventually the world caught up to the mind of Sir George Cayley.

What's in a Name?

Before we continue looking at the early experiments in aviation, it might be interesting to think about how the flying machine came to be called the "airplane" in the English language. Certainly, even into the 1900s, there were many different words or terms used to characterize a flying vehicle. "Flying machine," "aerial craft," "aerial navigation vessel," "air vehicle" and "aircraft" were some of the most common terms in the English language. But it is clear that by the end of his work, Sir George Cayley had also coined the term "aeroplane" as being a brief yet descriptive name for his heavier-than-air fixed-wing flying devices. This clearly differentiated these gliding machines from balloons or helicopter-like devices. It was also thought that this name gave an indication as to how the devices worked. Remember that Cayley, and for that matter, almost all up to and including the Wright brothers,thought that even a cambered or curved wing functioned under "the principle of the inclined plane." By this it is meant that a surface pushed on at an angle will tend to move sideways as well as in the direction of the push. Although the use of the term "flying machine" persisted into the World War I era and slightly beyond, by the 1920s "airplane" had become the commonly used term. Of course "aircraft" still survives, but technically it includes balloons, blimps, dirigibles, gliders, helicopters, and anything else that can get a person off of the ground, in addition to airplanes.

The interesting point is that the term is wrong. Airplane wings are not planes. They are all curved or cambered surfaces. And they do not work as planes. Rather than push air down with their lower surfaces, they achieve most of their lift from air drawn down from above. This fact, however, was not clearly documented until Horatio Phillips patented his airfoils in 1884. He explained, "a partial vacuum [was] created over a portion of the upper surface" of his cambered wings. Even then this fact was not widely known in aviation circles for another twenty-five years. They knew that to be efficient and controllable, wings had to be cambered, but except for a few people they did not know why. By the time the true mechanism of cambered wing lift became common knowledge, the term airplane had been accepted.

Is this a big deal? Certainly not, and I don't mean to make it one. It's just amusing to see why the subject of this book and of so much else written and spoken around the world has, for nearly two centuries, been called by an erroneous name in the English language (and originally in French also). We will find in Chapter IV that the Wright brothers, like nearly all of their predecessors, would have argued that "airplane" is a perfectly accurate description of how their machines worked. However we will also find in Chapter II that at least three of the early experimenters knew full well how cambered wings work, and believed that the name given to winged vehicles was misleading. One even proposed changing it.

The Early Gliders

The latter half of the nineteenth century saw widespread experimentation with powered and unpowered heavier-than-air flying machines. But there was an unfortunate dichotomy that was characteristic of the work done during this period. It seems that those who concentrated on gliding without the added complication of engines made the most advances in aerodynamics, while most experimenters having the savvy or means to create or obtain good engines were either more inept or less concerned with aerodynamics and flight control. As this dichotomy continued into the 1890s, the achieve-ment of manned, powered flight had to wait for the dawn of the next century.

In the 1850s a Frenchman, Jean-Marie LeBris, became interested in emu-lating bird flight. His approach was to build a machine that copied the shape of birds as closely as possible. He studied the albatross in particular since it seemed to him that this bird flew with ease. In his *Progress in Flying Machines* Octave Chanute recounts that LeBris dissected an albatross and held its wing in the wind to determine its lifting properties. This led him to believe that the wing not only lifted up but that it was capable, at the proper angles, to pull it-self forward into the wind. He therefore erroneously concluded that sustained flight without power was possible if the wing were shaped and angled just right.(8/105)

Figure 5: LeBris' Glider

By 1857 LeBris had constructed a gliding vehicle that did indeed look very much like an albatross. In fact, he called it his "artificial bird." It had a 50-foot wingspan and was to be launched from a horse-drawn cart. (8/105-110) It also featured cambered, tapered wings and a moveable cruciform tail for stability and control. Although the first glide was a success, on the second attempt LeBris crashed heavily and broke a leg. Some years later he built an-other similar machine. It too showed initial success, but soon it also crashed. Although not seriously hurt, this time LeBris threw in the towel.(17/95)

It has been recorded that on at least one of these machines LeBris had incorporated the feature of wing warping, the ability to bend a wing in the direction of the airflow in order to alter its lift or drag for turns. (20/67) This appears to be the first use of this form of control and, along with the moveable cruciform tail, the first attempt at control over all three directions of motion. LeBris obtained a patent for his wing warping in 1857.(18/69)

In 1870 Alphonse Penaud began building flying models that were assisted in their launch phase by pusher propellers powered by large, twisted rubber bands. Some of his models had adjustable horizontal and vertical aft-mounted controls and incorporated dihedral in the main wing for lateral stability. For longitudinal stability he used the Cayley method of a forward center of gravity offset by a negatively-loaded horizontal tail.(8/117) Although generally small (less than 2 feet long), his models were stable and capable of flying over 100 feet. He also built a small helicopter based upon the Launoy/ Bienvenu - Cayley concept, but powered by a twisted rubber band. This device is said to have become quite popular and was duplicated by the thousands by French toy makers.(23/55) In 1876 he patented his detailed design for the first flying wing.(18/87) Evidently Penaud was a prime example of becoming too wrapped up in one's work. It is claimed he committed suicide when he learned the French Aeronautical Society was not going to build his man-carrying design.

Figure 6: Penaud's Models

In 1868 an English experimenter, Mathew Boulton, patented wing flaps that moved in opposite directions to control an aircraft in roll.(21/134) These "ailerons" are precisely the way aircraft roll has been controlled to this very day. Unfortunately, Boulton's other ideas on aerodynamics and control were not as successful. He apparently never made any manned flights.

Just three years after Boulton was granted his patent, Charles Renard began flying multi-winged gliders in France. Although these gliders were unmanned, Renard incorporated separate little "winglets" on either side of the fuselage which were automatically activated by a pendulum for roll control.(16/16,18/88) So already we have three examples of successful schemes for roll control over thirty years before the Wrights developed and patented theirs. Not only that, while the Wrights' method of bending or warping the wing itself would soon die out, the method pioneered by Boulton of using separate moveable surfaces would go on to become the standard method of roll control used throughout the world.

Another Frenchman by the name of Goupil followed LeBris' example of building a vehicle that faithfully duplicated the shapes of birds. In 1883, with this machine, he also discovered the advantages of cambered wings. In fact, he was so impressed with the phenomenal lifting power of his glider that he turned to studying various camber shapes in detail. (8/155,158)

By the 1880s word of the aviation experiments being conducted in France and England had reached the United States. Some Americans attempted to duplicate, to the best of their knowledge, what was being done in Europe. One, William Beeson, even took out a U.S. patent on his design for a glider. (8/163,164) It had cambered wings and both horizontal and vertical tail surfaces that could be controlled by the pilot in flight. Evidently the vehicle, if it was ever actually completed, was not flown with any degree of success.

This brings up an interesting point. During the nineteenth century a number of patents were issued both in the United States and Europe for flying machines that were never built or never demonstrated to work. It seems this was common practice in other areas as well as in aviation. Some of these devices could not possibly have worked. So one needs to be careful if searching patents to determine what experimentation was done. In some cases the work amounted to nothing more than words and sketches of unfeasible schemes.

The most significant glider development during the 1880s in the United States was done by a professor from California named John Montgomery. He began by building modest gliders and making hops of up to 600 feet in length. At first he didn't even use curved wings, but soon he became a firm believer in the use of camber. In 1885 Professor Montgomery actually conceived of a circulatory flow all around a cambered wing section to which he attributed its creation of lift. This was 17 years before Kutta and Jukowski showed it to be true theoretically. He eventually adopted tandem wing designs similar to the layout used later by Professor Langley of the Smithsonian on his "aerodromes." Montgomery concentrated much of his effort on controllability, and he ultimately became quite successful at it. Although his second glider had hinged ailerons, he also developed a form of wing warping that varied wing camber for lateral control.(20/48-51)

These are just a few examples of literally dozens of experimenters who constructed gliding vehicles or attempted to construct them during this time period. Many of these were just small-scale models, and some were unsuccessful. The most successful, built during the 1890s, will be discussed in the next chapter. But even the examples here show that numerous vehicles were being designed and flown throughout the latter half of the nineteenth century. And some of these machines were both reasonably stable and somewhat controllable in flight.

The Search for Power

The steam engine had been around in various forms since the late eighteenth century, but many aviation experimenters, from Cayley on, recognized that it would be almost impossible to achieve the power-to-weight ratios from steam engines that were required for flight. Although Etienne Lenoir is usually credited with having invented the gasoline engine in 1860, any such engine approaching the power and reliability needed for a flying machine, or for that matter a ground conveyance, was decades away. So, in desperation and with no alternative, some went ahead and tried to power their machines with steam anyway.

In 1842 worldwide notoriety was given to beautiful sketches of a magnificent steam-powered aircraft design published by an English contemporary of Sir George Cayley, Mr. William Henson.(3/4) Henson's vision was a cambered single-winged (monoplane) aircraft with two pusher propellers and tail-mounted control surfaces. The design shows some awareness of the aerodynamic properties necessary for flight and looks as though it might have been possible for it to achieve stability in flight; however it probably would have been too heavy for its wings to support. In other words, it would have had a hopelessly high wing loading.

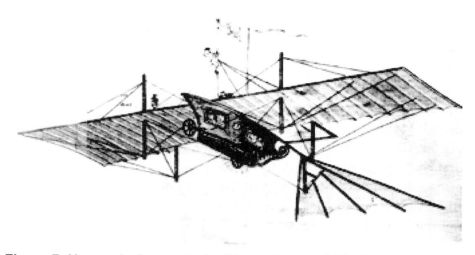

Figure 7: Henson's Concept of a Steam-Powered Airplane

As previously discussed, Henson approached Cayley for advice and financial support. Cayley declined the financial support but did offer advice. (7/188-199) He reiterated his judgment that steam power would, in all likelihood, be too heavy for flight. He also suggested that Henson abandon the hopelessly flimsy monoplane design and adopt a configuration with three stacked wings (a triplane) in order to achieve the requisite lift while retaining structural integrity. Henson never found the needed backing and, as a consequence, never built the aircraft. However, as was common practice at the time, he was granted a patent for the design in the United Kingdom in 1843.

Figure 8A: Stringfellow's Engine

Figure 8B: Stringfellow's Airplane

Although Henson gave up, his assistant, John Stringfellow, never did. In spite of Cayley's advice, Stringfellow pressed on with the development of a lightweight steam engine. By 1848 he had created a small engine weighing only 14 pounds, which was capable of developing one horsepower. This was an astounding power-to-weight ratio for the time, but far too small an engine to power a manned aircraft. Although some historians maintain that Stringfellow's aircraft did barely manage some short hops, it was the opinion of Octave Chanute that neither of his aircraft actually flew on their own. (20/21) Years later, in 1875, another Englishman, Thomas May, built steam-powered models that also barely flew.

In France, Victor Tatin built and flew powered models during the 1870s. He used compressed air to power tractor (front-mounted) propellers. (20/32,33) Both the wings and the propeller blades were cambered, and he used a negatively set horizontal tail for longitudinal stability.(8/141) Tatin was not just a cut-and-try experimenter. He did extensive calculations of the work, energy, and power required by his models, as well as analyses of wing loadings, lift-to-drag ratios, engine efficiencies, etc.(8/141) As a result, Tatin's models were quite successful flyers, reaching speeds of near 20 miles per hour and being fairly stable in flight.

Figure 9A: Tatin's Powered Model

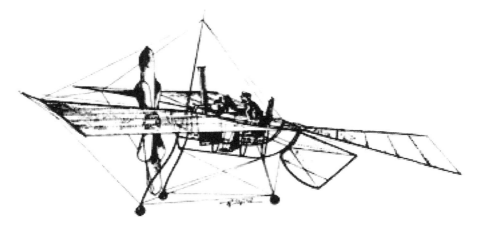

Figure 9B: duTemple's Airplane

Figure 9C: Mozhaiskie's Airplane

Others were actually making short manned hops with steam-powered aircraft. The Frenchman Felix duTemple, having built steam-powered models, built one large enough to lift a man in 1874.(3/4,5) It had both horizontal and vertical tail surfaces, and it featured wheeled tricycle landing gear. However, with a weird peaked camber shape and forward sweep to the wings, the aircraft's lifting capability and stability seem very questionable. Perhaps duTemple was fortunate that all it ever did were short low hops.

A Russian, Alexander Mozhaiski, also built a steam-powered monoplane large enough to carry a man.(3/5) Although it appears to have had little or no real camber to the wings, this may be the fault of the illustrator who, no doubt, had no appreciation of subtle curves on the machine. It was otherwise what was becoming a fairly standard configuration: a monoplane with tail-mounted control and stabilizing surfaces, dihedral in the wings, and pusher props. He also tried adding a tractor propeller to the mix. Like duTemple's craft, Mozhaiski's could make relatively short hops, but only if launched on an inclined runway.

These experimenters were by far not the only ones questing after powered flight. In the first forty-eight pages of his *Progress in Flying Machines*(8/1-48), Octave Chanute presented the work of dozens of experimenters who tried both man-powered and mechanically powered flapping wings, all to no avail. He also discussed the work of dozens of those who designed vehicles with horizontal lifting screws or propellers. Some looked a lot like helicopters, but others looked amazingly like daVinci's airscrew concept of four hundred years earlier. Nevertheless, both the pace of work and the frequency of partial successes were beginning to pick up, and by the end of the period it was becoming evident that the advent of manned powered flight was not too far off.

The Basic Researchers

Not all of those interested in the phenomenon of flight had the resources to build full-sized test vehicles, or the courage to try to fly in them. During the last half of the nineteenth century a number of people were doing basic scientific research into the aerodynamics of flight. They used analytical techniques and laboratory test equipment such as whirling arms, wind tunnels, or fleets of small-scale flying models. Many were astute enough to build upon the groundwork laid by Sir George Cayley. By the 1860s so much was going on in England that it became evident that those involved in aviation research and experimentation were in need of a specially dedicated forum for the exchange of ideas and information. So in 1866 the Aeronautical Society of Great Britain was formed(3/6) Its purposes were "to foster the development of heavier-than-air flight through meetings for the exchange of ideas and results, and to publish and distribute these in papers and journals." All this serious interest and dedication at the time of, or just after, the United States Civil War! And remember, we're talking about airplane flight here, not balloons.

The Aeronautical Society was an immediate success. In 1868 they held an exhibition in London. Experimenters from all over the world came to participate. In fact, there were a total of seventy-eight exhibitors at this event. (8/161) Obviously, even at that early date, those who were truly knowledgeable believed that manned powered flight was not only possible but likely in the near future. A similar organization, the French Society of Aerial Navigation, was formed in 1871.(18/86) Its goals were similar to those of the society in England.

At the first meeting of the Aeronautical Society of Great Britain in 1866, one of its members, Francis Wenham, presented a paper discussing his research on wing center of pressure locations, lift-to-drag ratios, and aspect ratios.(37/82-113) Wenham pointed out that most of the lift of a wing was developed on the forward portion. He also discussed the structural advantages of multiple superimposed wing configurations such as biplanes and triplanes. (8/100-103) (Although Cayley had used the triplane configuration some years earlier, at this time his work was still not widely known.) Wenham was the first to propose that an airplane should turn by generating more lift on one side and tilting, and presented a design which featured triangular winglets for banking the aircraft into turns.(37/105) Identical devices were used decades later by Glenn Curtiss for the same purpose.

Although Wenham did not discuss cambered wing profiles anywhere in this paper, he presented two drawings of a glider which clearly indicated that it had cambered wings.(37/105) Later on he became well aware of the value of curved or cambered wings. He also mentioned John Smeaton's work on the drag of flat plates perpendicular to an airflow, and said that Smeaton measured a drag of twelve pounds on a one square foot plate at fifteen miles per hour. Interestingly, this yields a value for Smeaton's coefficient exactly half way between that used by Otto Lilienthal and what the Wrights considered to be the correct value.(37/87) The significance of this will be seen in our fourth chapter.

However what can be considered to be his most significant, and certainly most unique, contribution to early aerodynamics appears in the very first paragraph of his 1866 paper. He stated the two primary properties of air, namely its "weight and inertia", and its "cohesion", or what we would call its viscosity.(37/82) These are indeed the two major characteristics that influence all airflows. In fact 17 years later Osbourne Reynolds achieved immortality by expressing these as a dimensionless ratio that indicates the degree of dominance of one of these two characteristics over the other. Early experimenters and "inventors" of the airplane did not concern themselves with such details. In fact most all, including the Wrights, seemed to take no notice of the viscous property of air, which is the key to the generation of lift. Nonetheless, his ratio, Reynolds Number, has become the most important parameter in aerodynamics, and is often used to determine the basic nature of an airflow, whether it is laminar (with viscosity dominating) or turbulent (with inertia dominating).

Wenham concluded his paper by strongly advocating that any experimenter gets a firm grounding in gliding flight before attempting powered flights. Over thirty years later Octave Chanute passed on this advice to the Wright brothers, who heeded it to their advantage. Wenham's work comprised the bulk of the first studies published by the Society. He and another member, John Browning, then returned to laboratory work proceeding to build the world's first recorded wind tunnel in 1871.(16/16) Their tunnel was powered by a steam engine.

In 1879 Richard Hart, also a member of the Aeronautical Society, published drawings of wing warping schemes and of moveable segments of the aft outer portions of wings which are now called by their French name of ailerons (little wings).(3/5) I find this work extremely interesting as Hart envisioned these devices not primarily as controls to roll an aircraft but more as devices to create differential drag and thus yaw the vehicle into a turn. With large deflections at the very low flight speeds then involved, that is their primary effect. In fact, this yawing effect is precisely what the Wright brothers found so baffling as soon as they attempted free flight. We will see in later chapters how much trouble this caused the Wrights, and how it drove many of their design corrections. We will also see that Hart's work and that by the Frenchman LeBris who was previously discussed, led Octave Chanute to testify under oath that "there is no question that the fundamental principle underlying wing warping was well-known before the Wrights incorporated it in their machine". (1/980)

Another member of the British Aeronautical Society, Horatio Phillips, built the second recorded wind tunnel. With it he developed a number of amazingly sophisticated airfoils.(3/5,6) Some of these were cambered and had incredibly modern shapes. A couple were of substantial thickness, with mild camber maximized at points from a third to half way back from the wing's leading edge (30% to 50% chord), and had nearly flat bottoms. Phillips patented at least seven of his wing section shapes in 1884 and 1891. His best section shapes were beyond anything the Wrights used and must have been capable of previously unheard-of lift-to-drag ratios.

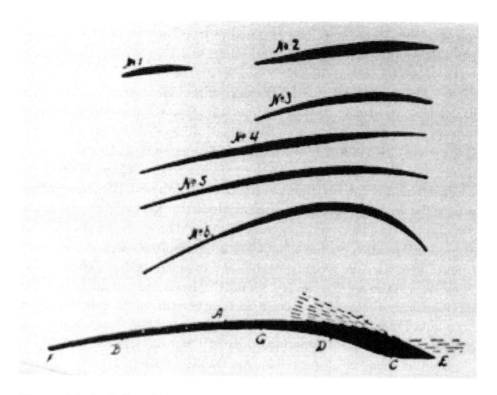

Figure 10: Airfoils of Horatio Phillips

The depth of Phillip's research and understanding is evident in his 1884 patent. In it, he states that his airfoils were designed in such a way as to "deflect upward the current of air coming into contact with the forward edges when under motion, so as to cause a partial vacuum over a portion of the upper surface of the blade, thus aiding the air below to support the weight". (8/166) Phillips published this same information in the August 14, 1885 issue of *London Engineering*. How did he deduce this? His tunnel was unique in the nineteenth century in that he used steam in the flow over the test sections to actually see the flow around them. A similar technique using streams of smoke or other observables is still used to this day.

Evidently his theory of lift was not quite correct in that, rather than seeing the lowered pressure on the top of the airfoil as the result of accelerated but attached flow (a la Bernoulli), it seems he envisioned it as a result of the flow being deflected upward from the upper surface, thus leaving a void of low pressure. Still, here is a far more correct understanding of cambered wing lift than the Wrights had, and it was published a decade and a half before they began.

In fact, in 1892 Freidrick W. Lanchester in England produced a theoretical derivation of the cambered wing section based solely upon mathematics and airflow considerations, yet another example of someone understanding the mechanism of lift on a cambered wing years before the Wrights began their work.(10/13)

Phillips couldn't resist the temptation to try to build and fly aircraft. (16/18) But, amazingly, for someone with his understanding of aerodynamics, his early creations could be considered monstrosities. They had dozens of vertically superimposed cambered slats for wings, sometimes arranged in two or three tandem arrays.(8/171) One of the Venetian blind-like contraptions did manage to lift a 72-pound dummy for brief periods, but it was unable to lift Phillips himself. Nevertheless, he kept at it over the years, eventually adopting more conventional configurations. By 1907 he was flying in a powered airplane of his own design.

It is evident that the wind tunnel was a reasonably well-documented aerodynamic research tool well before the turn of the twentieth century. In 1896 an M.I.T. student, Albert Wells, made the first recorded wind tunnel in the United States. In fact, by the time the Wrights were developing their tunnel Dr. Albert Zahm had a relatively huge wind tunnel operating at Catholic University in Washington, D.C. It had a six-by-six-foot test section 40 feet long. Even though it was driven by a suction fan, it still employed screens and vanes to insure uniform straight flow. It also had a built-in manometer to accurately monitor flow speed.(41/297) Although the tunnels of Phillips and Zahm were, in some ways, more sophisticated than the Wrights', they didn't produce anything like the volume of practical design data that the Wrights did with their tunnel.

During this period there were many other researchers active throughout the world. I discussed these few examples because of their relevance to claims often made concerning the work of the Wright brothers. In this regard there is one other area of early research that must be mentioned. That is the development of the cambered, twisted propeller.

It is "common knowledge" that the Wrights were the first to realize that the propeller should properly be considered to be a spinning airfoil lifting itself (and the aircraft) forward and that it should be designed accordingly. However, according to Chanute's "Progress in flying Machines", this basic concept was presented at an Aeronautical Society of Great Britain exposition in 1885. At this event Sidney Hollands reported on his experiments, indicating that a cambered, twisted, and tapered propeller was more efficient than flat or flat twisted ones.(8/162,163) This information was also published in the Society's journal. Then, in the period near the turn of the twentieth century, at least three designers of ship's propellers developed mathematical procedures for the design of air propellers as a series of cambered sections.(3/79) These men were Friedrick Lanchester in England, Stephan Drzeweicke in France, and Kudwig Prandtl in Germany.

There is one other amazing development that took place during this period. It falls under the category of designs that were patented but not built, but it also definitely falls into the category of "nothing new under the sun." In 1862 Luther Crowell designed what we would today call a convertiplane, and he obtained a U.S. patent for it. The vehicle was to have large propellers rotating in a horizontal plane for takeoff and landing. After lift-off these props, along with a small pair of wings, were to gradually transition 90 degrees in order to pull the aircraft forward. The process was to be reversed for landing. (8/111) Today we would immediately recognize this as the general configuration of the V-22 Osprey, the first production aircraft of this type in the world. The Osprey is just now entering into deployment, nearly a century and a half after Crowell first conceived of it during the time of the American Civil War.

Pictures of only a few of the most important early aviation vehicles appear in this book. However for those interested in seeing more, reference 18, *Aviation, Th e Pioneer Years* contains an amazing collection of photos of nearly all of the 19th and early 20th century air vehicles.

In this chapter we have already seen a surprising amount of progress toward the development of a flying machine by 1890. By that time there were aviation societies in both England and France which held expos involving many dozens of participants. But the last decade of the nineteenth century saw such a flurry of activity in both the United States and Europe that it is worthy of an entir chapter itself.

CHAPTER II

So Many, So Close: 1890 to the Wright Brothers

The Status in 1890

By 1890 essentially all the basic ingredients of flight had been discovered except for lightweight power. Cambered wings of reasonable aspect ratio, horizontal and vertical tail surfaces and wing dihedral for stability in all three axes of rotation, as well as methods of control in all three axes were known. Trimming with a forward center of gravity and a negatively set horizontal tail had been used. Unfortunately, the best solutions for these aerodynamic challenges were often lost within a myriad of poor or impossibly bad ideas causing many experimenters to still launch off into unfruitful directions.

Similarly, in the structural area, although many had found ways to build sufficiently light yet strong vehicles, others built machines that demanded way too much from their fragile wings and potential powerplants. And lastly, in the 1890s those experimenting with power were still pretty much stuck with the steam engine. Internal gas combustion was just reaching the point where a multi-cylinder engine of sufficient power, smoothness, and reliability was becoming a possibility. And those struggling with these problems were not the same people as those tackling the aviation challenge. So, although it can be said that all the components of a successful powered, controlled airplane were known, they were not all known by the same person or team. Only after the turn of the century would one team, the Wright brothers, put together a combination of solutions that would allow success. Even so, as might be expected, not all of their solutions were the best either.

A Long Hop?

The 1890s saw the last two great attempts at manned, steam-powered flight. The first was by a Frenchman, Clemet Ader. In 1890 He designed and built a 1,000-pound monoplane with a 46-foot wingspan(23/61) This aircraft, which he patented, included wing warping and apparently featured a propeller with cambered sections.(18/100) This vehicle was capable of lifting itself and Ader from level ground. Witnesses confirmed that on October 9, 1890 Ader flew the craft a distance of 165 feet. It only rose to an altitude of a couple of feet, thus remaining well within ground effect (see Appendix 2), but witnesses testified under oath that it did not touch the ground during this entire distance. The length of this flight was not limited by the performance of the aircraft, but rather by the length of the field.(18/101)

Figure 11A: Ader's First Airplane

Figure 11B: Ader's Third Airplane

The following year Ader constructed a second aircraft which incorporated a number of modifications that he felt would improve its performance over his first craft. It turned out that the second vehicle was not as capable as his first, its tests being curtailed after a brief unsuccessful period. Nevertheless, Ader somehow convinced the French War Ministry that he could build an aircraft capable of reliably delivering a load of bombs. The Ministry gave him a grant of nearly a million francs to do just that.

Accounts differ as to whether the third Ader aircraft ever actually left the ground. Some say the vehicle made a few hops before it crashed.(20/35) Others maintain that it crashed on takeoff during its first flight test.(23/62) Some sources claim it actually flew 1,500 feet.(33/117) But historians seem united on a few points. In spite of the fairly well confirmed flight on October 9, 1890, his claims of success were often somewhat inflated. Moreover, his vehicles were essentially uncontrollable and thus incapable of sustained flight. Still, Clemet Ader can claim at least one undisputed aviation first: he was the first to obtain a government grant well into six figures.

History records one other interesting story concerning Ader. It seems Octave Chanute, the great American glider builder and mentor of the Wright brothers, tried to buy an Ader aircraft for the Wright brothers to fly.(20/35) Not being able to actually provide one, Ader declined the offer. It's no doubt just as well since the Wrights would have wanted nothing to do with his or anybody else's machines anyway.

Speaking of Chanute, in his 1894 compilation *Progress in Flying Machines* he devoted more space to an Australian aviation inventor, Lawrence Hargrave, than to any other. Although not attempting to fly himself, Hargrave experimented with a tremendously varied assortment of kites and powered models during the early 1890s. Some of his models used propellers, while others used flapping wings. His power sources included rubber bands and small steam and gas combustion engines. Hargrave's notes show an amazingly detailed understanding and approach. He experimented with many different camber and planform shapes and determined the locations and movements of their centers of pressure. His models regularly flew quite successfully. Although many of Hargrave's successes went unwitnessed, Chanute, who was no easy sell, was of the opinion that Hargrave deserved success more than any other. (8/218-233)

Another Frenchman worth mentioning here is Pierre Mouillard. He made unpowered but manned glides during the 1890s. His significant achievement was the use of wing warping.(1/980) Although, as we have seen, he was far from the first to use this feature, he was the most successful with it for his time, actually making controlled turns. By 1896 he was making numerous glides in a machine with warping tips. Believing he was the first to perfect the feature, and being aware of a number of other aviators using or planning to use it, he proceeded to patent it in France. But he went further to protect his find. With Chanute's help he obtained a patent for wing warping in the United States in 1897.

Figure 12: Mouillard's Last Airplane

A Maxim(um) Effort

By far the most spectacular attempt at steam-powered, manned flight was made during the 1890s by an American, Hiram Maxim. He was an educated engineer and a world-renowned inventor, having been the chief engineer of the first U.S. electric company and the inventor of the machine gun. His machine gun patents had brought him a fortune. In aviation experimentation he found a way to unload a substantial chunk of his wealth.

Having established permanent residency in England, Maxim joined the Aeronautical Society and soon became its most active member. Consequently, his aviation experiments conducted at Baldwin's Park in Kent were well observed (8/133). He began by using a whirling arm device to test flat and cambered sections at various angles of attack. By 1890 he was experimenting with a huge apparatus consisting of two flat-bladed propellers which were used to drive large planes around a 200-foot circular track at various angles of attack for lift measurements.(8/133) Eventually he rejected this device in favor of a wind tunnel. His tunnel was capable of generating airspeeds up to ninety miles per hour. (38/50) In it he tested numerous cambered wing sections, some with nearly flat bottom surfaces.(38/39) Maxim came to believe that Phillips was wrong about there being a void of air above cambered surfaces and that lift was primarily due to the air being directed downward at the rear of a cambered wing.(38/40,41) Although true from a momentum standpoint, Maxim's explanation does not explain how the substance of the machine was actually held aloft.

Maxim then began construction of his signature aviation machine, a monster of a vehicle weighing over 7,000 pounds.(23/66-71) This behemoth was nearly 200 feet long and had a wingspan of about 110 feet. Its total wing area was 5,500 square feet.(8/234) Nothing approaching this scale had ever been attempted before, and the vehicle had gained world attention before it was even tested.

But why did Maxim make his vehicle so large? Sure, he had a lot of money, but he was a serious and capable engineer, not a showman. He wouldn't have built such a monster without a technical reason. It appears that the reason was what many would call efficiencies of scale, or what some modern aeronautical engineers call trade studies (short for tradeoff studies). As many, going back a century to Cayley had determined, steam engines had the problem of being heavy for the amount of power they put out. He considered using "oil" engines, but any of sufficient size would have been prohibitively expensive. (38/47,48) Maxim decided that if a vehicle were made large enough, the power output of steam engines would increase faster than their weight, allowing a ratio that would be sufficient for flight.(38/28) Accordingly, he developed two 180-horsepower steam engines that were each light enough for him to lift.(23/68) Maxim claimed these to be the most efficient steam engines yet, and believed that if steam pressure were increased from 200 to 300 psi he could get as much as 300 horsepower from them. This was, he believed, enough power to drive his vehicle to 100 miles per hour.(8/235)

However these numbers were very misleading. The 180-pound weight was really just the engine itself; the cylinder, piston, crank, and their housing, and associated valving. But in addition to this a steam engine requires a large supply of water or a condenser, a boiler, and all the associated piping and fuel for the boiler. There is no doubt that accounting for all this equipment raised the propulsion weight substantially.

The engines were to swing two slightly cambered 18-foot propellers that delivered over 2,000 pounds of thrust.(38/42,43) This in itself must have been an awesome sight for the time. And these propellers were to perform double duty; they were to propel the aircraft and turn it. Maxim intended to turn the aircraft by differential throttling, speeding up one engine and pro- peller and/or slowing down the other.(8/239) This was neither the first or last time an inventor attempted turning by using differential prop speeds. The scheme was never to prove manageable, but Maxim's machine never got that far anyway.

The aircraft's main wings appeared to be perfectly flat. Indeed Maxim himself referred to them as "planes." Why he would have used flat surfaces is perplexing. He supposedly tested both flat and cambered sections with his whirling arm and wind tunnel, and certainly was aware of the advantages of cambered wings. No doubt his wings developed some curvature under air loads. He did incorporate substantial dihedral in the wings' outer panels in order to achieve lateral stability.

Figure 13: Maxim's Airplane

His writings show that Maxim gave quite a bit of thought to both stability and control.(8/235) Not only had he addressed lateral (roll) control with dihedral and directional (yaw) control with differential props, but he came up with a completely unprecedented scheme for longitudinal (pitch) control. He used both fore and aft horizontal surfaces which were to be controlled by an automatic system using a gyroscope for horizontal reference.(38/51) This appears to have been the first attempt at an autopilot, and was apparently the first use of a controllable canard for pitch. It would have been interesting to see how well this pitch control system would have worked in the air. It seems Maxim's primary reason for using both fore and aft horizontal control surfaces was that he had visions of the machine losing power in the air and being able to float down flat with a symmetrical planform.(38/46)

The machine did not have a vertical aerodynamic stabilizer. The differential props were to be the only method of directional stability. This would have, no doubt, been an even more interesting feature to observe. Apparently Maxim himself had his doubts about this system of control, saying that if the differential props proved inadequate he would add a vertical tail rudder.(38/45)

Maxim was not about to let such a huge investment in time, effort, and money run free before the machine was reasonably proven and they had learned how to operate it. So he constrained the vehicle's motion by building a dual set of tracks nearly 1/2 mile long in Baldwin's Park. The first half of the tracks had constraining rails. The constraints were spaced so that the vehicle could actually lift off the lower tracks a few inches before it's motion was constrained.(8/234)

The machine carried a crew of three on most test runs.(8/245) Maxim felt this many people were necessary to operate the vehicle, observe its characteristics, and observe and record any test equipment onboard. In view of the overall gross weight, crew weight was certainly not a problem. The tests involved increasing the vehicle's speed in increments and observing the overall lift generated as well as the fore and aft (pitch) balance of the machine.(8/238, 239) By early 1893 they had recorded lifts of 2,800 pounds on the rear wheels and 2,500 pounds on the front.(8/244) In these early tests only the aft stabilizer was connected to the automatic pitch control. The fixed canard was to be activated only if pitch control proved inadequate without it.(8/239)

Finally, on July 31, 1894 Maxim upped the ante once more on steam pressure and started another run. The monster took off down the track like never before. When it got up to about 35 miles per hour it lifted off of the supporting tracks and pulled up against the restraining rails. In fact it lifted so hard that the rollers broke the restraining rails loose. For a brief moment Maxim and his crew were airborne. They had just about enough time to become aware that they were off the ground (covering a distance of over 300 feet in about seven seconds) when a piece of the upper track, pried up by the roller strut, stuck through one of the wildly spinning 18-foot propellers. There immediately followed a rapid degradation in the flying ability of the machine. Maxim cut power and he and his crew got out with their lives.

Having decided that his 7,000-pound machine actually was unnecessarily large, Maxim had plans for another appreciably smaller one.(38/44) However he decided that he had squandered enough money for one lifetime. By then he had spent about $100,000 on aviation experiments without really having success.(10/34) He had run out of the funds he had allotted for aviation experimentation, and there was little prospect of private or government funding in the foreseeable future.(38/52-55 &10/88) It's probably just as well as there is no evidence that the monster could have been controlled once it got into the air. Most revealing was a statement Maxim made shortly after the fatal crash of the English glider Percy Pilcher. Maxim admitted that he never really trusted his ability to balance his grand machine if it had ever actually flown. (10/43) Aside from that, numerous minor failures indicated that the machine would not have held together structurally under flight loads. Nevertheless,

Maxim's impressive machine and its tests achieved great notoriety around the world, further convincing many that manned powered flight was not far away.

The Great Gliders: Otto Lilienthal

During the final decade of the nineteenth century three men, a German, a Scotsman, and an American, took the science of gliding to new heights….and distances. They made thousands of glides, developing unprecedented levels of expertise. Ultimately, as had others before, two of them paid for their obsessions with their lives.

The German, Otto Lilienthal, began his lifelong obsession with flight in 1861 in Pomerania when he was thirteen years old. His first naïve attempts at flight were with separate wings strapped to his arms.(39/76) Although Otto's brother Gustav has usually gone unrecognized, probably because he didn't actually fly, he was an active participant in their investigations from the very start.(9/XIV) Otto studied science and engineering at the Potsdam Technical School, graduating with the highest grades ever achieved there.(9/XIII) He went on to do graduate studies at the Berlin Technical Academy. After a number of successful employments, he established his own engineering and manufacturing company in 1880. (39/75,76) The company specialized in marine signaling devices and steam engines, and Otto generated enough income from his innovations that eventually he was in a position to spend much of his time pursuing the study of flight.(9/XXI)

Lilienthal studied bird flight extensively, particularly the large storks so prevalent in many areas of Germany. He actually raised baby storks so that he could observe the steps involved in their learning how to fly.(39/85) Soon he became convinced that birds were so perfectly adapted for flight that any attempt at flight that did not closely follow their example would be doomed to failure.(9/23) He noticed the changes in the incidence angle of birds' wings between the down stroke and upstroke as had Francis Wenham, and like Wenham he correctly concluded that this allowed their wings to generate lift even on the upstroke.(9/96-98,37/103) As Cayley had done before him, Lilienthal resolved the dynamics of flight to the four basic forces of lift, drag, weight, and thrust. He even calculated the energy and work involved in bird flight.(9/7-23) Eventually he was able to show analytically that man was not capable of sustaining this level of effort.(9/121)

Otto recommended dissecting the problem of flight into its basic components and attacking each element in sequence.(38/7) Interestingly, he pointed out the similarity of maintaining the balance of a flying machine to learning to ride a bicycle.(38/10) His point was that experiments as well as theory were necessary to conquer the problem of flight.(39/78) If they were aware of this it must have given additional encouragement to the Wright brothers. However he went on to caution that "One single blast of wind can destroy the apparatus and even the life of the person flying."(38/9) This advice also stuck with the Wrights, although they may have gotten it through Octave Chanute.

Lilienthal largely mitigated the danger of flying his vehicles by first making small models of each one and test flying these. He made dozens of these models and in this manner was able to optimize the shapes of his vehicles, maximizing lift and minimizing drag. He strongly recommended this approach to others, pointing out that models could be built and tested quicker, cheaper, easier, and more safely.(39/96,97) Although the Wrights took a similar approach in 1899 with their five-foot kite model, it is unlikely this was a result of Lilienthal's advice. They flew the kite only a couple weeks after becoming aware of the existence of the material containing his recommendation.

In the 1860s Lilienthal constructed a whirling arm test device seven meters in diameter. With it he could test sections up to one square meter in size at speeds up to twelve meters per second.(9/46/64) From 1866 through 1889, using this and other large test machines, he studied various camber shapes, their lift and lift-to-drag ratios, as well as the effects of different aspect ratios and the planform or overall layout of wings.(9/43,60,61,65,66) He found that higher aspect ratios gave better lift-to-drag ratios and correctly ascribed this to reduced wing tip losses. He recommended using aspect ratios between five and eight and used the exact middle of this range, 6½, to generate extensive lift and drag data.(8/203) To further minimize tip losses, he determined that wings should be tapered toward the tips.(9/60,61) This appears to be the first time anyone understood the aerodynamic impact of wing planform to this degree. Although others before had used tapered wings, they were either mimicking birds or were doing it for structural reasons. The prescience of this discovery can be appreciated when one realizes that it was not taken advantage of by aircraft designers until three decades later and remains a basic tenet of aircraft design to this day.

Lilienthal became the most prominent member of the German Society for the Advancement of Aerial Navigation, and in 1889 published a book summarizing his 23 years of research. The book, Reference 9 for this work, is titled *Birdflight as the Basis of Aviation* and of course was written in German. Both it and his 1893 report to the German Society made it quite clear that wing camber is the secret to successful flight and that efforts to fly using flat surfaces were foolhardy.(8/279) In fact, he chided the French Society for failing to investigate cambered wings. Lilienthal determined that most birds have about seven to eight percent of camber in their wings, and while this was reasonable for small wings, larger ones, such as those to carry a man, should have more like five percent camber.(9/64 & 8/289,290) He also noted that at higher speeds wings with lower cambers perform better.(9/68)

In his book he went even further explaining why the smooth arc was the best shape for wings. He believed that the cambered wing section was better because it turned the air down gradually and thus didn't produce the turbulence that a flat plate did. Not only that, he believed that gradually redirecting the air above the cambered wing into a curved path created centrifugal forces within the air that tended to pull it away from the wings upper surface. Thus the air above the wing was stretched or thinned creating a "suction" on the top surface of the wing, and this played a major role in generating lift.(9/59) He pointed out that a proper wing section should be "more curved toward the leading edge and get straighter toward the back", and that the resulting suction on the upper surface was stronger on the forward portion of the wing, another correct deduction.(9/24,59) However, he cautioned against making the camber too steep near the leading edge of the wing.(8/290) Although he often referred to his camber profiles as parabolic, he also frequently added that they were very near semi-circular in shape(39/92)

Interestingly, Otto developed an acoustic method to aid in analyzing the efficiency of various cambers and aspect ratios. He would carefully listen to the sound of the wake from the wing models whirling by on his test machine and could hear differences from one to another due to the amount of turbulence they generated. He found this correlated very well with actual force measurements. For example, he noted that lower aspect ratio sections, which produced lower lift-to-drag ratios, made a "stronger rushing sound" than did better performing higher aspect ratio wing models. (9/59,60) He also noted that the planforms with tapered tips produced less sound indicating lower turbulence and losses.

Lilienthal's findings on wing planforms, aspect ratios, and section camber generally hold good to this day. Indeed, we will find out that most of the trouble that the Wrights had in 1900 and 1901 in generating lift and control-ling pitch were because of too steep camber at the leading edges of their other-wise nearly flat wings—this in spite of the fact that they often claimed to have patterned their early wing shapes after Lilienthal's.

In his 1889 book *Bird Flight as a Basis of Aviation* Lilienthal included the major results of his 23 years of research up to that point. He made graphs of lift and drag coefficient (or force) ratios for a number of cambered wing pro-files at angles of attack from less than zero up to ninety degrees. These ratios are referenced to the drag on the same test sections held perpendicular to the flow. The document also reiterated Newton's findings that drag was propor-tional to the cross-sectional area of an object and to the square of its velocity through the air.(9/12)

It seems curious that a successful experimenter like Lilienthal would have made thousands of glides and never have used a powerplant. This is partic-ularly perplexing since he had a successful major business centered on the manufacture of steam driven devices. The main reason he didn't try a pow-ered craft early in his flying was that he believed control was such an impor-tant problem that it must be solved first.(8/282) But not only that, before he began flying he became convinced that a source of power or thrust was not absolutely necessary in order to sustain flight most of the time. His ground test devices had led him to believe that natural wind had some kind of innate upward current in it and, if this were properly exploited, level flight could be maintained most of the time without using power.(9/122,123) He conclud-ed that "The design of practical flying machines is not absolutely dependent upon the provision of powerful and light motors".(9/123) Lilienthal was not the first experimenter to conclude this, which raises the question: what could their reasoning possibly have been?

Aviators from Cayley to Lilienthal had all experienced the fact that their gliders needed to descend in flight in calm air in order to maintain momen-tum. This was obvious ever since Cayley explicitly showed the dynamic forces involved in flight. Some portion of gravity's pull was needed for a glider to overcome aerodynamic drag, and this could only be accomplished by point-ing the aircraft's nose down and descending. But in nature there seemed to be an exception to this. Soaring birds appeared to be capable of flying end-lessly without expending the energy of flapping their wings. Of course today we know that they do this by using thermal updrafts or updrafts created by topography or large buildings. However, in the 1800s Lilienthal and most all of the others were unaware of localized updrafts, either thermal or otherwise. (9/90,91) Certainly they had seen that soaring birds tended to fly in circles. But on occasion these birds seemed to glide off straight and still not lose altitude. So apparently circling had nothing to do with it. It seemed they just circled because they liked to stay in groups or had spotted something interesting on the ground.

So what could explain the apparent contradiction between gliders that needed to descend in calm air and endlessly soaring birds? Well, certainly if one took the air in which a glider (or bird) was flying and gave it a slight upward motion, the vehicle (or creature) wouldn't have to come down. The upward moving air would compensate for the downward glide and the object would maintain altitude. To many that seemed the only possible explanation. Natural winds must generally have an upward motion in addition to their horizontal movement. In fact Lilienthal's test equipment, some of it over thirty feet high, convinced him that normal breezes had an upward component of three to four degrees.(9/78-81) Lilienthal, among others, concluded that if a glider were designed and flown just right it should be capable of being flown indefinitely without power.(9/111) The wind may not blow all the time, but in most places there was some at least 90% of the time. So evidently unpowered extended flight should be possible at most locations nearly all the time.

Of course, this seems ludicrous to us today. Why would all winds blow slightly up? And if they did, how is the air at ground level replaced? And where is it going? Is it piling up at some high altitude? It must be coming down somewhere. But to nineteenth century aviators this theory had a great deal of appeal. The only powerplants available, steam engines, were heavy and expensive. It would have been wonderful if they were unnecessary.

Lilienthal remained convinced of this theory, at least until he had flown for a while.(9/122,123) He referred to this as "the peculiar lifting effects of wind".(9/128) Otto's only explanation for this was that much higher speeds of the winds at high altitude must draw the lower air up. In his *Progress in Flying Machines* Octave Chanute entertained the idea enough to present a mathematical analysis showing that winds would have to have an upward component of about 4 miles per hour in order to hold a glider like Lilienthal's up in level flight.(8/209,210)

The funny thing is that at the locations at which many of these early experimenters flew, they did have updrafts. They launched off of hills into the wind, and of course the wind was diverted up the slope of the hill, so their prophesy was fulfilled. They were in updrafts and could glide level, at least for a short time.

It is yet more testimony to the wisdom of Sir George Cayley that he never fell for this misconception. He was aware from the very start, in the 1790s, that some form of propulsion would be necessary for sustained flight. He never wavered from this conclusion. In fact, he spent more years trying to develop a propulsion system than he did an airframe. In notes published in the 1896 edition of *The Aeronautical Annual* Hiram Maxim pointed out that soaring birds did so by circling in localized thermal updrafts, rising columns of warm air.(38/31-35) So there were a few nonbelievers in the idea of endless unpowered flight.

Although for a long time Lilienthal bought into the lifting wind theory, eventually, after he was actually flying, he moderated his position somewhat, accepting the fact that although "the occurrence of calms is rare", "light motors" really would be necessary for prolonged flight.(8/289 & 9/121) Finally in 1894 the Lilienthals did try a powered aircraft. They used a small steam engine but, since Otto was convinced that emulating birds was the way to go, they had it rigged up to flap the model's wings rather than drive a propeller.(8/289) On its initial trial the device failed structurally, beating itself to pieces.(9/XIX) Although he had initially thought flapping wings to be more efficient, Otto later changed his mind and allowed as how propellers might be better.(9/30 & 8/290) Unfortunately he never got around to trying a propeller before his untimely death.

Between 1891 and 1896 the Lilienthals produced a total of sixteen gliders. The thirteenth and fourteenth of these, flown in the fall of 1895, were biplanes. His machines weighed from 33 to 55 pounds and achieved glide ratios of eight to one in calm air.(38/10) They were all of the hang glider type with the pilot hanging vertically by his armpits. Otto was aware of the advantage of the prone position, but didn't regard it as practical. Although some of his gliders had dihedral for lateral stability, he could impose roll control by shifting his weight from side to side, something that couldn't be done from the prone position. It has been recorded that on a couple of his gliders he could flex or warp the wings, but he still relied heavily on weight shifting.

Lilienthal once described his technique for making turns as shifting his weight to one side causing the machine to bank, then letting it slide sideways toward the low wing until the cross wind on the vertical tail caused the craft to turn into the bank.(8/286) But eventually he became aware that just the act of forcing one wing to drop increased its effective angle of attack and thus drag, pulling the aircraft into a yaw turning into the low wing.(39/81) Modern tailless hang gliders are turned in this way. Shortly before his death he was making 180-degree turns in this manner even though he was greatly concerned about the high landing speeds resulting from going with the wind. He even had plans to begin attempting circling flight with his weight shifting machines.(38/17)

Lilienthal preferred the added stability afforded by the hanging pilot's low center of gravity. And of course, the vertical position allowed him to save weight by using his legs as takeoff and landing gear. Still, he was well aware that aerodynamic means would be necessary in order to control larger aircraft. (38/14,15) In fact, he was collaborating with three other German experimenters who were investigating aerodynamic means of stability and control by flying unmanned models.

Although leery of dihedral, he used both horizontal and vertical tail surfaces for stability, using a forward center of gravity and setting the horizontal surface at a negative angle for positive longitudinal stability.(8/278,285) By the 1890s these had become more or less standard features on all successful gliders.

Figure 14: Lilienthal's Gliding HII

Figure 15: Lilienthal and Glider

Figure 16: Lilienthal in Flight

Figure 17: Lilienthal Maneuvering

In 1894 Otto had a 60-foot high, conical artificial hill built near his home just outside of Berlin. From it he could take off into the wind no matter what direction it was coming from. He could also store folded up gliders in a chamber built within the top of the hill. But soon he decided that this hill was not high enough, so he started flying from the Rhinow Hills, naturally formed 200-foot high hills just outside of Berlin. From these he was achieving glide ratios of ten-to-one and making distances up to 1,000 feet.(39/81) In 1896 Otto was killed in one of these glides.

Lilienthal was basically a cautious man. He preceded his manned gliders with flights of small-scale models to verify the basic stability of each design. (38/14) His calculations indicated to him that he could not safely control a machine with a wing greater than about 160 square feet in area merely by shifting his weight. For shorter span biplanes he was willing to use total areas up to about 190 square feet.(38/12-16) He was reluctant to exceed these limitations even though other calculations indicated that larger wings would perform better. He also was careful to limit his flying conditions to winds of less than 20 miles per hour. (8/288) These precautions served him well for five years and over 2,000 flights. But on August 9th of 1896 Lilienthal was determined to fly even though the weather was somewhat gusty. It seemed to be nothing he hadn't handled before. Witnesses said he began a typical glide, but partway through, at an altitude of about 50 feet, the glider suddenly pitched up, then dove into the earth. The crash was severe and Lilienthal's back was broken. He died of internal injuries the next day.

Even with the rudimentary knowledge of aviation then existing, those close to the subject knew what must have happened as soon as they heard a general description of the crash. A sudden gust of wind must have thrown Lilienthal toward the rear of the vehicle, causing the tail to drop. The aircraft then nosed up, lost speed, stalled, and then the nose "fell through" and the craft dove headfirst into the ground.(3/7) After all, Lilienthal was approaching the age of fifty, a ripe age in the nineteenth century. He was not as quick and strong as he used to be. And this was not the first time something like that happened. In 1894 while flying in gusty winds he crashed fairly heavily as the result of a stall. He admitted that his loss of control was primarily due to fatigue. Otto referred to this as his only really bad crash in thousands of flights. (39/92,93) Later that year he suffered a similar crash that received much more publicity in the world press. He believed this one was due to excessive curvature of the wings. Although its eight percent camber gave great lift, the machine had unmanageable pitch characteristics.(39/93,94) Subsequently Lilienthal was to use only cambers of about six percent or less.

Anyone who has flown a hang glider, even a modern one, can attest to how strenuous it can be, particularly in tight turns or in gusty winds requiring rapid recoveries. And Otto, hanging vertically, could really only swing his legs, not his whole body as in a modern hang glider, so the explanation seems logical now as well as then. The Wright brothers stated many times that it was this understanding of the crash that caused them to retain their highly unstable forward pitch control long after they found out that the configuration was in fact not stable and barely manageable.

But here is a prime example of the enigma concerning the Wrights' apparent failure to heed information that should have been available to them. As we will see, Octave Chanute was the Wright brothers' primary source of information concerning aviation research and testing that had been accomplished prior to their efforts. And Chanute was well aware of a totally different explanation for Lilienthal's fatal crash. It seems Lilienthal had a close friend and fellow aviation and gliding experimenter, Wilhelm Kress from Vienna. Herr Kress was familiar with Otto's tests and equipment, and had just visited Lilienthal a week or two prior to the accident. According to Chanute's recollection, Kress told him that he was dismayed at the dilapidated condition of the biplane glider with an adjustable tail that Otto was determined to fly. Lilienthal recognized this but said he had a new one coming along and wouldn't be flying the old craft much longer. It was in this neglected glider that he was killed. According to some witnesses it was a structural failure of the tail support bracing that precipitated the crash.(32/14)

Chanute received this information directly from Kress.(32/Chapter 1) And Herr Kress was certainly a qualified source. He had begun experimenting with rubber band powered models in 1877 and went on to build a number of manned gliders.(18/89) By 1901 he had built a triple-tandem-winged sea-plane powered by a 30 horsepower Daimler engine. On his first takeoff attempt Kress swerved to avoid a stone jetty, turning the craft over and destroying it, thereby losing his chance to make the first powered flight.(18/115) He went on to eventually fly powered aircraft of his own design.

In view of the Wrights' obvious concern Chanute reported this information to them. Still the Wrights proceeded for some time as though they never heard this account of the tragedy, instead maintaining that Lilienthal had lost control of a perfectly sound glider. Considering the negative impact their canard design had on their commercial success, this error must rank right up there as one of the Wrights' major research oversights. Indeed in one of the documents that the Smithsonian recommended in 1899 for them to read, *The Aeronautical Annual of 1897*, Augustus Herring, one of Chanute's cohorts, clearly stated that Lilienthal's fatal crash was due to a biplane glider that had been "allowed to deteriorate and get out of repair"(39/57)

Photos and stories of Lilienthal's exploits appeared in newspapers and magazines around the world. He had made about 2,000 glides in two biplanes and numerous monoplanes.(3/7 & 16/18) Some of these flights were nearly 1,000 feet in length and 1 minute in duration.(24/23) He showed the world that air was indeed capable of supporting man and machine for an extended period. Among those following aviation developments, the era of widespread skepticism regarding the possibility of manned flight was essentially over.

There is an interesting anecdote concerning the two gentlemen we have just discussed, Hiram Maxim and Otto Lilienthal. While relations between aviation experimenters were, for the most part, supportive and congenial, occasionally rivalries did crop up. In his concluding editorial to the 1895 *Aeronautical Annual* James Means recounted a rather hostile exchange of written comments between the two great experimenters. In September of 1894 Maxim wrote that Lilienthal was nothing more than a "parachutist" and a "flying squirrel". Three months later Lilienthal replied saying that the only thing Maxim had accomplished in aviation was "to show us how not to do it". (37/169) Unfortunately I could find no further record of how or if the feud continued or was resolved.

The Great Gliders: Percy Pilcher

Another of the "Great Gliders" of the 1890s was a Scottish engineer named Percy Pilcher. Pilcher began his experiments not long after Lilienthal, and he no doubt had gotten at least some of his inspiration from reading about Otto's exploits. Pilcher began building and testing manned gliders in the early 1890s but met with limited success. So in 1895 he solicited an invitation from Lilienthal to come to Berlin and see the German's equipment and techniques first hand. Lilienthal was gracious enough to show Pilcher everything he had done. He even gave Percy gliding lessons on his machines.(23/80,81 & 39/146) Upon returning to Scotland, Pilcher added cruciform tails to his gliders that were similar to what Lilienthal was using. Subsequently, he met with vastly increased success.(39/144)

On June 25, 1895 Pilcher wrote a letter to the Australian aviation experimenter Lawrence Hargrave revealing an interesting insight into his overall philosophy of flight. He wrote, "Stability, strange as it may seem, is a thing I am very much afraid of. I like the machine practically neutral so as to be perfectly under control, or rather, more susceptible to the control movements of my body".(10/55) He went on to use the example of wing dihedral in a crosswind. Although dihedral tends to keep the wings of an aircraft level in calm air, in a crosswind, the air can push on the bottom of the upwind wing and cause the craft to bank away from the wind. This would be particularly troublesome in a hang glider like Pilcher's where, without aerodynamic control, he would be totally dependent upon swinging his legs. This is the other side of the stability versus control argument, that stability, while seeming to be a good thing, can work against a pilot's ability to control a vehicle. Eventually Pilcher dropped the use of dihedral in favor of a gullwing configuration wherein the inboard portions of the wings rise up but the outboard sections droop slightly. He felt this configuration handled much better in cross winds.(39/144,145) Interestingly, even though they flew lying prone and had aerodynamic controls, the Wrights went even farther with Pilcher's philosophy, creating aircraft that were unstable to the point of being difficult to fly.

In 1896 Pilcher built his fourth and most famous glider, the "Hawk." Again he used a cambered wing with some dihedral, but this time he made the horizontal and vertical tail surfaces moveable in flight. Once more he had made a substantial improvement, and *Scientific American* magazine reported that he made glides of up to 820 fet with this vehicle.

Figure 18: Pilcher's "Hawk" Glider

By 1898 Pilcher was convinced that he was ready to try powered flight. In June of that year he was constructing a gasoline internal combustion engine. Testing the following year revealed that the engine was only capable of about 4 horsepower, but Pilcher was hopeful that more could be coaxed out of it. He proceeded to test the engine with a propeller, also of his own design. (10/102,124) Along with the engine, he had designed and constructed a new, larger airframe to lift the increased weight. The vehicle was a triplane with the horizontal and vertical tails that were conventional by that time.

Throughout this period Pilcher was bedeviled by a lack of money. Development of an engine, propeller, and a new and larger airframe had caused him to expend funds at an ever-increasing rate.(10/118,122) If his work were to continue, he would need to find outside sources of funding. So he decided to put on a flying exhibition at Stanford Park. This was to be his last exhibition before attempting powered flight. Numerous members of the Aeronautical Society of Great Britain were in attendance, as were members of the nobility. Among these were a number of potential financial supporters, so it was imperative that the event proceeded smoothly. (10/128,129) Contrary to some accounts, the powered aircraft was not to be part of this event. The engine had broken down some time before and was undergoing repairs at the time.(10/128)

As is often the case in the British Isles, September 30, 1899, the day of the demonstration, dawned extremely damp and foggy.(23/81) Overnight his glider, made of woods and fabrics, had soaked up a substantial amount of water. This of course increased its weight by a considerable amount. However Percy decided that the show must go on, and as soon as the weather began to clear he commenced gliding demonstrations. On his first couple attempts the glider was so heavy that the launching line broke leading to brief hops. But on the third attempt Pilcher got a good strong launch. Shortly into the flight the crowd heard a snap and watched the tail structure collapse.(10/130) The aircraft dove into the earth severely injuring Pilcher. He died of head and back injuries two days later. Although the initial cause was different, the accident was eerily similar to Otto Lilienthal's, at least as Wilhelm Kress related it.

Few accounts of aviation's early history give adequate coverage to Percy Pilcher's accomplishments. Most don't mention him at all. But it is evident that in the field of gliding Pilcher achieved a level of skill comparable to those obtained by Lilienthal or Octave Chanute's team. He had made nearly 1,000 glides, some almost 1,000 feet long. But what's more, it is clear that in the fall of 1899 Pilcher was within a couple weeks of attempting the first powered, manned flights.

The Great Gliders: Octave Chanute & Augustus Herring

During this same period of time, in America the third of the "Great Gliders" was having unprecedented success on the sand dunes along the south shore of Lake Michigan. Octave Chanute, a French immigrant, had achieved a good deal of success as a civil engineer. He became the chief engineer of the Hudson River Railroad and later established his own prestigious and financially lucrative engineering firm.(20/46) Then, in 1876 he saw an article by the French aviation experimenter Alphonse Penaud that appeared in the Aeronautical Society of Great Britain's annual report. Chanute immediately became hooked on aviation, the obsession lasting the rest of his life. He studied everything from Cayley's 1809/1810 *On Aerial Navigation* to Lilienthal's *Bird Flight as the Basis of Aviation* as the material became available. He corresponded with individuals and organizations all over the world, eventually assembling the most extensive compilation of aviation information and literature in existence.

By the early 1890s, he had published many magazine and journal articles concerning all known aspects of aviation research. Then, in 1894 he published a compilation of these in a book titled *Progress in Flying Machines*. Chanute was subsequently recognized both in the United States and Europe as the world's preeminent authority on aviation history and experimentation. He became the focal point for the exchange of information among aviation experimenters throughout the world. He was nothing less than the nineteenth century version of a "World Wide Web" for aviation information. Later, his book became the basis of the Wright brother's reference material.(23/84)

By 1894 Chanute was in contact with a number of Americans who were interested in aviation and who were experimenting or who wanted to begin experimenting. He told some of them about the ideal gliding conditions that existed on the sand dunes along the southern shore of Lake Michigan near Miller, Indiana just east of Chicago. He pointed out that there were many dunes up to 300 feet in height, and that the sand was very forgiving on both man and machine when the inevitable crashes occurred.(39/32) Not only that, the breezes were steady and usually of just the right magnitude. Initially the group used the 70-foot dunes just a couple miles north of Miller. But the following year they went by boat to a more remote location a few miles farther east to avoid the throng of onlookers that had developed near Miller. (39/40,41) Having gotten some gliding experience under their belts, the group looked forward to the higher dunes at the new location.

With most of the financing provided by Chanute, this group proceeded to build and test both his and their own ideas for how to build flying machines. By this time Chanute was in his sixties, so he left the actual flying to the younger men and concentrated instead on theorizing, design, his worldwide information exchange, and the bulk of the group's financing.

It is interesting to follow the evolution in Chanute's thinking during this period regarding the function of wing camber. Early on he subscribed to the common theory that flat planar wings could give acceptable lift simply by reacting to pushing air down when shoved forward at a positive angle of attack.(8/172) Like many before him, he initially believed that even cambered wings such as those on birds developed lift in the same manner.(8/213) Later, he came to the conclusion that cambered wings definitely gave better lift-to-drag ratios, and that it was "not impossible" that cambered wings would be found to be necessary for successful flight.(8/192,251) He even concluded that while cambered wings would produce more lift by smoothly building up higher pressures on their underside, they would also produce "a rarefaction" or lowered air pressure on their top surface. Not having done this kind of testing on his own, Chanute probably derived this knowledge from his compilation of the works of Horatio Phillips and Otto Lilienthal which he reported in his book.(8/157,166,170)

Also in his book, Chanute presented the opinion that "almost all experiments with aeroplanes have hitherto been flat failures." He believed this was because of the difficulty of maintaining the equilibrium of that form of apparatus, "both sideways and fore and aft".(8/73,257) He stressed that even birds have to constantly struggle to maintain their balance in flight. (8/75) He also believed experimenters should direct their attention to gliding or "soaring" flight, and that the "maintenance of equilibrium … was by far the most important" aspect of flight yet to be solved. His conclusion was that any manned aircraft should have "automatic" or inherent stability to the maximum extent practical, and that until this was accomplished "it would be premature to … apply a motor". (39/30) Chanute's philosophy can be seen in the many designs his group created. It can also be seen in the Wrights' overall approach to flight.

The members of Chanute's group built gliders of both their own, and his, designs. In this regard, the group's members seemed often to work separately, each on his own projects. Some of Chanute's own designs were the most outlandish of the bunch. One was a multi-cell, multi-wing design, and another, the Katydid, had three tandem sets of biplane wings.(23/87)

Among the men that came to Miller, Indiana to work with Chanute was a fellow of exceptional capabilities named Augustus Herring. He was an extremely capable and insightful young man and made a significant contribution to what he called "the problem of the century". He was absolutely convinced of the importance of gently cambered wing profiles and was aware that "what is spoken of …as a pressure on the underside is chiefly a partial vacuum over the upper surface"(39/56) In fact, Herring proposed actually changing the name of the "aeroplane" to the "aerocurve". He pointed out that the chief advantage of the airplane over helicopter-like designs was the thrust multiplying effect of the airplane's lift-to-drag ratio, allowing it to lift a weight equal to many times the thrust from its propellers.(39/56) Herring was very pleased with the location Chanute picked for flying, and by 1897 recommended sand dunes facing a large body of water to all experimenters due to the more uniform winds in such a location.(39/58)

By the summer of 1896 Herring had developed, built, and flown what was to become the Chanute group's most successful aircraft. It was a straight-winged biplane with moderate smooth camber and horizontal and vertical tails.(23/88,93) As with all the group's designs, it was a hang glider with the pilot in the vertical position. Chanute often stressed that the pilot should always be in the upright position since that was "the natural position of man". (8/217) The vehicle evolved to have an "automatically adjustable" horizontal and vertical tail as well as a method for roll control. Herring referred to these as his "regulating" mechanisms and was cautious not to reveal details of their workings as he was applying for a patent on them (39/67-71). This vehicle proved to be an extremely safe and reliable glider, and the Wrights patterned their biplane wing planform, spacing, and structural truss work after it. It was truly a classic of its time. With an enclosed fuselage and a propeller it could almost have passed as a miniatur Wold War I airplane.

Figure 19: Chanute/Herring Biplane Glider - 1896

By 1898 Chanute was beginning to experiment with aerodynamic control. One of the more innovative things he tried briefly was independent variable wing sweep for both roll and pitch control.(10/101) If the sweep of both wings were increased, the aerodynamic, or lifting, center was moved aft allowing the nose to drop and visa versa. If the sweep of only one wing were increased, it would develop less lift closer in and the aircraft would roll toward it. Although variable sweep introduces structural vulnerabilities, its use for attitude control is not as outlandish as it may seem. Some birds use this type of planform modification for flight control. Seagulls and pelicans can be seen to fold up a wing in order to roll to that side when diving for fish. In fact, since gulls are plentiful along the shores of the Great Lakes, this may well have been where Chanute got the idea. In any case the scheme seems to have been unsuccessful for a manmade aircraft, probably because of pitch and yaw reactions to the sweep increase on one wing only.

As far as the need for power was concerned, it appears that Chanute didn't really buy into the idea of typical surface winds having some innate upward current. He acknowledged that upward currents must occur at some locations for birds to be able to soar for such long periods, but he correctly ascribed the updrafts to either thermal effects or surface features on the ground.(8/189-192) Thus, like Pilcher, he was convinced of the need for a powerplant in order to perform sustained flight. However he remained a strong advocate for learning to balance an unpowered aircraft first and adding a motor later. (8/261)

In 1894 Chanute stated the opinion that state-of-the-art steam engines should be about 10 pounds per horsepower. (8/8) Although this figure is substantially better than the Wrights achieved ten years later with their gasoline engine, he probably didn't account for water or a condensing system. Based upon these numbers, Chanute was of the opinion that powered flight using an engine and propellers was imminent.(8/48,49) But oddly, he felt his team was not yet ready to try it.(10/87)

Nevertheless, Herring was eager to try a powered aircraft. By the summer of 1898 he had one nearly ready for flight. Perhaps the best description of the plane is in a letter Chanute wrote to Percy Pilcher on June 3,1898.(10/101) In it he describes Herring's machine as being a biplane with a compressed air engine which drove both a pusher prop and a puller, or tractor, propeller. The engine, actually a horizontally opposed two-cylinder design, was capable of putting out up to 5 horsepower and drove two propellers that were about 5 feet in diameter.(39/72) The craft had both horizontal and vertical tail surfaces and incorporated Herring's version of "automatic stabilization." Its horizontal tail was moveable and spring loaded against air loads. The aircraft had a wingspan of 18 feet, wheels for takeoff and landing, and supposedly had an empty weight of only 88 pounds.

Later that year Herring made a couple of short hops in this powered aircraft. In one case he flew about 50 feet into a 20-mile-per-hour headwind, and in the other recorded flight he went 75 feet into a 26-mile-perhour wind. (10/107) Neither flight was actually long enough to prove that the plane could really support itself and maintain altitude. But those were to be the only flights of the vehicle. Once more fate cruelly turned back a nineteenth century effort at powered flight when Herring's craft was lost in a fire that destroyed his entire workshop. He never recovered from this loss in time to beat the Wright brothers into the air with a powered machine.

Chanute's small group tallied more than 1,500 glides, many of them hundreds of feet in length.(19/45) Although some of the designs, particularly those of Chanute himself, were somewhat bizarre, other designs, in particular Herring's biplane glider, were quite prescient, setting the basic pattern for aircraft designs for the next thirty years. But no doubt Octave Chanute's greatest personal contribution to the development of aviation was providing a focal point for the worldwide compilation and exchange of information. He provided, to anyone who asked, a foundation of proven techniques from which future designers could progress. Perhaps if the Wright brothers had taken even more advantage of this than they did, they could have designed somewhat differently and had more success in the burgeoning aircraft industry.

During the 1890s aviation experimenters were also active in England, France, and Italy.(20/32) In Poland, Czeslaw Tanski was constructing and flying gliders. In fact, in his 1894 book Chanute discussed nearly one hundred aviation researchers and experimenters. But the three "Great Gliders," Lilienthal, Pilcher, and the Chanute/Herring team, were by far the most advanced aerodynamically and made the greatest contributions to aviation knowledge. They were basically just hang gliders and had little means of control other than shifting body weight. This limited the size and weight of the gliders that they could control. As a result, except for Pilcher's last untested vehicle, and Herring's last and barely tested machine, they had no propulsion. But they convinced the educated public that flight was possible, powered flight imminent, and that future claims should be taken seriously. And they provided motivation and a great deal of information to get the Wright brothers started.

Maybe He Almost Did It

Up to this point we have looked at the work of aviation pioneers who clearly preceded the Wright brothers, individuals whose work either did or should have influenced the Wrights. But there was another very famous aviation pioneer from this same period who also became a contemporary, and indeed a competitor, to the Wrights. In fact, his work became obliquely involved in the Wrights' subsequent struggle for control of the aviation industry.

Samuel Pierpont Langley, although largely self-taught, became an astrophysicist. For twenty years he was professor of astronomy and physics at Pittsburgh's Western University. He was a member of the National Academy of Sciences, the Royal Astronomical Society, The Royal Society of London, the French Academy, and many other prestigious scientific organizations. He received honorary doctorates from the University of Wisconsin, the University of Michigan, Harvard, Princeton, and Oxford. Later he became Secretary of the Smithsonian Science Museum. He was obviously no dummy, nor was he merely the arrogant blowhard that some historians have made him out to be.

Langley was also susceptible to the aviation fever widely circulating among technically aware people during the later nineteenth century. He constructed his first whirling arm test apparatus in 1887.(39/12) From 1887 to 1896, he conducted extensive tests with the whirling arm and over a thousand free-flight tests with nearly a hundred different model configurations.(3/8 & 21/3) At least thirty of these models were powered by propellers driven by twisted rubber chords.(39/15) These, as well as airfoil and wing tests, were made in a well-manned and instrumented laboratory within the red brick Smithsonian "castle" in Washington, D.C. Langley even traveled to Berlin to study Lilienthal's work first hand.(21/97) He finally settled on a configuration having cambered rectangular tandem wings with dihedral, horizontal and vertical tail-mounted stabilizer/controls, and two counter-rotating pusher props. With a wing on each corner and the weight of the engine and pilot slung low between them, this configuration appeared fairly easy to stabilize. Actually, this is not necessarily true. A great deal depends upon the incidence angles of the wings, the location of the center of gravity, and the setting of the tail surfaces, just as on any other configuration. In any case, once Langley settled on this configuration, he never looked back.

Langley's first large unmanned steam powered models were failures large-ly owing to excessive weight and structural weaknesses.(39/17-19) Much of his problem stemmed from the tandem wing layout having the lift at the extreme ends of the vehicle with the weight masses of the engine and pilot concentrated in the center. (These structural problems were to plague him to the very end.) Even when the models didn't completely collapse they would deform so much that they were no longer airworthy and crashed.(39/23) Fixing these "aeroelastic" problems resulted in his aircraft typically sporting countless struts and guy wires.

Having launched so many laboratory models by hand, Langley assumed that larger craft would have to be launched in similar fashion. This would re-quire some initial elevation and a clear area out for some distance. Launches would also always have to be into the prevailing wind, and it would be nice if the vehicles could land on some soft surface. Langley's solution to all of these problems was to launch his larger models and manned vehicle from a power-ful catapult on the roof of a large houseboat anchored on the Potomac River. (39/20) The location he picked was a fairly secluded and particularly wide spot on the river about thirty miles south of Washington.

His launchers were powered by large springs. Although seemingly simple in operation they were a continuous source of problems. In 1893 and 1894 Langley made fifteen attempts to launch unmanned models and they were all failures.(39/21,22) Either the model would get snagged or it would sim-ply collapse from the extreme initial acceleration from the large compressed springs and subsequent air loads.

Finally, by 1896 Langley was regularly having success. Alexander Bell de-scribed flights he witnessed on May 6th of that year. A thirteen-foot model, Langley's "Aerodrome" number five, made a number of spiral climbing flights of about a minute and a half duration. Bell said the vehicle rose in 100-yard wide circles and attained an altitude of about 100 feet. It then ran out of steam (water) and glided smoothly back to the river unharmed.(39/26,27)

Later that year Langley's team built a 17-foot unmanned model with the same tandem winged configuration and fitted it with a larger steam engine. (3/8) They launched it off of the roof of the houseboat having set it to fly in a much larger circle. It proceeded to do just that, continuing for over a half mile. He then built a similar model that had a gas engine. On November 11th of the same year this one made a similar flight of three quarters of a mile.(39/28,29) Both models flew beautifully until they ran out of fuel and then gracefully glided into the Potomac, thus proving their inherent stability both with and without power. The Wright brothers claimed that they were highly motivated by these flights as they proved that mechanicaly-powered flight was possible. (1/1010)

Figure 20: Langley's Powered Model

At this point, having proven that powered flight was feasible, Langley drew his aviation experiments to a close. He wrote, "I have brought to a close the portion of the work which seemed especially mine. For the next state....it is probable that the world may look to others".(3/9) But the "world" quickly looked back to Langley. The U.S. Army had seen the usefulness of aerial reconnaissance, having successfully used observation balloons during both the Civil War and the Spanish-American War. However, it had also seen the extreme vulnerability of balloons. A smaller, faster, more maneuverable aerial observation platform would be just the ticket. So the War Department offered Langley a $50,000 contract to build a manned flying machine.(3/11) He couldn't resist.

Langley augmented his aviation staff and began scaling up his successful powered model. He hired an engineer from Cornell, Charles Manley, to oversee the critical area of engine design and construction. Manley took the engine project over from the Balzer Company of New York and came up with the world's first radial internal combustion engine. It weighed 184 pounds and put out 52 horsepower, a power-to-weight ratio that would not be exceeded for another fifteen years.(3/12)

An exact copy of the machine exists at the National Air and Space Museum Annex near Dulles Airport. Although the overall size and layout of the vehicle are impressive, detailed examination reveals numerous structural details that would have severely degraded its airworthiness. The most glaring of these is the use of external wing spars across the top of the wings. Certainly, with a thin wing of essentially zero thickness, the spars had to be external. But to run them across the top surface of the wing over the entire span, along very nearly the maximum camber line, is tantamount to creating a flow spoiler to destroy much of the lift that could be generated. Evidently, Langley, as did most others at this time, subscribed to the theory that wings produce lift on their undersides, and thus put the spars across the tops of the wings to keep the flow smooth along the lower surfaces. But knowing as we do now that lift is primarily generated by the smooth flow along the top surface of the wing, one can only conclude that Langley's external spars would have severely compromised the lifting ability of the wings.

The "Aerodrome," as Langley called his machine, would also have had severe drag problems. Even for its time, it looks like a veritable porcupine of external bracing poles. There are dozens of them, many being 5 feet or so in length. These, in turn, were guyed by nearly 100 bracing wires, some running 15 feet or more in length. Unfortunately, all this drag was to be offset by two wildly inefficient flat propellers. Of course the engine had plenty of power as proven by extensive ground testing. So perhaps it could have overcome the poor lift-to-drag ratio and primitive propellers. Still, it's a shame to see such an elegant basic design cluttered with such a profusion of parasites. But such construction was considered necessary and not outlandish at that time.

Finally, by October 1903 the launching catapult atop the houseboat had been greatly expanded and everything was deemed ready for the first flight. Manley lived up to his name and volunteered to be the pilot. Just how he could possibly have intended to learn how to fly the thing before it hit the water 30 feet below, no one knows. As far as anyone was aware, he had never even left the ground on a pogo stick. Yet he was optimistic enough to sew a large compass onto his right pant leg so he wouldn't get lost during his maiden flight. In any case, there was no time to lose practicing anything. Both Langley and the Wrights were aware of each other's status. To each it looked like the other could make a successful flight any day.

On October 7th Manley climbed aboard, warmed up the engine, revved it up, and was launched. The machine left the launcher, pointed its nose down, and went straight into the river. Everything, including Manley, was pulled out, dried out, cleaned up, and readied for another try. On December 8th the machine and Manley were launched for a second time. It immediately crumpled, pointed its nose up this time, stalled, and fell backwards into the river. (3/14) That was enough for Langley, Manley, the War Department, and the Smithsonian who had poured another 20,000 dollars into the effort. Nine days later the Wright brothers flew, and the race was over.

Figure 21: Langley's "Aerodrome" on Launcher

Figure 22: Langley's First Launch

Figure 23: Langley's Second Launch

With no Federal Aviation Administration or National Transportation Safety Bureau, the controversy surrounding the causes of these crashes was never really resolved. Some say the plane couldn't fly. Others say Manley couldn't fly it. Langley always maintained that the launching mechanism fouled the machine, damaging critical structure on both launches. Although Langley's explanation had its supporters, to many this seemed to be a dubious claim. The motion of the aircraft in one crash was exactly opposite of its motion in the other. How could the cause be the same in both?

Eleven years later the Curtiss Aircraft Company examined the vehicle and proclaimed it to be the most exquisite example of craftsmanship they had ever seen.(21/26) So failure was probably not due to poor construction techniques. Design, however, is another matter. It is not impossible that at some point, in sizing up from the successful models, Langley's group fell victim to the scale effect. Generally, anything made twice as big has four times the area and eight times the volume and weight. Since this vehicle had to support its own weight in the air, many pieces would have had to be made roughly eight times as strong. Additionally, for the same flight speed, the wings would have had to be at least four times as large, requiring even more structure. Sometimes this is very difficult to accomplish when spaces close in on each other. Of course, aircraft design is not this simple. But still, care must be used to fully account for scale effect on each piece when resizing a vehicle. Langley's notes indicate that elaborate stress tests were done on the full-sized aircraft in critical areas during fabrication.(21/18) Nonetheless, structural questions remained.

In both cases there were photos taken of the "Aerodrome" just after launch and before impact. On October 7th the date of Manley's first attempt, the second half of the launching ramp appears to have collapsed. So unless the launch rail was designed to drop away as it did, insufficient takeoff run could well be the primary cause of failure. Additionally, examination of the aircraft shows the forward wing to be twisted or washed out such that it would have been developing far less lift than the aft wing. This in itself would cause the aircraft to pitch down toward the water. The negative angle of this wing with no change in dihedral or sweep angle would seem to indicate a structural design weakness rather than a catastrophic failure caused by snagging the launch rail. The tail surfaces appear to be in a neutral position, so over control does not appear to have been a factor.

The photo from December 8th, the second attempt, indicates that the launch rail maintained a level position throughout its length, however, immediately in front of it the aircraft is pointing almost straight up. By this time the aft wings had completely collapsed and the front wings were beginning to do so. The aft part of the fuselage had been bent up nearly 90 degrees, and the tail surfaces had been almost totally destroyed. It seems odd that the launch mechanism would still have been designed poorly enough on the second attempt to cause all of this damage. But no matter how it was designed, a spring-driven launcher of this size must have had fairly violent initial acceleration. Certainly the 1903 Wright flyer launched by this device would have left it as a pile of wreckage.

The causes of failure of Langley's "Aerodrome" vehicle are of interest because not long after the Wrights' first flights they got into a protracted battle with the Smithsonian over who had the first manned aircraft "capable" of sustained flight. For a long time the Smithsonian accepted Langley's contention that his airplane had been fully capable and that the only problem was the launcher. The Wrights maintained that his craft was neither controllable nor structurally sound. Numerous red herrings were thrown into the argument, and it continued on and off for forty-five years. In 1909 no less than Octave Chanute, who had been a mentor of the Wrights for eight years, weighed in, testifying under oath that "there is no doubt that if the Langley machine had been properly launched it would have flown". (21/37) That statement, along with numerous depositions Chanute had to give in legal cases concerning the invention of wing warping, severely damaged his relationship with the Wrights.

Later, as we examine the Wrights' machines in detail we will see that in some ways Langley's aircraft was superior to theirs. It had an engine that was over four times as efficient and could easily run ten times as long. As demonstrated by his models, Langley's basic design was undoubtedly much more stable and may have been easier to control. Nevertheless, although they may not have done it perfectly, the Wrights did eventually make the first manned powered controlled flights. They did it first, and that's that. Unless maybe....

Maybe He Did It

There are a number of accounts of aviators who supposedly flew powered aircraft before the Wright brothers' flights of December 17, 1903. But the most persistent of these claims concerns a Bavarian born immigrant to

America named Gustav Whitehead (Weisskopf). Numerous newspaper and magazine articles have been written about his research and supposed flights of 1901 and 1902. The books on Whitehead most often referenced are *Lost Flights of Gustav Whitehead* and *The Story of Gustav Whitehead, Before the Wrights Flew*, both by Stella Randolph. Although these accounts are almost universally discredited by aviation historians, at the least they make for an interesting story.

Whitehead was an educated engineer whose technical qualifications exceeded most of those involved in aviation. Having become interested in aviation by 1890 while still living in Bavaria, he went to visit Otto Lilienthal in 1893 and 1894. Like a number of others, he learned a great deal about how to build a successful glider from Herr Lilienthal. In 1895 Whitehead came to the United States and ended up in Connecticut. He joined the Aeronautical Club of Boston and was hired to build and fly gliders by a man named J.B. Millet. Soon Whitehead became a successful builder of engines and was able to finance his own efforts.

Whitehead was amazingly prolific, and by 1901 he had built twenty different models and gliders. However, number 21 was to be his first powered, manned aircraft, and the first in the world. It was a cambered- and tapered-winged monoplane not unlike the classic form shown to him by Lilienthal. It had a suspended tapered boat-like fuselage for the pilot to sit in and only a horizontal tail surface. The tail was moveable to control pitch, and the wings had dihedral to stabilize roll. Roll control was to be primarily accomplished by shifting the pilot's weight from side to side, but Whitehead had also rigged a rope that would allow him to warp the wings for positive aerodynamic control should it prove to be necessary. He claimed body movement was sufficient control on his early flights but that the warping did work when he tred it later.

Figure 24: Whitehead's Powered Airplane

Whitehead proposed to achieve turning in the same manner as Hiram Maxim had, by differential throttling of two counter-rotating tractor (pulling) propellers, one on each side. As in Maxim's machine, this was accomplished by having a separate engine for each propeller. In Gustav's case these engines were internal gas engines of about 10 horsepower each. But his real innovation was incorporating a third engine of the same type and size. This one was geared to the ground wheels. It was to help the machine accelerate to takeoff speed and contributed nothing but weight to the aircraft once it got up in the air. This may seem like a ridiculously extravagant arrangement until one realizes that without driven wheels aircraft engines have to be oversized to provide the power necessary for takeoff. So, in that sense, aircraft carry around extra engine weight beyond that needed for level flight anyway. (At that time any climbs and maneuvers would have been very moderate and probably within the capabilities of his two flight engines.)

The big day came on August 14, 1901. Early, even before sunrise, Gustav was ground testing the machine which was tethered into the wind. Later in the morning at least a dozen spectators arrived at the large flat field just outside of Fairfield, Connecticut. Although a reporter from the *Bridgeport Herald* was there, oddly enough it seems no one had a reliable camera. It was said that Whitehead made four powered flights that day. According to the *Herald's* reporter, Dick Howell, one flight was nearly a half mile long and reached an altitude of about 50 feet. Howell's article refers to pictures of number 21 in flight, but these may have been detailed drawings rather than photographs. Reports of these flights also appeared in the *Boston Transcript* and *New York Herald* newspapers.

Whitehead is said to have gone to work immediately on an improved version of number 21, which he called—what else—number 22. It was to be very similar, but had about twice the power. It is claimed that this airplane was flown twice on January 17, 1902. It supposedly reached an altitude of 200 feet and flew for a couple of miles, partially over Long Island Sound. That seems like a gutsy, if not downright foolhardy, thing to do in January.

Of course the big question is: did all this really happen? As previously mentioned, no photos of the aircraft in the air exist. However, there are excellent pictures of it on the ground which, in itself, seems suspicious. The photos seem to show a well-executed, reasonably designed, and possibly airworthy craft. Whitehead certainly was as qualified as many others to have built such a machine. Randolph's book *Lost Flights of Gustav Whitehead* cites signed affidavits by fourteen observers who claimed to have witnessed his flights of August 1901. He had many witnesses, but then so do flying saucers. However these statements include contradictions and clearly disprovable claims. (1/1165) According to the *Washington Post*, the official position of the Smithsonian on this question of Whitehead's flights has been "we don't know." Operating under the gag order placed on them by their 1948 agreement with the Wright family, the Institution's generous position is that they looked at the information, and it was "inconclusive."

Perhaps the strongest indication that there may have been some truth to the story is the successful flights of reproductions. In 1986 a replica of Number 21 was constructed and successfully flown. Although the airframe was claimed to be as faithful a reproduction as possible, modern engines of supposedly comparable power were used. It certainly could be that modern technology made these flights possible, but it should also be noted that no one has had success in trying to precisely duplicate the 1903 machine and flights of the Wright brothers. Only one faithful reproduction of the Flyer has managed to fly about 130 feet once, yet the reproduction of Whitehead's Number 21 is claimed to have flown twenty times. Not only that, in 1998, a German project made a reproduction of Number 21, and it also flew. But again, modern technology might have played a role.

There are numerous other claims of powered airplanes that supposedly flew before the Wright brothers. These claims are usually negated by specifying that the vehicles were not controlled and that there are no photographs or reliable witnesses. As we will see, the Wrights' claim to have had "control" of their 1903 aircraft is questionable. There were witnesses to their 1903 flights, but like Whitehead's, their statements contain numerous contradictions and obviously false claims. There were photographs taken of the Wrights' 1903 flights, but the most often published pictures of these flights, while pretty, really don't prove much. One shows the aircraft a couple feet up but still over the end of the launch rail. Another shows it past the rail but with one wing tip on the ground. The best photographic proof is a seldom-published fuzzy shot claimed by Orville Wright to be of the last flight on December 17, 1903. It shows the plane on or very near the ground with its engine stopped (evident on blowups) a few hundred feet past the end of the launch rail. But even if this photo didn't exist, the numerous observations and photos of their flights at Huffman Prairie the following year imply some success in 1903. Fortunately, the Wrights were avid photographers, and they went on time and again to take photos in 1904 and 1905 proving that they could fly. And, until 1906, they ere the only ones who did.

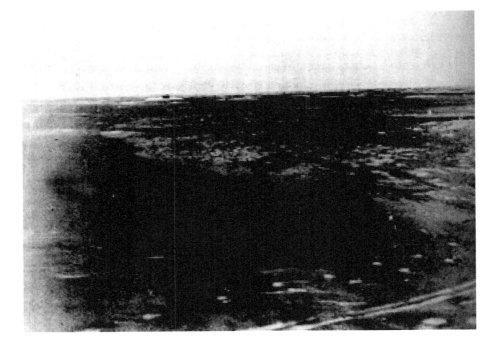

Figure 25: Final 1903 Kitty Hawk Flight

The Stage is Set

In 1895 a bill was introduced in the 54th Congress of the United States offering 100,000 dollars to anyone who could develop an airplane capable of lifting 400 pounds at a speed of 30 miles per hour.(38/80) Another provision offered 25,000 dollars for a flight of one mile. The bill was not passed, but it is a strong indication that aviation experimenters were being taken seriously.

Actually there were those who saw well beyond the mere invention of the airplane. In an 1898 speech to the Aeronautical Society of Great Britain, a Mr. G.L.O. Davidson predicted transcontinental airliners and airports near all major cities.(10/103) In a meeting of the Military Society of Ireland on January 21, 1897, far more ominous predictions were offered. Captain Baden-Powell, the honorary secretary of the Aeronautical Society of Great Britain, stated, "If we can only get a machine which will travel about in the air, and be able to go a good many miles through the air at a considerable height up, a great deal could be done, not only in the way of observation of the enemy, but also in the way of attacking fortifications from above." Major General Frankfort, the district commander, countered, "Two people can play at that game, so that if we had our machine in the air, probably some enemy would have their machine also, and it would probably come to the two machines trying to get at each other." Thus, in one meeting in 1897 the three major combat rolls for aircraft were delineated: those of reconnaissance, bombing, and air-to-air combat. All this took place years before the first true airplane was "invented".(10/67-70)

In these last two chapters we have seen that flight was defined theoretically, mathematically, and experimentally to an amazing degree well before powered manned flight was actually accomplished. To anyone familiar with the subject it was apparent by the end of the 19th century that manned powred flight was imminent.

CHAPTER III

Working With the Wrights: 1899–1905

I n this chapter and the next we will examine the Wrights' work leading to the success of the early Wright Flyers through 1905. First in this chapter we follow along with the Wrights: their studies, experiments, mistakes, and successes. We will see things pretty much as they recorded them, following a fairly traditional view of their understanding and reasoning at that time. But already it will start to become evident that much of the conventional wisdom concerning what they did and why they did it is wrong. In the next chapter we will go beyond their understanding of flight, but only to the extent possessed by their various predecessors. This will allow a more critical examination of their attitudes, decisions, work, and machinery. There we find out exactly what the 1903 Flyer was and was not, and why. And we will see that almost all of the conventional wisdom concerning their work is wrong.

Gathering Data

The origin of the Wright brothers' interest in flight is often cited to be a toy helicopter given to them by their father in 1878 when they were young boys. It's true that they wore it out along with a number of replicas of it they made, but they went on to start a printing business in 1888 and then a bicycle business in 1892. They claimed that the real start of their serious study of aviation was reading about the exploits of experimenters in 1896 while Orville was convalescing from a bout with typhoid.(20/63) Up to that time they had been absorbed with their bicycle business and their previous stint as local journalists. But as Wilbur read to the recovering Orville, they closely followed the experiments of Otto Lilienthal in Germany. These were extensively covered in newspapers and journals throughout the United States during that year. Other experimenters such as Ader, Pilcher, Chanute, Maxim, and Langley also received occasional coverage. Soon Orville got rid of his typhoid bug, but by then Wilbur had become permanently infected with the aviation bug. Lilienthal had shown that manned fixed-wing vehicles could fly, and Langley had proven that mechanically powered ones could fly also. To Wilbur it seemed all that remained was to combine the two and add a system of control over the machine.

On May 30, 1899 Wilbur wrote the Smithsonian Institution in Washington, D.C. requesting all available information on any publications, records, and other information having to do with heavier-than-air flight.(1/4) He soon received a list of books and publications on the subject along with four reproductions of articles. The Smithsonian's list included papers and books by the experimenters mentioned in the previous paragraph along with some by Cayley and Phillips.(1/6) Also included in the list was the all-important *Progress in Flying Machines* by Octave Chanute. The Wrights claimed to have been impressed at the time by the number, qualifications, and status of those who had worked the problem; however, they were much less impressed with the work done by these men since, in the Wrights' opinion, they had all ultimately met with failure by not having produced and flown a powered aircraft.(2/11)

The Wrights found that these experimenters could be divided into two schools of thought. The first group started with powered machines right away, apparently intending to learn how to fly and control them once they became airborne. The second group believed in learning how to operate unpowered flying machines first, possibly adding an engine later. But to that point, none of the power-first group had cleanly gotten off the ground, and none of the glide-first group had progressed or lived long enough to try powerplants. The Wrights, probably somewhat influenced by Lilienthal and Chanute, chose the second method. As they put it in 1908, they disapproved of the "wasteful extravagance of mounting delicate and costly machinery [engines] on wings which no one knew how to manage".(2/82) In fact, they wrote that at this time they were only interested in gliding as a sport. Still, I find it hard to believe that at least in Wilbur's mind there weren't vague dreams of the limitless flight possible with power.

The brothers were also impressed at how many of these pioneers had lost their lives pursuing flight. In particular, they were struck by the apparent fact that both Lilienthal and Pilcher had been killed because of stalls.(1/7) The initial information they had indicated that the loss of control in both cases was due to inadequate flight control, not structural failure. This explanation seemed reasonable since Lilienthal's and Pilcher's primary means of control was by shifting body weight fore and aft and left and right. The Wrights concluded that this method was totally insufficient, and they resolved to avoid their fate by devising a system of positive aerodynamic control.(2/12)

On the 13th of May, 1900 Wilbur established contact with the great American aviation authority Octave Chanute.(1/15) The gliding experiments being conducted by Chanute's small team were occurring only about 200 miles from Dayton, and information from Chanute seemed to be an excellent way to jump-start their own efforts. Wilbur wrote Chanute, "For some years I have been afflicted with the belief that flight is possible to man. My disease has increased in severity and I feel it will soon cost me an increased amount of money if not my life." The first sentence strikes me as odd. The material they had on hand should have clearly indicated that Lilienthal, Pilcher, and Chanute's group, with something like four thousand glides between them, had already proven that gliding flight by man was not only possible but fully accomplished. The second sentence clearly shows their concern for safety from the very beginning. Wilbur went on, "It is possible to fly without motors, but not without knowledge and skill." He continued, "My general ideas of the subject are….that what is chiefly needed is skill rather than machinery." Already here we have a clue to the direction their aircraft development would take; flying skill would be used to overcome design deficiencies. Unfortunately, years later potential customers wouldn't feel so comfortable with this approach.

Chanute's enthusiastic reply began a friendship and mentoring relationship which was to last for nearly ten years. He was particularly impressed with their apparent sincere scientific interest evidenced by their stated lack of financial motivation. Years later Wilbur wrote, "When he [Chanute] learned that we were interested in flying as a sport, and not with any expectation of recovering the money we were expending on it, he gave us much encouragement".

(2/83) He agreed with their emphasis on developing flight skills, and was able to provide them with a great deal of data on previous aviation research beyond that which the Smithsonian had recommended. Also, although the Wrights had already gotten wind data for the Chicago area, Chanute recommended the sand dunes of the Carolina and Georgia coasts as probably being the best gliding grounds.(1/21)

It is clear that, through the Smithsonian and Chanute, the Wrights were in possession of information on most of the significant work that preceded them. If they followed up on the list of titles the Smithsonian sent, they were in possession of even more information. It would seem that the logical approach would have been to gather all of the available information and study it thoroughly. Then, combining a decent internal combustion engine and propeller with a machine that incorporated the best flying qualities and handling techniques of those that preceded them, they would have the world's first successful manned, powered, controlled flying machine—not that that would be easy. In any case, that is not really what they did.

1899: Flying a Kite in Dayton

Wilbur began their research by studying buzzards in flight in the Dayton area. In his first letter to Octave Chanute written May 13th, 1900 Wilbur discussed his observation that birds regain their lateral balance by twisting their wing tips in opposite directions to create more lift on one side and less on the other.(1/18) Wilbur was also obviously impressed by the basic fact that the harder birds turned, the more steeply they banked or rolled into the turn. Evidently, controlling this roll through some aerodynamic means had to be the key to both straight and maneuvering flight. Oddly, years later Orville was to state "I cannot think of any part bird flight had in the development of human flight except as an inspiration".(1/1168) This is just one of many contradictions one encounters throughout the Wrights' statements and writings.

As previously recounted, a century earlier Sir George Cayley had devised dihedral as a method of keeping an airplane from tipping sideways. (To briefly recap, by having the wings bent up into a shallow V, an airplane, when tilted, would have the lower wing more horizontal, thus developing more vertical lift than the other, and thereby tilting the aircraft back level.) But with dihedral any sideways wind, either from a gust or from a slight misalignment of the aircraft with its flight direction (yaw), would cause a plane to tilt away from the crosswind. This is a trait many aviators had found to be advantageous. The Wrights, however, wanted to be able to fly straight and level and not be turned or tilted at the whim of a crosswind or gust. They felt strongly enough about this to write that "a flyer founded upon it [dihedral] could be of no value in any practical way".(2/82) They wanted a way to keep the wings level under any conditions by exerting positive control.

The story of Wilbur discovering biplane wing warping by twisting on a cardboard bicycle inner tube box is well known. With the wings of a biplane twisted in the spanwise direction, one side would be at a greater angle to the onrushing wind (higher angle of attack) than the other side. This would cause the wing with the greater angle to develop more lift. So if the aircraft became tilted, the lower wing could be made to rise up and tilt (or roll) the aircraft back toward level. (See Figure 26) If a means could be devised to allow a pilot to twist the wings in this way, he should be able to keep the machine level without the aid of dihedral. And, Wilbur figured, the vehicle's flight direction and equilibrium would no longer depend upon the whims of crosswind.

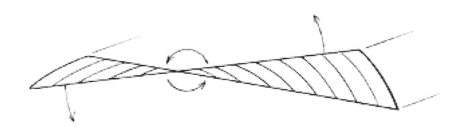

Opposite Forces Tilt or Roll Wing and Aircraft

Figure 26: Wing Warping

They considered this idea such a conceptual breakthrough that Wilbur immediately built a model to test the technique. He adopted Chanute's (actually Herring's) biplane wings, but scaled them down to a span of only about five feet.(2/13) A horizontal tail surface was mounted some distance behind on a stick that came off perpendicularly from the aft center vertical support between the wings. The device did not need to be big enough to lift a man since it could be controlled through the tethering lines when flown like a kite. It was to be restrained and controlled by four lines coming forward, one from each wing tip. On each side the upper and lower lines were fastened to opposite ends of a stick that was to be held vertically. One man could fly the device by holding a stick in each hand. The machine was constructed in a flexible manner so that if the sticks were tilted opposite each other, the wings would twist or warp. If the sticks were tilted in the same direction, one wing would slide ahead or behind the other.(1/9) This would tilt the uprights, which would deflect the horizontal tail surface up or down. So, although the device was constructed primarily to test the warping and thus lateral control, it could also be directed up or down to some degree.

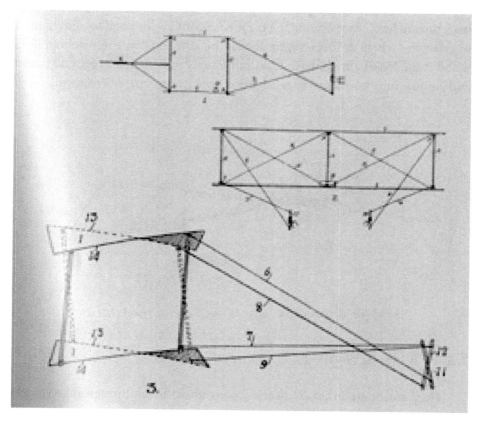

Figure 27: Wrights' 1899 Test Kite

The device was ready for testing by late July 1899. Orville was on a family camping trip a few miles north of Dayton, but Wilbur just couldn't wait to try out his idea. So on one of Dayton's typically breezy summer days at the end of July, Wilbur took the glider/kite out and flew it. As he tilted the sticks back and forth in opposing directions the wings twisted and, sure enough, the machine tilted right and left. It was easily recovered with opposite twist and thus seemed completely controllable in roll. Wilbur also tried its pitch characteristics, but due to the control lines the vehicle was less responsive in this direction. Still, since roll control was the major objective of the test, it was deemed a rousing success.(2/13)

Wilbur couldn't wait for Orville's return to deliver the good news. He traveled to Orville's campground and they discussed the event the whole day. They decided to build a full-sized vehicle and begin learning to glide the following year. After its single day of testing, the 5-foot model was never flown again.

1900: It Flies Better Backwards!

Convinced that they had a control scheme good enough to allow them to fly without killing themselves, the Wrights proceeded to build a full-sized glider which would be, they thought, big enough to ride on. But they needed a better place than Dayton, Ohio for their experiments. Some have suggested that at this early date they were also seeking seclusion. Although this was probably true in later years, at this point it is doubtful that they felt they had anything to hide, except possibly their vanity.

Acting on Chanute's recommendation, they had written the U.S. Weather Bureau and found that indeed the winds in the Kitty Hawk area should be quite favorable. In September the daytime wind speed averaged 16 miles per hour. Considering the heights of the dunes and the forgiving nature of the soft sand, the site seemed ideal. Kitty Hawk, North Carolina it was.

By late summer of 1900 they had completed the preliminary design of their first manned glider. It too was similar to the Chanute/Herring biplane glider of 1896 but was to have a wingspan of 18 feet and a chord of five feet for a total area of both wings of 185 square feet. The wing size had been selected in accordance with their interpretation of Otto Lilienthal's data and an airspeed of 16 miles per hour.(2/13,83) The wings had a maximum camber of five percent and incorporated Wilbur's scheme of warping for lateral control. This camber meant that the maximum height of the hump in the wing, as measured from a straight line from the front edge to its aft edge, would be five percent of the straight-line distance between the edges. (See Figure 28) This maximum height or camber occurred only about ten percent of the way back from the front to the rear of the wing. Apparently, the horizontal stabilizer or pitch control was, at least provisionally, to be mounted in front of the main wings instead of behind as on the previous year's test machine. The reasons for this will be discussed shortly. There was no vertical surface.

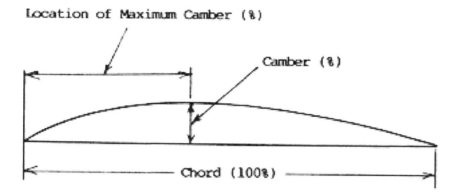

Figure 28: Wing Camber Measurement

Orville stayed behind for a while to tend to the bicycle business while Wilbur went on to Kitty Hawk to perform the final fabrication and assembly of the machine there. Upon arrival Wilbur found that the 18-foot spruce boards called for by his design for wing spars were unavailable. The closest he could find were 16-foot pine, so the final aircraft had a span, with tips, of 16 feet, an aspect ratio of 3.4, and a total wing area of 165 square feet. It weighed, with Wilbur onboard, about190 pounds.

Figure 29: Wrights' 1900 Glider

Acting on another of Octave Chanute's recommendations, their intentions were to first fly the vehicle tethered with a ballast weight onboard instead of a pilot.(39/52) By manipulating the tethering lines they could somewhat maneuver the vehicle and verify its stability and controllability. If successful they would proceed to manned, tethered flight and finally to free glides. The first thing they learned was that the craft could come nowhere near generating enough lift at 16 miles per hour to get one of them off of the ground. This was baffling as a check showed their design to be reasonably consistent with Lilienthal's data. In any case, manned free flights by the Wrights were basically out of the picture for 1900. The best the machine could do was to barely lift Wilbur with a wind speed of 25 miles per hour while held at a relatively high angle to the wind.(1/41) So they continued on with tethered testing, using about 75 pounds of chain as ballast.

The second thing they found during these tethered tests was that the wing warping scheme did appear to be working reasonably well. The tethered vehicle would bank sharply right or left as expected. When banked, it tended to slide off sideways toward the low wing. But this could easily be corrected by opposite application of the wing warping. Lateral control appeared to be solved.

But the third thing they found was almost as troubling as the lift problem. With its moveable (actually bendable) forward mounted horizontal control surface, the vehicle seemed to be unstable in pitch, constantly trying to bob its nose up or down.(2/17) Since this motion was somewhat constrained by the tethering lines it was difficult to determine the real magnitude of the problem. So they decided to take the machine down to the large dunes in Kill Devil, North Carolina further south. There, with a strong wind, they would perform some unmanned free-gliding tests to see just how bad the pitch problem really was.

Only about a dozen of these free glides were made, all near the end of the 1900 test series. The total flight test time for 1900 was only twelve minutes and barely two minutes of that was untethered.(26/66) But still it was enough to reveal the extent of the pitch instability. Aware that their predecessors had seemed to prefer aft stabilizers, they decided to try something radical. They loaded some ballast aboard and launched their glider down the hill backward! To their amazement it flew much better, exhibiting almost no pitch instability. As Orville put it in 1920, "In our 1900 experiment we had even found the inherent stability much improved....by gliding it....with the trailing edge of the main planes [wings] forward and the elevator trailing behind".(2/17) This certainly provided food for serious thought. Imagine having put so much study, thought, and effort into building and testing something, and then finding out it works better backwards.

An extensive discussion of the Wrights' use of a forward-mounted pitch control, or canard, will be presented in the next chapter. However, this is an appropriate point at which to discuss the canard's advantages as the Wrights saw it.

Everyone who looks at the Wright brothers' airplanes first notices how spindly they seem. But just as quickly, viewers tend to notice a shape we are not used to seeing, a large structure sticking out far in front of the main wings with a small, horizontal, wing-like surface mounted at its foremost end. Not only has such a device hardly ever been used since the time of the Wrights, but it hadn't been used before them either (except for Maxim's machine which never really flew). It performs the same general control function on their aircraft as the aft horizontal surface does on any other. Its movement pitches the nose up or down. But whereas the aft-mounted horizontal surface stabilizes an aircraft, the forward surface on the Wright vehicles made them highly unstable. The effect was so severe that many pilots of early airplanes considered Wright Flyers nearly unflyable. So why then did they choose such a configuration?

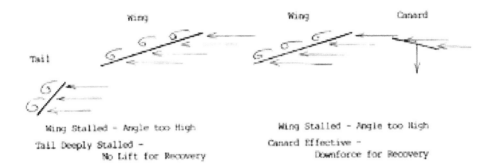

Figure 30: Stall Recovery

They originally put the pitch control (or horizontal "rudder" as they referred to it in their earlier years) in front of the wings for three reasons. The most important was for trans- and post-stall pitch control. A stall occurs when the main lifting wing(s) gets to such a high angle of attack to the oncoming air that the air no longer follows the shape of the wing. In a complete stall, all lift is lost and the airplane pitches its nose down and plummets. If an aft-mounted surface is to push the aircraft's nose down to avert a full stall, it must push up on the tail. But to do so, it must be turned to an even higher angle than the main wing. In this situation the tail could stall first, dropping down, raising the nose still further, and completely stall the wing(s). Then the whole aircraft would either slide backward or pitch nose down and plummet.

On the other hand, if the horizontal (pitch) control is in the front of the aircraft, upon sensing a stall, the pilot would turn it to a lower, safer angle of attack to bring the nose down, thus avoiding a full stall and the resulting high-speed dive into the earth. (See Figure 30) Since the Wrights believed that both Lilienthal and Pilcher had been killed by diving headfirst into the ground after stalls, this became, in their minds, an absolutely indispensable design feature of their airplanes.(2/12) The Wrights were to retain this attitude for many years, even after they learned that the real reasons for Lilienthal's and Pilcher's crashes were structural failure as Wilbur revealed in his September 1901 speech in Chicago.(1/102)

The second reason the Wrights chose a forward elevator (also called a "canard") was that they wanted a near neutrally stable machine. They knew that a highly stable vehicle would react strongly to gusts and wanted to minimize this effect. They had information indicating that as a flat or nearly flat surface is tilted to higher angles of attack to the oncoming air, the center of pressure or lift (the point along its length at which the forces from the air balance out) moves aft.(2/17) This seemed reasonable since when edge-on to the airflow the center of pressure is on the front edge, and when perpendicular to the flow the center of pressure is at the midpoint. So why wouldn't the center of lift move directly from one point to the other as the surface is tilted up? If this were the case, the relatively large wing would produce such a strong stabilizing force that the aircraft would overreact to gusts. (See Figure 31) They believed that putting the horizontal surface in front at a negative angle of attack would diminish this effect. As Wilbur put it in his speech in Chicago in 1901, "the horizontal forward surface or canard was placed in such a position that the wind upon it would counterbalance the effect of the travel of the center of pressure on the main surfaces".(1/104)

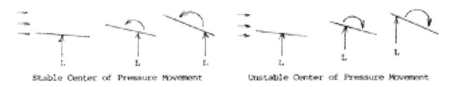

Figure 31: Centers of Pressure

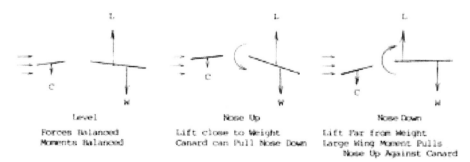

Figure 32: Wrights' Original Incorrect Stability Concept

The Wrights' stability concept would have worked like this: Picture the airplane operating with the main wing at a small positive angle of attack with the canard at a moderate negative angle. The aircraft's center of gravity would be placed some distance behind the center of lift of the main wings, with the stabilizer up front pushing down to balance out the aft weight. If the vehicle pitched up, the center of lift would move aft closer to the center of weight. This would reduce the upward pitching moment from the wing but also reduce the downward pitching moment from the canard. Likewise, if the nose pitched down, the center of lift would move forward farther away from the center of gravity, increasing the nose up pitching moment from the wing, but also increasing the downward pitching moment from the canard. (See Figure 32) Thus longitudinal balance of the vehicle would be maintained. Unfortunately, as the Wrights were to find out the following year, the center of lift on a cambered wing did not move in this manner, and that is primarily why their aircraft were so unstable in pitch.

The third reason the Wrights gave for preferring the forward pitch control (or elevator) was because of a fault they believed the rear-mounted horizontal stabilizer/control had in normal flight.(2/82) Long before the Wrights, back actually to Cayley's time, he determined that to stabilize an airplane in pitch one could put the center of gravity slightly ahead of the center of wing lift and set the aft-mounted stabilizer so as to push down slightly. Thus, the downward pushing tail balances out the forward weight with the wing pushing up between them as shown in the drawing in the left portion of Figure 33. As explained in Chapter I, the advantage of this is that if the airplane were tipped nose up, the tail would come to a nearly zero angle and would quit pushing down. That would allow the weight to bring the nose back down to level again. Similarly, if the nose were tipped down, the tail would get to an even more negative angle and would push down harder, bringing the nose back up. Thus the vehicle is self-righting or, in engineering terms, longitudinally stable. (While it is true that a horizontal tail can also tend to stabilize an aircraft when trimmed with the center of gravity at, or even behind, the center of lift, such a configuration loses the natural dynamic stability that results from having the center of gravity ahead of the center of drag.)

The problem with this setup is something designers now call phugoid oscillations. On some airplanes designed like this, if the craft is speeded up, the tail, being at a negative angle, will push down harder. This could also happen as the result of a slight downdraft. That would bring the nose up, making the airplane climb, which would slow it down. But having slowed down, the negatively-set tail wouldn't push down as hard. Then the nose would drop, and the plane would descend, gaining speed in the process. Soon the higher speed would make the tail push down harder again, bringing the nose back up beyond level. At this point the airplane would be back where we started, climbing and slowing down. Thus the cycle of roller coaster or porpoising motion repeats over and over. (See Figure 33) All this occurs without any input from the pilot, in fact, without any change in the aircraft's controls whatsoever. The oscillations can be kicked off by a headwind or tailwind gust, by an up or down gust, or even by an inadvertent movement of the tail surface. The Wrights were adamant about eliminating the possibility of phugoid oscillations since they had resolved to make their design as "inert as possible to the effects of change in wind direction or speed".(2/28) The importance of this approach to the design of their aircraft and the consequences of it cannot be overstated.

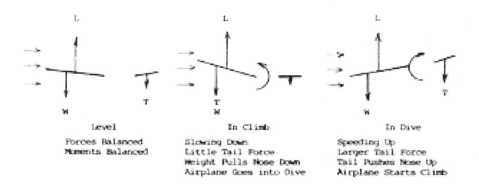

Level

Forces Balanced
Moments Balanced

In Climb

Slowing Down
Little Tail Force
Weight Pulls Nose Down
Airplane Goes into Dive

In Dive

Speeding Up
Larger Tail Force
Tail Pushes Nose Up
Airplane Starts Climb

Figure 33: Phugoid Oscillations

All this begs the question: If, during the 1900 test session and the following year, the Wrights found out that the forward elevator made their aircraft so unstable, why didn't they change it? Why not correct the problem by putting the stabilizer in back? Well, it's not like they didn't think about it. On September 23rd, just before the 1900 tests, in a letter to his father, Wilbur said that the vehicle was going to have a fixed horizontal tail for stability. (1/26) After the "backwards" tests a month later, they thought seriously about it again. But by November 26th Wilbur described their glider to Chanute as having "neither a horizontal or vertical tail". (1/46) After that, no further reference is made to a horizontal tail surface. So evidently the final decision was made between mid-October and mid-November 1900. One of Chanute's cohorts, Augustus Herring, wrote in his diary that the Wrights still considered switching the elevator to the rear of their vehicle in 1901, but no record of this can be found in the existing records of the Wrights.

In the end they elected to continue with the elevator in front mainly for two reasons. The primary one was still safety. They believed that positive pitch control during stall recovery was essentially guaranteed with a forward elevator. The second reason was that they thought they could make it easily manageable. They held out hope that a correctly shaped wing section would eliminate or even reverse the travel of the center of lift. But even if it didn't, they felt the frequency and magnitude of corrections required would be something one could handle with enough practice. After all, they manufactured bicycles which were all the rage in the 1890s. The fact that these were totally unstable did not seem to dampen public enthusiasm for them at all.

In later years there was yet another reason for retaining the forward elevator, one which they never mentioned. They were locked into it by their patent. Any change to their configuration would have jeopardized their claims to exclusivity. But that will be covered in detail in the next chapter. In these early days, they were concerned with surviving the invention of the airplane, and Orville has written more than once that positive pitch control when near or in a stall was the main reason they retained the forward elevator. So at the end of the 1900 test session they were not displeased with the vehicle's sensitive response to their pitch control.(1/106)

1901: Can't We Trust Anything?

The Wrights came back to Dayton from the 1900 tests having detected no problem with wing warping for lateral control and believing that any pitch instability could be effectively controlled with their canard. In any case the instability was worth tolerating for safety from stall-induced dives. But the machine's lack of lifting ability had to be addressed if a vehicle was ever to carry them aloft, much less with an engine. They had to determine whether the problem was wing shape, size, or both.

They devised a crude apparatus that could give some degree of comparative measurements. It was a V-shaped device that was mounted horizontally and was free to pivot about a vertical hub at its apex. (2/15) By mounting miniature wing shapes at each tip of the V and setting the device in a brisk wind, they could determine which shape gave how much more lift by measuring the angle at which the V trimmed out. With this they compared dozens of flat and cambered shapes. The results indicated that larger wings were necessary and led them to doubt the validity of Lilienthal's lift data even more. Still, they claimed that at Chanute's instigation they again adopted a Lilienthal wing camber shape for their 1901 glider. In his court deposition of 1920, Orville claimed the maximum camber height was about 8% and located about a third of the way back from the leading edge.(1/15) However photos show something quite different, maximum camber once again at no more than 10% chord but with the rest of the profile slightly reflexed. But more about that in the next chapter.) In any case, they hoped the new camber shape would alleviate the previous year's pitch problem. And just to be sure they would have enough lift, they nearly doubled the wing area from the previous year to 290 square feet. But with a span of 22 feet and a 7-foot chord, the aspect ratio was even lower at 3.1 rather than 3.5 .(1/1184)

This year the brothers resolved to avoid the chilly weather at Kitty Hawk by arriving during the summer. With the expectation of warmer weather for this test session, the Wrights wrote a letter on May 12th inviting the aging Octave Chanute to come to Kitty Hawk to observe the tests.(1/54) The Wrights arrived around July 10th and immediately discovered that they had made a huge mistake. The mosquitoes were unbelievable. The lengthy description Orville gives of them to his sister in a letter on July 28th is absolutely chilling.(1/72-75) He described the experience as sheer misery, saying that his bout with typhoid was nothing compared to this. The little monsters got through clothes, nets, blankets, everything. The only relief the men found was to confuse the little buggers by eating and sleeping in the smoke provided by burning moist tree stumps.

The first day of gliding in the 1901 machine was July 27th. Wilbur made over a dozen flights that day.(1/75) The first thing they discovered was that this vehicle still wasn't capable of lifting one of them at the typical speeds at which the winds blew.(2/83) Running launches were necessary, and manned, tethered tests in the milder summer breezes were completely out of the question. The second thing that was immediately evident was that the new wing section shape (camber) did nothing to reduce the pitch instability. The craft constantly bobbed up and down at least as much as the previous one had.

Figure 34: Wrights' 1901 Glider Launching

By this time Octave Chanute and two of his associates were in camp at Kitty Hawk with the Wrights. Edward C. Huffaker had a graduate degree in physics and had done aerodynamic research, including extensive studies of center-of-pressure locations with professor Langley at the Smithsonian. He had left the Smithsonian and had become an assistant to Chanute.(41/118, 42/111) Dr. George Spratt was trained in medicine but had devoted himself to the study of aviation. Chanute, Huffaker, and Spratt constituted a highly educated advisory team, and their contribution to problem solving, although minimized by previous authors, should not be underestimated.

Both Spratt and Huffaker suggested to the Wrights that the reason their vehicles had so much instability was that the center of lift didn't move with angle of attack in the manner that they thought it did.(2/17) So they devised a simple experiment using one wing from the glider and a moveable ballast. These tests proved conclusively that on cambered airfoils at the angles of attack used in flight, the center of pressure, or lift, did indeed move forward with increasing angle, just the opposite of what the Wrights had thought. But the Wrights had seen data indicating that on a flat plate it moved aft. So they still believed that their solution would be to come up with a section shape that would have the center of pressure characteristics they wanted and would produce lift.

They installed a third spanwise wing spar with the appropriate rigging to press out any camber except for that at the very front of the wings.(1/81,83) The accompanying photos in Figure 35, both of the 1901 test vehicle as modified, show the added spar and the section shape. It is evident that the maximum camber still occurred within the first 10% of the wing, and the remainder actually had a slight reflex shape (negative camber). This is evident in both the flying shot with full air loads and in the photo of the machine at rest on the ground. Unfortunately, not only did this alteration not help the pitch problem, but the vehicle had worse gliding characteristics than the previous year's machine. It couldn't match the lift-to-drag ratio of the previous model.

Figure 35: Wrights' 1901 Glider in Flight and on Ground

Yet another problem was the vehicle's sensitivity to crosswinds. With no vertical surfaces, it had no directional stability. So although they tried to launch and fly directly into the wind, unavoidable diversions in direction would occur, sending the aircraft traveling somewhat across the face of the hill. Then, as the breeze blew up the hill it would get under the windward wing, tilt it up, and the vehicle would slide toward the low wing and stick it into the sandy hill. Even if the craft hadn't turned, the somewhat conical shapes of the hills could let a crosswind under a wing with the same result.

The Wrights actually started gliding at Kitty Hawk in 1900 with a slight dihedral in their wings, but, realizing that it aggravated the crosswind problem, they took the dihedral out. Soon into the 1901 season they decided to avoid the crosswind problem completely by rigging the craft so that the wings bent down toward the tips.(1/27) With this negative dihedral, or anhedral, the wind couldn't get under a wing as easily. Even if it did it would raise the wing nearest the hill, and thus tend to roll the aircraft away from the hill rather than into it. (See Figure 36)

Dihedral   Anhedral

Figure 36: Dihedral versus Anhedral on a Hill

(This has led to a rather amusing present-day situation. Many who see the 1903 Wright Flyer replica at the Smithsonian Air and Space Museum in Washington, D.C., see the downward droop of the wings and wonder why the museum doesn't take better care of such a valuable aircraft by supporting it properly. They don't realize that that is precisely the way the Wrights rigged and flew it.)

But the real corker of the 1901 test session was the wing warping. It was working exactly opposite of what they intended. As they put it in a 1908 article, the effect was "just the reverse of what we were led to expect when flying the machine as a kite".(2/83) When the wings on the lower side were given a greater angle of attack they went further down, while the higher wings with lesser angle went further up! This was often followed immediately by a sideslip and spin of the aircraft toward the low wing and into the hill. With stronger application of the roll control, the vehicle would turn or spin into the hill even more violently. How could something that was working so well, now, when it was really needed, turn out so bad? And this on top of everything else!

Finally, they determined what the problem must be. When the wings were warped to correct a tilt, the side with more angle of attack, which was expected to go up, generated so much more drag that it was pulled back by the airflow. Consequently it slowed down, and the slowing reduced its lift dropping the wing farther and turning the aircraft toward it. At the same time, the wing on the other side sped up enough to generate more lift even though it was at a lesser angle. The result was that the aircraft banked even more toward the already low wing, which was at the higher angle, a complete reversal of control. The plane would then slide sideways toward the ground like a plate sliding off of a tilted table. This effect was magnified by the anhedral. Sometimes the wing with downward warp would initially start to come back up, but right away it would fall behind and down. (1/82)

When the test vehicles had been tethered with lines tied to the wing tips, they couldn't turn, or yaw, toward either side, slowing one wing and speeding up the other. Then the warping worked perfectly. So what could be done that would nail down a free-flying aircraft so that it wouldn't yaw? Soon someone at the camp came up with a possible answer. To keep it pointed straight ahead they only needed to keep it pointing into the wind, just like a weather vane. That's it! The old vertical tail used by so many of their predecessors.

But could they do it? No! They simply didn't have the materials and tools on-site to make such a major modification. Not only that, the balance of the entire machine would have to be readdressed if a tail were added. Any solution to the wing warping roll reversal problem would have to wait for their return to Dayton and the construction of another machine. So they continued on at Kitty Hawk, making several hundred glides and many measurements as best they could.(2/17) They even found that if the wing warping were used promptly and sparingly, one could somewhat avoid the reversal phenomenon.

By the end of the 1901 test session much more gliding experience and data had been gained. Still, for the Wrights it was a disappointing and unnerving year. It seemed that most of what they knew and relied upon had proven wrong. The lift coefficient tables they were using, supposedly the best in existence, were apparently seriously in error. They had proven the movement of the center of lift to be the exact opposite of what they had read. As a result, pitch control was still very difficult. Although their predecessors had almost all relied upon dihedral, they were finding that the exact opposite, anhedral, was better for their gliding. And worst of all, their beloved wing warping scheme that had looked so promising in tethered flight was now acting unreliably and often backwards in free flight.

In a letter to Chanute, written soon after they got back to Dayton, Wilbur referred to their testing status as a "muddled state of affairs".(1/85) It is often claimed that while in a mood swing on the train ride back to Dayton, Wilbur exclaimed that man would not fly for another thousand years.(3/11) However his actual statement was that "man wouldn't fly for another 50 years".(14/77,79) It was much later that Orville changed it to "another thousand years."

Octave Chanute is often given credit for keeping the Wright brothers involved in aviation during this period. Some believe his prodding to give a speech to the Western Society of Engineers got Wilbur reengaged. Others point to Wilbur's reading the inspirational writings of Mouillard provided by Chanute.(18/92) Probably after a rest and regrouping they would have soon resumed their aviation research anyway. Nonetheless, Chanute's encouragement was no doubt welcome.

Winter 1901–1902: When the Going Gets Tough

These tough guys got going again, apparently not long after they got back to Dayton. But now they realized that devising a successful flying machine was not going to be a cakewalk. They were going to have to devote much more of their time to research and ground testing. In fact, they made the fateful decision to dismiss any theory or data that they could not verify themselves. As Orville put it in a 1908 magazine article, "We saw that the calculations upon which all flying machines had been based were unreliable, and that all were simply groping in the dark. Having set out with absolute faith in the existing scientific data, we were driven to doubt one thing after another, till finally, after two years of experiment, we cast it all aside, and decided to rely entirely upon our own investigations. Truth and error were everywhere so intimately mixed as to be indistinguishable".(2/84) So now they would do their own experiments and develop their own empirical data. Actually, they had some of this go-it-alone or do-it-my-way attitude right from the start, but now it became doctrine. In subsequent chapters we will see this approach had both positive and negative effects on their long-term success. For now we will continue along with the Wrights quest to create an airplane.

The first tests the Wrights conducted after their return to Dayton in 1901 were with a device similar to the V-shaped one they had used almost a year earlier. They mounted a free-turning bicycle wheel horizontally over the front wheel of a bicycle. On this wheel they mounted airfoil test sections and a flat plate and drove them through the air at about fifteen miles per hour. Thus they could evaluate the effectiveness of various camber shapes. The results convinced them that they had to significantly alter their wing design. But to arrive at the optimum shape much more precise tests would be required. (1/123,124)

They had discussed the problem of generating data with Octave Chanute, Dr. Spratt, and Edward Huffaker while at Kitty Hawk. It was determined that the best method would be through the use of a wind tunnel. Although construction of the basic device was relatively straightforward, the trick would be to get straight uniform airflow and to make accurate measurements.

They first built a proof-of-concept device consisting of a fruit crate with the ends removed, and a prop driven by their shop engine to blow air through the box. But most of their actual testing was done in their second tunnel, a square cross section smooth wooden device roughly 16 inches on each side. An improved fan was capable of blowing air through the tunnel at up to 35 miles per hour. Although at least ten wind tunnels had been used before theirs, this tunnel apparently had the most sophisticated force measuring system yet built. In this tunnel the Wrights felt they were able to control wind speed to within a 1/2 mile per hour and make measurements accurate to between an eighth and a quarter of a degree.

Figure 37: Wrights' Wind Tunnel

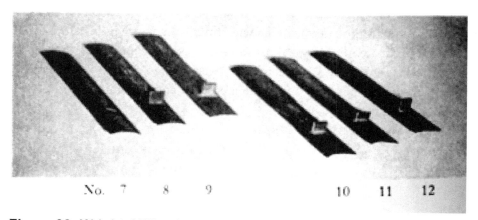

No.   7   8   9   10   11   12

Figure 38: Wrights' Wind Tunnel Models

Using their ingeniously designed "balance" devices to compare the forces on various wing test sections against reference sections, they examined about fifty different "surfaces" or airfoils in their tunnel. These were tested at 2½ degree intervals from 0 to 45 degrees of "incidence" or angle of attack. They tested variations in leading edge radius, camber shapes, camber depth, locations of maximum camber, wing thickness, and aspect ratio. They also tested the effects of multiple wings in tandem and as biplanes. And they were able to measure the all-important lift-to-drag ratios. They concluded by carefully tabulating most of their results, although they did not publish them.

Without doubt, the most important thing they did with the wind tunnel was solve their lifting problem. For two years their suspicion of Lilienthal's coefficient tables had been growing. Now with their wind tunnel they thought they would be able to show once and for all how wrong his data was. But yet again the hidden intricacies of aerodynamics had confounded them. By the time their wind tunnel tests were completed Wilbur had concluded "....for a surface....like that described in his book [Lilienthal's] table is probably as near correct as it is possible....with the methods he used".(1/169)

Analysis of the tunnel results showed that their test wing having five percent camber and an aspect ratio of six had the "highest dynamic efficiency" of all those tested. This is exactly what Lilienthal had concluded, and shows amazing agreement between two totally different early test devices and techniques.(42/111) In any case, the Wrights had finally solved their lifting problem. (Many authors have claimed that from their wind tunnel testing the Wrights found major errors in Lilienthal's data allowing them to correct their lift deficiency. Obviously I do not accept this view. But keeping with the intent of this chapter, I will save further explanation for the next one.)

The wind tunnel tests were completed well before Christmas 1901 and appeared to be a rousing success.(26/76) The Wrights now had wing sections that they believed would give better lift-to-drag ratios and relieve some of the pitch instability. They could also confidently calculate the wing area required for any needed amount of lift. They had settled on the trailing fixed vertical stabilizer as the solution to the roll control reversal problem, and they could use anhedral to deal with crosswinds. Armed with this bag of tricks, they were ready to design and build their next glider for the 1902 season at Kitty Hawk, North Carolina. Their confidence had been restored through intense, methodical, organized research. Now nothing could go wrong. Right? Wrong!

1902: As Good as It's Going to Get

By the fall of 1901 it had become apparent to the Wright brothers that conquering the air was going to take much more time and financial commitment than they had originally envisioned. They would have to let their bicycle business slide somewhat. From 1896 to 1900 they had built and sold around three hundred bicycles.(14/30) But with the invention of the automobile it was obviously only a matter of time until bicycles would no longer be a basic mode of transportation anyway. (In five years they would dissolve their bicycle business.) It would be great if they could come up with a practical flying machine and figure out a way to make their fortune from it. They felt it would probably be by selling them as sporting machines. The Wrights could not yet see much practical value to an airplane. Anyway, at that point they were still struggling to come up with a glider that could fly straight and reasonably steady.

For 1902 they came up with an improved design that they felt just might do it. At 310 square feet the wings were barely increased in area over the 290-square-foot 1901 glider. But the chord was cut from 7 feet to 5, and the span stretched from 22 to 32 feet. These changes more than doubled the aspect ratio from 3.1 to 6.5.(1/1185) And, in a further return to the Chanute/Herring wing shape, the camber was given a much smoother arch from front to rear of the wings. Maximum camber was reduced to four percent and located about a third of the way back from the leading edge. They hoped this camber reduction and reshaping would provide more lift and help alleviate the pitch instability.(2/18)

The forward elevator was of course retained but was altered to give smoother control by increasing its size and the amount of load it carried. And, most importantly, two fixed vertical tail surfaces were added to keep the aircraft flying straight whenever wing warping was used to control aircraft roll. (2/18) They rigged the craft with straight wings in hopes that their improved control system could handle crosswinds without anhedral. This was also the first vehicle to use their famous hip cradle to actuate the wing warping. (14/89) It was a wooden U-shaped device they would lay in and slide sideways by shoving their hips to the left or right.

It was almost September by the time they were ready to ship the parts to the camp at Kitty Hawk. As usual, final assembly had to take place there. It looked like, as in 1900, they were going to need their share of firewood, but at least they would not have so many mosquitoes to contend with as in the previous year.

Ever cautious, they also made the first tests of the 1902 machine unmanned, ballasted, and tethered, or as they called it, "flying it as a kite." As before, each man stood some distance in front of and below each wing tip with a line (or lines) going to the tip(s) on his side. The strong coastal winds were dependable as usual. The first thing they noticed was that instead of flying with the lines trailing back at about 45 degrees, this glider flew with the tethering lines nearly vertical. This meant that this vehicle was lifting its own weight, plus ballast, while generating very little drag. They also tested wing warping, rolling the machine from side to side. It showed no evidence of wanting to turn or change direction.(2/18) Evidently, the vertical stabilizer was working as planned. The prospects for successful gliding looked great.

Figure 39: Wrights' 1902 Tethered Test

The next step was free gliding. Wilbur had finally decided that this vehicle was safe enough to let his brother begin flying. Up to this point Orville had only done tethered flights.(34/169,170) Actually, Orville was probably the

most physically fit of the two, having won a number of medals as a bicycle
racer. Nonetheless, he did not make free flights until September, 22, 1902. No
doubt Wilbur, having been largely responsible for the design of the machines,
felt responsible for his brother's safety.

Finally, with the reshaped wing, they had enough lift for extended manned
glides. But here in these free flights, as before, the troubles cropped up. The
new machine handled worse than the previous year's glider. It was now going into stronger spins from which they couldn't recover.(2/19) Re-rigging
the aircraft to have anhedral didn't help. In fact it made the handling even
more vicious. The problem was that if the vehicle got tilted for some reason
it would, as before, slide sideways toward the low wing. The slight anhedral
that had been added aggravated this tilt and slide. But now the sideways slide
caused air to push on the trailing vertical stabilizers, pushing them away and
the nose toward the slide. The differential drag caused by wing warping was
also twisting the nose toward the slide when recovery was attempted. So then,
with all three effects being additive, the glider would immediately steepen the
bank, turn into it, and spin into the sand. As they put it in a 1908 magazine
article, "The addition of a fixed vertical vane in the rear increased the trouble,
and made the machine absolutely dangerous".(2/83) Their fix to last year's
troubles had made things worse instead of better.

Octave Chanute and his associate Dr. Spratt were visiting the 1902 Kitty
Hawk test session as they had done the year before. But this time Augustus
Herring was along in place of Mr. Huffaker. (1/279,280) Although not having
the degree of formal education and laboratory experience that Huffaker had,
Herring had designed and built the Chanute team's most successful glider and
had extensive gliding experience. These three and the Wright brothers constituted a formidable five-man brain trust to tackle any problems. It is not completely clear who in this group actually first conceived of the answer to the
spin problem. In his diary entry of October 3, 1902, Orville wrote that during the previous night he "studied out a new vertical rudder".(1/269) Orville
later claimed that by this, he meant that he had conceived of the idea as opposed to just figuring out how to make it work. This is somewhat surprising
since Wilbur was usually a step or two ahead of his brother in aerodynamic
thinking, as was Dr. Spratt.

In any case, it was deduced that if air blowing on one side of the vertical
stabilizer aggravated the problem, it might be helpful if air could be made to
blow on the other side of the surface. It certainly seemed logical enough. But

how could air be made to blow on the side away from the slide? Well, what if the vertical stabilizer was on hinges and could be turned away from the slide, or low wing, like a rudder? Then, when the low wing was given more angle of attack to bring it back up, the rudder could be turned to keep it from dragging back and falling farther. The vertical stabilizer, now a moveable rudder, would keep the craft from turning, holding the low wing forward and making it lift as desired.(2/19)

But a moveable rudder created another problem. The pilot was already using his arms to constantly adjust the forward elevator and using his feet to swing his hips from side to side to control wing warping. (Remember, he laid in a sideways sliding cradle that was connected to the warping cables.) He had nothing left with which to manage a third control, to say nothing of the mental overload that would be involved. The Wrights recognized that even they, the most experienced flyers alive, couldn't do it. So if the rudder were going to move, it would have to do so without any more pilot input than was already available.

Then a thought occurred to Wilbur. Since their whole objective was to be able to fly straight and level, rudder movement would only be needed to counteract adverse yaw. And this only occurred when the wings were warped. So why not connect the rudder and warping together, making what we now call coordinated controls? They quickly devised another system of ropes and pulleys to do this. Fortunately, by 1902 they had enough supplies on-site or had located enough nearby sources of materials to make such alterations at Kitty Hawk.

Now, after a little tuning to adjust the amount the rudder turned, they were really in business. Flying straight and level was no longer a problem. (2/19) The craft still bobbed up and down constantly, but by now they had learned to cope with that fairly well. They reckoned they made about a thousand glides in 1902, close to eight hundred of them with the coordinated rudder.(2/84,85) Some of these glides lasted 30 seconds and covered over 600 feet. Actually most glides covered very little distance since the vehicle's airspeed was little more than the wind speed. The Wrights preferred this as measurements were easier to make and they didn't have to carry the glider back so far for a relaunch.(1/358) On the 23rd of October Orville cabled his sister and said, "In two days we made over 250 glides."

Figure 40: Wrights' 1902 Glider in Flight

Finally, they knew they had an aircraft design that they could control well enough to put an engine on it. Not only that, it had the best glide ratio yet. (2/18) (It gave up less altitude to go a given distance.) Considering the disappointment of the previous year, knowing this and just gliding to gain more experience must have been pure joy. They wanted to cram in as much gliding as possible before they risked flying with something as valuable as an entire propulsion system. As Wilbur put it the following summer, "[One thousand] glides is equivalent to about four hours of steady practice, far too little to give anyone a complete mastery of the art of flying".(1/324)

Although already designing a larger machine to carry a propulsion system, they had one more alteration to try on the 1902 glider. An engine and propulsion system would need a rigid framework to hold it, but their whole vehicle twisted with the wing warping. So they decided to re-rig the aircraft so that the three center sections would remain rigid, and only the two outer sections, about forty percent of each wing, would twist with warping. (2/19,20) The only question was, would control response still be sufficient to maintain equilibrium? They tried this and found that roll response was almost unaffected.

Now everything was in place as far as the airframe and controls were concerned. The final version of the 1902 glider was good enough for propulsion if only it could have lifted the weight. So all that remained was to go back to Dayton and scale up the airplane....and come up with an engine....and a drive system....and propellers. That's all!

Early 1903: We Have to Make an Engine Too?

The Wrights realized by this time that aircraft design was actually an iterative process. Adding an engine would add weight, which would require the airframe to be bigger. This, in turn, would require more power, which would mean a bigger engine with more weight, and so on. Still, at some point the design had to be at least temporarily "frozen" so that work could progress on the airframe and engine at the same time. This basic design approach is still used today, although these days so much of the design process is hidden in computers that many people think the process is more sophisticated than it really is.

The Wrights determined that they would need about 500 square feet of wing area to lift the vehicle, a pilot, and a propulsion system weighing no more than 250 pounds. Of this, the complete engine could weigh no more than 180 pounds.(3/82) They calculated that about eight horsepower should be sufficient to propel such a machine through the air in straight, level flight. With their power requirement specified, they sent inquiries out to locate and buy an engine.

The only engines made at that time for which weight was any consideration at all were those for cars and motorcycles, so they sent their requirements to a number of these manufacturers in hopes of a favorable reply. Well, at least according to the Wrights, there weren't any such engines. This seems hard to believe. They were only asking for an engine weighing no more than 22 pounds per horsepower. Still, they claim they couldn't find one. What's more, for a sale of only one or two engines to some struggling bike makers, no company was interested in custom designing and fabricating one.

A couple of years earlier the Wrights had designed and built a one-cylinder gasoline engine to drive the lathes and drills in their bike shop.(3/82) The thing was still running pretty well too. So, they figured, why not build their airplane engine themselves? By this time they were of a frame of mind to not rely on anyone else for anything anyway. It wouldn't be easy, but it looked like that was the only way they were going to get the kind of engine they needed. Besides, what had been easy so far? If they could just come up with a good design, Charlie Taylor, their shop machinist, assured them he could make it.

It has been said that they used a Pope-Toledo automobile engine for design inspiration, and it's true that there are similarities.(20/69) Nevertheless their design is unique, and shows original thought and solutions throughout. Although Taylor credited much of the basic design to the Wrights, many details of the design were up to him.(3/82) The engine was developed largely through the cut and try method. There were no detailed drawings. In fact, when they built their second engine the following year, they had to take the first one apart to get measurements.(3/82) They ended up with a four-cylinder engine of four-inch bore and stroke weighing 179 pounds and capable of putting out a maximum of 12 horsepower at about 1,100 rpm.(3/86) It laid horizontally and was not a complete engine in the usual sense. It had no fuel pump, no oil pump, and no water pump. It had no carburetor or fuel injection. Lubrication of the "lower end" was by splashing oil from the crankcase onto the bearings and cylinder walls. Lubrication of the "top end," the valves and camshaft, was by hand with an oilcan. This all tended to limit the maximum running time of the engine from 1 to 2 minutes.(24/66) By then the cylinder heads were red-hot. Also enforcing the running time limitation was the fact that the cooling water was circulated through the block purely by convection. Fuel was fed by gravity and vaporized by first being passed by the outside of the hot cylinders.

Figure 41: Wrights' 1903 Engine

Although these simplifying features severely limited the engine's running time, any mechanic familiar with old engines knows that by eliminating all these pumps and the carburetor, they had eliminated most of the major sources of problems. They usually ran the engine at about 800 rpm at which it put out between eight and nine horsepower when warm. They had previously determined that this was enough to drive their aircraft in straight and level flight.

Of course, to get from shaft horsepower of the engine to thrust on the aircraft they were going to have to come up with propellers. The creation of a reasonably efficient twisted, airfoil-shaped propeller is often stated as their grandest achievement. It certainly was the most intellectually challenging. In a December 1902 letter to Dr. Spratt, Wilbur indicated that they were already studying the propeller problem.(1/292) Reasoning that a propeller needed to do the same thing as a wing but in a horizontal, spiral path, they decided to make it shaped like a wing, i.e., cambered rather than flat in cross section. It would have to be twisted like any other propeller, but how much twist at any radius point depended upon rotational speed, airplane speed, and prop wake slippage, all of which vary throughout a flight. The chord, overall diameter, and total swept area were also variables to be considered. The Wrights developed a methodology to account for all of these, and from that they created design reference tables from which to select compatible parameters for a propeller.(2/85) A generally similar propeller design procedure was used right up to the jet age.

Almost equally challenging was the fabrication of these twisted, cambered shapes. First, three perfect spruce boards were glued together with absolutely no voids. Shaping was done with hatchet, drawknife, and file, checked against templates every few inches of the way for 8. feet. The grain and gluing of the spruce had to be perfect. It was found in later years that failure of a propeller in flight could mean death. And of course, when it was all done the prop had to balance perfectly at the hub. These propellers truly were marvels of hand craftsmanship.

Figure 42: Wrights' 1903 Propellers

Another problem to be solved was getting the power from the engine to the propellers. The props were put behind the wings so that the spiral flow coming out of them would not degrade the lift of the wings. Counter-rotating the props canceled torque reaction, but that is not why the Wrights used two propellers. That was done to limit diameter and rotational speed.(3/80) Of course, two pusher propellers also made room for a center structure for the tail assembly. Engine timing chain was used to transmit the power since bicycle chain was not strong enough. But this was no mean feat. When one considers the torsional vibration or jerking back and forth caused by occasional misfiring of the chokeless engine, the size and weight of the eight-foot propellers, and the fact that on one side the chain had to reach over seven feet and crisscross itself, it had to be a pretty robust system. Bicycle chain would not have been up to the task. Certainly, failure at a bad time would mean disaster.

At this point the Wrights found themselves in a position that would be envied by any modern designer. They had more available power than they thought they needed, so they could pile a bit more weight onto the airplane. They beefed up structural parts, adding about 150 pounds to the Flyer.(2/85) Had they known what a marginal flyer it would turn out to be, they might have been more cautious about adding weight. After arriving at Kitty Hawk about a month before beginning flight tests, the Wrights did fairly extensive structural testing of the reassembled machine. Only some minor re-rigging of truss wires was required.(1/382)

1903: We Did It

Even though they somewhat neglected their bicycle business in 1903, creation of the new craft along with its propulsion system, was not completed until the fall. Arriving at Kitty Hawk in late September, they first had to build a "hangar" in which to assemble and house the new machine. The glider from last year had been stored in the original building. So, while awaiting arrival of the crates containing the new machine, they brushed up their piloting skills by gliding in the 1902 vehicle. This practice was interrupted by a number of bad storms. Still, these glides were the best they had ever done, some lasting over a minute. (1/373) Although they were building up to an attempt at something that had never been done before, their confidence level was high. Yes, their aircraft were tricky to handle, but they had mastered that. Their aircraft were not maneuverable, but that could be tackled later. At least now they were relying only on their own theory, testing, and workmanship. There should be no more major surprises.

But there was no time to lose. Although Langley's first attempt at manned powered flight on October 7th had been a dismal failure, he hadn't given up yet. He was going to try again soon. So the Wrights dropped their original idea of test-gliding the 1903 machine without its engine and propellers, and pressed ahead to install the propulsion system before any unpowered test flights with the new vehicle.

Some authors have indicated that the Wrights also had noteworthy competition in 1903 from a French army captain named Ferdinand Ferber. It's true that in 1902 and 1903 Ferber was experimenting with a powered biplane. (23/139) He was testing the full-sized airplane which hung in mid-air from a giant whirling arm. Although the craft had a reasonably reliable 6-horsepower engine, it was but a crude approximation of a Chanute/Herring type biplane with a hopelessly inefficient flat paddle-type propeller. The vehicle was incapable of lifting its own weight, so Ferber attempted unsuccessfully, through Chanute, to buy the Wrights' 1902 glider. Thus the Wrights were well aware that Captain Ferber, though highly motivated, was no threat to their aspirations to be first.(1/299)

Nevertheless, the Wrights still had one major problem to work out. All of their gliders up to that time had been launched with the help of ground crew. One man at each wing tip would drag the machines into the wind as fast as possible. But if the 1903 Flyer was to be credited with the first unassisted powered flight, it would have to take off under its own power. The new vehicle was basically a scaled up version of the 1902 machine with a slightly reduced aspect ratio of 6.15.(1/1187) However, with a 40-foot wingspan and a takeoff weight of about 750 pounds, this machine was no longer something two men could drag into a strong wind. Wheels were out of the question on the soft sand, as were skids or runners. Their solution was to build a metal-clad wooden track upon which the vehicle could roll.(24/60) The track was portable in four 15-foot sections which could be placed on any level ground and into the prevailing wind. The aircraft would be set on a wheeled dolly which could roll down the track on rollers similar to wire wheel hubs. The final problem was solved.

Now they were ready. The machine was completely assembled. They had even installed test instrumentation to measure flight duration, maximum airspeed, and total engine revolutions. All they had to do was just fire up the engine a few more times, check out the controls, set her on the track, and let her go.

November 5, 1903 saw the final checkouts begin. The darned engine, with no real choke, was running even rougher than it did in Dayton, particularly when it was cold. And it was really getting cold. The engine backfired a lot, backlashing the chains and jerking the propellers. The props could not turn smoothly. Soon they didn't turn at all. The propeller hubs had torn loose from the mild steel tubular shafts and had scored them so badly that the shafts would have to be remanufactured.(1/376,377) Since no spares had been brought, the shafts had to go back to Dayton for Charlie Taylor to repair them. Dr. Spratt, who along with Chanute was visiting the camp again, generously volunteered to take the shafts to Norfolk and send them on to Dayton from there. It was November 20th before the shafts were returned, but Charlie had worked his magic and the propellers gripped more firmly than ever. Now they were really ready.

The next day they fired up again. The propellers again quit turning. But his time the shafts weren't turning either. The chain sprockets that drove the shafts had come loose.(1/386) Fortunately, this was a problem they could handle on-site with some bonding material. In a couple days that was fixed. Then the weather turned sour.

Finally, on November 28th they were ready again. It was decided to put the Flyer on the rail and let her go if all seemed well. Time was becoming critical. Langley was ready to make his second attempt any day. The engine was fired up again for a few tests and everything was turning. Even though the engine was still running roughly, the sprockets and propellers were holding. But what was that? One of the propeller shafts seemed to be whipping as if it were bending. The machine was shut down. Examination showed the shafts had cracked badly from torsional vibration, the constant twisting back and forth from engine roughness.(1/388) The mild steel tubes were simply not up to the task.

Two days later Orville left for Dayton with the shafts. They would have to be redesigned and made out of solid tempered, rather than mild tubular, steel. In the meantime Langley was loading his "Aerodrome" aircraft onto the roof of the houseboat. At the bicycle shop, Taylor was machining the tempered steel as fast as he could. In Washington, Langley was towing the houseboat back out into the Potomac. Finally, Orville was buying a ticket and Taylor was packing the new shafts. Then on the December 8,1903 Langley launched his aircraft again. And again it fell into the river, this time structurally destroyed. He was through, at least for the foreseeable future. Orville read the news about Langley's second effort on the train back to North Carolina. Much of the pressure to fly quickly was off. But still, winter was approaching. It could be very harsh on the coast. Already the ponds had been frozen many mornings. And both they and their minister father expected them home in plenty of time for Christmas.

Three days after Orville's return the shafts were in and the track laid. They were ready to fly. On the morning of December 14th, 1903 they flipped a coin and Wilbur won. He was to make the first try. This seemed fitting since all along Wilbur had taken the lead in theorizing and innovation. Making the world's first powered airplane flight would be a fitting reward for him. But the breeze was moderate and they knew takeoff would be marginal under such conditions. Wilbur revved the engine and slipped the restraining chord. He let it run the full length of the rail to get airspeed. But when he pitched the elevator to lift off he over controlled, stalled, and crashed.(1/392) He had only gone a little over 100 feet in the air. The left wing, skids, and elevator frame were slightly damaged. These were repaired, and in three days they were ready for another ty.

Figure 43: Wilbur Wright's December 14, 1903 Crash

December 17th dawned cold and windy. Once again there was ice on the puddles and the wind was now blowing at least 25 miles per hour.(1/394) It was rough weather, but actually not a bad day for their airplane to fly. Since Wilbur had blown his chance on the fourteenth, it was now Orville's turn. The wind was even blowing a little harder at the first launch, and Wilbur was able to trot alongside all the way down the launch rail. When Orville pulled up near the end, the aircraft rose up to about 10 feet, dipped down to just a few feet, rose up to 10 feet again, then dipped down all the way into the sand.(1/395) Orville had only gone a few feet farther than Wilbur had on the fourteenth, about 120 feet, but nothing major was broken and after a couple minor repairs the airplane was still operable. Plus, one of their local assistants had taken a good photograph just as the aircraft rose off the track, although he wasn't sure of it at the time. It turned out that the photo clearly showed the aircraft in the air.

Figure 44: Orville Wright's December 17, 1903, "First Flight"

Three more flights were made that day with the brothers alternating piloting. The second flight, Wilbur's first that day, was about 175 feet long. Next,
Orville made it to about 200 feet. But then, on his second flight, Wilbur make
a flight they recorded as 59 seconds and 852 feet.(2/21) With the 25-mile-
perhour headwind, the aircraft was making a ground speed of only about five
miles per hour. In these flights the machine was almost always undulating up
and down. Orville later admitted that it was essentially uncontrollable, each
flight actually ending in a minor crash.(1/395,396) In fact, the last flight
crashed so hard that considerable damage was done to the elevator supports,
and flying had to be terminated for the day. The damage could have been repaired and the aircraft flown again in a couple days, however the wind was
getting even gustier. Finally, one gust rolled the vehicle end over end, pretty
much demolishing it. It was clear that flying was done for the year.(2/85,86)

It has been claimed that the Wrights were considering additional flight
attempts of up to miles in length before the wind wrecked the airplane. But
these are ludicrous statements for a number of reasons. Each time the Wrights

flew on the 17th of December it was a constant struggle to obtain control. Only on the last flight did they claim Wilbur achieved fairly steady flight for a brief period. They found the 1903 aircraft almost uncontrollable for a good reason. In a letter to Dr. Spratt written on the first of June while the powered craft was under construction Wilbur said that they were "greatly increasing the size of the front rudder (the elevator)." They also moved the pivot point back too far giving the control an "over center" feel which pulled the control much farther than intended.(1/312)

There were even better reasons that the plane could not have gone further than it did. At a ground speed of less than ten miles per hour, it would have taken 12 minutes to go a couple of miles. Not only did they not carry enough fuel for that, but their engine would overheat and seize solid in no more than about two minutes of operation. They also could not turn the 1903 vehicle and had little control over how crosswinds turned it.

Nevertheless, they decided that the deed had been done. A manned, powered machine had taken off, sustained itself in the air on the last trial, and landed again over level ground. Although Chanute and Dr. Spratt had left the camp in November, the Wrights had witnesses of forthright character, and they had *photographs* of the machine in the air.(2/21) They immediately sent a telegram to their father in Dayton announcing their success. Then they packed up their gear, secured the camp and buildings, and got home in plenty of time for Christmas. Little did they know it would be five years before they would return to their camp at Kitty Hawk.

1904: Beginning to Get the Hang of It

Most accounts of how the Wrights "invented the airplane" conclude at the end of 1903. However the Wrights themselves knew better and kept working at it for another two years before they felt they had created a real airplane, something worth protecting and showing the world. They knew that all of their 1903 powered hops had been prematurely terminated by loss of control. As Orville put it years later, "We decided to build another machine with stronger landing gear and to continue the experiments to acquire more skill in the handling of the machine, the lack of which had terminated each of the four flights at Kitty Hawk on December 17th, 1903".(2/45) Amazingly, they still felt the handling deficiency was in their flying skill and never gave much thought to altering the basic configuration of their vehicles to make them stable.

They realized that if they were to develop the flying skill that their powered machine demanded, a couple of changes would have to be made. First, they would need to develop a better engine, one that could run for more than a minute or two. Also, they would need to do their flying near their shop in Dayton. They'd had it with the distance, remoteness, and brutality of testing at Kitty Hawk. The wind there was great, but if this new engine was more powerful they might be able to fly without so much wind (and enjoy much better accommodations).

During early 1904 they designed and built two new 4-cylinder engines. It turned out that they hadn't documented their 1903 engine design in their customary methodical fashion. As stated earlier, they had to take the old engine apart and measure the parts to make the new engines.(1/414) They dabbled with the design of a V-8, but it was not completed. The new fours had oil pumps as well as improved cooling systems. As a result, they were capable of running reliably for 5 minutes or more.(1/463) One was to be used as a developmental test engine in the shop. The other was mounted in a new larger airframe. Initially these engines were capable of developing a maximum of 16 horsepower at about 1,200 rpm.

Members of the Wright family had on occasion taken the trolley east to Springfield, Ohio, about 15 miles away. Just a few miles east of Dayton one could change lines at Simm's Station and head south to Yellow Springs. Next to Simm's Station was Huffman Prairie, a large dairy farm owned by Dayton banker Torrence Huffman. He agreed to let the brothers fly on a flat, open section of his land that was separated from the trolley line by a scattered row of tall trees. They could even build a storage shed there if they wished. Just don't hit any cows. This land is now in the center of the sprawling Wright Patterson Air Force Base complex.

For 1904, although the airframe was about the same size as the 1903 Flyer, takeoff weight was now over 900 pounds.(2/45) The days of a couple guys launching their machine by hand or testing it as a kite were long gone. But even though they were no longer on sand, the use of wheels was shunned. The field was too rough for their fragile machines. They would still use a track and dolly for takeoff, and land on spruce skids.

The story, as told by Orville for a 1908 article in *The Century* magazine, is that for the very first test flight on the 23rd of May, they invited all the Dayton press to observe.(26/123) They asked only that no photographs be taken. While wanting the event verified and recorded, they claimed they did not want to draw the huge crowds that widely disseminated photos would attract. About a dozen reporters and a few dozen other observers showed up. The crowd eventually became impatient as the Wrights wrestled with the new engine which was acting quite temperamental. Although the light wind was probably insufficient for takeoff, they decided to give it a try. The machine ran off the end of the track without lifting an inch.(2/86) A few of the reporters returned the next day, but again the engine acted up and the wind was insufficient. That was the last of the newspaper people.

Takeoffs were proving to be a real problem. According to their father Milton Wright's diary, the brothers tried to fly on a few occasions in late May but the weather wouldn't cooperate.(1/436) In a letter to Chanute, Wilbur said that they made a number of attempts in June but could only make distances of less than 200 feet.(1/441) They found that even with the new more powerful engine working well, the 1904 Flyer couldn't take off in less than a 200-foot run without heading into at least a 12-mile-per-hour headwind. But with the prairie shielded by huge hills to the north and south, and the occasional tall tree, it wasn't often that they had that much breeze at ground level. And, as mentioned, their Flyer was way too big for a couple of guys to push around.

Finally a tower was constructed that contained a huge weight that was attached by a rope that ran down and up twice through a system of pulleys, and then out to the end of the launch rail and back to the airplane.(24/71) When the 1,600-pound weight was dropped, the other end of the rope was pulled sixty feet along the rail and the airplane was launched into the air. This catapult could be adjusted to add up to 25 miles per hour to the launch speed of the vehicle. Best of all, it was too simple to give much trouble. And now they could fly in any weather that wasn't inclement. The device was first used on the 7th of September, three and one half months after their first takeoff try at Dayton.(1/455)

From that point on, their 1904 flight testing was only briefly interrupted by a trip to the St. Louis World's Fair. Chanute had told them of a $100,000 prize being offered there for the best demonstration of flight. It turned out that the rules laid down by the prize contributors were beyond the capabilities of even the Wrights' 1904 Flyer. Besides, by this time they had visions of patenting their flying machine, so they didn't want to reveal their technology prematurely. But they decided to go anyway, just as observers, to see if the large prize had smoked out any real competition. Although there wasn't any, just the mere existence of the prize indicated that at least some thought the time for powered flight had come.

The Wrights chalked up a total of 105 flights comprising 45 minutes in the air during the last half of 1904, but they were still far from satisfied with the handling of their machine.(1/467) They couldn't turn or really control its direction of flight.(24/70,71) And, as had all their machines, it was still bobbing up and down incessantly. They tried to reduce the pitch instability by relocating the center of gravity farther forward, thus further increasing the loading on the canard, but this only helped a little.(1/446)

As the engine broke in they were nearing flight speeds of 40 miles per hour. This seemed to help the turning problem somewhat, but they still had difficulty attaining any altitude above 30 feet.(24/73) For some reason they once more rigged anhedral into the wings, which promptly aggravated the turning problem again. By late August they were making flights over the maximum length of the field, a little over a quarter of a mile.(1/452) But if they were ever to go farther, they would hav to learn how to turn.

Figure 45: A Wright 1904 Flight

The very first attempt at a gradual turn on September 15th ended in a crash.(1/455) The problem with turning wasn't so much getting into a turn as getting out of it. When put into a shallow turn the vehicle would continue to bank more and more steeply, tightening the turn until it spun into the ground. If opposite wing warp was employed to control the bank angle, the craft would spin or sometimes nose up and stall. Fortunately, since the plane couldn't yet fly higher than about 35 feet, damage was usually minor. Even so, they did significant damage to the aircraft on October 15th and again on November 3rd. (1/461,463)

The Wrights felt that at least some of their problems were simply because they were not getting high enough to execute turns. There was some truth in this, but not for the reasons they thought. In any case, they experimented with a number of propeller designs, eventually coming up in September with props that significantly increased thrust on the airplane.(3/81) With this added thrust and altitude they began to have more success sustaining shallow banks and making gradual turns. On September 20th they flew their first full circle. (1/460) It took 1 minute and 30 seconds and covered three quarters of a mile, but they did it. On November 9th, and again on December 1st, they managed over three full circuits of the Prairie in shallow turns. These flights were also the two longest of the year at over 5 minutes each.(24/74)

But they were still not happy with an airplane that took the better part of a minute and almost a half mile to make a U-turn, and then couldn't get out of it! In fact, on both the 5th, and 15th of October, and then again on November 3rd,they crashed trying to get out of shallow turns.(1/461-463) At some point one of them must have realized that they had to use wing warping in the opposite direction just to sustain a turn. In turns the outer wing was moving through the air faster, so it developed more lift than the other and tried to throw the plane deeper into the bank and turn. Their beloved anhedral was adding to the problem since the outer wing was more level causing it to develop even more lift. Significant opposite wing warp was needed to counteract all this. Then they would try to exit the turn by adding even more opposite wing warp. But all this time the vertical rudder, which was still connected to the warp, was deflecting toward the outside of the turn. This was often throwing the nose of the banked airplane out and up, and the plane into a slip and stall.

Now what to do? The very thing that kept wing warp reversal from spinning the machine when trying to fly straight, was now causing it to slip and stall when trying to turn. Well, the first thing to do was to verify that the rudder was actually the problem. So they disconnected the rudder cables from the wing warping and lashed it down straight. Sure enough, old problems were back. But the aircraft could now be brought out of a shallow banking turn without pitching up or skidding.(1/469-471) So the coordinated rudder was indeed the problem. But how to have their cake and eat it? There was really no choice. Control of the rudder would have to be separated from wing warping. It could then be used to varying degrees at the discretion of the operator. It would take some time to devise and fabricate a manageable scheme for three separate flight controls, but by this time it was mid-December and time to quit flight tests for the year anyway.

Also, the pitch problem remained. Throughout the 1904 tests the Wrights tried everything they could think of short of putting the elevator in back. They changed wing camber, the shape and camber of the elevator, and they moved the center of gravity forward. The center of gravity relocation seemed to have the greatest beneficial effect.(3/49) Still, the airplane undulated constantly. But by now they were so quick at catching and correcting it that, unless they were distracted, the pitching motions were hardly noticeable. Of course, the frequent flapping of the elevator was a dead giveaway to the constant attention required to fly the vehicle.

1905: Now We Can Turn

Much of the first half of 1905 was spent designing and constructing the third version of a powered flyer as well as maintaining the bicycle business. Although the 1904 Flyer had been very similar to the 1903 machine, this time a number of changes were made, most with a view toward creating a vehicle that actually could be turned. The Wrights were well aware that they wouldn't really have a useable airplane until its direction of flight could be fully controlled by the pilot. One thing they had noticed in 1904 was that in a banking turn, some of the lift was being used to pull the aircraft toward the inside of the turn. This took away from the lift available to hold the vehicle up in the air. Unless this lift was replaced by putting the wings at a higher angle of attack to the wind, the aircraft would descend. And since they could only fly at altitudes below 40 feet in 1904, and they had a 40-foot wide airplane, any descent meant an almost immediate crash.

But putting the aircraft at a steeper angle of attack also increased the drag, and thus more power was required. In 1904 the extra power just wasn't there. However, shop testing in the spring of 1905 revealed that the 1904 engine was now putting out about 20 horsepower due to being more completely broken in.(3/86) It was spinning a little faster and evidently the piston rings and valves were sealing better. Later they found that this additional power, along with appropriately redesigned propellers, was enough to get them near 40 miles per hour and, finally, above 40 feet of altitude. (At this time the Wrights were not aware of the phenomenon of ground effect. This is discussed in detail in Appendix 2.) They also added fuel and oil pumps to the engine as well as further improvements to the cooling system.(1/479) Their latest engine was capable of essentially unlimited operating duration.

Aerodynamic modifications for 1905 included increasing the maximum wing camber depth from four to five percent of the chord length. Although the wing's dimensions were about the same, the forward and aft flight control supports were extended, adding 7 feet to the length of the vehicle and increasing its pitching moment of inertia and the effectiveness of the controls. (1/1190) To further reduce pitch instability the center of gravity was moved still further forward, largely by increasing the girth of the skids and elevator supports. This also increased their strength and would hopefully reduce repair frequency. The canard, or forward elevator, was increased in area to handle its increased loading, and also for better control response with less movement by the operator.(3/50) And yet again they started the flight tests with a slight droop rigged into the wings, their precious anhedral.

But by far the most significant change to the airframe was the abandonment of their soon-to-be-patented coordinated rudders. The vertical rudders were still there, but now they were controlled independently of wing warping. (1/471,2/46) By the end of 1904 the Wrights had determined that this was essential in order to hold and exit a turn.

By midsummer of 1905 the Wrights were ready to resume flying at Huffman Prairie near Dayton. The first flight on June 23rd lasted for just 272 feet and ended in an out of control crash. The fourth, sixth, and eighth flights also ended in crashes.(1/449,450) They were again having trouble maintaining and exiting turns, and sometimes even in initiating them. It was tricky to start a turn without overbanking. Then, throughout the turn the aircraft wanted to overbank and descend. And when they tried to exit the turn the vehicle would spin in. After the eighth flight they determined that the rudder needed to be more responsive. So they tried a trick they had learned a few years earlier with the forward elevator; they moved the pivot points back within the rudders instead of having them at the leading edge. (1/500) They were, in effect, creating what would come to be known as aerodynamically balanced controls. (This trick had been used on boat rudders for many decades.) This design allows the control to be deflected with much less effort or, conversely, gives more deflection with the same effort on the control making it feel more responsive.

Then, on July 14th the ninth test ended in a dangerously heavy crash. But this time the problem was an old one, loss of pitch control.(1/501) Although they had largely come to terms with their vehicle's pitch instabilities in level flight, now that they were trying to turn, the workload of controlling the vehicle in all three axes was sometimes more than even they could handle. They decided they needed a better understanding of the aircraft's pitch characteristics. So they went back to their wind tunnel and, for the first time, attempted to make measurements of the fore and aft location of the center of pressure on airfoils, as well as its movement with varying angles of attack.(1/502,503) However this tunnel testing was very brief and it is questionable how much of practical value the Wrights learned.

They resumed flying in late August, and although they still had problems even initiating turns, at least there were no real crashes for the next few flights. Nevertheless, they decided that they needed still more directional control, so on the 30th and 31st of August they fitted new, larger vertical rear rudders.(1/507,508) They even tried the radical step of hinging them aft of their centers of pressure. This gave the rudders an over-center feel which would have made them overly responsive if not downright dangerous. The brothers passed on no further information regarding the duration or success of this modification.

The next half-dozen flights in early September were rather uneventful, although the Wrights were still unsuccessful at consistently turning and returning to level flight. Then, on both flight numbers 27 and 30, they had minor crashes due to stalling in turns. Finally, on flight number 34 on the 15th of September they crashed due to an inability to stop the vehicle from turning. (1/511) They had to face reality. Although they liked the crosswind effect given by anhedral, it was destroying any chance they had of making and exiting turns. Any time they initiated a banking turn, the anhedral was throwing them deeper into the bank, requiring extreme control in the opposite direction just to maintain the desired bank angle, often eliminating any chance of returning to level flight. Moreover, the higher bank angles resulted in a substantial loss of lift, requiring flight at angles of attack dangerously close to stalling. So, no longer having to worry about the strong Kitty Hawk crosswinds tilting them and blowing them into hillsides, they finally took the droop out of the wings and re-rigged the aircraft to have dihedral.

The positive results of dihedral were immediate. In late September and early October they made more flights, pretty much turning and leveling out at will. They even discovered a trick of pushing the nose down somewhat at the end of a turn to gain speed which gave them more rudder power and, most importantly, avoided stalling the slower inside wing when it was put to a higher angle of attack for the rollout.(1/512) A number of flights continued until the plane ran out of gas. The longest flight, on October 5th lasted over 38 minutes and included thirty laps around the field.(1/514 & 2/46) It, too, was terminated only by fuel exhaustion. This flight covered a total distance of about 25 miles, their longest ever.

They made a total of fifty flights by mid-October 1905. Since by then they were flying much higher, they were attracting the attention of many highway and trolley passengers and other onlookers. But they wished to keep the details of their machines secret until their patent was approved and contracts for substantial sums of money could be secured. So they decided that it would be prudent to terminate their testing. They had flown a maximum distance of 25 miles at speeds approaching 40 miles per hour, and had exceeded 100 feet in altitude. They could fly as long as they wanted and wherever they wanted. They now had a real airplane. The only airplane. And they knew it.

Figure 46: A Wright 1905 Flight

CHAPTER IV

A Critical Look: 1899 - 1905

I n the last chapter we followed along with the Wrights through their research and testing, from the beginning to the achievement of a reasonably flyable powered aircraft by 1905, the first in the world. We followed
their reasoning and saw their problems and the solutions as they saw them.
But this time, with the advantages of hindsight and a better understanding of the phenomena involved, we will examine their work more critically.
We will look at the problems they encountered with a depth of understanding that the Wright brothers simply did not have. But we will be careful
not to take advantage of knowledge that was nowhere in existence at that
time. Instead we will see that the knowledge necessary to avoid or better
solve their problems was indeed in existence and well recorded before the
Wrights began their work. We will find that had they made more extensive
use of existing information they had, and not been so quick to discount
most all of the work done before them, they no doubt would have achieved
a much better result even sooner. They probably would have actually accomplished some of the things by 1903 for which they have erroneously
been given credit. And they may well have achieved the long-term leadership of the aircraft industry that they so desperately came to want.

Rather than follow along in strict chronology as in the last chapter, in this
one we will divide their work into specific technical areas and examine each
in turn. Since many of the same events and problems were discussed in the

last chapter, these discussions may, at times, seem repetitive. But here we will discover that many of the problems the Wrights encountered were created by themselves, some they didn't admit to. We'll see problems they didn't even realize they had. And we will reveal many more of the misconceptions concerning their work and the capabilities of their machines.

It is worth reiterating that this chapter is not intended to belittle or denigrate the Wright brothers' work. They accomplished the magnificent feat of creating the world's first real airplane and did so in an amazingly short time. The analyses presented in this chapter are merely intended to set the historical record straight.

The Wright Mindset

The Wrights' attitude seemed to be that the outside world should not always be trusted. There were those who were incompetent and careless. What's more, some sought to take advantage of them, to dupe them out of what should rightfully be theirs. Only family members were to be fully trusted.(14/20)

Although this may seem at first like a rather severe portrait of humanity, it was not an uncommon attitude at the end of the 19th century. At that time a wave of immigrants was washing westward across America and many of them couldn't speak English. They were consequently victims or perpetrators of misunderstandings or intentional misdeeds. Americans had few of the protections available through modern technology and law enforcement that we now enjoy, and some were quick to take advantage of this situation.

Even so, it seems their father, Milton, took his attitude to an extreme. He was engaged in battles with other members of the clergy within his own church. In fact, he was even involved in a lawsuit within the church at his own instigation.(14/26) Growing up in this somewhat paranoid environment could explain many of Wilbur and Orville's actions later in life, including many of their social, scientific, and legal struggles.

But this attitude also brought benefits to the Wright family. They moved to Dayton during Wilbur's senior year of high school, which precluded his receiving a diploma in spite of his excellent work throughout school. Soon after the move, Wilbur, while playing hockey, suffered a severe injury to his face which he feared would badly disfigure him for life. It didn't, but nonetheless he stayed home for some time struggling with depression. Then, when his mother fell ill, he continued to stay at home taking excellent care of her and Katherine, his child sister.(14/25)

By the time their mother died, Katherine was fifteen years old and capable of caring for the household. However, in the late nineteenth century, with school and her father and brothers, this was no easy task. But then, upon completion of high school Katherine was rewarded with the opportunity to get a college degree, a rare accomplishment for a woman back then. Actually, both Wilbur and Orville also had thoughts of going to college, but with the depression of the 1890s and their successful printing and bicycle businesses, they drifted away from the idea.(14/25-27) But Kate did go to college, getting a teaching degree in 1898. After teaching in the local high school for some years, she quit to devote herself full-time to Orville's recovery from his 1908 Ft. Meyers crash, and then to her brothers' burgeoning airplane business.

So sticking together and contributing to the family's well-being while viewing others with suspicion reaped some rewards. But we will see that this attitude was carried to such an extreme that it eventually contributed to Wilbur and Orville's difficulties in later life.

The Spark

The toy wind-up rubber band helicopter given to the boys by their father when they were young teenagers was mentioned in the last chapter. Since they related the story on occasion as their first brush with flight, this has often been quoted as the beginning of their interest in aviation. They, however, never really claimed it as such. When the toy wore out, they did build a few replicas of it. They even tried to see how much bigger they could make it. But being unfamiliar with the scale effect, their larger versions were failures.(1/3) (The scale effect, you may recall from a previous discussion of Langley's Aerodrome, is the term used for the geometric fact that, in general, if something is made twice as big in linear terms, it will have four times the area and eight times the volume or weight, thus requiring eight times the strength in many areas and roughly eight times the power in order to lift itself.) In any case, as teenagers often do, they soon lost interest and turned their minds to other things.

Others have claimed that the boys developed their fascination with flight from watching soaring birds in the Dayton area. To my knowledge neither of the Wrights ever claimed this to be much of a factor either although Wilbur did mention in a letter to Chanute that he thought he saw birds twisting their wingtips. Like anyone who has observed bird flight even briefly, Wilbur noted that all birds bank or tilt in order to turn. However he indicated that they never really studied bird flight until they went to Kitty Hawk.(1/34-36) There, the soaring flight of buzzards, pelicans, gulls, and frigate birds fascinated the Wrights much as they do many of us who visit the beach. By then they could understand much more of what they saw. Still Orville maintained that they got very little from watching birds.(14/34,51)

Actually, without a telescopic, high-speed cini-camera, it is very difficult to learn much about how birds propel and control their flight. The movements are extremely subtle and quick, and hard for the naked eye to accurately perceive at a distance. As Wilbur put it in a speech to the Western Society of Engineers on September 18, 1901, "The bird has learned this art of equilibrium, and learned it so thoroughly that its skill is not apparent to our sight". (1/100) Most use versions of wing warping for roll control and turning. However, some will shorten one wing by bending it at the "elbow." Gulls and pelicans do this for tight turning when diving for fish. Others will trail a tip back and bend it much like an aileron. And many will twist and deflect their broad tails to use them like a rudder to initiate a yaw to turn or control roll. And to really confuse the issue, some birds use dihedral while some use anhedral. Many birds will draw from this bag of tricks whatever seems to suit them at the moment. So any observer of birds, particularly those laymen using the naked eye, may well end up more confused than enlightened. Although during the 1880s Jules Marey obtained some rapid sequence photos of birds landing, these would have been of little use to the Wrights who, in any case, were unaware of them.(18/94).

As mentioned in Chapter III, the Wrights claimed their interest in aviation was actually ignited in 1896 when Wilbur read of the activities of previous experimenters to Orville in the evenings while Orville was recovering from his bout with typhoid. Wilbur was very impressed by Lilienthal's work and heavily influenced by his conclusions, in particular that the last remaining problem to be solved was that of maintaining equilibrium in flight. (8/211) It seems that from this point on, Wilbur's interest in manned flight never waned. Although at first Orville seemed to be less driven and technically interested than Wilbur, he eventually became a capable and productive member of the duo.

Basic Research

During the late 1890s Wilbur scoured the Dayton library and began a collection of newspaper and magazine articles, gathering everything that came his way on aviation and the experimenters and their exploits. This database took a giant leap forward after Wilbur wrote the Smithsonian in Washington, D.C. on May 30th, 1899 requesting a listing of pertinent information.(2/11) In response to his request he received four reprints of articles along with a list of titles of relevant material. Four books on the list, Octave Chanute's *Progress in Flying Machines* and James Means' *Aeronautical Annuals* of 1895, 1896, and 1897, contained virtually everything up through Lilienthal's accident.(14/38) Eventually, with this and additional material provided by Chanute, the Wrights certainly should have had material on Cayley, Henson, Stringfellow, LeBris, duTemple, Penaud, Mouillard, Phillips, Lilienthal, Pilcher, Chanute's own team, Maxim, and Langley. Although some of the reporting was occasionally erroneous and sensationalized, this still must have comprised a tremendously broad and solid base of information from which to depart.

However, it is questionable just how much of this material really influenced the Wrights' thinking and choices. In his letter to the Smithsonian Wilbur said, "I have some pet theories as to the proper construction of a flying machine," indicating that he already had some preconceived notions about the design of an aircraft. Not only that, their first test device, the five-foot biplane kite, was flown shortly after they first requested data. Its wings were obviously patterned closely on an Augustus Herring design, as were those of their subsequent aircraft. Its aspect ratio, wing spacing, and structure were all quite similar to the Herring/Chanute 1897 machine, which was that team's most successful design. But of course the Wrights' version included wing warping. The operation, testing, and results obtained with this device were sufficiently described in the last chapter. The point to be made here is that it was completed and flown only a few weeks after Wilbur first requested information from the Smithsonian. They were still gathering and studying material recommended by the Smithsonian after the 1899 flight test.

They eventually did study much of the material. For example, in correspondence with Chanute in December of 1904 Wilbur discussed some of Cayley's work that appeared in the 1809 and 1810 articles and praised the accuracy of Cayley's calculations.(7/42) Yet the Wrights paid no heed to

Cayley's warnings that a horizontal tail was absolutely essential for stability or that an airplane engine would need extra power for takeoff.(7/49) Cayley's statement, made a century earlier, was that it was absolutely necessary to have both "side-to-side" and "up-and-down" controls mounted behind the lifting wings.(18/48) For that matter, four centuries before that Leonardo daVinci had sketched a stabilizing tail for his manned glider concept (see Figure 51).

Not one of the aviation experimenters preceding the Wrights had used a forward-mounted elevator on any of their manned or unmanned vehicles. (Although Maxim's machine had a forward elevator, the vehicle never really flew and the surface was never employed.) All of the previous experimenters who built gliding models had used aft stabilizers. And of course their models were stable in flight. They had to be. They had no pilots. Their work included hundreds of models, flying for over a hundred years. The "great gliders," Lilienthal, Pilcher, and Chanute's team all used tailed configurations and made thousands of manned glides, some lasting for nearly a minute and 1,000 feet. It took a couple of pretty headstrong guys to conclude that all these men had done it wrong for over a century. To say nothing about the birds. They all had tails. Had they been doing it wrong too?

In one area of their basic research the Wrights were actually too trusting of their predecessor's conclusions. Unfortunately, it was and is the most basic principle of heavier than air flight: how cambered wings generate lift. We have seen in Chapters I and II that all of their predecessors except Horatio Phillips, Otto Lilienthal, and Augustus Herring had gotten it completely wrong. The others all thought that lift was due to the impact of air on the bottom surface of wings. The Wrights also bought into this theory. And, hard as it may be to believe, the inventors of the airplane still believed it long after they had created their first powered Flyers.

In the Wrights' master patent granted in 1906, a document they had worked on and refined for over three years, they stated that their aircraft was "....supported in the air by reason of the contact between the air and the *under surface* of one or more aeroplanes [wings], the contact surface being presented at a small angle of incidence to the air".(4,1) (The italic and bold emphasis is mine.) In other words, to them, lift was nothing more than the reaction of a slanted surface being impacted upon by countless air particles, just like the way water supports a skier. This line of reasoning appears in many places throughout their work. In fact, they believed that the function of wing camber, or curvature, was to present the front portion of the upper surface to impinging air particles in order to create a downforce on the front to keep the wing from flipping over backward.

The Wrights had put a great deal of effort into their 1906 patent in order to cover, in the greatest and most correct detail possible, all aspects of their machines' operation. They knew their entire future success depended upon it. Certainly, if they understood lift they would have included a proper explanation of how their vehicle was able to fly in their patent. But it is not there, and it does not exist anywhere else in their writings.

In a paper presented to the Western Society of Engineers on September 18, 1901, Wilbur maintained that the reason the center of lifting pressure on a cambered airfoil moves aft with decreasing angle of attack was that at the lower angles, air hit on more of the forward upper surface, thus pushing the front of the wing down harder.(1/109) (The real reasons for this lift movement are that at lower angles, the airflow is accelerated, and thus the pressure reduced, over a longer stretch of the wing's upper surface, and also any flow separation and resulting lift loss from the aft upper surface is diminished.) Later we will see what severe problems this misunderstanding of how cambered airfoils work created for the Wrights, not only in developing the airplane but also in marketing it.

I have found only one indication that they may have even suspected that there was lowered pressure above an airfoil. In a letter to Chanute on December, 1ˢᵗ, 1901, in the midst of their wind tunnel testing, Wilbur explained some lift curve anomalies (actually slight bumps in the lines) by writing "Possibly this is due to the fact that at small angles the lift is chiefly due to the rarefaction on the back, while at larger angles the incidence on the lower side produces the predominating pressure, or visa versa".(1/169,170) Even here it is evident that Wilbur was not sure what was going on. He seems to think there is a lowered pressure somewhere on the "back" of the wing section, but he is not sure if or how it would play a role in affecting or producing any lift. This letter contains the only reference I have found to the possibility of their awareness of the existence of a lowered pressure above the wing. And it is referring to minor fluctuations in lift, not the basic production of it.

Statements made years later by Wilbur reveal his continued belief in the pressure-on-the-bottom theory. In a letter to Chanute on April 12, 1905, he indicated that he believed that birds flew by "keeping the pressure constantly on the underside" of their wings.(1/486) Wilbur wrote an article for a French magazine on July 19, 1907 comparing the operation of his flying machine to blimps and balloons. In it he stated that, as opposed to a blimp, "the flying machine, on the other hand, is constructed on the principle of the inclined plane".(1/801) In other words, lift was merely the sideways reaction of a surface to being pushed on at an angle. This incorrect explanation of lift was offered seven years after they began flying and nearly four years after their first powered flight.

There is yet another confirmation of the Wrights' misconception concerning how lift is generated by a cambered airfoil. It occurred to me while examining the Wrights actual wind tunnel test models at the Franklin Institute in Philadelphia. This one has been glaring, unnoticed, for a century. The airfoil models used by the Wrights in their wind tunnels had mounting tabs soldered onto them at right angles to the wings but aligned with the airflow. Although these tabs were necessary, they were, no doubt, put on in a manner intended to cause the minimum disruption to the airflow that was critical to the generation of lift. Any modern-day aerodynamicist would use a long pole or "sting" mounting from behind the test sections, or at least mount them from their lower surfaces to avoid disturbing the critical flow over the tops of the sections. But in every case the Wrights soldered the tabs onto the top surfaces of their test sections. Obviously, they didn't want to disturb the flow below the sections because they believed that was the key to the generation of lift. (1/550.6 to 550.10)

The phenomenon of lift on a cambered wing can be explained from an energy standpoint using Daniel Bernoulli's relationship which describes the tradeoff between a subsonic flow's kinetic energy (that due to its motion, or speed) and its inherent pressure energy. Depending on its temperature and density, air contains only so much total energy for its motion and pressure to draw upon. As the air accelerates across the curved top of a cambered wing it thins out and draws kinetic energy from the total available, thus reducing the pressure energy, or simply, the pressure.

From a molecular standpoint, as the air speeds up to cover the greater distance across the convex upper surface of the wing, the air molecules spread out leaving fewer molecules to electromagnetically repel a given segment of the wing surface's molecules. This results in less pressure on the surface thereby creating the lift on a cambered wing. (The acceleration of the air at subsonic speeds also lowers its temperature reducing the random motion of its molecules and the resulting electromagnetic pressure on the wing's molecules, but that small effect is not of concern here.)

Perhaps the simplest way of picturing this is through an analogy of air flowing over a wing to the flow of traffic on a highway. Each car pushes down on the street with its weight. When the traffic flow is stopped, the cars are close together and the weight on a given segment of road is high. But when the traffic speeds up, the cars spread out and the weight on the same segment of road diminishes. Now think of the cars as particles (molecules) of air and the road as the top of a wing. That is similar to the way air above a wing is thinned out as it speeds up, and the pressure on top of the wing lowered to create lift.

Interestingly, Bernoulli published this physical relationship over 160 years before the Wrights began their experiments. However you can't really fault the Wrights for not seeing the relationship between this law and the functioning of a cambered wing. I have seen no indication that any of their predecessors or contemporaries did either. Even so, Horatio Phillips published the relationship between lift and lowered pressures above a wing fifteen years before the Wrights began. Although Phillips' work was pointed out to the Wrights by the Smithsonian, and his explanation is presented in three places in Chanute's 1894 book, which the Wrights had, it could be glossed over amidst the numerous references to inclined planes and such.(8/157,166,169)

What is perhaps even more surprising is that Otto Lilienthal pointed out in his 1889 book that, although there is a higher pressure on the bottom surface of a thin cambered airfoil, there also is a "suction" on its top surface which plays a more significant role in the development of lift. He envisioned this suction being caused by the air being forced to flow in a curved path over the airfoil. He believed that centrifugal force would tend to draw the air away from the convex upper surface, thereby stretching or thinning the air and lowering the pressure on the surface. This concept is extremely close to what actually happens and is actually closer to the truth than was Horatio Phillips' explanation a few years earlier. Lilienthal even correctly deduced that the "suction" was stronger over the forward portion of a cambered airfoil.(9/59)

Early on, the Wrights put more faith in Lilienthal's work than any of their other predecessors, so it may seem surprising that they did not take note of this, perhaps his most profound conclusion. But the explanation is disarmingly simple. Otto Lilienthal wrote in German and the Wrights could not read German. The only translations they had early on were provided by Chanute on the 29th of September,1901. Chanute had received them from Professor Langley, and they consisted of only thirteen sections from Otto's 42-section book. Unfortunately the translations did not include the section wherein Lilienthal gave his explanation of the generation of lift.(1/139,140) In a May 6th, 1903 letter to Dr. Spratt, Wilbur pointed out that he couldn't read Lilienthal's book because it was in German. Nonetheless he proceeded to give his presumption of why Lilienthal preferred cambered wings and it was completely wrong. In the letter Wilbur wrote only in terms of impact and deflection of the airstream, saying nothing about suctions or lowered pressures.

It seems like the Wrights, and almost all other early aviation experimenters, were only concerned with the inertia or momentum aspects of air, but totally unaware of, or unconcerned with, the viscosity or cohesive aspects of air. This is unfortunate since it is the viscus quality of air that is primarily responsible for its ability to generate lift.

But there was yet another proper explanation of lift that the Wrights certainly should have read. In 1899 the Smithsonian recommended that they read, among other things, James Means' series of *The Aeronautical Annuals*. In the 1897 edition Augustus Herring's article included the statement that "what is spoken of….as a pressure on the underside [of a cambered wing] is chiefly a partial vacuum over the upper surface".(39/56) Considering the problems the Wrights' misinterpretation of lift caused prior to their wind tunnel testing near the end of 1901, not heeding this correct statement must be considered yet another unfortunate shortcoming of their initial research effort.

Lanchester had published a mathematical derivation of the lift on a cambered wing in England not long after Chanute's book was published.(35/124) Also, by 1902 Wilhelm Kutta and Nikolai Jukowski had published their circulation theories of lift. These theories indicate that a lowered pressure above a cambered airfoil is the key to lift. But these findings were widely publicized too late to do the Wrights any good, so they uncharacteristically went with the majority opinion and began by copying a successful wing design, albeit with some major errors as will be explained shortly.

Eventually the Wrights became distrusting of all their predecessors' work. By the fall of 1901 they had decided "that all the calculations upon which all flying machines had been based were unreliable….all were groping in the dark".(2/84) And then they added "Finally, after two years of experiment, we cast it all aside and decided to rely entirely upon our own investigations." The argument could be made that they were largely doing that from the start. Even so, it seems that occasionally their struggles to achieve lift and control of their machines wore them down and they returned to the material generated by their predecessors for help. In fact, they were still consulting Cayley's work as late as the winter of 1904/1905.(1/475)

Although the Wrights deduced much from their gliding tests at Kitty Hawk in August of 1901, and from bicycle tests during that fall in Dayton, the most famous of the Wrights' research tools were their wind tunnels. Actually there were three, the first being little more than a proof-of-concept prototype. (1/548,550) Most testing was done in the second tunnel. Usually both the concept and design are credited completely to the Wrights. Neither is true. The idea came up in conversations with Chanute, Spratt, and Huffaker at the Kitty Hawk camp during the summer of 1901. In fact, Chanute showed the Wrights photos of wind tunnel components.(1/134) Not only that, the Wrights returned to Dayton armed with a scheme for a test apparatus, a force "balance" suggested to them by Dr. Spratt. It was basically a flexible parallelogram device mounted horizontally in the tunnel which would allow vertical test sections to translate and exhibit the ratio of the lift and drag forces imposed on them by the airflow without changing the critical angle of attack of the test sections. The Wrights also adapted the concept to measure the forces on airfoils against flat plate drag, but the basic scheme to measure lift-to-drag ratios, the true merit of an airfoil, was Dr. Spratt's suggestion. Orville readily admitted this in a letter to Dr. Spratt and in his sworn legal deposition of 1920. (1/554 & 2/18)

The Wrights were indeed fortunate to have the benefit of consultations with Octave Chanute who had been the chief engineer and bridge and trestle designer for the Hudson River Railroad, and was the world's foremost compiler of aviation research, Edward Huffaker who had a degree in physics and substantial aerodynamic research experience with professor Langley at the Smithsonian, and Dr. George Spratt who had also extensively studied aviation research methods and results. These three constituted a formidable resource. The Wrights' records provide evidence of the contributions these men made to the Wrights' knowledge base, but this is almost universally overlooked by historians. Still, the Wrights' records reveal that these men assisted them with assembling an initial data base, recommending they first make unmanned tethered tests of vehicles and then master controlled gliding flight, suggesting the Georgia or Carolina coasts for a test site, the design of light trussed biplane wing structures, wing shapes, centers-of-pressure location and movements, wind tunnel design, tunnel measuring systems, and the all-important catapult design. Chanute even repeatedly tried unsuccessfully to convince the

Wrights to adopt a more stable airplane configuration, something they finally had to do almost ten years later. Considering all these inputs, it is quite possible that without them the Wrights would not have achieved success as soon as they did, if at all.

It might seem that, with all the testing the Wrights did in their wind tunnels, they should have correctly understood the mechanism of wing lift. They made many hundreds of runs in their tunnels, testing dozens of cambered shapes. They also investigated many planforms, aspect ratios, tip shapes, multi-wing configurations, and even a delta wing. But the forces on these shapes were always compared one against another, or against flat plate references. The closest they came to making actual pressure measurements were comparative measurements of total lift. Only in two tests in 1905 were center of pressure measurements made.

Knowledge of the patterns of airflow around an airfoil might have clued the Wrights as to the mechanism of lift. But as far as flow patterns were concerned, they had no means to see them in their tunnels and they merely made intuitive guesses as to what was going on. Unfortunately, this was one of the times their intuition failed them. Phillips, on the other hand, used streams of steam to actually see airflow patterns.(8/166) Consequently, his appreciation for how a cambered wing actually produces lift was far more accurate than the Wrights'. But apparently even without such visual clues, Lilienthal and Herring came to still more accurate understandings of how lift was generated. Although as Orville put it in 1921, they had generated more data "than all of our predecessors put together", they did not have as good an understanding of the physical causes of these data as did Horatio Phillips, Otto Lilienthal, or Augustus Herring years earlier.(1/551)

It has been asserted that the Wrights were, after all, "engineers, not scientists", and as such were not concerned with exactly how things worked, but rather with what actually worked, or worked best. Although this assertion was made to me from the highest level of the Smithsonian's Air and Space Museum, I have never heard it made by a real engineer, and believe it does a disservice to the Wrights as engineers. While it is certainly true that engineers use empirical data in the design process, it is not possible to properly use this data without an understanding of the basic physics behind what they are creating. Indeed, modern engineers spend nearly all of their academic years (and some a great deal of subsequent research) developing this understanding. I am sure the Wrights were well aware of this requirement, and thought that they did understand how the various components of their machines worked. This is what distinguished them from most of their predecessors. To say that they didn't really care how things worked is far more demeaning to them as engineers than is my assertion that they thought they knew but in some cases were wrong.

Before discussing the results of their wind tunnel testing we should be absolutely clear on one thing. The Wrights used the correct wing area for their 1901 vehicle months before they even began building their first wind tunnel. Finding out that the 1900 glider with 165 square feet of total wing area produced nowhere near the lift required for manned flight, they nearly doubled the area to 290 square feet on the 1901 machine. I have seen no computational justification for the exact magnitude of this increase. The total wing area of the 1902 glider was essentially the same at 305 square feet. So whatever happened in the wind tunnel at the end of 1901, it had nothing to do with a changed Smeaton's coefficient changing the wing areas of their machines. Actually the idea of 300 square feet of wing area being appropriate for manned gliding had been around for a century. Sir George Cayley used it in his 1804 "man carrying" glider, and he published this requirement in his third article in *Nicholson's Journal* in 1810.

Over a 23-year period Otto Lilienthal used his test equipment to generate plots and tables of lift and drag coefficients for various wing shapes over a wide range of angles of attack to the airflow. The Wrights claimed to have used Lilienthal's data and wing shapes to design their 1900 and 1901 gliders. (The shapes are crucial because different wing cambers and planforms give vastly different lift.) This is why many have written that the reason the Wrights could not generate enough lift with their early machines was that Lilienthal's lift data were wrong. For a century the story has been told about how the Wrights used their wind tunnel to correct errors in Lilienthal's data, and how this finally allowed them to design wings of sufficient size and lift to proceed with powered flight. Others claimed that, following his lead, the Wrights used the wrong value of Smeaton's coefficient, and that this error was revealed by their wind tunnel testing. My research revealed that none of these claims are true.

Lilienthal used a whirling arm machine to generate most of his lift and drag data, and presented the results as graphs or "plates" at the end of his book *Birdflight as the Basis of Aviation*. The airfoils he tested had semicircular cambers or curvatures with aspect ratios of 6.5 and maximum cambers of 0, 2.,

4, and 8⅓ percent of the chord length. But for the airfoil with camber of 8⅓ percent, tests were also conducted on a fixed wing section in a strong "natural wind", and these data were also presented.(9/143-150) Unfortunately none of these plots were among the translated sections of Lilienthal's book that Chanute had and provided to the Wrights. All the Wrights had was a table of Lilienthal's coefficients that Chanute obtained from his German contact, Major Moedebeck, and then published in the 1897 issue of James Means' *Aeronautical Annual*. (1/140, 39/115) This was a tabulation of the natural wind data for the eight and one third percent camber semi-circular section, although these conditions were not specified on the table.

So a few things are immediately noteworthy. First, the data the Wrights used were for a semi-circular section with maximum camber at the fifty percent chord point, not at the ten percent point they chose. Second, the data was for a section with maximum camber of eight and one third percent, not the five percent Lilienthal recommended and the Wrights used. Third, Lilienthal's data were for wings with twice the aspect ratio that the Wrights were using. And finally, the Lilienthal data the Wrights had was derived in a straight natural wind; a whirling arm machine had nothing to do with it. Although the tapered shape of Lilenthal's test wing was not specified on the coefficient table, its significance would not have been apparent to the Wrights until after their wind tunnel testing anyway. So more about this later.

(The next five pages are most easily followed by those with a basic familiarity with algebra and aeronautical engineering. For those not interested, skip ahead to the last paragraph on page 142. No information essential to a basic understanding of the Wrights' lift problem will be lost in doing so.)

Before getting further into the results of the Wrights' wind tunnel tests, it is important to have an understanding of the factors involved in the generation of lift and drag on a wing, and their relationship to each other. The discovery of these factors is credited to some of history's most illustrious scientific minds. By 1500 Leonardo daVinci had determined that the drag force generated on an object moving through air is proportional to its crossectional area, and by 1638 Galileo had found that the force was also proportional to the density of the surrounding medium. Then, in 1669 Christian Huygens, and in 1673 Edme Mariotte, determined the drag to be proportional to the square of the relative velocity between the object and the medium through which it is moving. Finally the master, Sir Isaac Newton, proved all of these relationships through pendulum experiments published in his 1687 *Principia*. (41/31-37)

If a body is not symmetrical about an axis in the direction of motion, the force on it resulting from its motion through air will most likely not be exactly opposite its direction of motion, i.e., not all drag. For a wing, the component of the force crossways to the direction of motion is much greater than the drag and is called the lift. So, since lift and drag are merely two different slices of the same force, lift is also dependent upon the same parameters. Consequently, for over a century engineers have used the relationships

$$L = \frac{1}{2}\rho \times V^2 \times S \times C_L$$

And

$$D = \frac{1}{2}\rho \times V^2 \times S \times C_D$$

where L is the lift, D is the drag, ρ is the air density, V is the velocity of the wing, S is its area as seen from above, and C_L and C_D are called the lift and drag coefficients respectively. (The x's merely indicate multiplication.) The 1/2 is there so that the term $1/2\rho V^2$ represents the kinetic energy of the flow per unit volume. Since this term has the units of pressure, it is also called the dynamic pressure. The coefficients at the ends of the equations are not constant and are whatever number it takes to make the equations work. Until recent times they were typically derived through physical testing wherein all the other factors were known.

During the nineteenth century all aviation experimentation was done near ground level, so the decrease in air density with altitude was not a factor. And, since minor effects on density such as temperature and barometric pressure were unknown or ignored, density was considered constant, leading early experimenters to use the relationships

$$L = k \times V^2 \times S \times C_L$$
$$D = k \times V^2 \times S \times C_D$$

The k was called Smeaton's coefficient and was determined from the drag equation by setting C_D equal to one and measuring the drag on a flat plate or disk set at 90 degrees to the airflow. This was the relationship for lift (and drag) used by Lilienthal, Langley, Chanute, and many others,

including the Wrights. (Since the drag coefficient of a flat plate perpendicular to an airflow was later determined to be 1.28 when the standard sea level
value for air density was used, early lift and drag coefficients do not equate
directly to modern values.)

To design an aircraft it is necessary to predict how much lift will result
from a given wing size and shape. To do so, the lift and drag coefficients of various wing shapes must be available. During the 1930s and 1940s the National
Advisory Committee for Aeronautics (NACA, the precursor to NASA) did
wind tunnel tests measuring the forces on a vast variety of wing cross section shapes, and used the first previous set of equations to calculate the corresponding coefficients versus speed. Much of this data was widely published
and generally available throughout the world. In the design process, a likely
wing shape can be chosen and the appropriate coefficients used to determine
other factors such as wing size, cruise speed or altitude, or allowable weight,
depending upon which of these have already been determined by requirements or other factors. If necessary, a number of wing sections can be tried
along with various planforms. These days modern high-speed computers using advanced computational fluid dynamics methods are capable of directly
calculating amazingly accurate values of lift and drag and their coefficients.
However wind tunnel tests of models, along with the appropriate scale and
flow corrections, are still usually considered the final word on predicting
these parameters for aircraft during the design process.

On October, 6, 1901, before beginning their wind tunnel tests, Wilbur
wrote a letter to Octave Chanute saying, "I am now absolutely certain
that Lilienthal's table is very seriously in error".(1/127) But then ten days
later he wrote, "It would appear that Lilienthal is very much nearer the
truth....".(1/135) On November 2, 1901 Wilbur wrote, "....there is reason in
nearly all he writes". He added that there were four categories of "apparent discrepancies between [the Wrights'] calculations based on [Lilienthal's] tables
and [their] actual experiences". These included "(1) errors of Lilienthal's for-
mula and tables; (2) errors in the use of them; (3) errors in anemometers and
other estimates of velocities; (4) errors of our own in overlooking or improperly applying certain things".(1/145) They went on to discuss Lilienthal's
"errors" referred to in item one above, and the only one that could possibly
have had significant impact on their work was too high a value of Smeaton's
coefficient. But notice that at least two, and possibly all three, of the other
"discrepancies" listed above were actually admissions of errors committed by

the Wrights in using his data. Finally, by December 1, 1901 Wilbur concluded that "....for a surface....like that described in his [Lilienthal's] book the
table is probably as near correct as it is possible....with the methods he used".
(1/169)

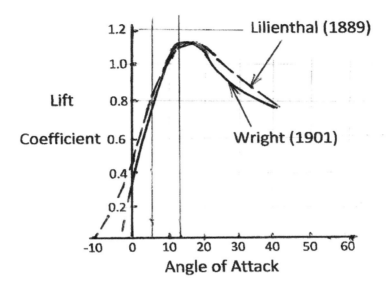

Figure 47A: Wright and Lilienthal Lift Curves

Study of both Lilienthal's lift coefficient data and the corresponding data
generated by the Wrights in their wind tunnel shows that, indeed, if one com-
pares similar camber and planform shapes, there is almost no difference between the two data sets at the typical flight angles of four to twelve degrees
angle of attack. (See Figure 47A) (34/146) In fact, in this region Lilienthal's
data are more consistent than some of the Wrights'.(34/146) In a letter to
Chanute, Wilbur admitted that "an error of a tenth of a degree in mounting
the [test] surface on the [wind tunnel's balance] machine would lead to an
error [in calculating lift coefficient] of nearly ten percent".(1/163) This is no
doubt why, after two months of studying, testing, and calculating, the Wrights
developed an appreciation for the accuracy of Lilienthal's work, concluding
that "....the table is probably as near correct as it is possible....".(3/21)

So there were no substantial errors in Lilienthal's data due to his test conditions. But what about his value of Smeaton's coefficient? Many have pointed
to his recommended high value of this parameter as the source of error in his

data. Well, it turns out that Lilienthal calculated his coefficients from lift and drag ratios without using Smeaton's coefficient. Since the areas and speeds were the same (or compensated for with ratios), he could present his data as ratios of the lift and drag coefficients with the wing profiles set at various angles-of-attack versus the value of the drag coefficient at ninety degrees. By this method the value of k is automatically consistent, drops out of the ratios along with speed and area, and is thus irrelevant. So not only is the ratio of the lift at any angle to the drag at 90° the same as the ratio of the lift coefficient at any angle to the drag coefficient at 90°, but since the drag coefficient at 90° was, at that time, taken to be one, the force or coefficient ratio *is* the value of the lift coefficient. Mathematically, the situation is

$$ L \,/\, D_{90°} = C_L \,/\, C_{D90°} = C_L \,/\, 1 = C_L $$

Actually, the Wrights' wind tunnel worked the same way. In a letter to Octave Chanute at the start of their tests Wilbur said that their balance gave lifts as a fraction of the drag on flat plates, in other words, as ratios rather than directly.

Lilienthal's plots (or tables of the same data) can be used in a couple of ways to calculate the wing area required for a vehicle (provided one is using a wing with one of his camber profiles and planforms). One way involves Smeaton's coefficient, and one does not. One could do so without k by simply making a measurement of the drag force on a model of the proposed wing at ninety degrees to the flow using any model size at any known airspeed. (Actually, for camber profiles similar to Lilienthal's even a flat model of the planform would do.) Then the area ratio from test wing to the aircraft wing could be calculated using the ratio of the required lift to the drag on the test wing at ninety degrees, the ratio of the speeds squared, and Lilienthal's appropriate lift coefficient. From a physics standpoint k is involved, but from a mathematics standpoint it cancels out and never appears. (Those who are mathematically enthused can verify this by dividing the equation for aircraft lift by the similar equation for model drag at ninety degrees and rearranging, keeping in mind that the drag coefficient of the model wing at ninety degrees was considered to be one.)

The other way to use Lilienthal's data is by using k explicitly. Here one would multiply Lilienthal's lift coefficient by Smeaton's k and by the anticipated flight velocity squared, then multiply all this by the appropriate wing area to give the required lift (in other words, solving the lift equation shown a couple pages ago). Apparently this is what the Wrights did in designing their first glider in 1900. But the problem is that, using this method, one must use the correct value of Smeaton's coefficient. The Wrights evidently chose the value Lilienthal recommended in his text and right on his data plots, namely 0.13 metric, which is equivalent to 0.00533 in the English system with speed in miles per hour.

But here is the rub. For some reason Lilienthal's recommended value for k was about fifty percent high. By this time Octave Chanute was aware of dozens of values for k ranging from 0.0027 to 0.0055, so it was far from an established number.(1/513) Francis Wenham presented numbers in 1866 indicating a value of 0.0044 (half way from Lilienthal's to the current value), and Sir George Cayley, a century before the Wrights, had determined it to be 0.0038.(37/87) The United States Weather Bureau was using 0.0040 and professor Langley at the Smithsonian had determined it to be 0.0033. (The modern typically accepted value is 0.00327.) Evidently in 1900 the Wrights were not aware of the 100% uncertainty in the value of k, nor were they aware of Langley's value. They have inferred that they just used what was recommended on Lilienthal's plot.

Anyone aware of the uncertainty in Smeaton's should have avoided using it by testing a model of their proposed wing at ninety degrees. The test could have been done using an accurate force scale and any size section at any speed. The force ratio method previously discussed would then yield a wing area solution without using k. (At this time no one corrected for speed or scale effects such as with Reynold's number.) Apparently either the Wrights did not think of this method or at that time they were unaware of the controversy surrounding Smeaton's coefficient, and the high k they used forced their 1900 wing area solution to be too low. One wonders if this is another example of insufficient preliminary research.

Realizing their 1900 glider had completely insufficient wing area to lift them at the airspeeds and angles of incidence to the wind (angles of attack) they envisioned, they made the tests in early 1901 with the horizontally mounted V-shaped device discussed in Chapter III. This led them to believe that Lilienthal's value of Smeaton's coefficient k they had used was way too high. According to Orville, to be sure they had large enough wings, they nearly doubled their wing area for 1901, that vehicle having 305 total square feet of area (actually 290 after the cutout for the pilot).

At that time their concepts and calculations were hindered by inaccurate measurements of angle of attack during gliding tests, and the belief that there could be a difference in the characteristics of air depending upon whether it was the air or the vehicle that was moving. Although this later seems unfathomable to us now, back then almost nothing was known for certain, and the idea that there could be a difference was entertained by both the Wrights and Octave Chanute.

Flight tests during the summer of 1901 at Kitty Hawk revealed that they still didn't have enough lift, and discussions there with Chanute, Spratt, and Huffaker, convinced them that more testing was in order. It's likely these gentlemen brought up the idea of a wind tunnel to the Wrights since there is no record of any previous mention of a tunnel by either of them. After returning to Dayton the first tests they did were similar to those done early in the year with the V-shaped device. But this time they compared plates to cambered wing models using a bicycle wheel mounted horizontally and free to turn over the front wheel of a bicycle. This convinced them that Lilienthal's k was about 40 percent too high. In a letter to Chanute on October 16th, Wilbur wrote "I see no good reason for using a coefficient greater than .0033,...." (1/124) But since this was essentially the value used to calculate the wing area for the 1901 machine, the lift problem had to lie elsewhere. Consequently, wind tunnel tests were begun on the 22nd of November incorporating the tunnel design information they got from Chanute, Spratt, and Huffaker at Kitty Hawk. (1/135,550)

The exasperating fact in this whole episode is that how the Wrights used Lilienthal's data is largely irrelevant because, as previously mentioned, they didn't use anything like his wing camber profiles or planform shape. The Wrights claimed many times to have used Lilienthal's camber for their 1900 and 1901 machines, but by this they really meant that they used his value for the maximum height of the camber arch, not his entire section profile. (26/69) Although both the Wrights and Lilienthal spoke of using "parabolic" camber profiles, the Wrights' wings were sharply curved at the very front and flat after that, whereas Lilienthal said he used "shallow parabolas [which did] not differ much from circular arcs".(9/58) Lilienthal, Chanute, and many others had already written that a cambered wing should have its point of maximum camber from one third to halfway back from the leading edge of the wing, and that the curvature should be as gradual as possible, both in front of and behind this point. An examination of Lilienthal's favored airfoils in Figure 47B shows this to have been the case. (9/64,65)

However, examination of the Wrights' 1900 and 1901 gliders in Figures 48A and B shows something quite different. There are a number of photos of these machines, both in the air and on the ground. In spite of statements by the Wrights to the contrary, the photos all show wings with a very sudden rise to a maximum camber located no more than ten percent of the chord back from the leading edge.(1/547) Then the later ninety percent of the sections are flat or, in the case of the 1901 vehicle, noticeably reflexed. This is particularly surprising since Lilienthal clearly stated that smoothly arched sections were better than reflexed surfaces.(9/53) Of course he stated it in German, and this too did not appear in Chanute's translations.

So the Wrights early wing shapes were nothing like the shapes from which Lilienthal calculated his data, or for that matter, the shapes preferred by Chanute, Pilcher, Langley, LeBris, or even George Cayley. Orville admitted as much in a letter to Griffith Brener written on June 30, 1938.(1/43) In it he said, "The profile [section shape] of our wings were somewhat different from those used by Lilienthal, Chanute, etc. The change we made in the profile was for the purpose of better fore-and-aft equilibrium." In other words, they made the change in an attempt to cope with the pitch instability caused by their forward elevator. (Just how this was supposed to work is explained in a later section of this chapter.) Wilbur was even more explicit on this subject. In his 1901 speech to the Western Society of Engineers in Chicago he said "Instead of using the arc of a circle, we made the curve of our machine very abrupt at the front".(1/109,110) These statements amount to a direct admission that **the Wrights did not use Lilienthal's wing shapes** on their 1900 and 1901 gliders. And that means that **his data did not apply to their vehicles.**

It is important here to look at the Wrights' own tunnel data and see what it revealed to them. Graphs of pertinent data are presented on pages 176, 177, and 179 of Reference One, *The Papers of Wilbur and Orville Wright*. This data reveals that at a typical flight angle of five degrees, a smoothly arched airfoil with its maximum camber about halfway back, like the test airfoils that the Wrights numbered five or six, yields a lift coefficient of about 0.28. On the other hand, an airfoil with the maximum arch at the ten percent point, as done on the 1900 and 1901 gliders and exemplified by test sections numbers 16, 17, or 30, gives a lift coefficient of 0.22 at the same angle. This indicated a loss in lift for the early Wright gliders of 25 percent just due to camber profile as compared to Lilienthal's wings. But in reality the loss was much greater.

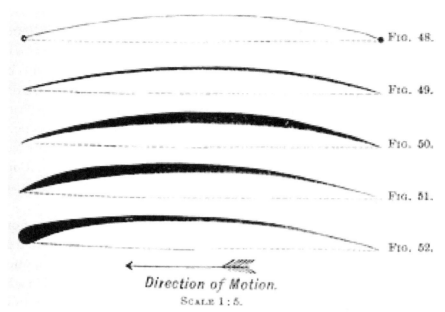

Figure 47B: Lilienthal's Test Wing Cross Sections

Figure 48A: Wrights'1900 Wing Cross Section Shape

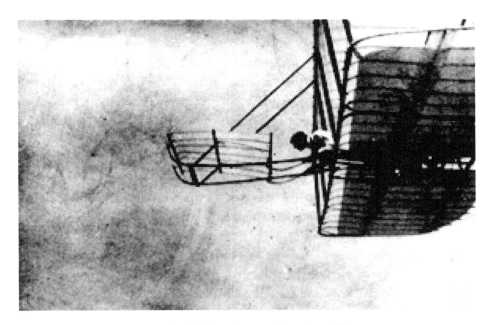

Figure 48B: Wrights' 1901 Wing Cross Section Shape

Figure 49: Wrights' 1902 Wing Cross Section Shape

These measurements, both for those resembling the Wrights' and Lilienthal's shapes, had to be taken from square planforms, i.e., aspect ratios of one. In these cases, the airflows around the test sections were totally dominated by edge, or tip, losses. For more practical wing shapes with aspect ratios much greater, the lift coefficient difference would undoubtedly be much more pronounced.

A better comparison can be made using the Wrights' own lift tables as published in Reference One. It is important to compare airfoil sections that were tested with the same aspect ratio (length to width). Although somewhat exaggerated, number 30 is the most similar to what the Wrights used on their 1900 and 1901 vehicles. For sections comparable to the Lilienthal sections shown in Figure 47, we should use the Wrights' numbers 18 and 19, which have their maximum cambers at 50 percent and 35 percent chord respectively. All three of these sections were tested with aspect ratios of four which allows direct comparison of profiles. At a five degree angle of attack, the number 30 section gave a coefficient of 0.25, while number 18 yielded 0.45, and 19 gave 0.43. This indicated that more gradual profiles like those Lilienthal favored could give up to 75 percent more lift than those on the Wrights' early gliders. (1/550.8, 560, 561, 564, 565, 579, & 581)

The Wrights believed that their tunnel measurements were accurate to at least a quarter of a degree in angle of attack, which translates to about 0.02 in lift coefficient.(1/549) So there is no doubt that they would have been struck by this loss in lift due to the weird curvature of their 1900 and 1901 wings. This is evidenced by the fact that for their 1902 glider, shown in Figure 49, the Wrights used wings that were drastically different in section profile, altered in fact to very near Lilienthal's favored shapes. Oddly, the section profile they actually used on the 1902 machine was not exactly any of those they tested, but rather a compromise between some of their best performing test shapes.(1/574)

Another measure of how bad the Wrights' early wing camber profiles were is achievable wing loading. This is how much weight a unit area of the wing can lift, the net average pressure on the wing if you will. For example, a 1,000-pound airplane with 500 square feet of wing area has a wing loading of two. Lilienthal recommended wing loadings of from 1.6 to 2.0 as being reasonably obtainable with a properly cambered wing.(9/123) However the lift of the Wrights' 1901 machine was so poor that it could generate a maximum wing loading of only 0.84, half of Lilienthal's recommended minimum.

The other major problem the Wrights discovered with their wind tunnel was with aspect ratio, the ratio of their rectangular wing's span to its width or chord. Their 1900 aircraft had an aspect ratio of 3.4, while the 1901 machine's was 3.1. These were also done in attempts to increase longitudinal stability. But Otto Lilienthal used wings with aspect ratios of 6.5 to generate his data. To get an idea of the Wrights' discovery of the significance of this difference, one can again go to their own wind tunnel data from 1901. The data do not allow an exact comparison of cambered sections, but for flat sections the plots on pages 175 and 179 of Reference One show a 20 percent lift improvement in going from an aspect ratio of four to one of six. This is an aspect ratio increase of 50 percent. But the difference between their 1901 aircraft and Lilienthal's test wings was from 3.1 to 6.5, a difference of over 100 percent. So in fact, the difference in lift due to differing aspect ratios would have been around 30 to 40 percent. These figures are also confirmed by the information in the Wrights' data tables.(1/558,578) Once again, they changed the design of their 1902 machine to that of Lilienthal's, adopting the aspect ratio of 6.5 that he used for his test wings.

Wilbur acknowledged the significance of camber and aspect ratio differences in a letter to Chanute written near the conclusion of their wind tunnel testing. He wrote **"It is very evident . . . that a table based on one aspect [ratio] and [wing section] profile is worthless for a surface of different aspect and curvature. This no doubt explains why we have had so much trouble figuring all our machines from Lilienthal's table."** Wilbur also pointed out that, at their typical gliding angles, a smooth arc was clearly superior to their 1900 and 1901 camber shapes.(1/163) These were obviously revelations for the Wrights, and these statements amount to nothing less than a clear admission that **their lifting problems were due to their own errors and not Lilienthal's.**

Although 1903 is celebrated as the advent of powered flight, and 1905 is considered by many to be the year when a controllable airplane was finally achieved, 1901 could be considered the year of the Wrights' biggest breakthrough. With their tests early in the year indicating larger wings were required, their Kitty Hawk tests during the summer revealing more ground testing to be necessary, their subsequent bicycle mounted tests in the fall determining Smeaton's coefficient, and finally their extensive wind tunnel tests near the end of the year revealing the proper wing shapes, it was really during

1901 that the Wrights determined how to build an airplane that could actually sustain itself in the air.

Finally, there is one other significant factor that I have never seen mentioned. Lilienthal determined his data for a single wing, not a biplane like the Wrights' vehicles. Since biplanes have four wing tips rather than two, and typically significantly reduced aspect ratios, they suffer much greater tip losses for the same total wing area. In the process they generate a more intense downwash. Since the wings share in each other's downwash they suffer greater induced drag than does a single wing of the same area. Estimates of this drag increase could run from ten to well over twenty percent depending on the aspect ratios and spacing of the wings. The Wrights tested for this loss in their wind tunnel, but had no way to account for it before 1902.

We now have a number of inescapable conclusions: First, any claim that the Wrights were using Lilienthal's recommended wing shapes in 1900 or 1901 is false. Second, the common claims that their lifting problems in 1901 were due either to errors in Lilienthal's data or to his use of a high value of Smeaton's coefficient are also false. And false is the idea that their tunnel data showed the need for bigger wings than used on their 1901 machine. What is true is that their wind tunnel investigations revealed the undeniable need to abandon their totally inappropriate wings and instead to use the wing cross-section shapes and aspect ratios actually used and recommended by Lilienthal (and Chanute, Phillips, Langley, Mouillard, LeBris, Cayley and others for that matter). These changes, not more wing area or corrections to Lilienthal's data or Smeaton's coefficient, solved their lifting problem for 1902. As we just saw two paragraphs ago, the Wrights admitted all of this.

A glance at the tethering lines to the 1900 and 1902 gliders clearly shows what an improvement was made. The 1900 machine is seen to be pulling back on the lines as hard as it is lifting while the 1902 vehicle is lifting its weight without hardly pulling back at all. In other words, the newer craft had a much-improved lift-to-drag ratio.

There are two questions begged by all of this. Why did Otto Lilienthal recommend such an erroneous value of Smeaton's coefficient? And if he used it, why did his gliders fly so well? His research was far beyond anything that had been done before, and it went on for decades. He was incredibly thorough and capable, using fairly advanced calculus to solve for the forces and bending moments on bird's wings.(9/26,27) Yet the first time he mentions the lift/drag equation and Smeaton's coefficient (k) in his book he simply states that the value of k is 0.13 metric (0.0053 English) with absolutely no discussion.(9/12) This is said to have been the accepted value for some time, but Lilienthal certainly had the means and, one would think, the motivation to verify it. He was capable of measuring lift and drag forces directly with his 25-foot whirling arm machine which he used for over two decades.(9/42) Simply measuring the drag, area, and speed of a plate perpendicular to the airflow would have determined k. I have seen no evidence that he performed these tests, and no evidence to explain why he used 0.13 metric for k.

Then there is the question of why did his gliders fly so well? Lilienthal did not begin flying until two years after he published his book, so it might seem tempting to propose that he eventually developed corrections to his methods based on his flying experiences. These corrections, not appearing in his earlier book, could have included reducing the value of k. However there is evidence that this didn't happen. His brother's Addendum, written over fifteen years after Otto's death, includes a mathematical analysis of the lift equation for the Wright brothers' two-seat Flyer. In it Gustav used 0.13 metric for Smeaton's k and still achieved a solution.(9/136) He did so because his estimate of speed was about ten percent low, his weight was 13 percent high, and the rest of the difference was made up by a lift coefficient that was about ten percent too low. (It is important to note that this ten percent difference in lift coefficient is equivalent to no more than one degree in angle of attack.) What this shows is that although the true value of Smeaton's coefficient was over a third lower than that used by the Lilienthals, this difference can be made up in the lift equation by minor errors in lift, speed, and angle of attack. And remember, speed is squared in the lift equation, so a speed error is more than doubled in the solution. Thus it becomes evident how relatively minor changes in other parameters can compensate for substantial errors in Smeaton's coefficient.

There are calculations in Lilienthal's book that indicate they may indeed have undervalued the effective angles of attack at which Otto flew, thus largely compensating for a high value of k.(9/136) In a December 15, 1901 letter to Chanute, Wilbur Wright agrees, concluding that Lilienthal flew at higher angles of attack, and thus higher lift coefficients, than his original data would have indicated.(1/173) In any case, all of Otto's lifting theory was overridden by the fact that he came to believe that he couldn't safely control wings greater than 15 square meters (160 square feet) by shifting his weight. (8/284) This, more than anything, rendered the value of Smeaton's coefficient moot as regards the design and performance of Lilienthal's gliders. All things considered, although he made thousands of glides it is unlikely that Lilienthal ever achieved anything near the lift-to-drag and glide ratios that the Wrights did in 1902.

In summary, the Wrights did not find errors in Lilienthal's lift data with their wind tunnel. His high value of Smeaton's coefficient was effectively eliminated from their work with the building of their 1901 glider long before the Wrights built their tunnel. What they found with the tunnel were errors in their own wing designs, specifically camber shape and aspect ratio, and that they had to pattern their wings after those recommended by Lilienthal.

I am well aware that these conclusions contradict previous works on this subject, and for that matter information presented in museums across the country. But even a cursory examination of photographs showing the obvious differences between the Wrights' 1900 and 1901 wing shapes and Lilienthal's, the similarity between their 1902 wing shape and his, and the consistency in total area of the wings of their 1901 and 1902 vehicles should lead one to question the previous "common knowledge" concerning the Wrights' findings from their wind tunnel testing. (That was indeed the original motivation behind the research that resulted in this book.) The data cited herein allows no conclusion other than the Wright brothers' wind tunnel research revealed that they didn't need bigger wings but rather that they had to abandon the bizarre wing curvatures and aspect ratios they had created in an attempt to cope with their canard-induced pitch instability.(1/226) In fact, their results showed them that they had to adopt wing shapes similar to those used by Lilienthal and many others who preceded them, and in a letter to Octave Chanute near the end of their testing they effectively said so.

Oddly, the Wrights' wind tunnel testing may well have contributed to an even more serious problem for them, one that hindered the marketing of their aircraft in later years. The excellent work they did in drag and lift-to-drag measurements in the tunnel allowed them to make calculations of unprecedented accuracy regarding the power that was required to propel their aircraft in level flight at extremely low altitude. Unfortunately, it was exactly this requirement that they used to size their first engine. This will be described more fully near the end of this chapter. But suffice it to say here that this use of their tunnel expertise to determine the minimum power necessary for level flight, and the resulting lack of excess power available for takeoffs, forced them to compensate for Kitty Hawk winds by employing an elaborate catapult arrangement to initiate flying speed. This complication, which they retained for years, greatly reduced the marketability of their aircraft.

Stability Versus Pilot Skill

There are widely held misconceptions regarding the design philosophy of the Wright brothers. Most anyone familiar with the subject knows that Wright gliders and airplanes were not hands-off machines. In fact, they were highly unstable. People seem fond of saying that the Wrights had no choice but to build their vehicles this way because that is the nature of flight. They assert that in flight, balance must be constantly reestablished and maintained by an operator. Moreover, they point out that the Wrights would see no big problem with this since they were builders and purveyors of bicycles, and these are totally unstable machines. We will find that, as is becoming usual, this interpretation could not be further from the truth. And anyone who has studied aircraft design, learned to fly, or even flown with someone else, should know it.

The flying qualities of an airplane are generally encompassed by the term "stability and control." Most texts on aircraft design have at least two long and intricate chapters on the subject. Any detailed discussion of an airplane will cover its stability and control properties. It seems sometimes as if it has become one word, "stabilityandcontrol." There really is an intimate connection between the two analytically because many of the mathematical terms used to calculate both stability and control effects are the same. However, this is unfortunate operationally since stability and control are really two entirely different aspects of an aircraft's flying qualities. In fact, they can be considered opposites. Stability refers to how well the aircraft flies straight and level on its own, with no pilot inputs. Control is how it responds to pilot inputs. An aircraft that is very stable is often somewhat resistant to control, or at least will respond sluggishly to control inputs. On the other hand, an aircraft that is highly responsive and maneuverable is invariably not very stable. Many modern aircraft have electronics that move aerodynamic controls to create false stability, or alter the pilot's inputs to achieve the desired maneuvers. But, absent these electronics, the previous statements hold true.

Engineers talk about two basic kinds of stability: static and dynamic. Static stability means that if you move something from a certain position or orientation and let it go, it heads back to, or very near, its original position. Dynamic stability is a measure of how fast and positively it moves directly toward its original or desired position. To animate it, something that is statically stable "knows" where it wants to be and stays there. Something with good dynamic stability is very "anxious" to achieve the original or desired state and goes directly there.

As one might expect, in these early days the Wrights never analytically addressed either one of these issues. What little attention they did give them was mostly of the experimental, or "cut and try" methodology. They were aware of the concept of the center of pressure, that point about which all the pressures acting on a body seem to balance out such that it won't rotate. It is crucial to locate this point in order to accomplish the basic balancing of an aircraft. But, except for one brief ground test in July of 1905, they didn't test for the exact location and movement of center of pressure locations.(1/502,503) In fact the Wrights were only able to achieve acceptable longitudinal balance of the 1904 machine by adding 70 pounds of iron bars to the front of the vehicle, something they must have been very reluctant to do after being careful to save weight throughout the airframe.

Wilbur briefly expressed their philosophy on the subject in an address to the Western Society of Engineers on September 18, 1901.(1/101) He said, "The balancing of a gliding or flying machine....merely consists in causing the center of pressure to coincide with the center of gravity." This is true as far as it goes. But there are two ambiguous key words in this statement, "balancing" and "causing." By "balancing" did he mean stably or not? And by "causing" did he mean by vehicle design or pilot operation?

Lilienthal, Pilcher, and Chanute's team produced gliders that were controlled by the manipulation of the operator's body weight. The Wrights were well aware of the limitations this imposed on vehicle size and maneuverability. So they resolved to control their vehicles by aerodynamic means, altering the vehicle's configuration appropriately, whatever that would turn out to mean, to cause it to regain balance. They also knew that many aviation experimenters had created inherently stable models and gliders before them. But after they found out that their configuration was unstable they decided that if they could work out a system of positive aerodynamic control, they needn't worry much about whether their vehicles had inherent stability or not.

There was one aspect of control that they uncompromisingly made paramount: the ability to avoid a dangerous swift dive or backslide into the earth after a stall. How they accomplished this, and its impact on their machines, will be discussed later in this chapter. For this section it is sufficient to point out that they were willing to completely sacrifice stability to achieve this goal. Moreover, they were willing to cope with the constant demands this decision would place on the operators of their vehicles. Unfortunately for the Wrights, few others were willing to pay this price. These others soon found ways to handle any stalling problem without sacrificing stability.

We know that throughout the previous century the Wrights' predecessors had found ways to achieve inherent aerodynamic stability. Since George Cayley they typically did so in pitch by having the center of gravity (along with its associated momentum) ahead of the retarding force acting at the center of lift and drag. (Think of an arrow with the heavy arrowhead forward and the feathers in back.) This then required a negatively loaded horizontal tail to achieve balance in pitch. For stability in roll they used dihedral, and for directional stability they adopted the vertical tail. But the Wrights asserted that they were dissatisfied with the tendencies of these devices to cause oscillations, what we would nowadays call dynamic instabilities. Wilbur claimed that dihedral was the reason Maxim's machine crashed and that Lilienthal got away with having it because he flew only in calm air.(1/334) Neither of these claims was true. By 1920 Orville was claiming that these oscillations were the reasons they rejected the use of horizontal tails and dihedral, and this may be, to some degree, true.(2/92)

It should be pointed out that much of the Wrights' problems with both stability and control were brought on by the peculiarities of their test conditions and their early gliders' complete lack of directional stability. They didn't find their warp-induced roll and yaw instabilities until they quit tethering their machines and began free gliding. Much of their pitch instability was certainly amplified by flying within 20 feet of the ground at Kitty Hawk, immersed in the turbulent wind gusts rolling up the bumpy hillsides. Moreover, any time their complete lack of directional stability allowed their gliders to get the least bit crosswise to the winds rushing up the hills, the updrafts would lift the windward wing and jam the other down into the hillside. In 1920 Orville justified their use of anhedral to counteract crosswinds by saying that "Under the peculiar conditions existing on the Kill Devil Hill....we found the advantage of the drooped wings more than overcame the disadvantages".(2/17) Had they flight tested in calmer more normal flying conditions, the virtues of inherent stability would, no doubt, have been more appealing.

So very early on, the Wrights not only rejected stabilizing features, but they reversed them by putting droop in the wings and placing the horizontal stabilizer in front. The results were gliders that were unstable in pitch, unstable in roll, and neutrally stable in yaw. This demanded constant corrections in multiple flight axes by the pilot, even in calm air. In his 1903 speech to the Western Society of Engineers, Wilbur said, "In all our machines the maintenance of the equilibrium has been dependent on the skill and constant vigilance of the aviator".(1/328) And on top of that, before 1905 their aircraft couldn't execute turns. All these problems were exacerbated by having inadequate power. Although they championed skill over stability, even with around a thousand glides and powered flights between them, until the end of 1905 the Wrights couldn't develop the skill required to keep their aircraft reliably in the air while maneuvering.

Octave Chanute, the last of the "great gliders" and their confidant and mentor, kept pounding on the Wrights about the virtues of inherent, or as he put it, "automatic" stability. And they kept answering back by extolling the importance of operator skill.(1/15) They had always believed that operator skill would be an important ingredient in maintaining balance in flight, but not nearly to the extent that it became necessary in order to fly their machines. Had they used dihedral (as they finally did in 1905) and aft vertical and horizontal tails (as they finally did in 1910), they might have had, as early as 1903, an aircraft that both they and others could have flown without crashing.

Fred Culick and Henry Jex jointly reported on the stability and control aspects of the 1903 Wright Flyer as a result of wind tunnel tests of precise models. A 1/6-scale model was tested at the California Institute of Technology, and a 1/8-scale model was tested in the tunnel at the Northrop Corporation. They concluded analytically that flying the 1903 Flyer required the same response time on the controls as balancing a yardstick on one finger.(3/35) They also found that at a 23-mile-per-hour flight speed, an almost undetectable up-gust of 1/2 mile per hour, if uncountered by controls, would stall the Flyer in less than 3 seconds.

In summary, to say that airplanes require constant balancing by the pilot and that the Wrights knew this going in is to cram two false statements into one sentence. As any aviation pilot, engineer, or enthusiast knows, up until the relatively recent advent of computerized electronic controls, all aircraft were designed to be capable of being trimmed to fly straight and level, hands-off, purely by virtue of their aerodynamic design. The Wrights knew this had already been accomplished fairly well by a number of their predecessors. But after accidentally failing to achieve it, they chose to do without it because of what they believed to be necessary safety considerations and because of the peculiarities of their testing conditions. Unfortunately, they didn't realize that these problems could have been handled differently in a stable airplane with sufficient power. And even more unfortunate for them, it wasn't long before others did just that and left them in the dust commercially.

Straight and Level

One of the most universally accepted misconceptions about the Wrights' early aircraft is that, with aerodynamic controls acting on each of the three axes of pitch, yaw, and roll, their 1902 glider and the succeeding powered aircraft could successfully complete turns at will. Since modern airplanes have three-axis controls and easily use these to make turns, people seem to assume the same was true for the Wrights' early vehicles. However, successfully turning an airplane, particularly a very low and slow one, is much more complicated than many realize. (Witness the fact that Ken Hyde, an experienced airline pilot, crashed and destroyed a Wright Model B Flyer exact replica the first time he tried to turn it.) It turned out that the Wrights had to struggle through these complications before they could reliably complete turns with their aircraft in October of 1905. Actually, until 1904 their entire effort was directed toward first being able to control their vehicles well enough to maintain level flight with a constant heading, i.e., to fly *straight and level.* That was, in fact, the original reason they adopted three-axis control. These facts are so contrary to conventional belief that an extensive examination of the evidence is warranted.

As with any examination of the Wrights' work, the best place to start is with Marvin McFarland's extensive 1278-page compilation of the Wright brothers' records, diaries, correspondence, flight test notes, sketches, data, speeches, and photos. McFarland presents 16 entries in his Index that represent 45 references by the Wrights to turning or circling that they had made by the end of 1905. However only three of these references to turning, and one for circling, were made before 1904. He also includes three photos of the 1902 glider in shallow banks of no more than ten degrees which he labeled as turning. Careful examination of each of these pre-1904 references reveals that they actually represent something quite different. It is important to re-member here that an airplane or glider can bank without changing heading, change heading (yaw) without banking, and, due to winds, change flight path or course without either rolling or changing heading.

McFarland's first citing on "turning" refers to an August 9th, 1901 en-try to Orville Wright's journal in which he recorded that "In two instances he [Wilbur] made flights curving sharply to the left....".(1/81) Orville said nothing about these course deviations being intentional, or what the actual heading of the aircraft may have been. He said that the flight paths curved, not that the aircraft was turned. He went on to describe the day's flying having been ended by a crash due to Wilbur's inability to recover from an inadvertent bank, most likely caused either by a wind gust or his attention having been di-verted to something else such as pitch control. This indicates that the sharply curving flights may well also have been the results of sudden wind gusts or diverted attention.

McFarland's second entry under "turning" is in a letter from Wilbur to Octave Chanute on August 22nd,1901 stating that "...our machine does not turn (i.e., circle) towards the lowest wing under all circumstances, a very unlooked for result, and one which completely upsets our theories as to the causes which produce the turning to right or left".(1/84) Here two things are apparent. First, the actions of their glider were not repeatable, it turning some-times toward the low wing, and sometimes not. Second, they were focusing on trying to figure out what was causing their machine to turn, not on causing it to turn themselves.

The third reference to "turning" is again from Orville's diary but in a September 29th, 1902 entry wherein Orville recorded sketches of two flight paths showing curves to the right away from the wind which he shows as hit-ting the vehicle on its front left quarter.(1/265) In one sketch the curve to the right ended the flight, while in the other the curve to the right was im-mediately followed by a curve back to the left which ended the flight. Nothing was included in Orville's text to indicate that these "turns" were intentional or what the actual heading of the aircraft may have been at any point. Actually, since their basic objective was to glide or "soar" for as long as possible while keeping landing speed to a minimum, the vehicle may well have been pointed generally toward the prevailing wind during the whole event. It appears that these curved paths were the result of wind gusts from the left simply blow-ing the glider sideways toward the right. Or, asymmetric drag resulting from warping the wings to recover from a tilt away from the wind could have caused the vehicle to yaw or turn to the right away from the wind. In one of the flights Wilbur may have attempted to recover his original flight direction but could not maintain control.

McFarland cites only one reference to "circling" before 1904, and this is in an October 7th,1903 letter from Octave Chanute to Wilbur Wright suggesting that he try flying in a circle.(1/361) Evidently the Wrights had not reported any turning or circling to Chanute up to that point (which was well after the three events just discussed). Wilbur made no reply to this suggestion in his subsequent letters to Chanute. Since Wilbur was normally very conscientious about addressing all of Chanute's concerns in their correspondence, it appears likely that he had no intention of attempting turns yet, and wanted to avoid entering into a lengthy written dialogue with Chanute on the wisdom of this decision. Besides, by this time they were preparing for their first attempt at powered flight.

Nothing in these statements indicates that any of the course or heading deviations was intentional. Rather, it appears that the banking, turning, or course deviations of the Wrights' gliders were inadvertent due to external causes, and that they were merely trying to figure out the various reactions of their machines and their causes.

In addition to these citations of written material, McFarland lists three 1902 photos under "turning" in his Index. These each show the 1902 glider in very shallow lateral banks of no more than ten degrees. The first, McFarland's Plate 49, is taken from the right side of the glider showing it in a shallow bank to the left.(1/230.11) There is no indication of warping being applied. That night, October 10th,1902, Orville wrote in his journal that Wilbur had come to a stop, banked, and then turned. This is a classic description of going into a stall, then, due to a crosswind or control movement, one wing drops and the glider spins in toward the low wing. Just the act of trying to level this aircraft with wing warping would yaw it into the bank due to asymmetric drag. Orville's description makes it clear that Wilbur was not making an intentional turn and was likely out of control on that flight.

McFarland's second plate, number 57, is the famous shot from October 24th,1902 showing the glider from directly behind in a slight bank to the right with the warping control in the recovery position. (See Figure 50) The photo does not indicate whether the bank was intentional or that the aircraft was changing heading. In fact, since the aircraft was still headed directly away from the camera and hundreds of footprints are evident in the sand directly in front of the camera, it seems likely that it was being brought back level from an inadvertent bank and had not deviated from its original heading.(1/230.15)

Figure 50: Wright 1902 Glider in a Right Bank

The third plate, number 58, also taken on October 24th,1902, shows the 1902 glider in a similar mild bank to the right, but this time the warping was into the bank.(1/230.16) Since the bank is so slight it is not evident whether the pilot was initiating the bank or had overcorrected from an inadvertent bank in the other direction. As in Plate 57, in 58 the aircraft is headed directly away from the photographer and again hundreds of footprints appear in the foreground, so evidently again it hadn't changed from its original heading.

Perhaps the determining factor is that in a letter written that night to his sister, Orville made absolutely no mention or inference of their having made any turns that day.(1/279,280) Since he had previously made note of any significant curves in their flight paths, this seems to indicate that the aircraft continued on basically straight ahead in both flights in which the photos were taken. Even more significantly, in Wilbur's next letter to Chanute he likewise made no mention of turning, even though that letter was a wrap-up of the year's gliding activity and accomplishments, and Chanute had been encouraging them to make turns.(1/281)

On page 671 McFarland himself draws the conclusion that the Wrights "met the wind gusts and steered as they willed". This is McFarland's conclusion, not a statement by either of the Wrights, and he doesn't say whether he thinks they "willed" the machine to go straight or turn. However by saying that they "met the wind gusts" he seems to imply that he thought they were able to maintain their original orientations unperturbed by the wind.

Years after the events just discussed the Wrights recorded additional statements concerning their objectives for their early aircraft. In their 1908 article for The Century magazine they wrote, "We would make it as inert as possible to the effects of change of direction or speed, and thus reduce the effects of wind gusts to a minimum".(2/82) Clearly their concern was that the aircraft would stay straight and level during wind gusts. This statement could be interpreted to imply that they intentionally designed for instability from the start. However it was written well after they ended up with a highly unstable aircraft and everything else contradicts that premise. It seems they were originally unaware that designing a vehicle that would be "inert" to wind gusts was equivalent to making it unstable. Nonetheless, in this 1908 article they were still taking pride in having done "just the opposite of what our predecessors had done".

Yet more evidence that the Wrights were not trying to turn in 1901 and 1902 can be found in the only two statements in Orville's 1920 legal deposition concerning roll control.(2/16) Previous authors have assumed that the Wrights were attempting to bank into a turn when they ran into the adverse yaw problem. However, in his deposition Orville opens the discussion by saying, "Sometimes in warping the wings to *restore lateral balance....*" and then goes on to describe the phenomenon of induced yaw and adverse roll. Obviously he is telling us that they were trying to regain *straight and level* flight from an unintentional banked position rather than entering into a banking turn from a level attitude. In his other reference to roll control Orville begins with "When the wings were warped in an attempt to *recover balance....*". (Italics in these statements are mine) Similar statements elsewhere beginning with phrases like "Sometimes the machine became tilted..." give additional confirmation.

One of the most conclusive sources regarding their objective for the control system on their 1902 glider is their 1906 patent on this vehicle.(4/All) This document is a painstakingly detailed description of the intent and functioning of their invention as any patent should be. On page three, lines 78 through 87 state that "....owing to various conditions of wind pressure and other causes, the body of the machine is apt to become unbalanced laterally, one side tending to sink and the other side tending to rise, the machine turning around its central longitudinal axis. The provision which we have just described enables the operator to meet this difficulty and to preserve the lateral balance of the machine". In other words, the original purpose of their wing warping "invention" was to bring the aircraft back *level* when the wind tilts it.

On page four, lines 16 to 45 give a lengthy discussion plainly stating that the purpose of the coordinated vertical rudder was to counteract adverse yaw (and thus adverse roll) created by wing warping, thereby keeping the aircraft flying *straight and level*. Page five, lines 25 through 27 state that by using the horizontal "rudder" the machine "may thus be directed upward or downward at the will of the operator and the longitudinal balance thereof maintained." Here the purpose given for the canard is to keep the machine flying level.

Certainly the clearest statement of the original objective of their control systems appearing in the patent is to be found on the first page from line 55 to line 61. It says "...owing to the varying conditions to be met there are numerous disturbing forces which tend to shift the machine from the position which it should occupy to obtain the desired results. It is the chief objective of our invention to provide means for remedying this difficulty...". Again, they are patenting the ability to counteract the outside influences that were acting to keep them from flying *straight and level*.

The only other statement concerning control objectives in the patent, and the only statement in the entire document that is conceivably ambiguous enough that it could possibly have been referring to turning, appears on page one, lines 16 through 20. It states, "The objects of our invention are to provide means for maintaining or restoring the equilibrium or lateral balance of the apparatus, to provide means for guiding the machine both vertically and horizontally, and to provide a structure combining lightness, strength [etc]...". Could "guiding" have referred to something other than straight and level? Out of context possibly, but considering the rest of the sentence, the rest of the document, and their explanations for everything they did, it is unlikely. Again, the intent here was to guide the machine to follow a straight and level path.

In addition to the Wrights' own words and photos, the design modifications they made in 1902 reveal their objectives. The vertical stabilizers for the 1902 machine were originally installed in a fixed straight position. This was their idea of how they could prevent their glider from turning when they used wing warping to regain level flight from an unintentional banked position.

When wing warping was employed to bring the tilted 1901 glider back to level flight, the downward warped wing developed more drag while drag was reduced on the upward warped wing. This caused the aircraft to yaw toward the downward warped wing. They installed the fixed vertical stabilizers on the 1902 glider to keep it flying straight ahead. It turned out that this didn't work because the machine would sideslip toward the low wing and the fixed vertical stabilizers mounted in the rear would cause it to weathervane or turn in the direction of the sideslip and enter into a spin. The solution to their problem was another modification, replacing the fixed vertical stabilizers with a single moveable one which would deflect away from the slip and force the aircraft to maintain its original heading. Since that was its only intended function, it was connected to the wing warping and only worked every time warping was employed.

So both the fixed and moveable vertical tails were installed to keep the machine flying straight, not to enable it to turn. This distinction becomes important in the upcoming section, "Banishing Rock and Roll". Had the Wrights been entering into a banking turn, the aircraft would have begun slipping toward the lower leading upward-warped wing. In this case the fixed vertical stabilizer originally installed would have helped turn the vehicle in the desired direction. But since they were actually trying to get out of an unintentional bank, their vehicles were slipping and spinning in toward the lower trailing downward-warped wing. In this case the fixed vertical stabilizers would have aggravated the spin, *which is what they said they did.*

An absolutely incontrovertible explanation of the purpose of their coordinated rudder is in a letter from their lawyer, Harry Toulmin, to the patent examiner, William Townsend. Townsend was confused as to the workings of the controls on the 1902 glider. Toulmin had spent many hours with the Wrights learning every detail of the construction and operation of the vehicle in order to write their patent application. His explanation of the control system to Townsend was, "....the vertical rudder is *in no sense a steering device,* but is simply for correcting the increased resistance offered by one end of the machine over the other arising from the different angles at which the ends of the planes [wings] are presented to the wind, and this it does automatically". (The italics are mine.) (43/33)

Next to the Wrights, Toulmin was an expert on how the vehicles were designed, and why. And his explanation is absolutely clear about the fact that the moveable coordinated rudder on the 1902 aircraft, and by similarity, the 1903 airplane, was only intended to prevent yawing, not to enable or enhance yawing or turning.

At Chanute's insistence, Wilbur made detailed presentations with extensive visual aids to the Western Society of Engineers in Chicago in both 1901 and 1903. He went into surprising and lengthy detail concerning the design, operation, and testing of their machines. The presentations were quite comprehensive, including both longitudinal and lateral controls, their operation, and their effects on the machines. Nowhere in either speech did he even mention turning.

Those familiar with modern airplanes may be thinking that actually the elevator is a key control in maintaining turns since, when an airplane is banked over heavily, pulling back on the elevator is the prime control forcing the turn. The Wrights certainly had a powerful if erratic pitch control in their moveable canard. However photos as well as motion pictures of their flights at Ft. Meyers and Centro Celle, Italy reveal that, as late as 1909, the Wrights didn't operate their aircraft at bank angles exceeding 15 degrees, almost always no more than about ten degrees. At these shallow bank angles the elevator wouldn't have been an effective turning agent.

To many it may seem odd that the Wrights wouldn't have wanted to accomplish turning early in their flight testing and instead seemed to be fixated on being able to fly straight and level through 1903. Not only did they have some good reasons for this, but much of the time they had little choice.

Typical winds at Kitty Hawk were at least 15 to 20 miles per hour when they flew. This was essentially the flying speed of their early gliders, and made it much easier for the "wingmen" that launched the vehicles, sometimes having to perform running launches many dozens of times per day. So often the gliders hung almost motionless in the air, what the Wrights called "soaring". (Of course the glider didn't have to be carried back to the launch point so far either, but this would not have been as bad as it may seem. As anyone who has hang-glided in the Kitty Hawk area knows, if you hold the glider at the right heading and angle to the wind it will pretty much pull you back up the hill.)

There were other advantages to soaring. Hanging relatively motionless in the air at just a few feet in altitude made it possible for the observer to make measurements such as glide angle, angle of attack, and such. Also, remaining near the observing brother made it possible for both of them to discuss wind gusts, control movements, and the resulting vehicle reactions. This would have been important since sometimes the observer would have a more objective memory of events than the struggling pilot.

However, flying on a hillside into a wind that matches one's airspeed places a maneuvering restriction on the vehicle. It can't turn. Any change in heading resulting in a loss of forward progress will result in the vehicle getting blown back into the hillside. So in that sense, the best gliding conditions at Kitty Hawk pretty much ruled out turning, and instead placed a demand on being able to maintain straight and level flight. This was no problem for the Wrights since they emphasized gaining flight experience by spending as much time as possible in the air rather than trying to cover long distances.

It is well known that the 1903 powered flights were all basically in a straight line. So the only logical conclusion from all available evidence, the letters, flight test notes, the diary, photos, depositions, speeches, articles, their patent, and their lawyer, is that prior to the flights of 1904 the Wright brothers made no serious attempt at intentionally executing turns with their vehicles. Indeed, as they found out in 1904 and 1905, none of their earlier vehicles were even capable of executing turns.

Ahead or Behind

Many who are familiar with airplanes are struck by a feature of Wright Flyers that is quite unusual. The Wrights' machines all have a small wing out in front of what are obviously the much larger main lifting wings. We are used to seeing these small horizontal surfaces mounted behind the main wings of airplanes. When in back these are called horizontal stabilizers. When they are in front of the main wings, they are more often called canards. Whether they are in the front or back of the plane, they can also be called elevators if they are moveable. (Canard means "duck" in French. It seems Santos-Dumont's 1906 aircraft, the 14bis, had a large box kite-like control way out in front on a long narrow "neck" of a fuselage. Thus it had a profile that, to some Frenchmen, resembled a duck in flight. Consequently the name was coined for his and all other airplanes with forward control surfaces.)(33/179)

A review of the models and gliders that were successful throughout the century preceding the Wrights' efforts, going all the way back to Cayley's 1804 glider, shows them all to have had the horizontal surface placed behind the main wing. As previously mentioned, even daVinci, in his sketch of a glider four hundred years earlier, placed the horizontal control/stabilizer at the rear. It's true that a few of the early aviators tried emulating the Wrights' use of canards, especially following Wilbur's spectacular demonstration in France in 1908. But these attempts were soon abandoned. So the obvious questions are: Why did the Wrights put the horizontal control in front? And why didn't anybody else?

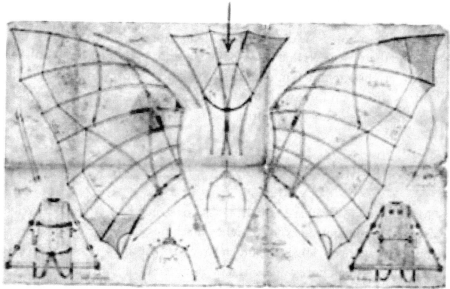

Figure 51: Leonardo DaVinci's Sketch of Glider Components, Circa 1500

To reconstruct the thought processes of the Wright brothers one must pay attention to when their various statements were made, how they were made, and in what context. Often in their writings the Wrights gave a reason for doing something and, within its context, it sounds as though that was the only or most important reason they had for doing it. However another document from another time will indicate a completely different reason for the same thing. To sort this out it is important to have both a modern understanding of aerodynamics and a knowledge of aerodynamics as the Wrights understood it. It is also vital to place the statements in the context of what the Wrights were trying to accomplish with each statement at the time it was made. Sometimes this had little to do with the technical merits of the item being discussed.

Also, it is important to be mindful of the terminology used by the Wrights during their testing. For example, for a century we have reserved the term "rudder" for the vertical control surface that makes an airplane yaw to the left or right. However, the Wrights, as did many others before them, used the term for both vertical and horizontal control surfaces, whether they were located in the front or rear of the vehicle. So references to the canard in their writings can be missed if one is deflected by the word "rudder."

The Wrights' decision to place the horizontal pitch control ahead of the main lifting wings was not made without some deliberation and second thoughts. Remember, their very first flying machine, the 1899 biplane kite, had the horizontal surface in the back. In a letter to Octave Chanute written on the 13th of May 1900, Wilbur stated that on their 1900 glider they were going to use an aft pitch control identical to that on the 1899 machine. (1/18) At this point they hypothesized that Lilienthal's fatal crash was due to having a moveable but uncontrolled horizontal tail, whereas theirs would be positively controlled.

Although all the other Wright aircraft were fabricated in Dayton, the 1900 machine was not only assembled but also partially fabricated at Kitty Hawk. Orville had stayed in Dayton, so Wilbur was responsible for the final configuration and fabrication of the 1900 glider. He constructed it during September, and in a letter to Chanute on the twenty-third, he stated, "The tail of my machine is fixed, and even if my steering arrangement should fail, it would still leave me with the same control that Lilienthal had at best".(1/26) This certainly indicates that as of late September the, or at least a, stabilizer was to be behind the wings. There is no record of either of the Wrights ever having referred to their canard as a "tail." When they used the term tail, they meant something behind the main wings. Also, the comparison with Lilienthal's machine would indicate a like configuration, i.e., one with a horizontal tail.

The early part of October was taken up with an abortive attempt to fly the machine in the wind while suspended from a "derrick," which they had constructed. But by mid-October they had gone back to tethering it by hand from the ground, what they called "flying it as a kite." By this time it seems they had made at least a tentative commitment to mounting the elevator in front. Existing photos of the 1900 device clearly indicate which edge of the main wings were the leading edges, and the elevator is ahead of the wings in every photo. Even so, it is clear from their writings that they flew the vehicle both ways, with the elevator in front and behind. In a letter to their sister, Orville recounted on the 17th of October,1900 that "We tried it with tail in front, behind, and every other way. When we got through, Wil was so mixed up he couldn't even theorize".(1/38) These tests were considered so significant that twenty years later Orville was to write, "In our 1900 experiments we had even found the inherent stability much improved when we tested the machine by gliding it down a hill loaded with a small sack of sand with the trailing edge of the main plane forward and the elevator trailing behind (in short, when flying it backward)".(2/17)

I find a few things interesting in these statements by Orville. First, in his letter to his sister on October, 18, 1900, he still refers to the horizontal surface as the "tail." It's possible that Orville was not used to it being in front because Wilbur had decided that on his own after he left Dayton. But it is more likely that, as of that date, over halfway through the 1900 test session, they had still not absolutely decided on the canard as their final configuration. It's true that in the statement written twenty years later Orville referred to having the elevator behind as being "backwards," but that was with the benefit of hindsight. Even more importantly, this late statement is in a deposition connected with a legal action and, as such, was worded for compatibility with the canard configuration described in their patent.

The other, perhaps even more significant point is that, if Orville's statement twenty years later is correct, they were apparently just turning the glider around and flying it backwards, not taking the elevator off and remounting it. This would mean that when the elevator was behind, the main wings were flying backwards also. Thus the camber of the main wings was reversed. If the point of maximum camber had been at the 50 percent chord point, or even around a third of the way back like most wings, that would be one thing. But on the 1900 and 1901 Wright gliders the maximum camber was at about the 10 percent chord point. All the camber was right behind the leading edge of the wings. The rest of the wing was flat. Reversing this camber profile must have made for some very unusual and possibly severe flow separation and pitching characteristics. The Wrights did not fully appreciate the significance of this since they were not familiar with all the intricacies of flow separation and never did wing pitching measurements. Had they a true understanding of the wing instability that the elevator had to overcome when in the aft position, they might have had a better appreciation of its stabilizing power and been less prone to abandon it.

Finally, I find it somewhat interesting that the wording in his letter to his sister seemed to put Orville in the position of reporter and Wilbur in the position of "theorizer." In later years, according to his recounts, Orville became a productive partner in the sibling brain trust, but at this time it seems that Wilbur, having been responsible for the fabrication of the 1900 machine, was intellectually in charge.

So exactly when and why did they conclusively decide to adopt the canard as their final configuration? A little further on in his letter to his sister, Orville described some unmanned flights they made on the 18th of October, in particular a few that ended up in fairly scary crashes. He described the glider's actions as follows: "After going about 30 feet out, it would sometimes turn up a little too much in front, when it would start back, increasing in speed as it came, and whack the side of the hill with terrific force. The result generally was a broken limb [on the machine] somewhere, but we hastily splint the breaks and go ahead".(1/38) This is a classic description of stalls. The aircraft noses up, loses speed, and either the nose falls down and the vehicle dives into the ground, or it slides down backward into a crash. With sufficient altitude, flight orientation and speed could have been recovered. But in the Wrights' case, with the craft stalling within 30 feet of the ground, the vehicle would hit while still in the post-stall dive.

Here they were seeing the vicious side of flying; the thing that they thought had killed Lilienthal and Pilcher. And, as Wilbur expressed to their father before they even began flying, "The man who wishes to keep at the problem long enough to really learn anything positively must not take dangerous risks".(1/26) Sure enough, after the 18th of October 1900, no further comments by the Wrights regarding the use of a horizontal tail are to be found in their records. In fact, in a letter to Chanute written on November 26th, shortly after their return to Dayton, Wilbur described their machine as simply having a "horizontal rudder projecting in front of the planes," or wings.(1/46) No mention was made to Chanute of ever having tried the vehicle with the horizontal stabilizer in back. (According to Augustus Herring's records they discussed moving the elevator to the rear in 1901 but nothing came of it.)

The Wrights' concern, at least in the early years, was not actually with stall recovery. They knew that their stalls would occur in such proximity to the ground that actual recovery would usually not be possible. They just didn't want to hit the ground halfway to recovery with the aircraft in an accelerating nosedive. This would have been particularly dangerous in their case since they planned on lying prone with their heads projecting in front of the main wings. They felt that if their vehicles could maintain pitch control, even while stalled, they could stay fairly level and float down slowly hitting the ground flat, a much safer situation. They considered all other stability or control issues to be secondary to this goal.

The forward elevator has a number of advantages that make it capable of doing what the Wrights were looking for. First, of course, is that it sticks out in front of everything, getting clean, undisturbed, non-turbulent air to work with. On an aircraft such as the Wrights', which had two wings, numerous struts and wires, as well as a man in front, flow aft could be quite turbulent. It's difficult for a control to get a clean "bite" in such confused airflow and thus have much effectiveness.

Also, an aircraft stalls because the main lifting wings are going too slowly, or more likely, are at too steep of an angle of attack for the speed at which they are moving. To recover, the nose must be pushed down. As mentioned in the last chapter, the canard does this by going to a safe lower angle of attack. A tail surface, on the other hand, must push the tail up by going to an even higher angle of attack than the already stalled main wings. So the tail could be ineffective, or worse yet, stall itself, dropping down and deepening the stall of the aircraft. (In practice, prop wash and downwash from the wings somewhat mitigates this problem, but it is unlikely the Wrights had any awareness of this.)

And finally, when approaching a stall an airplane is typically going up and slowing and must be sent back down to regain speed and recover flight. A canard recovers by immediately generating a down-force in the direction in which the airplane needs to go. But a horizontal tail must generate an up-force, just the opposite of where the aircraft needs to go So the plane must wait until it rotates to a nose down attitude and starts to descend in order to begin regaining flying speed. This can cause the aircraft to lose even more altitude during recovery. When close to the ground, this difference can be critical.

The Wrights were convinced that the ability of the canard to keep the vehicle level, post-stall, and allow them to "pancake" flat into the sand was their key to surviving their early years of experimentation without having a severe accident. And in this regard, their judgment seems to have been vindicated. In the summary of their 1901 flight tests presented to the Western Society of Engineers, Wilbur pointed out that indeed the situation of stalling too low to recover, yet high enough to be dangerous, had occurred a number of times. But as they had anticipated, with their forward elevator or canard, the aircraft simply fluttered down flat to the ground, making a soft landing with little or no damage to man or machine.(1/108,109)

By 1905 the Wrights had enough power in their aircraft to fly out of ground effect and were routinely flying at altitudes of around 100 feet. This would have been enough altitude to recover a 30-mile-per-hour low wing-loading aircraft from a stall, even with an aft-mounted elevator. But still they kept the canard. Later in this section I will discuss further why they kept it, and what they could, indeed should, have done.

The second most important reason the Wrights chose a canard layout was their desire to stabilize the up or down pitching motion of the aircraft's nose. They claimed that all the material they had at the start of their experiments indicated that the center of pressure was near the leading edge of a surface at zero angle of attack and gradually moved back to the midpoint as the surface was angled up to perpendicular to the airflow. In a way, this would appear logical. The end conditions seemed right, so why wouldn't the center of pressure move gradually from one place to the other? If that were the case, as it approached zero angle of attack the center of pressure (lift) of a cambered wing would move forward and cause it to want to pitch back up more and more. But at the same time their negatively set canard would attain a more negative angle causing it to pull down stronger against the wings increased pitch up, thus stabilizing the aircraft. Conversely, if the angle of attack increased and the center of pressure moved aft, the wing would want to pitch up less. But at the same time the canard would achieve a reduced negative angle and pull down less and thus the balance of the aircraft would be maintained without the pilot even having to move the pitch control. (This is depicted in the diagram of Figure 32.)

Well, on a cambered surface the center of pressure does not move like that, and by that time at least some experimenters knew better. Aviation researchers like Francis Wenham or Horatio Phillips could not have determined the cambered wing characteristics they did without becoming aware of correct center of pressure locations and movements. In fact, their reporting indicates an awareness that most of the lift of cambered sections was developed on the forward upper region.(23/56, 8/166)

In reality, when operating cambered wing sections of the type used by the Wrights and their predecessors, and within the useable flight range of angles of attack, the center of pressure (or lift) moves forward with increasing angle. It actually moves from well aft at near zero lift angles, through mid-chord, up to a point about a quarter of the way back from the leading edge of the wing at typical flying angles.

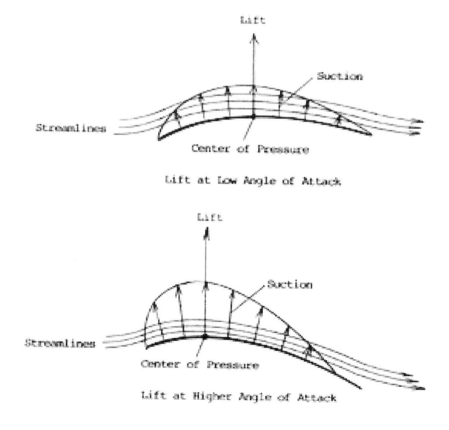

Figure 52: Centers of Pressure (Lift)

Why is that? As a cambered wing is rotated to higher angles of attack (higher angles to the oncoming air), the air is forced to accelerate sooner and harder in order to follow the more angled curvature of the upper surface. And, as Bernoulli noted 160 years earlier, the more air is accelerated, the more it will drop its pressure. So at higher angles a cambered wing develops more lift on its forward portion, thus moving the overall center of lift forward. (See Figure 52) Sometimes this effect is even more pronounced due to flow separation from the aft upper surface destroying lift there. But remember, the Wrights, along with many others at their time, weren't aware of the importance of the upper surface of a wing in developing lift, so there was no way they could deduce these characteristics.

Well, what was happening to the Wrights' vehicle is now apparent. At the angles of attack used in flight, the center of lift moved forward on the wings with increasing angle. This pulled the wings toward an even higher angle of attack. So the wings were longitudinally very unstable, and the canard aggravated it. But oddly enough, due to a peculiarity of the Wrights' early testing, they didn't really come to grips with the true severity of this problem until the fall of 1901. For the most part they tested their 1900 glider by tethering the wing tips on each side. So although they could warp the wings and make the vehicle roll, it was not free to yaw and was also somewhat limited in pitch motion. Consequently, the severe degree of pitch instability was not readily apparent. The Wrights didn't understand the true magnitude of the pitch instability until they undertook extensive free glides toward the end of their 1901 testing.

Both brothers recorded statements directly saying that their canards were in large part the result of their erroneous concept of the movement of the center of pressure on a wing. During his speech in Chicago in 1901 Wilbur stated "Our peculiar plan of control by forward surfaces instead of tails was based on the assumption that the center of pressure would continue to move farther and farther forward as the angle became less".(1/110) In his legal deposition of 1920, Orville recalled their perplexity over the situation: "Our elevator was placed in front of the surfaces [wings] with the idea of producing inherent stability fore and aft, which it should have done had the travel of the center of pressure been forward [with decreasing angle of attack] as we had been led to believe".(2/17)

Throughout 1900 and most of 1901, the Wrights believed that the unexpected movement of the center of pressure on their wings was due to a peculiar property of the shape of their wing cross sections, i.e., incorrect camber shapes. So they struggled to find a shape that would not exhibit the anomaly. Unfortunately, in doing so, they were greatly hindered by their misconception concerning how wings generate lift. In a previous section we saw that they thought only in terms of air impinging on surfaces. So they believed that the travel of the center of pressure with changes in angle of attack on a gradually curved wing section was due to its presenting substantially more or less of its upper surface for the wind to impact upon.(1/109) Consequently, their solution to limiting the adverse movement of the center of pressure was to put all of the rising camber at the very front of the airfoil. Then, they reasoned, moderate changes in angle of attack would not change how much of the upper surface the airflow would impact. And this would pretty much cause the center of pressure to stay put. (See Figure 53) All that would then be necessary to achieve stability would be to properly locate the vehicle's center of gravity.

As Wilbur explained it in his 1901 speech in Chicago, "Instead of using the arc of a circle, we made the curve of our machine very abrupt at the front so as to expose the least possible area to this downward pressure".(1/109,110) He also acknowledged this approach in his 1908 article in *The Century* magazine. He explained that they set out to achieve "fore-and-aft stability by giving the aeroplanes [wings] a peculiar shape [camber or cross section]".(2/82) This would have also fit nicely with their goal stated nearby in the article. That was to make their aircraft "as inert as possible to the effects of change of direction or speed, and thus reduce the effects of wind gusts to a minimum"(2/82)

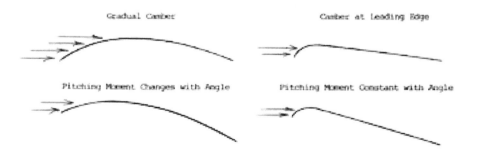

Figure 53: Wrights' Incorrect Concept for a Stable Airfoil

Unfortunately, as seemed to happen so often, their solution had just the opposite effect of what they desired. By curving the wing section over only the first 10 percent or so and making the remaining 90 percent of the wing profile nearly flat, they had created, both in their 1900 and 1901 machines, a very sudden airflow separation characteristic resulting in what modern designers would today call departure. This means that the flight characteristics departed from what was expected or desired. Instead of the flow separating over the last 10 percent or so of the upper surface and the separation point gradually creeping forward as it does on a smoothly curved surface as angle of attack is increased, it would more suddenly separate, or reattach, over a substantial portion of the large flat section of their wings.

Figure 54: Wrights' 1901 Glider with a Third Spar

While building the 1901 machine, the Wrights told Chanute and his associates of their pitch instability problem and their planned solution. Both Spratt and Huffaker informed the Wrights that they believed they would still have the same problem; the center of pressure would still move forward with increasing angle of attack.(1/110) Here again is more proof that the true movement of the center of pressure was already well-known. Chanute and his two associates were present at the Kitty Hawk camp later that year when, sure enough, the Wrights were struggling with the same (if not worse) problem.

The Wrights had even tried flattening the wing still further by pressing down the mid-chord area with a third spanwise spar shown in Figure 54.(1/111) Finally Dr. Spratt suggested some tethered tests with various center of gravity locations and angles of attack. These would determine once and for all where the centers of pressure locations actually were. And again, sure enough, Spratt and Huffaker were right. The center of pressure was indeed moving forward with increasing angle of attack. That settled it. The mystery was solved. The 1900 glider had flown better backwards because the design was backwards, because the theory they used was backwards. All this, the Wrights maintained, was through no fault of their own.(2/17)

Nevertheless, the Wrights were not going to abandon the canard. In fact, in his September 1901 presentation to the Western Society of Engineers a month after the end of the Kitty Hawk tests for that year, one of the conclusions that Wilbur presented was that aircraft absolutely do not need horizontal or vertical tails.(1/117) This statement seems doubly perplexing since they then immediately went back to Dayton and began designing the 1902 glider with a vertical tail, which they had already decided was necessary to counteract the wing-warping-induced yaw.

As was pointed out in the previous section, the Wrights were well aware that an aircraft could easily be made to be inherently longitudinally stable, i.e., stable in pitch. They also knew that many of their predecessors had done it. However they found fault with the primary method that had been used to achieve this stability. To briefly recap, others had stabilized their aircraft in pitch by having the center of gravity located slightly ahead of the center of lift and drag, and using a negatively loaded horizontal tail. If the nose tilted up, the tail was at a less negative angle, thus pushing down less and allowing the weight to pull the nose back down. If the nose pointed somewhat downward, the tail, being at a more negative angle, pushed down harder, bringing the nose back up. That is the immediate effect. But there can be a more long-term effect. As the nose pointed up, the aircraft, running "uphill," soon slowed down. This also reduced the downward push of the tail, allowing the aircraft to nose over and start running "downhill." The resulting increase in airspeed then pushed down harder on the negatively-set horizontal tail, bringing the nose back up, in some cases up past level. This caused the airplane to run "uphill" again. (Movements of the main wing's center of pressure can modify these motions somewhat.) The Wrights' complaint was that sometimes a perturbation in speed or angle of attack could start these excursions, creating cycles or oscillations of pitch instability. The aircraft would continue on just like a roller coaster. These cycles, you may remember, are called phugoid oscillations.

Phugoid oscillations can be nearly unnoticeable, or they can be quite large. Some modern large aircraft have gone through phugoid excursions approaching 1,000 feet in altitude over periods of 30 seconds or more. In extreme cases, gliders with this problem can approach stalling conditions on the upswing. Fortunately, many ways have been found to minimize or eliminate the problem. The most effective way is relocation of the center of gravity, although changing speed, or the size, location, or angle of the horizontal tail are also effective. Some of the Wrights' predecessors had discovered these fixes, so it would seem that even if the Wrights had not read of these remedies, they would also have been able to discover them. Perhaps had they done experimentation with flying models before going to full-scale aircraft, they would have. But then, first experimenting with flyable models would have also solved a lot of their other problems earlier and easier.

Actually, there is no record of the Wrights having discussed phugoids or any other pitch oscillations during their early testing. The first explicit reference to "constant undulation" caused by the tailed configurations appears in Orville's 1908 article in *The Century*.(2/82) However there is the following statement in Wilbur's 1901 address to the Western Society of Engineers: "After much study we finally concluded that tails were a source of trouble rather than assistance; and therefore we decided to dispense with them altogether".(1/104) Certainly one thing he was referring to was the post-stall dive. But if that were all, it seems he would have used a stronger word like "danger" rather than "trouble." So maybe he was also thinking of phugoids, and it really was an early concern of theirs.

But there is yet another reason for their preferring the canard that I believe was more important than the Wrights ever let on. That is the positive psychological effect of having their lifesaving control out there in front of them where they could see it. With these horizontal control surfaces pivoted about a third of the way back, it seems all one needed do to control pitching (as a first approximation anyway) would be to move the canard surface such that the leading edge stays near or just above the line of the horizon. One might even be able to judge the load on it by bulging of the fabric. It would also function as a lateral bank indicator. Without something out ahead it might have been difficult for a pilot lying prone to judge the attitude of the aircraft in time to make needed corrections. Remember, the California Institute of

Technology and Northrop wind tunnel tests showed the 1903 Flyer to be as difficult to control as balancing a yardstick on one finger. Try doing that without seeing where the top of the stick is going!

There is a fifth and very pragmatic reason why the Wrights stuck with the canard configuration long after they should have. They were locked into it by their patent. This will be discussed more extensively later, but suffice it to say here that, what with trying to extend their wing warping concept to ailerons, winglets, and all other forms of roll control, and having abandoned other features of their 1906 patent, all they needed to do would have been to change the overall configuration of their airplane to that used by their competitors and they wouldn't have had a leg to stand on in litigations.

Their original patent, number 821,393 granted in 1906, was specifically written to cover their 1902 glider, but it also covered the airframe configuration of their subsequent aircraft since they were constructed in the same manner, and it mentioned the aircraft could be mechanically powered. Lines 28 through 31 of page five of the patent state, "Contrary to the usual custom, we place the horizontal rudder (sic) in front of the aeroplanes [wings] at a negative angle and employ no horizontal tail at all".(4/5) They are saying here that one of the things that is unique about their vehicle is the canard. Moreover, they are admitting that the horizontal tail is the "usual custom" and therefore really not patentable. So, were they to convert to the usual and customary configuration, their vehicle would, in this respect, lose its patentability. (Remember that by the end of 1902 the vehicle described in the patent, the 1902 glider, did not have its canard negatively set and loaded, but in fact it ended up with a substantial positive load on it, as did the 1903 machines and later ones. Thus the specific idea covered in the patent had already been abandoned by the time it was submitted.)

Finally, we really should consider what role the Wrights' psychological attitude might have played in their use and retention of the canard surface. At the start I'd like to say that I believe the Wrights were basically thorough and pragmatic in their research and testing. But they were also human and therefore susceptible to other motivations as well. In the first place, I think they were far too quick to discount, in fact largely ignore, much of the work that had been done before them. In his 1908 magazine article Wilbur wrote, "We saw that the calculations upon which all flying machines had been based were unreliable, and that all were simply groping in the dark." A little farther on he said "We cast it all aside, and decided to rely entirely upon our own investigations".(2/84) Aside from the first statement being absolutely not true, the second statement shows an amazing willingness to discard a century of work done by dozens of well-qualified men.

Perhaps the real extent of Wilbur's disdain, if not downright arrogance, is evident in his comment about one of Langley's successful unmanned, powered models. In a letter to Octave Chanute, Wilbur referred to it as a "toy". (1/217) Remember, this was an unmanned powered aircraft that had flown smoothly eight years previously, executing a turn for nearly a mile, and stopping only when it ran out of fuel. It then glided smoothly and gently to the earth. When the Wrights finally accomplished this years later it was with a wobbly, unstable, barely manageable vehicle.

However, when it came to blind arrogance Orville typically outdid Wilbur. In 1944 he said "Henson, Stringfellow, and Marriott made no contributions to the art or science of aviation worth mentioning." He went on, "Every feature of Henson's machine had been used or proposed previously. His mere assemblage of old elements certainly did not constitute invention." (35/36) This comment is astoundingly thoughtless since, this exact criticism applies perfectly to what he and his brother did. Except for their chain drive of propellers and interconnected rudder and warping which soon had to be abandoned, every major feature of the Wrights' machines had been used or proposed previously, even their canard elevators and engines. This statement actually disqualified himself and his brother as inventors.

Elsewhere in the 1908 article, in a discussion about the longitudinal and lateral stability of their machines Orville states "We therefore resolved to try a fundamentally different principle. We would make it....just the reverse of what our predecessors had done".(2/82) This is presented as though the decision was made at the start, before they had even been to Kitty Hawk. So it can't be ascribed to the severe testing conditions there. One could almost rewrite all these statements as follows: "None of those guys knew what they were doing, so we showed them how to do it. Not only that, we did it by doing just the opposite of what everybody else did." Once you've set yourself up in this position, it's pretty hard to turn around and say, "Ah, never mind. We decided their way was better anyway."

There is one other factor to the psychological aspect. The Wrights, particularly Wilbur, seemed to believe that they had fought their way through a maze of blind alleys and had discovered the only way to make a successful airplane, and they had concluded that any and all other ways must be wrong. Therefore, unless someone else went along the exact same path as they did, and discovered the same remedies, they would not be successful at designing an airplane. This is best exemplified in Wilbur's 1906 letter to Chanute in which he says, "We do not believe there is a chance in one hundred that anyone will have a machine....within five years. It is many times five years".(1/729,730) It's like the brothers thought they had struggled so hard for so long to get to the point that they were by 1906 that there couldn't possibly have been other easier and better ways to have done it. If that had been true, Wilbur's prediction would have had a pretty firm statistical basis. Unfortunately, it was far from the truth, and within a couple years they had pretty stiff competition in the air.

This brings up another non-technical, but quite possibly additional, reason the Wrights didn't abandon their forward elevators for a decade. Since May of 1900, Octave Chanute had kept them advised of their competitors' progress in aviation research. He informed them of the accomplishments of over a dozen serious researchers, in particular the Smithsonian's Samuel Langley with whom he had regular contact since the early 1890s.

Chanute also advised Langley of the success the Wrights were having with their gliders, and Langley soon approached the Wrights in 1902 requesting to visit them at Kitty Hawk. The Wrights declined, saying they would be returning to Dayton within a few days.(1/283) Langley told Chanute he was particularly interested in the Wrights control scheme. By July of 1903 Wilbur asked Chanute not to give Langley any advanced notice of their experiments, and in early December Chanute cautioned Dr. George Spratt that the Wrights didn't want Langley to know they were going to attempt flight with a motor soon.(1/337,377)

The Wrights' major effort from the summer of 1901 through most of 1902 had to be to figure out how to develop the necessary lift and control to keep their vehicles in the air. Their next major problem was to develop a propulsion system. These efforts, plus their competitors' progress, may have convinced them they had no time to abandon their canard and develop a totally reconfigured vehicle. Instead, by the end of 1905 they had refined their canard machine well enough to keep it in the air and complete turns.

Then, for the next several years, they both concentrated on intense efforts to market their vehicles and construct enough of them for demonstrations in the U.S. and Europe. Again there was little time to develop a new configuration. Only after securing some sales contracts and licensing deals in 1909 did they turn to developing a new more stable conventional design, the model B Flyer.

Summarizing this section so far, the strongest and most valid reason the Wrights had to mount their horizontal control in front of their aircraft was to maintain pitch control during and after a stall. This enabled them to slowly flutter down to the ground flat as opposed to crashing into it headfirst in a fast dive. They gave secondary reasons of wanting to achieve near-neutral pitch stability and avoid pitch oscillations. But these goals could have been achieved with tailed aircraft by other means, and a number of their predecessors had already done so. Although the Wrights barely mentioned it, I believe seeing the pitch control out in front made it easier to judge the attitude of their aircraft. And, it is important to remember that by 1906 they were locked into the canard configuration by their patents and the numerous legal battles involving them. Also, psychological factors involving ego and fear of competition prevented them from giving any other configuration a serious try later on. Finally, the progress of other aviation experimenters was such that, if they took the time to reconfigure and retest their vehicles, they may well not have been the first into the air.

I have not presented these seven reasons for the Wrights' canard configuration as a laundry list of possibilities from which to pick favorites. I believe that at various times each one of them was an operative factor. Of the three reasons most often cited by the Wrights, only one of them, avoiding post-stall dives into the ground, had any real validity. Their stability considerations were incorrect, and phugoid oscillations were not an insurmountable problem with tailed configurations. Moreover, when one considers the number of stalls resulting from the tricky handling caused by the canards, it is questionable, at best, whether they really were a safety feature. They probably eventually caused more crashes than they prevented.

But even if one is willing to grant that the canards were beneficial, that would only have been true through 1903 or 1904. By 1905 they had enough power that they were routinely flying at about 100 feet over Huffman Prairie. These altitudes were probably limited by their unwillingness to be seen by trolley and highway passengers. So by 1905 they could achieve such altitude and speed that stalling or even recovering from stalls should have been no problem with a conventional horizontal tail instead of the canard. Therefore, even if they didn't start out with a conventional horizontal tail, they could have converted to that configuration after 1904. But after they finally achieved a reliable turning capability during the last week of testing in 1905, they didn't fly again for nearly three years. Rather than improving their product, they spent these years filing patents and hurriedly trying to sell their aircraft before something better came along.

So what was the result of their decision to use the canard? Wildly unstable aircraft that even they could barely fly. Over the years, from 1900 through 1905, they tried to modify their aircraft to be less unstable. Most of these changes consisted of moving the center of gravity forward and putting a heavy positive load on the canard. By 1903 their canard was carrying twice the loading per square foot that the main wings had.(1/351,352) (In an aerodynamic sense, this converted their configuration toward that used by Langley's much maligned Aerodrome, i.e., a tandem wing configuration.) This allowed them to affect the balance of the aircraft with much smaller control movements and also insured that the canard, when in the neutral position, would stall before the main wing did, a feature that helps prevent total aircraft stalls. But still, Wright Flyers remained the most difficult aircraft to fly, primarily because of pitch instability. Films of Wright Flyers in flight in 1909 clearly show periods of frequent elevator movements, often with a frequency of about once a second, sometimes even quicker.(3/37,38)

A modern analysis of the 1903 Flyer revealed that its center of gravity was at the 30 percent wing chord point, and its neutral point was at about the 10 percent chord point.(3/25) If the center of gravity is at the neutral point, an airplane is aerodynamically neutrally balanced, i.e., a slight perturbation in angle of attack generates no pitching moment. For longitudinal (pitch) stability, the center of gravity must be kept ahead of the neutral point. The distance from the neutral point forward to the center of gravity is called the static margin. It is measured as a percentage or decimal portion of the wing chord, positive being stable and negative unstable. So by modern terminology, the 1903 Flyer had a static margin of -20 percent. To give an idea of how unstable this is, most modern fighter aircraft with digital electronic stability control systems are designed to be aerodynamically unstable for high maneuverability in combat. And they typically have static margins of around -5 to -7 percent.(3/25) In other words, the 1903 Wright Flyer was three or four times more unstable than the most unstable airplanes we build today with the help of automatic digital electronic flight control systems!

And what was the result of that? Many pilots considered even the improved versions of Wright Flyers to be nothing less than killers. One of the major reasons that the U.S. Army was reluctant to buy Wright Flyers was the difficulty of flying them, again largely due to their pitch instability. Finally, after seeing the proliferation of aircraft in foreign militaries and knowing the Wrights' patents had the U.S. market largely locked up, the U.S. Army acquiesced and began to buy Flyers and have pilots trained. But within 16 months eight of the first fourteen U.S. Army pilots had been killed.(26/48)

The Wrights established an exhibition team to make money and promote their product. The Wrights themselves trained the nine pilots comprising the team. Between June 1910 and November 1911, five of the nine pilots were killed in crashes.(14/199) Henry Villard recorded that although dozens had entered the aircraft manufacturing business worldwide, eight of the first thirty-three people killed in airplanes were killed in Wright Flyers.

It would seem the difficulty of flying early Wright aircraft would be well known, particularly by those interested enough to build flyable replicas. Apparently this is not the case. In May of 2003 Ken Hyde, a retired airline pilot, supposed to only be doing the first taxi test, took off in a very expensive Wright Model B replica. Even though the B was much improved over the 1903 vehicle, Ken crashed it almost immediately trying to turn around and return to the field. The crash was apparently due to failure to correct for the wing warping reversal described in this book. Ken suffered a broken arm and other minor injuries, but the aircraft, including one of only two original Wright engines, was a write-off. Then in November, in preparation for the centennial celebration, Terry Queijo crashed Hyde's 1903 replica less than two seconds into its first flight attempt. The repaired aircraft failed to leave the ground at the Kitty Hawk centennial event in front of over a thousand onlookers.

On October fifth of 2007 Mark Dusenberry crashed his replica of a 1905 Flyer at Huffman Prairie. Then on October first of 2009 he again crashed the repaired aircraft in his second attempt to prepare for a reenactment. This time he was severely injured and at least temporarily crippled, giving up his effort.

But it gets worse. On July 30th, 2011 Don Gumm and Mitchel Cary were killed when they crashed their Wright Model B "look alike", ironically while flying near the Dayton Wright Brothers Airport south of Dayton. In fact, as of this writing, no one has successfully flown a truly accurate replica of the original 1903 powered Wright aircraft 150 feet, under control or not.

It beggars the imagination of this aeronautical engineer that so many people with appreciable resources, skill, and knowledge of the Wrights' work could invest the time, effort and money to build accurate reproductions of their earliest airplanes, and yet apparently have little or no appreciation of how difficult, indeed nearly impossible, it is to fly the aircraft, particularly with no headwind or practice. These recreators of early Wright Flyers would like us to believe they are honoring the Wrights by attempting to build and fly their aircraft. But this engineer resents the hubris and arrogance of these people for thinking they could immediately duplicate the Wrights' accomplishments without going through the years of study, thought, and thousands of ground and flight tests it took the Wrights to get there. Even as late as 1910 Grover Loening saw Wilbur, with hundreds of hours of flying experience, sit in his aircraft on the ground practicing and memorizing maneuvering and recovery procedures on the controls.

Certainly, no one should expect the very first manned, powered airplane to have been perfect or even good. But that's not the point. The point is that the Wright brothers desperately wanted to lead, if not sew up, the aviation industry for the foreseeable future. But once they chose to more or less abandon further technical development and instead rely on invoking their patent to retain dominance of worldwide aviation, they were essentially locked in to their original configuration. And the continued use of the canard, along with the instability it induced, kept the Wrights from achieving their long-term goal. It led to their failure to compete commercially with the other aircraft that soon became available. Along with performance deficiencies, Flyers were simply too difficult to fly. A disproportionate number of men died trying. Finally, in 1910 the security of some sales contracts, and competing designs, drove them to abandon their unstable canard layout, and they adopted a conventional aft stabilizer configuration for their first volume production aircraft, the Model B. But by then they were hopelessly behind other aviation developments, and they never achieved the huge commercial success they dearly sought.

Banning Rock and Roll

In order to stabilize an airplane in flight one must not only prevent pitching of the nose up or down, but it must also be prevented from rolling, or tilting, to the right or left. Typically, a straight cambered wing by itself tends to be stable laterally (in roll) and unstable longitudinally (in pitch). Also, anyone wanting to get up off of the ground has to immediately tackle the pitch control problem. Since most of the nineteenth century aviators barely managed to get

off the ground, if at all, they invested more effort devising means of pitch control than for roll control. Observing this, many have considered the Wrights'
aerodynamic roll control to be their greatest contribution to the science of
flight, other than propulsion. Of course, it had been obvious to anyone who
contemplated bird flight even briefly that birds needed to stay level in order to
fly straight and to bank in order to turn. So, as we saw in Chapters I and II, others before the Wrights had experimented with, or at least considered, active
aerodynamic means of controlling roll, including ailerons, winglets, and wing
warping. In fact, versions of these devices had already been patented before
the Wrights began their aviation experiments.

It is generally considered preferable if unintentional tilting or rolling of an
aircraft can be prevented automatically by some inherent aerodynamic design
feature rather than requiring constant attention and frequent inputs from the
pilot through a control device. We saw that by 1809 Sir George Cayley had figured out that if the wings were set at an angle, like a shallow V as seen from the
front or back, the craft would automatically tend to right itself from a rolled
position.(3/31) (By now you probably remember that if an airplane with this
feature is tilted toward one side, the low wing becomes more horizontal, generating more lift and thus pushing the craft back toward level.) Many birds
have this shape, at least on the inboard portions of their wings. This feature,
called dihedral, was used to achieve lateral stability by most of those who preceded the Wrights and has been used on most airplanes since then.

Many nineteenth century experimenters were also aware of an added
advantage to dihedral. In addition to keeping an aircraft level when going
straight, it can assist in turning the vehicle in a banked turn. By employing a
vertical rudder, an airplane can be made to slide or skid toward one side. Once
skidding, the leading wing will be blown up by air hitting its bottom surface,
while the trailing wing will be blown down by air hitting its top. (In actuality,
with dihedral the effective angle of attack of the leading wing of a yawed airplane is increased due to spanwise flow inboard, while that of the trailing wing
is decreased due to spanwise flow in the outboard direction.) Consequently,
the craft will roll away from the slide or skid and into a banked turn, albeit still
with some skidding. This is not the most comfortable and certainly not the
most efficient way to turn an airplane, but it works. Few before the Wrights
had gotten far enough to attempt turns. Still, many learned to appreciate the
inherent stability provided by dihedral.

On their first glider the Wrights initially rigged in a few degrees of dihedral.(34/94) But upon seeing the machine's reaction to the strong gusty Kitty Hawk crosswinds, they took it out. They eventually wrote things indicating they did not like dihedral from the start. Perhaps the best example of this appears in Orville's article in the 1908 *Century* magazine. "After considering the practical effect of the dihedral principle, we reached the conclusion that a flyer founded upon it might be of interest from a scientific point of view, but could be of no value in a practical way".(2/28) A little later it says, "We would make it [the aircraft] as inert as possible….by arching the surfaces [wings] from tip to tip".

This could give the impression that the Wrights had decided to use anhedral before they even started flying. That is not true. Both the 1899 kite and the 1900 glider, after removal of its initial dihedral, had wings that were spanwise perfectly straight. During these years they were totally engrossed in verifying the roll control capability of their wing warping idea. However, as soon as they attempted regular free glides at Kitty Hawk in 1901, they sat up and took notice. They were okay as long as they were pointing straight down a hill and into the wind, but when they encountered a crossing gust or began traversing a slope even slightly, the wind, pushed up by the sloping hill, would come up under the windward wing and tilt the leeward wing down. The airplane would then slide down sideways toward, and finally into, the hillside.

The Wrights decided they had to do something with the design of their machine to help them cope with this problem. This seemed particularly urgent since, as we will soon see, their roll recovery mechanism wasn't working at all. Obviously, dihedral would make this particular problem worse. So they decided they would adjust the rigging so as to bend the wings in the spanwise direction with the tips slightly drooped down, i.e., anhedral. Then a crosswind coming up the hill would hit the windward wing tip pretty near edge on and would even tend to lift the leeward wing. The aircraft would then no longer roll into the hillside, but it would actually roll away from it, if at all.

Although this part of the idea seemed to work, unfortunately, as so often seems to be the way with airplanes, this solution created a whole new problem for them. Now, in addition to being highly unstable in pitch because of the canard, the aircraft and those that followed were also unstable in roll, even in calm air. When the airplane banked even slightly, the high wing was now more level than the low one, creating more lift and tilting the vehicle farther into the roll. If not corrected in some way, it would quickly slide off sideways toward the low wing, just like a coin sliding off of a bowling ball. Soon the low wing tip was in the sand, and the flight was over. Now, with both pitch and roll instabilities, flying the aircraft was like trying to sit atop a giant beach ball. To make matters worse, their roll control, for which they had such high hopes, had a few surprises for them too.

A famous story tells how Wilbur inadvertently discovered wing warping in 1899 by absentmindedly twisting on a small, long cardboard box that had no ends. By pinching opposite corners together on one end, and the other opposite corners on the other end, the surfaces of the box could be made to twist such that the top and bottom on one end were at a different angle from those on the opposite end. He realized that wings that could do this should cause an airplane to bank or tilt toward one side or the other. What is less well known is that before this they were trying to figure out ways to twist entire rigid wing halves relative to each other in order to achieve lateral control.(1/8) This followed from a design that Lilienthal had concocted. But like him, they never found a structurally sound way of doing this.

They decided that if they made biplanes, they could figure out a way to twist or warp the wings opposite of each other just like the cardboard box twisted. Then one side would have a higher angle of attack than the other near the tips and should generate more lift. This would cause the wing and aircraft to roll toward the wing with the lower angle of attack, and in this manner they would bring their aircraft back level when it became tilted.

There is evidence that the Wrights initially believed that they were the first to come up with a practical means of actively controlling roll and certainly the first to devise wing warping, this in spite of the fact that the English experimenter M.P.W. Boulton had already patented wing flaps that moved in opposite directions to control roll (i.e., ailerons), and a Frenchman, Charles Renard, had come up with separate winglets that worked in a similar fashion. (21/134 & 16/16) Later, Chanute told the Wrights more than once that wing warping was not original either, citing Mouillard's 1897 U.S. patent for just that.(1/981,982) However the Wrights were unphased by all this and preceded to not only use the idea but to patent it themselves and, they alleged, all other methods of roll control. But more about that later.

In Chapter III we saw that in 1899 Wilbur built a 5-foot span biplane kite which he tested using two sticks and four lines tied to the wing tips. Twisting the wings by tilting the sticks opposite each other produced such wonderful roll response that Wilbur couldn't wait to tell his brother. But the important thing to remember here is that Wilbur didn't notice any difference in pull on the sticks when the wings were twisted. The forces generated by this device were small, but perhaps if he had flown it for more than a few minutes on one day he would have noticed a difference.

The following year, 1900, they built a machine of a size that they thought would be big enough for manned flights. It was a biplane with a 17-foot wing-span. It turned out that in any reasonable amount of wind it couldn't support a pilot, so they had to test fly it as before, unmanned with the wing tips tethered by lines. But this machine was so big that each brother had to handle the lines for one end of the wings. Again the vehicle showed good roll response to the wing warping, but neither man could tell if his side was pulling less or harder than the other side. And of course, because of the tethers, the machine could not yaw or turn at all. Later in the year, toward the end of the test session, the winds at Kitty Hawk grew even stronger. Finally, with winds well over 20 miles per hour, they attempted a few free manned glides. But in these condi-tions it was difficult to detect any handling vices the machine may have had. Besides, except for the last few glides, they had the wing warping tied off and inoperable.(34/99) So they decided to stick with the same basic configura-tion for the following year.

For 1901 they upsized the wings to a span of 22 feet and slightly altered the wing section shape in hopes of improving the aircraft's pitch characteris-tics. They were disappointed to find that the vehicle still didn't have enough lift and that the pitch characteristics were not improved. If anything, the pitching problem was even worse. Then, as soon as they abandoned the teth-ers and began free gliding the machine, their wing warping roll control began to work backwards. When the vehicle became tilted and they tried to right it, instead of coming back level it would bank even more steeply, turn toward the low wing, and slide or spin into the sand. 1901 was turning out to be some test session. There was still not enough lift. And not only had the pitch character-istics gotten worse, but the previous year they had found that their design flew better backwards. And now the roll control was working backwards!

To fully understand why their wing warping was causing the aircraft to spin in, it is necessary to take a quantitative look at the peculiarities of extremely slow flight as presented in Appendix 1. But the qualitative factors are these: A wing's lift and drag increase in proportion to its angle up from the direction the wind is coming from, the angle of attack. Lift and drag also increase with the square of the flight speed, i.e., twice as fast gives four times as much lift or drag. Although the speed and force relationship had been well established many years earlier, the Wrights, at least early on, did not seem to really appreciate the ramifications of this squared relationship. Wilbur told the Western Society of Engineers in 1901 that, in an aircraft, twice the power would give more than twice the speed.(1/115) In reality, twice the speed would result in nearly four times the drag, requiring about four times the thrust and, since power is thrust times speed, eight times the power to overcome it.

At the low flight speeds of the Wrights' early vehicles, the consequences of the proportionality of aerodynamic forces with the square of speed are quite surprising. In their case, with the wings warped, although the wing with more angle of attack initially generates more lift, it also generates much more drag. The other wing, being at a lower angle, initially reduces its lift and drag. So if a vehicle like the Wrights' 1901 glider, which had no directional stability, became tilted and warping was applied to bring it back level, it would initially start to roll back level, but it would also immediately begin to rotate about its vertical axis toward the low higher-angled wing. Soon, due to the rotation, the higher wing with less angle of attack would be going so much faster than the other that it would develop more lift throwing the aircraft farther into the original bank. This could not be corrected or even stopped, and the aircraft would slide or spin into the ground. To make matters worse, although lift is almost exactly proportional to angle of attack, drag is, at higher angles, more proportional to the square of angle of attack. So applying more warp caused a more drastic increase in drag on the higher angled wing, further accelerating the yaw and control reversal, resulting in an even more violent spin. In some cases the yaw rate could accelerate to the point where the higher angled wing had almost no airspeed or lift at all. The anhedral added to this problem. (Again, for a more detailed quantitative explanation of these phenomena see Appendix 1.)

The brothers soldiered on, struggling through the remainder of the 1901 test session as best they could. They made more glides, attempting to refine their handling of the pitch control and trying to avoid the roll and spin problems. They managed to make glide ratio measurements, although, due to a reduced aspect ratio, this machine didn't even have as good a glide ratio as the previous one. They probably had already thought of a solution to the warp reversal and spin problem while still at Kitty Hawk. Nevertheless, Wilbur, the stronger theoretician of the two, was still anguishing over the problem as they were returning to Dayton. It was just as well though, since they didn't have the materials or fabricating capability at Kitty Hawk that they would have needed to create a fix.

They managed to design and fabricate a significantly different biplane glider for the 1902 test session at Kitty Hawk. As compared to the 1901 machine, the new one had a wingspan increase to over 32 feet along with a chord reduction to 5 feet, changing the aspect ratio from 3.1 to 6.5. It also sported a totally different more smoothly distributed wing camber profile with maximum camber occurring about a third of the way back from the leading edge.

But there was another entirely new feature. The Wrights had figured out that their warping reversal problem was caused by the yawing rate that warping induced. So they determined that if they could keep the vehicle pointed straight ahead, like it did when it was tethered, then they would get the desired roll response. So why not keep it pointing into the wind the same way a weather vane does, by putting a big vertical fin trailing behind the aircraft? Well, that's exactly what they did. Actually, to make for a more compact and rigid structure, they made two 5-foot-high vertical stabilizers mounted side by side only about 4 feet behind the trailing edge of the main wings. These stabilizers were rigidly mounted with no provision for adjustment. Remember, the objective at this time was to fly straight ahead.

Ever cautious as usual, they did their first tests at Kitty Hawk in 1902 with the vehicle unmanned and tethered. And, as usual, the tethered tests gave them reason for optimism. The vehicle seemed to be behaving much better in all three axes of motion. And it was lifting like crazy. So the Wrights undertook manned glides in September.

The new gradual wing cross-section shape with maximum camber moved from the 10 percent chord location back to about the 30 percent point, along with the larger aspect ratio, were vast improvements. They finally had enough lift. Not only that, pitch instability wasn't as vicious as on the previous machines. But wouldn't you know it, another well-thought-out aerodynamic scheme turned into a complete disaster. Their new aft vertical stabilizers had made the spin problem worse. The reverse rolling was about the same as last year. But the tendency of the vehicle to turn into the roll and spin was much stronger. As they put it in the 1908 magazine article, "The addition of a fixed vertical vane in the rear increased the trouble, and made the machine absolutely dangerous".(2/83) To make matters worse, the increased aspect ratio of the wings, over twice that of the 1901 machine, along with the anhedral on the increased span, accentuated the warp-induced yaw and adverse roll-in.

This is an opportune point at which to correct another misconception. To describe this spin-in to the sand the Wrights coined the term "well digging." Although it's not a major point, I have often read incorrect descriptions of these events and even heard an incorrect description of them by a narrator at the National Air and Space Museum. In fact, the description was just the opposite of what really happened.

Those in error start from the premise that the Wrights were starting from level flight and trying to bank into a deliberate turn using wing warping. Secondly, they appear to be aware of the increased drag on the downward-warped wing but unaware that in a very short time, this drag asymmetry induced a yaw rate that caused a substantial lift imbalance in favor of the upward-warped wing. As a result, they think the aircraft was banking into the upward-warped wing and then yawing away from it, resulting in a slide or slip into the lower, leading, upward-warped wing, eventually sticking it straight into the sand. This straight sideslip does not particularly remind one of "well digging."

In fact, the Wrights, in both the 1908 article in The Century as well as Orville's 1920 deposition for the Mouillard case, made it quite clear that (1) they were trying to regain level flight with an already inadvertently banked aircraft, and (2) the aircraft would actually roll and yaw farther into the lower downward-warped trailing wing. The final result was the aircraft descending and spinning about the low downward warped wing resulting in a swirling or auguring of the low wing tip into the sand. Thus the term "well digging". (2/19,83)

This is certainly not a major point in the extensive and complex story of the Wright brothers' exploits. But I do believe we owe the Wrights the honor of reading their words carefully and recounting their explanations correctly. That is, after all, the reason for this book. Additional information on the effects of wing warping on the Wrights' gliders can be obtained from Reference One, pages 82, 84, 85, 256, and 259, and from Reference Two, pages 17, 19, and 83.

Once more the Wrights had to stop and try to figure out what went wrong. By this time both their brother Lorin and Dr. Spratt had joined the Wrights in their camp. Chanute and Herring were on their way. But, according to Orville's journal, he was the one to come up with the solution a couple days before their arrival.(1/269) The problem was that as the plane tilted it would slip off or slide sideways toward the low side. This caused a side wind to blow on the fixed rudders, pushing the tail away and the nose toward the slide. But the vehicle was already turning into the slide because of the warp-induced high drag on the low wing. So now the two yawing effects were additive, causing the vehicle to turn in more than before. The tails worked like a weather vane all right, but the wind was coming from the side toward the slide, not from straight ahead. (Actually there was an additional yawing effect. The downward motion of the low wing increased its effective angle of attack, increasing its drag even further.)

Somehow they had to figure a way to get the wind to push the nose away from the slide and toward the original direction of flight. For that, the wind would have to push on the other side of the vertical tail, the side away from the slide. But that could only be done by turning the stabilizer away from the slide. Then the glider would be held in the original direction just like it was by the tethers. And that should make the warping work like it was intended.

That all sounded great, but they both knew that they already had just about all they could handle in the air, constantly coping with the aircraft's pitch and roll instabilities. How could they take on another control on a third axis of flight? According to Orville, it was Wilbur who came up with the solution to this problem. He realized that the only reason they needed the rudder at all was to counter the yaw brought on by the use of wing warping. (Remember, at this time they were trying to fly straight, not turn.) So why not connect the two controls? Well, that's what they did, and the new co-ordinated rudder was an immediate success. All that was needed was a little tuning. Now, when tilted, the aircraft could be brought back level with little or no change in the direction of flight. The Wrights were so ecstatic that they glided to exhaustion. They were now making over a hundred glides a day, to-tallying up nearly a thousand glides for the year. Many, if not most of these, were nearly stationary flights directly into the wind, what the Wrights called "soaring". True, the pitch and roll controls required constant attention, but at least now they worked. The plane could be kept reasonably straight and level most of the time.

They felt almost ready to make a powered aircraft, but there was one more thing that they needed to check out. A propulsion system could not be made flexible. So most of the craft could not be allowed to twist with the wing warp-ing as it had been doing. Consequently, they re-rigged the machine so that only the aft portion of the outermost wing panels could flex. But would the control still have enough authority to give sufficient roll response? It turned out there wasn't much difference. Now they were really ready.

It's important to understand something about flight tests such as these. The actions of the Wrights' aircraft were not precisely as I have described here in every instance. Variations in conditions and operation occasionally caused the vehicles to act or react somewhat differently. The speed, direction or duration of wind gusts, the airspeed and altitude of the vehicle, or the timing, magnitude, or duration of control applied to the aircraft are all primary influences on exactly how it may have reacted. Consequently, a detailed reading of every available description of every flight will, on occasion, describe a phenomenon somewhat different from what I have been describing here. That is to be expected and is why, to this day, flight tests are often repeated over and over to achieve meaningful results. However, the actions of the Wrights' vehicles I have described here are the ones typically exhibited in their tests and the ones that caused them to make the design changes they did.

Proceeding on to 1903, the first powered Wright aircraft was structurally and aerodynamically basically the same as the final version of the 1902 glider, but bigger. It had a wingspan of 40 feet. However, due to slight changes in center of gravity location and control pivot points, and considering pilot comments, there is reason to believe that its flying qualities were worse, and operator demands more severe, than were those for the 1902 glider. Not yet knowing this, the Wrights practiced for an attempt with the powered machine by gliding the 1902 aircraft. It had been left assembled in their Kitty Hawk shed and still flew well. Soon they renewed their confidence in maintaining the precarious balance of the unstable aircraft they had created. They felt ready to risk their valuable handmade one-of-a-kind propulsion system by taking it into the air.

Even with all that practice it is still a fact that all of the powered flights of 1903 ended in minor crashes, two of them severe enough that testing had to be curtailed for repairs. The 1903 vehicle was, or ended up, out of control in every flight. Although this was primarily due to pitch instability, lateral instability was the major contributor to ending the third attempt.(1/396) They recorded a total flying time for all five events of less than 2 minutes, most of that being attributed to the last trial.

One of the points I keep drumming home in this book is that through the end of 1903 the Wright brothers were totally occupied with making their vehicles capable of flying straight and level regardless of outside influences.

They did not attempt to execute intentional turns until the fall of 1904. Even then their first thirty flights were basically straight flights of less distance than that claimed for Wilbur's last one in 1903.(1/450) But when they did try to turn they immediately discovered more problems. The 1904 aircraft, basically the same as the 1903 but with a little more power, would enter into turns fairly well, but then it wanted to keep banking steeper and steeper into the turn. Often, when the Wrights attempted to prevent this, or if they tried to return to level flight, the aircraft crashed. (Sometimes you just have to stop and admire these guys for punching ahead no matter what, and not throwing in the towel.)

When any airplane is put into a banking turn, the outside wing moves faster than the inside wing. In modern situations this is seldom a problem because the basic airspeed is so much greater than the wing speed difference due to turning. But in a Wright Flyer the wings are so wide, the speeds so slow, and the turns so tight, that the resulting difference in lift of the outer and inner wings is substantial. Don't forget, lift is proportional to the square of the speed. As an example, a 1904 Flyer attempting a turn with a 200-foot radius would be generating half again more lift on its outermost wing panels as on its innermost panels just due to the difference in speeds of the inner and outer wings. Most planes don't turn that tight, but that's not unreasonable at all for a 30-mile-per-hour vehicle. Also, most airplanes counteract this effect somewhat by having dihedral. But remember, as usual, the 1904 Flyer had anhedral, which also caused it to want to fall into a bank ever more steeply. Together, these two adverse effects would place stringent demands on the best control system.

There was yet another factor that was making the problem even worse. Remember, the Wrights still had their rudder tied in with the wing warping. They could not use one without getting the other. So when they applied lots of opposite warp to counteract the overbanking, they also got a lot of rudder toward the outside of the turn. Sometimes the resulting yaw was enough to raise the nose up and toward the outside of the turn, putting the aircraft into a sideslipping stall, resulting in yet another crash. This was further aggravated by the plane being very near a stall anyway since it didn't have enough excess power to hold airspeed at the increased angle of attack necessary to turn. In a banked turn, the vertical lift of the wings (that portion counteracting gravity) is reduced since the wings are tilted over. That vertical component of lift has to be replaced by going to a higher angle of attack. But that generates more drag, and thus, there is the need for more power to maintain airspeed. Either that or the plane has to give up altitude and fly "downhill" to hold speed. But a plane that can't get out of ground effect doesn't have much altitude to give up. In 1904 they were doing their flying within about 30 feet of the ground.

The Wrights struggled with the turning problem all through their 1904 test series at Huffman Prairie and never did solve it. But by the fall of 1905, they had brought three new factors into play. First, they finally got rid of the anhedral and actually put in a little dihedral. Second, they had more power, so much more that they now finally could climb out of ground effect. And third, they disconnected the vertical rudder from the wing warping.(1/471,2/46) So then, not only did they not have so much of an overbanking problem, but also they had enough power to hold altitude in a turn, and they had a sophisticated enough control system to allow them to consistently get out of each turn. In fact, they had enough altitude that they developed a technique of going into a little dive at the end of a turn in order to gain speed to avoid stalling the inside wing when it was given a larger angle of attack for the rollout to level flight.(1/521) After finally getting everything together and learning how to turn and return to level straight flight reliably, they practiced it for a week. Then they quit flying for three years.

The turning problem of 1904 and 1905 is an interesting example of different writings of the Wrights giving different impressions. Following their individual accounts of 1904 flights written as they occurred, it is evident that they suffered quite a number of minor and a few not so minor crashes in turns or trying to get out of them. These accounts paint a picture of a struggle in learning how to redesign the vehicle in order to fully execute turns at will. But in their first rebuttal deposition in their case against Augustus Herring and Glen Curtiss, they wrote as though they had very little trouble turning the 1904 vehicle.(1/472) It merely says, "On a few occasions the machine did not respond promptly and the machine came to the ground in a somewhat tilted position." This is in contrast to 1904 postflight test notes. These contained comments like "unable to stop turning and broke engine, and skids and both screws [propellers]," or "darted into ground and broke upper [wing] spar, and skids, and screw," or "broke screws and rear lower spar" at the end of a circle, or various comments about "unable to stop turning".(1/454,456) I bring this up not merely to cast suspicion on the Wrights, but to point out that one has to be very careful in quoting them or in drawing conclusions from any particular writing of theirs. Sometimes careful analysis is required to resolve conflicts or contradictions, and in some cases it is just not possible.

Now let's take a look at what the Wrights might have done differently to achieve better results. But it is meaningless to do this with the advantage of hindsight or a complete modern understanding of aerodynamics. Rather, we must do it by putting ourselves in their shoes and considering what they had to work with.

Although the use of drooping wings, anhedral, may have made their aircraft less sensitive to crosswinds along the sloping hills of Kitty Hawk, it was still a poor choice. Why give up stability for normal conditions in order to have somewhat reduced aircraft reactions to unusual conditions? The Wrights have written that they believed gusty crosswinds to be the normal state of affairs. That may have been true at ground skimming altitudes at Kitty Hawk, but anyone, whether they fly or not, knows this is not generally true. It just doesn't seem to make sense to force yourself to constantly rebalance an aircraft just so it doesn't react quite so much to a crossing gust.

It didn't make sense to anyone else either. No one before the Wrights had used anhedral. In fact, the vast majority of them used dihedral. And I sometimes wonder if that isn't the clue to their thinking. The Wrights took a great deal of pride in their assertions that everyone before them had done it wrong and that they would achieve success by doing just the opposite.(2/82) And the use of anhedral is a prime example of this. In so many ways, they seemed like such pragmatic guys. Yet, it is very difficult to come up with a practical argument for their use of anhedral, particularly after 1902. The 1903 and later flights were over level ground, so side gusts pushing them into the side of a hill was no longer a problem. In any case the anhedral really didn't have much impact on either their short- or long-term success. If anything, the roll instability gave urgency to their achieving a workable roll control during 1901 and 1902. Anhedral only became a serious liability in 1904 when they tried to make turns. Since they quickly got rid of it early in the 1905 testing, it really didn't hold them up that much. And they never went back to it.

As far as their lateral or roll control scheme is concerned, unfortunately, the Wrights made the worst choice possible. Wing warping, ailerons, and winglets had all been devised and documented before the Wrights began. The Wrights' much-lauded wing warping was by far the least desirable of the three, increasing the angle of whole wing sections on one side while decreasing them on the other. This created the worst possible drag imbalance and led to all of their induced yaw and control reversal problems. Ailerons, by deflecting only a small portion of the wing, would have generated less trouble. However, using separate winglets would have avoided these problems entirely. These flat panels can be set to a zero angle to the airflow at normal flight conditions. Then deflecting them equal but opposite amounts for roll control would generate no drag imbalance whatsoever. Thus the Wrights could have avoided all of the control reversal and associated slipping and spinning problems they fought from 1901 into 1905. Later Flyers would have handled better also. But eventually they would have had to come up with a moveable vertical rudder anyway, so perhaps it's just as well they did it because of wing warping. (Spoilers, panels on the tops of wings that flip up, both diminish lift while increasing drag thereby creating favorable yaw into the roll. But they hadn't been invented yet.)

The fact that their airplanes were all biplanes magnified the roll reversal problem even more. They had four wings changing angle of attack rather than just two. This made the problem more severe than it would have been on a single-winged plane.

But there was yet another problem that plagued every aircraft the Wrights produced. You'll remember that their fix to the induced yaw and roll reversal problem was to install the moveable vertical rudder and tie it in with the warping control. But then they separated the rudder and warping controls in 1905 in order to successfully make turns. All of their aircraft to follow, into 1915, retained wing warping and a separate rudder control. So although their aircraft all still needed a lot of rudder input to avoid roll control reversal, this input had to be done manually rather than automatically. This requirement, along with the constant attention to pitch attitude demanded by the canard configuration, put a substantial workload on the pilot of a Wright Flyer, more than was necessary to fly other aircraft.

Some of the problems the Wrights had with lateral control of their airplanes had more to do with patents than with technology. Their primary patent, number 821,393, was drafted in 1903. Granted in 1906, it actually was a patent of their 1902 glider's final configuration. As such, it specifically describes the coordinated linkage of the moveable vertical tail with the wing warping system. Unfortunately, they found out in 1904 and 1905 that they couldn't successfully turn with the coordinated controls, so they had to abandon the system. But they couldn't cover the independently operating rudder with a new patent since many before them had used such a device. This caused them problems in later litigations when it was pointed out that the Wrights themselves were not using the control methods described in their own patent. (I haven't found anything indicating that anyone noticed that the Wrights had also reversed the loading on their canards to highly positive from the negative loading called for in their patent.)

Before leaving the subject of roll control, it is important to acknowledge the devastating impact patenting wing warping had on the Wrights' ultimate success in aviation. By 1911 the Wrights were facing stiff competition and had abandoned coordinated controls, the launching rail, and the canard pitch control. The only major feature of their patented design that they still retained was wing warping. But wing warping could only be done with very thin and rather flimsy wings. And by 1911 designers were beginning to see the advantages of thicker, more rigid wings. The true mechanism of how cambered wings develop lift had become common knowledge, and the aerodynamic advantages of filling in the bottoms of wings were becoming evident. Also, these thicker wings were stronger, allowing higher maneuver loads, and provided spaces that eventually were used for storing such things as weapons or fuel. Finally, in 1915 Orville had to abandon wing warping and go along with the trend. But by then he was hopelessly behind in this and many other design aspects. At that point he had abandoned every major feature of their main patent. Two years later, and a year after the United States entered World War I, the federal government forced him to drop litigations concerning the patents.

So then, if wing warping was such a bad choice, and other methods of roll control were known, why did they use it? After all, they gave a number of reasons for using the canard instead of a horizontal tail. But I have found no statements of theirs as to why they would have used warping rather than ailerons or winglets. Even after they ran into so much trouble with warping reversal and the resulting crashes, they never mentioned any other forms of roll control. It seems like they were never aware of them, never read or thought of them, at least not until 1907 or so when others began flying powered airplanes with ailerons or winglets. But by then their patent had them locked into wing warping.

Evidently, this is another example of how the Wrights could have benefitted from more research into the work of their predecessors. After all, Boulton and Hart had written about ailerons, and Renard had used winglets on his models. But Wilbur tested warping in 1899, about the time they were obtaining much of their research material. Still, why wouldn't they have tried something else in 1901 or 1902 when problems with warping surfaced? Well, as we are learning, the Wrights found it difficult to believe that there could be a fundamental flaw in any of their thinking or methods.

The negative impact of making and retaining the unfortunate choice of wing warping for roll control cannot be overstated. This ranks right up there with choosing and keeping the canard pitch control and the catapult launch system. Yes, they did create the world's first powered airplane in spite of these drawbacks. But had they chosen another method of roll control they might have been more competitive in the aircraft industry after abandoning the canard and catapult in 1910, and they might still have achieved a piece of the commercial success they so desired.

We Need Power

In this section rather than going into a detailed critique of the Wrights' engine or propeller designs, I'll discuss their propulsion situation more from the standpoint of power required and available. In Chapter II we saw that the engine Charles Manley developed for Langley's Aerodrome, the first radial, was capable of putting out over four times the power of the Wrights' first engine at the same weight. The Wrights probably should not be held to the same standard as Manley and Baltzer as they were neither college educated engineers nor engine manufacturers. Still, the engines were contemporaries, and the specifications stand.

I find it hard to believe that the Wrights could not find a suitable engine already in existence for their 1903 aircraft. The specifications, 10 to 12 horsepower from an engine weighing less than 200 pounds, were not beyond the state of the art at that time. It appears that the Wrights also found it hard to believe. In a September 1900 letter to his father, Wilbur expressed his opinion that once they developed a controllable flying machine, finding a suitable engine would be no problem.(1/26) When he addressed the Western Society of Engineers in September of 1901, Wilbur reaffirmed his belief that an engine meeting their requirements of about 18 pounds per horsepower would be readily available from a number of manufacturers. He stated that "Indeed, working motors of one half this weight per horsepower (9 pounds per horsepower) have been constructed by several different builders".(1/114) Although I've seen little to directly verify this, I believe cost was a major factor in their decision to build their own engines, particularly since they thought they had a good chance of destroying at least one of them.

While the Wrights exhibited a great deal of practical engineering capability and determination by developing and building their own engines and propellers, they also boxed themselves into a situation fraught with problems. Glide slope measurements at Kitty Hawk, along with their wind tunnel results, gave them an unprecedented capability to calculate the drag and lift-to-drag characteristics of their vehicles. This knowledge allowed them to make a relatively accurate calculation of the power required to keep their aircraft in level flight. Unfortunately, that is precisely the requirement they designed their first engine to meet. They created an engine that was just barely capable of overcoming the drag of their aircraft in level flight at ground-skimming altitude. But a true airplane must also have sufficient extra power to take off, climb to a maneuvering altitude, and turn. The 1903 Flyer had none of these capabilities. In fact, it didn't have enough power to climb out of ground effect. (The ground effect is a phenomenon whereby airplanes flying extremely close to the ground develop lift much more easily than they do at higher altitudes. A detailed explanation of this effect is presented in Appendix 2.)

An obvious question is: how high does ground effect affect an airplane? And the answer is that it depends. It depends mostly on size and aspect ratio of the wing (length versus width), and secondarily, it depends on angle of attack and speed. The closer to the ground an aircraft is, the stronger the effect, and it tapers off gradually as the vehicle rises. In most cases it is effective up to an altitude equivalent to about the span of the wing. For the 1903 and 1904 Wright Flyers, this would be up to about 40 feet of altitude. The 1903 flights were all within about 15 feet of the ground. Photos from 1904 all show the Flyer within about 35 feet of the ground. In fact most show it less than 20 feet up. So the records indicate that neither of these aircraft climbed out of ground effect. They simply didn't have the power to sustain themselves against the higher drag they would have generated in totally free air. That's because the Wrights never measured the drag of their aircraft in totally free air, only within ground effect. And that's apparently because, even with all their glides, the Wrights were not aware of ground effect.

In the discussion session following his presentation to the Western Society of Engineers in June 1903, Wilbur was asked whether he thought there was more upward lift at 6 inches above the ground as opposed to 20 feet of altitude (people often think of ground effect as giving more lift rather than less drag). Wilbur replied, "I do not think there is very much difference". (1/333) Of course, it's perfectly reasonable for the Wrights to have been un-aware of the ground effect. Never having been out of it, how were they to know that they were in it? And don't forget, they never studied flow patterns around wings to any significant degree. Perhaps they should have mustered up the courage to fly higher out of ground effect as Lilienthal had done. But of course, he got killed and they didn't. Even so, the effect gradually increases as one nears the ground, and it seems that they should have noticed some dif-ference in glide slopes or the angles of the tether lines between, say, 5 feet and 20 feet of altitude. You can certainly feel it in a modern hang glider. Obviously someone in that 1903 lecture audience had their suspicions, or they wouldn't have asked the question. It would be interesting to know what they had done, and what they knew.

As previously mentioned, the Wrights' propeller designs represent a state of understanding and design capability well ahead of other aviation experimenters. Along with this, the Wrights are always given credit for be-ing the first to realize that a propeller should be made like a spinning cam-bered wing lifting forward and that it can be designed by considering it as a succession of many such small sections varying in size, shape, and pitch over its blade length, i.e., what's called the blade element theory. But both of these statements are incorrect. Maritime propellers had been in existence for decades, and some of the more capable designers of ship propellers had worked on applying their techniques to air as well as water. Frank W. Caldwell pioneered research in high speed flows on propellers and created the variable pitch and constant speed props. He was recognized as a world-class propeller designer at Hamilton Standard, at the time considered by many to be the world's foremost manufacturer of propellers.(41/256-259) His historical research revealed that "Some time before any actual flights in airplanes, a theory of the air propeller was evolved more or less indepen-dently by Lanchester [in England], Drzweicki [in France], and Prandtl in Germany. This theory is based on the conception of the airplane propeller as a series of wing sections moving in a spiral path. The Wright brothers ap-parently evolved this theory independently without knowledge of the work of earlier scientists".(3/79) So it seems that while the Wrights' creation of an airfoil-shaped propeller may be considered original in the sense that they evidently did not rely on anyone else's previous work, it is not original in the sense that it had never been done before.

Actually, as pointed out in Chapter I, the concept of a propeller having twisted cambered blades can be traced back much earlier. Sketches indicate that Adder used cambered propellers on his 1890 vehicle, and Hollands documented the advantage of cambered, twisted, and tapered propellers in a paper for the Aeronautical Society of Great Britain in 1885.(8/162,163) In fact, Hollands' recommendations for the amount of camber and twist for a propeller appeared in Chanute's book that the Wrights had by 1900. But long before that, Sir George Cayley, in his 1809 magazine article, discussed and presented a sketch of a helicopter-like model with which he had experimented. It had two four-bladed propellers with blades made of stiffened, cambered, tapered bird feathers.(6/Nov.,1809) He must have recognized the efficiency of this shape in producing lift or thrust, having rejected the use of flat blades.

According to a letter Wilbur wrote to Dr. Spratt on December 12, 1902 the Wrights had already started experimenting with propellers by that time. Six months later Octave Chanute visited the Wrights in Dayton on June 6, 1903 on his way back from Europe.(1/314) Part of their discussions must have concerned propellers because the following day, upon his return to Chicago, Chanute forwarded copies of his holdings on the subject to the Wrights.(1/315) As was his custom, Chanute had gathered together a collection of material published by propeller researchers and designers, including fairly comprehensive papers written by Drzweiecki in 1900 and 1901. That same day, June 7, 1903, the Wrights wrote a letter to Dr. Spratt indicating that they had completed their propellers.(1/313) If that was the case, and these were the only propellers made in 1903, only the material on Hollands in Chanute's book could have influenced the Wrights' work. A month later Wilbur was moved to write a critique of Drzweicki's techniques in a reply to Chanute.(1/337) He particularly criticized Drzweiecki's failure to properly account for the forward motion of the vehicle, as well as the acceleration of the air just before it enters the props, what the Wrights called "throwdown."

So, according to these facts and dates, the Wrights independently evolved their own procedures for propeller design. In any case, their process was evidently more accurate than any other technique in existence. Unfortunately, it was never completely documented and remains sketchy in many areas. But, contrary to the impression given by almost all aviation historians, they did not originate the concept of airfoil-shaped propeller blades nor of designing it as a twisted series of such cambered sections. Once again, although they did great work, they could have saved some time and effort by more diligent pursuit and study of work done previously by others.

Orville noted in his diary in early December, 1903 at Kitty Hawk that before he and Wilbur actually attempted to fly the powered plane they did what would later be called taxi tests. They fired up the engine and ran the airplane down their 60-foot launch rail.(1/391) (On one run the aircraft's tail structure snagged on one of the rail supports and broke, an eerie similarity to what Langley claimed had doomed his manned flights.) They soon found that their sprocket-propeller combination loaded the engine too heavily and it could not wind up much more than about 800 rpm.(1/379,380) Although they viewed this as a problem at the time, it really wasn't. They were not reaching flight speed in these tests so the engine was capable of revving higher once in the air.

When they actually measured the overall thrust the props could put on the airplane they regained their optimism. They had calculated the aircraft would require about 95 pounds of thrust for level flight, and their propulsion system seemed to be capable of over 130 pounds.(1/389) So it looked to them like they had plenty of cushion with which to work. In reality, I doubt that they had anything like this nearly 40 percent excess of available power. The performance of the 1903 Flyer certainly didn't indicate so.

Rather astonishing claims have been made concerning the efficiency of the Wrights' first propellers. Some claim to have made tests showing efficiencies in excess of eighty percent. These claims seem particularly bizarre in view of the inappropriate reverse taper of the Wrights' early propellers. Having the widest chord at the tips results in excessive tip loadings and aerodynamic losses just as it would for a reverse taper wing. The Wrights themselves claimed their 1903 propellers were only 66 percent efficient.(2/85) In 1905 they improved their propellers by cutting a wedge out of the leading edge of their tips. This eliminated some of the reverse taper and probably reduced tip losses. These became known as the "bent end" propellers. They had made four different sets of propellers during their 1904 flight tests mostly due to crashes. But their shapes were also altered in an effort to improve performance.(3/81) Evidently once again the Wrights have been made to look perfect when in fact they were merely the best in the world.

The Wrights recorded five takeoffs in 1903. Four of these would have been into headwinds of at least 25 miles per hour. Consequently, the engine and propellers were required to add no more than another five miles per hour for the aircraft to take off. Had the wind been any less, the machine could not have flown. Too little wind was certainly a major factor in Wilbur's failure to keep the plane aloft on December 14th. After takeoff on the 17th the aircraft didn't have enough power to rise above ground effect. But they deemed the last test sufficient to establish that they had indeed made the first manned, powered, and, at least briefly, somewhat controlled flight. Also, it was a very impressive demonstration of efficient, integrated, precision design, quite impressing for the first example of a whole new form of locomotion.

In the last section we saw how the Wrights struggled throughout the 1904 and 1905 test sessions to figure out how to turn an airplane. We saw how they modified the control system in order to solve the problem. But it was also largely a power problem, i.e. getting enough power to climb out of ground effect, and overcoming the additional drag generated by replacing the lift lost in banking turns. They created a new and improved engine for 1904 which, running at higher rpm with new propellers, raised their maximum power output from about 10 or 12 horsepower to about 16 horsepower. This same engine was putting out 20 horsepower by the end of the 1905 test session, largely due to being better broken in.(3/86) With that they could easily climb to 100 feet, clearly beyond ground effect. The engine still had the problem of overheating the bearings after about five minutes of operation, but better lubrication solved that. Later flights in 1905, one lasting 38 minutes, were limited by fuel (and possibly pilot) exhaustion.

Their marginal power supply caused them another problem in 1904 and 1905. They didn't have the reliable 25-mile-per-hour headwinds of Kitty Hawk to take off into at Huffman Prairie. They extended their launch rail to over 100 feet, and eventually increased it to over 200 feet. But still it was not enough to ensure takeoffs with the power they had available. They needed some sort of accelerating device to boost their aircraft into the air. Fortunately they either remembered Chanute's letter from a couple years earlier dated July 29, 1902, or he reminded them of it in more recent discussions. In that letter he had told the Wrights of "a method of imparting initial velocity to a glider by using a falling weight".(1/242) Chanute had gotten the design from a fellow gliding enthusiast, Albert A. Merrill, a prominent member of a gliding group called the Boston Aeronautical Society.

The variant of this device that the Wrights created was a 25-foot-high wooden quadripod, or derrick that suspended up to a 1,600-pound weight. (27/128) The weight was hung by a rope which, through a system of pulleys, converted a 20-foot drop of the weight to a 60-foot pull on the other end of the rope. This rope was strung out and back along a Kitty Hawk style launch rail. The device was capable of gradually accelerating a 1,000-pound machine up to 30 miles per hour in about 50 feet.

The Wrights were quite pleased with their launcher. With it they were able to fly even when there was no wind whatsoever. In fact, these were the best times to fly at Huffman Prairie since there was no turbulence from wind blowing over the nearby hills and the trees that lined the pasture. Their cata-pult was simple, reliable, and inexpensive to build. And unlike Langley's large springs that imposed huge initial acceleration loads, gravity acting on the fall-ing weight slowly built up speed on the Wrights' vehicles.

Unfortunately for the Wrights, in later years no one else thought much of the catapult idea. Were you supposed to erect a 25-foot derrick, a 1-ton weight, a couple hundred feet of rope, and 50 or 100 feet of track every place you wanted to fly? And what about eight men, a couple of horses, or a car or truck to position the airplane and pull up the weight? What if you set down someplace unexpected on a whim, or had to land because of fuel depletion or weather? Would you have to sit there until the ground could be leveled and all the launch equipment could be mustered, delivered, and set up? And then would you have a crew knock it all down and ship it to the next place?

Any substantial sales of aircraft at that time were going to be to armies. Storm clouds, as they say, were definitely on the horizon in Europe. The armies of Great Britain, France, Germany, Austria, Italy, and Russia all wanted reliable, operational aircraft as soon as they could be developed. But they were particularly leery of buying equipment with such limitations and logistics headaches as the Wright aircraft with their catapults.

Besides, it was becoming apparent to these governments that they would soon have alternatives to what the Wrights were offering and at much less cost. In these countries, native sons were feverishly working to develop indig-enous aircraft. And these all had wheels along with the power to take off from any reasonably smooth pasture or field. This was primarily for two reasons. Internal combustion technology was progressing faster in Europe than in the United States at that time, resulting in lighter, more powerful engines. Also, no doubt the earliest European aircraft designers did not have the relatively precise design integration capability that allowed the Wrights to design to such accuracy. So they just made sure their airplanes had plenty of power. The excess power of these engines then provided the capability to make unassisted takeoffs, wheels and all. Of course, the U.S. Army was well aware of this, and it accounted for much of their reluctance to buy the early Wright designs.

But true to their typical stubbornness, the Wrights did not convert their aircraft to wheels until 1910, even though they probably had sufficient power to discard the catapult by 1908 or 1909. Incredibly, on June 30, 1908 Orville wrote a letter to the publisher of *Scientific American* magazine saying that he thought that in the future all aircraft would start from rails rather than wheels. (1/905) One wonders how big he thought airplanes could get and still be handled this way. But this degree of hubris was typical of the Wright brothers. They didn't adopt the aft horizontal stabilizer until 1910 either, long after all others had done so. And they didn't abandon their wing warping until even later, 1915. By then they had lost all credibility as state of the art or even competitive designers. No doubt much of their reluctance to change was due to their patent battles. Still, they always seemed to fixate on their solutions as being the very best, if not the only ones. Anyone else's were either inferior, rip-offs from theirs, or both. This attitude was probably their biggest mistake.

Consequences

The purpose of Chapter III was to review in detail the traditional story of the Wrights' struggle to invent the airplane. But in Chapter IV we did a careful examination of what exists of their records to determine what really happened and why. We took an objective look at their choices, and explored how using other knowledge that was available to them at that time might have led them to better decisions. This was not an effort to diminish their magnificent accomplishments that, for a few years, set them on a technical level far above any others in aviation. Rather it has shown that, as with anyone struggling to create something new, not all their decisions were the best ones, and that history has greatly exaggerated their accomplishments while overlooking those of others. Moreover, these decisions were not without consequence to their future success in the aviation business.

We saw that there are numerous indications that the Wrights made somewhat limited use of the vast quantity of research their predecessors had done. Although they had access to most of this material, their records and work indicate that except for some data from Lilienthal and Chanute, they paid little attention to much of this information before they started experimenting. They were far too quick to discard the results of their predecessors and to consider them all complete failures. The Wrights understandably took pride in going their own way. But sometimes they seemed to carry this pride to arrogance by refusing to abandon their early ideas, even when numerous others had demonstrated better solutions. It may well also be that Chanute, keeping them abreast of the progress of others, created a sense of urgency in the Wrights to proceed with what they already had rather than make revisions that would slow their marketing progress.

The combination of a desire to make stable vehicles with canard elevators, along with their incorrect concept of how wings generate lift, led them to use unusual and ineffective wing shapes on their 1900 and 1901 gliders. Consequently these vehicles couldn't lift Wilbur in any but the very strongest Kitty Hawk winds. Then, in the summer of 1901 at Kitty Hawk, Chanute, Spratt, and Huffaker showed them how to make a wind tunnel that convinced them to adopt traditional wing shapes that solved their lifting problem in 1902. Both the Wrights and their biographers have been content to let all of the blame for their early wing deficiencies fall on the data from Otto Lilienthal. However their own statements, data, and photos reveal that because of their admittedly totally inappropriate wing shapes, the responsibility for the lifting inadequacies of the 1900 and 1901 vehicles rests firmly on the Wrights and no one else.

They had determination, bordering on belligerence, in refusing to let their creations operate at the mercy of the elements such as gusts or crosswinds. As a result, they put up with constant instability in their vehicles and refused to change them, even when it became apparent that the rest of the world would not tolerate such machinery. Their use of a canard made their aircraft more unstable than some modern aircraft which can only fly with automated electronic flight controls. And their choice of wing warping for roll control, even though better methods had already been invented, forced pilots of Wright Flyers to simultaneously correct with other controls to avoid deadly spins. These serious handling vices contributed to the fact that most of the army pilots and most of their own demonstration pilots were killed in Wright aircraft within their first fifteen months of flying.

Much credit has been given to early Wright Flyers for being the world's first fully controllable airplanes. But this is true only within strict limits. Movies exist of Wilbur's flights at LeMans, France and Centrocelle, Italy, and Orville's at Fort Meyer near Washington D.C. during 1908 and 1909. In all cases their aircraft were not allowed to exceed 15 degrees of bank or pitch during these flights. True, extreme maneuvers are not to be expected from the earliest airplanes. But by 1910 there were a number of other designs that could easily exceed the level of maneuverability demonstrated by Wright Flyers.

Within six years of having perfected their control system, their roll control was shown to be impractical for use on the thicker wings appearing on newer aircraft. Yet, with typical obstinacy, they refused to change it until after the start of World War I. By then they had abandoned all the features of their patent, and still their designs were hopelessly behind the state of the art.

Unfortunately, they used their unique wind tunnel testing and computational capabilities to size their engine to a condition that their aircraft couldn't reach on its own. Although within a couple years they did have enough power to execute gradual turns, their aircraft were chronically underpowered relative to most of their competitors. While the Wrights created reasonably efficient propellers, much of the concepts and theory they developed were already in existence.

An immediate and continuing result of their underpowering was that they had to adopt a cumbersome device to launch their aircraft into the air. This, along with dangerous pitch instability and tricky roll control, made their airplanes far less useful than their competition. Many considered them less practical than other designs for both civilian and military use alike. Even on this matter, the Wrights' pride was such that they refused to abandon their catapult until it was too late to make much difference.

After inventing the powered airplane, the Wright brothers became so convinced of their exceptional wisdom, so confident in their prescience, that they were willing to go out on a limb with rash predictions about the future design of airplanes. Just a couple pages ago we noted Orville's prediction in *Scientific American* that all aircraft of the future would take off from rails rather than use wheels.(1/905) Two years later the Wrights abandoned the launch rail and catapult and went to a wheeled undercarriage. Not long before his death, Wilbur wrote that Octave Chanute's biplane configuration would be a part of airplane design "forever." The monoplane had established its performance superiority within just a few more years.

As we will see in a couple of chapters, one of their biggest mistakes was abandoning the considerable inventive power of their brains and relying instead on the dubious security of international legal systems to stifle the progress of others in order to insure their long-term dominance of aviation.

After all this criticism I want to reiterate an important point. Hindsight is wonderful, and certainly the first version of anything so complicated as an airplane can't be perfect, particularly since it was a whole new form of locomotion, free to move and rotate in all three directions. But that is not the point. The point is that even intellects as powerful as the Wrights are capable of oversights and mistakes. By seeing the story like it really happened, perhaps some pitfalls of the type that the Wrights encountered can be avoided by inventors, designers, engineers, and others in the future. Aggrandizing everything they did may inflate our patriotic pride, but not our knowledge. But much worse, it trivializes the six year struggle during which the Wrights had so solve a myriad of problems to finally create the worlds first controllable airplane by October of 1905.

CHAPTER V

Everybody's Doing It

This chapter presents an overview of airplane development from 1906 until shortly before World War I, the "Great War." Contrary to the Wrights' wildest expectations, within a few years there were many in both the United States and Europe who were developing airplanes with flying qualities equal or superior to theirs. This chapter covers this period in year-by-year sections. But rather than attempt the impossible task of an exhaustive account of all developments during the period, enough significant technology and performance milestones are included to make a comparison of the Wrights' development with that of their competitors. More complete accounts of aviation during this period can be seen in some of the references in the source listing for this book. References 14, 18, and 35 are especially good in this regard. But just from what is covered here it will become evident that the Wright brothers overestimated the uniqueness of their engineering abilities. They were caught flatfooted in a totally defensive posture by an industry that was racing ahead at a pace that few could have foreseen.

1906

The Wrights focused most of their efforts in 1906 and 1907 in two areas, trying to market a slightly updated version of the third powered Wright

Flyer, and further development of engines. During 1905 they had contacted the U.S. Department of War (now Defense) and the war ministries of some of the major European powers. (Pages 135 to 150 of *The Wright Brothers, and the Invention of the Aerial Age* by Crouch and Jakab give a detailed description of the Wrights' efforts in 1905 and 1906 to sell aircraft to the Europeans, particularly the French.) Although many of the agencies contacted showed some interest in the Wrights' offers, negotiations were hampered by the conditions the Wrights imposed upon them. First was price. The brothers were unwilling to enter into any contracts for less than six figures, a pretty hefty sum of money in anybody's currency in 1906. They also wanted exclusivity in airplane production guaranteed by patents in each of the countries with which they were negotiating, including the United States. Many foreign governments were reluctant to agree to this since their own countrymen were whispering in their ears that they could soon build flying machines too.

By far the biggest impediment to the Wrights' success at selling their machine early on was their penchant for secrecy. Not only would they not demonstrate their Flyer, initially they were reluctant to let anyone even see the machine without a contract. But no government with any degree of accountability to its citizens would spend substantial resources on a device claiming to do something so spectacular, something that had never been done before, without even seeing it work.

Why were the Wrights so secretive? It seems hard for us, looking back a century later, to believe that anyone could hope to keep all the ways to build an airplane secret. But, by the end of 1905 only the Wrights had done it. All others had failed. So the Wrights were convinced that their way was the only way it could be done. They believed that unless someone stumbled upon their exact methods, conducted their series of tests, and devised their exact solutions, they couldn't fly. So they thought that the only way competitors could succeed any time soon would be to steal their design.

An exchange of letters between the Wrights and Octave Chanute in 1906 is particularly enlightening in this regard. On the 10th of October Wilbur wrote Chanute saying that they were holding to their six-figure price for their Flyer. He rationalized, "We are convinced that no one will be able to develop a practical flyer within five years." He added, "We do not believe there is a chance in one hundred that anyone will have a machine....within five years. It is many times five years".(1/729,730) Wilbur even had the audacity to tell Chanute that he did not appreciate how difficult developing an airplane was. Chanute immediately wrote back saying, basically, don't be so sure. It didn't take you more than five years, and there may be a number of solutions to flyable shapes and configurations.(1/730) This was not the only time Chanute's prescience exceeded that of the Wrights. Within two years the Wrights had stiff competition. Within two more they were obsolete.

The only area of technical development that the Wrights appear to have worked on in 1906 was engine development. The tests of 1904 and 1905 showed them how important an abundance of power was to being able to maneuver an airplane and to being able to recover from precarious situations. And of course, engine reliability was the key to pilot longevity, which was always paramount in their minds. So the Wrights each took off on an engine project of his own. Wilbur worked on an improved version of the previous horizontal 4-cylinder engine. However, Orville seemed to really find his niche in engine design. He developed a vertical in-line four with oil pump, water pump, and a high- tension ignition system. In its original form it produced 28 horsepower, but eventually Orville worked it up to 40 horsepower.(3/87) The engine produced this power while adhering to the original 180-pound weight limit.

The Wrights took one of their infrequent breaks from the shop during September of 1906 to take the trolley down to the Dayton Fair on the south side of town. They decided not to pass up the opportunity to see "Captain" Tom Baldwin demonstrate his dirigible, one of the few rigidly shaped lighter-than-air ships in existence. The brothers worked their way to the front of the crowd, right behind the airship's ground handlers. The day was extremely windy, but Baldwin, sensing the crowd's impatience, attempted a flight anyway. According to Seth Shulman's book, the airship quickly went out of control and the ground crew had to run to secure its lines, the Wrights right along with them. Baldwin thanked everyone involved, and once he realized the Wrights were there he hastened to introduce his engine builder to them. (21/84,85) He knew the young engineer from New York, Glenn Curtiss, had been hoping to meet the Wrights while in Dayton.

During the 1890s Curtiss had become, like the Wrights, interested in the new "safety bicycles" having equal-sized wheels. He was even more fascinated with engines and speed. So he set out putting engines on bicycles and racing them. His success in achieving high speeds led to brisk sales of his motorcycles and renown as a builder of light yet powerful engines.(24/126) By the time Curtiss met the Wrights, he had set numerous world records and had gone over 130 miles per hour on one of his motorcycles. He wanted to meet the Wrights in hopes of selling them engines.

The Wrights, in an unusually unguarded fit of generosity, invited Curtiss to their workshop and even showed him photos of their 1904 airplane in flight, discussing its features and their functions.(33/186) Curtiss was immediately captivated by the idea of winged flight and was soon to become totally preoccupied with the design, construction, and piloting of airplanes. Typically, the Wrights underestimated the ability of this motorcycle builder to develop a flying machine. Within two years Curtiss had won the Scientific American trophy for the first public flight of an airplane over the distance of 1 kilometer. (21/142) The following year he soundly trounced three Wright Flyers to win the Gordon Bennett speed trophy in Reims, France.(21/163,164) No doubt these developments reinforced the Wrights' conviction that their penchant for secrecy had been justified.

By the fall of 1906 Octave Chanute was becoming increasingly uncomfortable with the Wrights' eagerness to make big money and their overconfidence in the inability of others. On November 1st he wrote to the Wrights informing them that he knew of at least ten different groups in Great Britain, France, and Germany that were working on manned powered aircraft.(1/733) He also pointed out that nearly all of these were using better engines than the Wrights had. For example, Levavasseur in France was making his V-8 engine available to aviation experimenters. It weighed barely over 200 pounds and put out a solid 50 horsepower, over twice as efficient as the Wrights' last engine.(15/37)

Chanute also noted that in France the son of a wealthy Brazilian coffee magnate, one Santos-Dumont, appeared to be about where the Wrights had been in 1903, i.e. making short semi-controlled hops of a couple hundred feet or so. Santos-Dumont's plane, the 14bis, had huge dihedral, winglets, and both horizontal and vertical canards in the form of an open box at the front of a long, narrow fuselage.(35/89) In one sense Santos-Dumont had already leapfrogged the Wrights on control technology since the 14bis, his first powered airplane, had the center of gravity well forward and a heavy load on the horizontal canard, something the Wrights didn't fully appreciate until 1905.(28) In his answer to Chanute's letter, Wilbur, with characteristic overconfidence, countered that only "If he has gone more than 300 feet has he really done something; less than this is nothing."(1/734,735) A week later, on November 12th, 1906 Santos-Dumont made a flight of 722 feet in the 14bis under three-axis control.(1/734) At the time, many in Europe believed this to be the very first flight by a manned, powered, controlled airplane. As it turned out, European progress was such that the only countries in which the Wrights were the first to fly were Belgium and Switzerland. (18/130,136,137)

Figure 55: Santos-Dumont's 14bis, 1906

Since 1904 two French brothers, Gabriel and Charles Voisin, had been flying gliders based upon descriptions of the Wrights' vehicles that Chanute had been allowed to publish.(30/6,7) The following year, under the sponsorship of the famous early French aviation enthusiast Earnest Archdeacon, they formed the world's first airplane manufacturing company, the Syndicate d'Aviation.(35/87) By 1906 they were building planes of both their own and others' designs. By 1907 they had produced a couple machines that flew rather well. Examination of one of their 1907 designs reveals how they achieved such rapid success. Their aircraft had plenty of wing area with gradual camber, aft-mounted stabilizers, and separate winglets for roll control. In short, they avoided all the major problems that the Wright brothers had to grapple with for up to fifteen years.

Figure 56: Voisin Taking Off, 1907

1907

When it came to methodically solving technical problems the Wrights were in their element. But in the fast-moving competitive world of big business they were naive and totally unprepared. So at the start of 1907 the Wrights were in negotiations with Mr. Charles R. Flint and Company, a New York investment firm associated with a number of wealthy investors. Flint's firm specialized in selling U.S. technology abroad. They had sold ships to Brazil, Japan, Russia, and Chile, submarines to Russia, and cars to France. (14/153) Flint offered the Wrights $500,000 up front and substantial royalties on sales thereafter.(1/749,750) The Wrights wisely signed on with Flint and Company.

By the summer of 1907 Wilbur was in Europe with representatives of Flint's company trying to sell their aircraft in Paris and Berlin. The French, and probably the English and Germans as well, were very leery of the six figure prices Wilbur was demanding since they had not even seen the machine, much less seen it fly. On August 24th Hart O. Berg, Flint's representative in France, and Wilbur withdrew their offer to France. They refused to pay the exorbitant bribe that the French representative wanted to grease the skids for the deal.(14/155)

Eventually the Flint people convinced Wilbur that in order to sell airplanes they would have to bring a Flyer to Europe for display and demonstrations. Already the strain of foreign negotiations was beginning to tell on Wilbur. His correspondence with Orville during July includes expressions of his frustrations with his brother for not being able to ship a completed airplane and instead attempting to meddle in his negotiations.(1/803-805)

During this time Orville had a full plate too, for he was building new aircraft in Dayton, Ohio and negotiating with the U.S. Army.(14/154) During the summer of 1907 Orville's negotiations with the army stagnated when the army asked for exclusive rights to all Wright aircraft.(14/154)

Technology wise, except for a slightly more powerful engine, the Wrights in 1907 remained precisely where they had been in 1905. An example of their continuing disdain for the inherent aircraft stability preferred by the Europeans appears in a letter to Chanute on June 2nd wherein Orville commented on a paper he had sent them. Orville wrote "The travel of the center of pressure fore and aft is one of the least troublesome things one has to contend with in flying, and it is therefore not wise to sacrifice the efficiency of the [airfoil] surface for a slight gain in fore-and-aft equilibrium".(1/767)

Meanwhile, in France the native aviators were really "hopping." The Voisin brothers built one of their aircraft for Henri Farman, an Englishman living in France. The Voisins included many of Farman's ideas, replacing their winglets with ailerons which proved to be significant improvements. On the 26th of October Farman flew it for over 1/2 mile.(15/32,33) Later, Henri Farman and his brother Maurice built their own airplane. This craft was successful enough to win a 50,000 Frank prize.(20/88,89) With this money and notoriety the Farman brothers soon set up a factory that eventually sold over a thousand aircraft, ten times Orville's estimate of the total production of the Wright Company.(20/89) Santos-Dumont and Robert Esnault-Pelterie, both of whom incorporated ailerons in their designs, were also flying their own aircraft in France.(15/34) The prophetic Louis Bleriot made several flights with his tractor (forward-mounted propeller) monoplane which had tail-mounted control surfaces and an enclosed fuselage, an incredibly modern configuration.(15/34) By the end of 1907, no less than eight aviators had flown their powered, controlled airplanes in France.(18/28)

The English were beginning to venture into the air as well. A fellow by the name of Alliot Verdon Roe won a fly-off competition for powered models in London. With his prize money he began constructing his first full-sized manned aircraft.(11/23) His firm was later to gain fame under the name Avroe. Also, Horatio Phillips, the guy who patented those beautiful airfoils in 1884, was making short hops in a successful glider in which he had mounted a 20-horsepower engine.(15/35)

A few years earlier Octave Chanute had sent descriptions and sketches of the Wright 1902 glider to various European publications and enthusiasts. Consequently, many of the first attempts in Europe were biplanes, many of these sporting canard control surfaces. Some authors cite such designs by Archdeacon, Santos-Dumont, Voisin, Delagrange, Farman, and even Glenn Curtiss in the United States, as proof that these aviators got their start by copying the Wrights.(14/150,162) (Actually both Santos-Dumont and the Voisins credited their boxed-in biplane wing shapes to Hargrave who in turn had credited Francis Wenham with the original concept.) But even if the Wrights were influential, these authors don't mention the fact that their cambered, trussed biplane wings were a direct copy of Chanute and Herring's very successful 1896 glider. Wilbur acknowledged their use of the Chanute/ Herring configuration in a letter in 1909.(1/972) Again in a 1910 letter he said they used Chanute's "double deck truss . . . adapting it to [their] own ide-als and principles of control".(1/1006) In other words, they added warping. Orville also stated this in a 1920 deposition.(1/8,9 & 2/12,13)

These early European machines also showed some interesting contrasts with Wright Flyers. As Chanute had preached to the Wrights in vain, the Europeans were all believers in inherent stability for their designs. They typi-cally incorporated dihedral, and while for a brief time some had emulated the Wrights' forward elevator, nearly all of them also had vertical and horizontal tail surfaces for stability. And they were way ahead in propulsion. For example, Lavavasseur, having created the very popular 50-horsepower "Antoinette" V-8 in 1906, later grafted two of these together end-to-end, creating a 100-horse-power V-16 powerplant.(24/102)

About the only area in which the Wrights could be considered to have a significant advantage was in flying experience and the resulting ability and confidence to manually coordinate flight controls, particularly in entering and exiting turns. Since October 1905, the Wrights could pretty well guide their airplanes around at will, at least as much as their limited power would allow. On the other hand, the Europeans, even in 1907, were largely constrained to extremely shallow wide turns, many using their rudders to yaw the craft, and relying largely on dihedral to give a modest bank as a result of the ensuing skid. Although some were trying wing warping, winglets, and ailerons, strong positive lateral control did not really gain universal acceptance in Europe until the famous Rheims demonstration by Wilbur in 1908.

Perhaps every bit as ominous for the Wrights as the developments in Europe was the formation in the United States of the Aerial Experiment Association by Alexander Graham Bell. Bell was, of course, well heeled by that time, and was convinced that aviation was going to be the next big technological development. He pulled together a group including U.S. Army Lieutenant Tom Selfridge, the graduate engineer Casey Baldwin, the brave experimenter Doug McCurdy, and most noteworthy, Glenn Curtiss as the director of experiments.(24/128) It was an extremely enthusiastic, innovative, and loosely controlled group. They produced a working airplane with three-axis control in five months.(24/128,130)

Seeing what was coming, on November 25th the Wrights made a new offer to the U.S. Army, lowering their price from $100,000 to $25,000.(14/156) Two days before Christmas, with some collusion from the Wrights, the army issued a set of requirements for an airplane. The major requirements were a maximum speed over 40 miles per hour and a flight duration of at least one hour. The Wrights submitted a bid a month later accepting these requirements.

Throughout all of this, the Wrights maintained their headstrong attitude of superiority. More than once they expressed to Chanute their disdain for the European accomplishments since they were flying in calm air as opposed to the 20-mile-per-hour-plus headwinds that the Wrights had to contend with when they were at Kitty Hawk.(1/769) Of course they were totally ignoring the fact that without the 25-mile-per-hour headwind, or a catapult, their aircraft couldn't have taken off.

1908

The Wright brothers entered 1908 with a great deal of confidence in their inevitable dominance of worldwide aviation. They had patents either granted or pending in the United States and all the major European countries and Russia. Although there was an absolute flurry of aviation development activity in Europe, particularly France, as well as in the United States, no one was eclipsing their achievements of two and a half years earlier. In a January 27th letter to Chanute, Wilbur claimed that no one would be able to prevent the

Wrights' ultimate domination of aviation since dihedral was no good and they had all of the positive methods of roll control locked up with their patents. (1/855) When Chanute questioned this, Wilbur replied that they had filed patents subsequent to their original wing warping one, and these covered all forms of roll control. These patents and the ensuing battles will be discussed in the next chapter. But they are mentioned here to point out that the "many times five years" lead that the Wrights believed they had just a couple of years earlier had already dwindled to a two-year lead protected by a few sheets of paper that were not universally recognized in Europe and were contestable in the United States.

It was shortly after this exchange that Octave Chanute's growing frustration with the Wrights broke out into the open for the first time. For eight years Chanute had been the Wrights' mentor, sending them information on predecessors and competitors, pointing them toward Kitty Hawk, funding the travel of himself and others for consultations, helping them solve their technical problems, encouraging them to continue when they were disheartened by setbacks, and doing his best to convince them that in order to be truly successful, an aircraft would have to have some degree of inherent stability. But it seemed that finally, in the face of their hunger for monetary success and their boundless arrogance, he could no longer keep silent. In a couple of newspaper and magazine articles published in 1908 Chanute was quoted as claiming that the Wrights were poor businessmen and that they wanted an exorbitant price for a machine, the usefulness of which was highly overrated. (1/898) Although the Wrights took notice, their relationship with Chanute continued for another year or so until it was nearly destroyed, primarily by his testimony against their position in patent suits.

The year 1908 proved to be the zenith of the Wright brothers' domination in both the United States and Europe. First they returned to Kitty Hawk to test a machine that was basically the 1905 vehicle but with a little more horsepower, upright seating for a crew of two, and a new set of pilot's controls.(1/873) Although they made twenty-two flights in May, they were all very brief. The U.S. Army was beginning to show serious interest, so Orville began preparation of the new machine for demonstration. The competition still looked weak to non-existent.

In Europe, although negotiations were painstakingly slow, Mr. Berg of the Flint Company had closed a deal with France.(14/156) Wilbur was there uncrating and assembling another of the new machines for a demonstration.

There was much skepticism in Europe regarding the Wrights' accomplishments, and this demonstration, to be held near LeMans, was being publicized all over. Although by this time many others were flying in Europe, Wilbur was confident that the refinement of their machine, along with his unequaled flying experience, would show the Wrights to be far superior.

Still, the pressure was on, and what greeted Wilbur's eyes upon opening the crates caused him to lash out at his brother in the most extreme recorded example of discord between the two. Finding broken wing ribs, torn fabric, a crushed radiator, missing fasteners, broken engine parts, etc., Wilbur wrote "I never saw such evidence of idiocy in my life".(1/900) Orville replied, blaming much of the damage on customs. However, he could not explain away Wilbur's numerous complaints about shoddy workmanship. Wilbur continued his diatribes in subsequent weeks, claiming that his brother "never [seemed] to notice requests or instructions." He wrote to Orville, "If you have any conscience, it ought to be pretty sore".(1/907) Wilbur seemed to have no appreciation for Orville's situation of having to deal with correspondence from all directions, new employees, patent proceedings, the U.S. Army, plus preparing two aircraft for acceptance demonstrations. Certainly, everyone has his or her character flaws, and the best of brothers have occasional tiffs. But it is worthwhile keeping in mind Wilbur's potential for volatility and vindictiveness when considering their patent battles in the next chapter.

Eventually things got back on track and Wilbur assembled the modified Flyer III employing a less troublesome French engine. This was accompanied by a great deal of publicity generated by a skeptical European press directed toward an even more skeptical citizenry. Initially Wilbur again had trouble holding and exiting turns. But this time it was merely a problem of getting used to the new control scheme.(1/919) Finally, on the 8th of August he was ready. He made two flights that day before a huge gathering of press, competitors, and others that set Europe on its ear. His demonstrations of obvious control and maneuverability were unprecedented and overwhelmed layman and competitor alike. On one flight he did a perfectly coordinated figure eight. On the other, near the end, heading straight for a stand of high trees, and with the crowd aghast, he pulled into a 180-degree turn, rolled out, and flared to a perfect landing.(1/912) The hundreds of spectators, including members of the press, went wild. Among them were France's most notable aviators: the Voisins, Delagrange, Santos-Dumont, and Bleriot. All were in utter amazement. Bleriot told the press "For us in France and everywhere, a new era in mechanical flight has begun. I am not sufficiently calm after the event thoroughly to express my opinion. My view can best be expressed in these words—it is marvelous!"(20/112)

Wilbur went on to fly 127 more times during the remainder of the year. He took up over forty passengers on the two-seated aircraft and actually taught three prominent personages to fly it.(14/172) Crouch and Jakab give a fairly comprehensive summary of Wilbur's accomplishments in Europe in 1908 in their book *The Wright Brothers, and the Invention of the Aerial Age*. (14/171-184) He took royalty and heads of industry into the air, setting nine world records along the way. His longest flight was well over two hours, and he reached an altitude of nearly 400 feet.(24/109) He was the undisputed king of the air, and all of Europe knew it. The pace of discussions with the governments of Great Britain, France, Germany, Italy, and Russia all picked up, and a number of production, sales, and licensing agreements were negotiated.

All the European builders and flyers were impressed with the expert craftsmanship evidenced throughout Wilbur's machine, a trademark of the Wrights from the beginning. But they were even more impressed with the control he exhibited, particularly with the obvious utility of positive lateral control. Those who had been using it refined it, and those who hadn't adopted it. The ability to bank a plane was obviously the key to making turns. However, most used ailerons or separate winglets rather than warping. In many cases this was probably because ailerons and winglets could be added to existing aircraft while wing warping couldn't. But few Europeans abandoned dihedral or aft-mounted stabilizers. Rather, they added the Wrights' superior control to their already stable aircraft, which proved to be the right way to go.

Meanwhile, back in the United States, Orville was on an almost concurrent schedule, preparing to compete for an army contract. The competition didn't really amount to much. No foreigners participated. Augustus Herring demonstrated a biplane that was not competitive. Baldwin brought his dirigible which had no chance of meeting the army's speed requirement. Bell's A.E.A. group was just getting started, still trying to master turning. Nevertheless, Orville hung it all out, setting records for speed, endurance, and altitude. He made numerous flights of over an hour duration.(14/167) These flights were open to the press, and reporting on them generated a great deal of excitement throughout both the United States and Europe. Although Orville had set a U.S. endurance record of 1 hour and 14 minutes, he struggled to meet the army's speed requirement of 40 miles per hour with two men onboard.

(20/115) Since both men were sitting upright all out in the breeze, the second man was a significant drag factor as well as added weight. Lt. Thomas Selfridge, in his official army capacity, was acting as onboard observer on some of these flights. Of course, all the while he was gathering useful information for his A.E.A. group.

Orville decided that possibly with different props he could develop more thrust and reach the required speed. Brand new propellers were fitted, but one of them soon developed a split. It was repaired with nails, glue, and a cloth covering.(1/921) One week and five flights later Orville and Lt. Selfridge were whistling along pretty good when one of the two bladed wooden propellers split causing one blade to unload. The resulting vibration tore the propeller shaft mounting brackets loose, allowing the prop to swing sideways and cut the guy wires for the vertical tail.(1/921) The plane went out of control and dove into the ground severely injuring Orville and killing Lt. Selfridge. He thus became the first known fatality of U.S. heavier-than-air aviation.

Available material on both Orville's and Wilbur's official post-crash analyses mention nothing about the repaired prop. But obviously either the other propeller failed because it also had been manufactured improperly, or, much more likely, Orville's repair failed. In a private letter the following year to Octave Chanute, Wilbur tried to take much of the blame upon himself because of inadequate strength testing of the props, tests that he himself had devised and conducted.(1/954) However, statistically this is a hard proposition to swallow since this was the only catastrophic in-flight propeller failure they had experienced over many years of flying.

Nevertheless, the army Signal Corps had already decided that it would be useful to have some eyes in the sky. So, in spite of the fatal crash they gave the Wrights another chance. As soon as they could build another craft they would be allowed to try once more to exceed the requirements. This is somewhat surprising in view of the fact that the Wrights still would not use a wheeled undercarriage. They were still using the launch rail and catapult for takeoffs, both in the United States and Europe. Just how useful an aircraft like this could be to the army or anyone else is a real question. All other aircraft throughout the world were using wheels. But true to their inimitable stubbornness, it was at about this time that Orville wrote his letter to the *Scientific American* opining that all future aircraft would start from rails rather than wheels.(1/905) Since by then aircraft gross weights and speeds were being pushed up about 20 percent each year, one wonders just how big and fast Orville thought an aircraft could be and still be landed on skids, much less be manhandled back onto a launching rail.

While 1908 was a great year for the Wrights, it was also a year of strong progress for their competitors. The French government was already having second thoughts about its contract with the Wrights since so many native designs were flying.(14/160) In the United States, Bell's A.E.A. group was going strong at Glenn Curtiss' facilities at Hammondsport, New York. Having abandoned Bell's own rather eccentric and unsuccessful ideas of how to design a flying machine, everyone was cut loose to do his best. Tom Selfridge came up with a vehicle first and called it the Red Wing. Next to fly was Casey Baldwin's White Wing. Third, but by far the most successful, was Glenn Curtiss' June Bug.(15/37,38) These were all pusher biplanes reminiscent of the Wright/Chanute/Herring configuration. While they had forward elevators like the Wright Flyers, they also had both vertical and horizontal tail surfaces for stability, just like the Chanute/Herring glider did. The June Bug also included a couple of innovations. Its biplane wings converged somewhat at the tips. That is to say, the bottom wing had curved dihedral, while the top wing had curved anhedral. Although this might mitigate wing tip aerodynamic efficiency losses to a small degree, I suspect it was done for structural reasons. The other major configuration difference was that, wanting to steer clear of the Wright's' wing warping patent, the A.E.A. aircraft used a form of separate wing tip ailerons, or winglets, for lateral control. Apparently the A.E.A. didn't know that in an effort to monopolize aviation the Wrights had claimed to have patented everything having to do with lateral control, whether they had used it or not.

Using one of Curtiss' typically lightweight but powerful V-8 engines, the June Bug was one of the fastest airplanes yet built, capable of nearly 50 miles per hour in level flight. It was this machine that Curtiss used to put on a number of well attended exhibitions, winning the Scientific American Cup for the first officially observed closed-course flight of 1 kilometer.(18/32) Of course, the Wrights had exceeded that many times over in 1905, but they had chosen not to compete in public with Glenn Curtiss. By the end of the year Curtiss' renown was such that he was building an improved version of the June Bug for sale nearly a year before the Wrights had sold any aircraft.(19/70)

During the summer of 1908 Henri Farman brought his modified Voisin to America in hopes of giving a demonstration tour and thereby gaining commercial success. His optimism stemmed from his achievements earlier in the year in France. In January he had won a 50,000 frank prize for the first officially observed flight over a 1-kilometer course in France. He followed this up with a cross-country flight of 17 miles, a feat that Bleriot also accomplished in his tractor monoplane with ailerons and rear stabilizer/controls. Unfortunately Farman, whose airplane also used ailerons, immediately ran into trouble with the Wrights who tried to have U.S. customs impound his airplane because of patent infringement.(36/575) It seems Farman did eventually manage to give some demonstrations, but these failed to draw much in the way of crowds or publicity.

By the end of 1908, although no one in Europe could yet contest Wilbur's mastery of maneuverability, many had progressed to the point that they could reliably give demonstrations. In addition to Farman and Bleriot, the Voisins, Santos-Dumont, Esnault-Pelterie, Fabre, DeLagrange, and Levavasseur were progressing rapidly. Levavasseur's aircraft are particularly interesting in that he had already begun using wings with curved upper surfaces and nearly flat bottoms, in other words wings with definite thickness, airfoil shapes as we know them today. His monoplanes had three-axis control, and were successful to the point that he sold five of them in 1908.(15/40)

1909

Eager to capitalize on Wilbur's highly successful and publicized flying at Rheims, France during the latter half of 1908, Orville and their sister Katherine came over to Europe to confer in January of 1909. After arranging a licensing agreement to have Model A Wright Flyers built in France, they fanned out, Orville and Kate going to Berlin and Wilbur to Rome. Aircraft orders were obtained and they concluded some production agreements. Their return to the United States in May was no doubt a well-deserved triumphant cruise. By the end of the year Wright Model A's were rolling off the lines in France and also in England where the Short brothers had reached a licensing agreement with the Wrights.

Back home in the United States there was still plenty of work to be done. Orville had failed to meet the army's specified performance in 1908 with an acceptance test that ended in tragedy. But he was being given another chance and desperately wanted to sew up the contract before any competition could emerge. It appeared their patents had locked everyone else out, but one could never be absolutely sure. So by early summer they had another craft ready and shipped to Ft. Meyer for testing. This time Orville was able to fly 10 miles at over 40 miles per hour with a passenger. He flew from Ft. Meyer down south to a pylon on Sutter's Hill just west of Alexandria, Virginia and back. By August the army had signed on and plans could begin for a stateside assembly plant.(24/154) Up to this point the Wrights had built just seven aircraft since 1907.(1/1193) But now they would have to build many times that amount. Just as the previous year had been the peak of the Wrights' demonstrated superiority in the air, 1909 was to be the peak of their commercial superiority.

But indeed competition was coming, patents or not. In the United States competition was primarily from Glenn Curtiss. As will be seen in the next chapter, with the aid of Henry Ford and others, he was putting up a spirited battle against the Wright patents. Confident that, as with autos, no one company would be able to stifle all others in a major emerging industry, Curtiss joined with Augustus Herring to form an aircraft manufacturing company. (15/54) He promoted it by staging a number of public exhibitions, something the Wrights had not yet done in the United States. He did city-to-city flights which the Wrights, with their elaborate launching equipment, would not find easy to do. And much to their chagrin, he not only made the first commercial sale of an airplane in the United States, but to foster sales he established the first flying school.(20/105)

In Europe, Lord Northcliffe, publisher of the *Daily Mail* doubled the prize he had offered the previous year for a cross-channel flight. In fact he offered the Wrights a bonus of three times the prize if they would accomplish the feat. They, however, preferred to concentrate on demonstrations directly related to sales of production rights.(35/109) With the Wrights out of the picture, it was widely believed that either Farman or Bleriot had the best chance of winning the prize since both had been doing cross-country flights of about the same distance. Of the two, Bleriot's planes were the most advanced, what with their single wings, front engines, partially enclosed fuselage, and tail-mounted horizontal and vertical stabilizers and controls. Although he had begun with ailerons, after seeing Wilbur's demonstration at LeMans, Bleriot decided to try wing warping.(15/52) He soon reverted back to ailerons.

Bleriot's first vehicle to use warping was the Model XI, and with this he felt ready to tackle the channel. Actually, Herbert Latham of France was the first to try the crossing, but he made it less than halfway, returning on a boat. (18/142) Then, six days later on the 25th of July, Bleriot made it all the way. (15/56,57) Having won the Daily Mail prize, his worldwide notoriety was such that it is claimed that over the next forty days he received orders for over one hundred aircraft.(35/126)

The exploits of the Wrights, Curtiss, Bleriot, the Farman brothers, and others had ignited flying fever all over the world. Throngs flocked to dozens of "air meets" in the United States and Europe to get their first look at a human being leaving the Earth. These became extremely profitable events. Many manufacturers were able to get started primarily with the funds earned from these shows. Not only that, but the competition between performers acted to accelerate development, particularly in speed and maneuverability.

The biggest of these air meets during 1909 was the one held at Reims, France in August. Coming just weeks after Bleriot's triumphant channel flight, the event was attended by 300,000 people including dignitaries and royalty from all over the world.(24/144) The event drew a total of thirty-eight entries, although only twenty-three actually managed to end up flying. Seven of these flew distances of over 100 kilometers, Farman actually flying one stint of 112 miles. Herbert Latham reached an altitude of 508 feet. Glenn Curtiss brought his third plane, the "Rheims Racer," to the event. Once again, he demonstrated his plane's superiority over Wright Flyers in front of hundreds of thousands of people. There were six Flyers entered in the speed event. Curtiss soundly trounced them all with a speed of 46.6 miles per hour.(15/58) Once again, even though prodded by the Aeronautical Club of America, the Wrights themselves had refused to participate.(35/117) One reason was obvious. Although the previous year Wright Flyers held the world records for speed, altitude, distance, and endurance, in 1909 at Rheims they took none. In four short years Wright Flyers had gone from the only airplane in existence, to merely the best one, to an also-ran. In fact, with only two exceptions, after 1909 European aircraft held all major aviation records until after World War I. The various meets, contests, and demonstrations of this period are recounted in amazing detail in Curtis Prendergast's book *The First Aviators*.

The Wrights did pull off one publicity stunt in 1909 that helped perpetuate their reputation. On the 4th of October Wilbur made a 20-mile round trip flight up and down the west side of Manhattan. He took off from Governor's Island south of Manhattan and flew up the Hudson River, around Grant's Tomb, and back down the river. He then circled the Statue of Liberty and came back across the harbor to land at Governor's Island. For this flight he lashed a covered canoe to the bottom of his aircraft for flotation in case he went into the Hudson River. It is estimated that over a million people in New

York and New Jersey witnessed this demonstration.(14/189) (Ironically, a century later Chesley Sullenberger became world famous for safely ditching his airliner in the same spot on the Hudson that Wilbur overflew while making the first major public demonstration of an airplane in the U.S.)

The year also saw a number of European designs enter series production. In addition to Bleriot, Henri Farman began production of his third design, a vehicle with ailerons and aft stabilizers. The Voisins had built fifteen aircraft by the end of the year.(15/52,53) In England, while the Short brothers had begun to build Wright Flyers under license, A.V. Roe was building a triplane of his own design.(20/122) The year 1909 also saw the debut of a new design by Santos-Dumont, the "Dragonfly," a monoplane with horizontal and vertical tails. It incorporated wing warping for lateral control, one of the last designs to do so. Even so, it was considered by many to be a superior design to that of the Wright Flyers.(28)

Unlike the Wrights, Santos-Dumont refused to patent his designs, instead believing in sharing technology with others in aviation. Of course, being from a multimillionaire family may have helped foster his generosity. Unfortunately, Santos-Dumont's aviation career came to a sad conclusion, as did his life. In 1910 he suffered severe head injuries when his "Demoiselle" aircraft fractured a critical structural wire at about 100 feet in altitude and plummeted to the earth. He never flew again. Even more tragically, some years later he was to take his own life. Some claim he became increasingly more despondent over the death and destruction brought on by military airplanes in World War I, and took personal responsibility because of his part in developing them (28).

By the end of 1909 there were at least forty licensed aviators worldwide.(20/126) In fact, aviation had reached such a state of maturity that in England the first edition of *Janes All The World's Aircraft* was published. It noted that an Englishman, Fredrick Handley-Page, had built the world's first swept-wing airplane.(19/77) Of course the moderate sweep was not needed for speed, but it would perform one of the same functions as dihedral since, when the plane was yawed or skidded slightly sideways, the leading wing was straighter to the airflow. It would then develop more lift than the trailing wing, and thus roll the aircraft into the yaw, establishing a banking turn. Handley-Page had other good ideas and his name survived for decades in British aviation, as did that of Geoffrey deHavilland who also started building aircraft in England in 1909.

1910

In 1910 the Wrights could still take pride in a number of commercial accomplishments. The army contract, along with a pile of other orders, enabled the Wrights to gather enough financing to build the Wright Company factory in Dayton, Ohio. They began production in the new facility late in the year with a new design, the Model B.(2/77) They had also continued engine developments which resulted in in-line four and six cylinder designs as well as a 481-cubic inch V-8 that put out 60 horsepower and weighed 300 pounds.(3/89)

Figure 57: Wright Company and the Model B, 1910

The Wrights set up a flying school in March 1910 near Montgomery, Alabama at the site of what is now Maxwell Air Force Base.(1/990) This allowed them to train new pilots year-round, in the summer at Huffman Prairie and during the winter in Alabama.(14/197) One of the more notable pilots they trained in 1910 was Eddie Stinson who was to go on as a manufacturer of light aircraft.(14/200) Eddie's sisters Katherine and Marjorie also became pilots and were active in aviation for many years.

In the spring the brothers finally found time for a project they'd had in mind for some time. At the Alabama facility they designed and constructed what is believed to have been the first true ground flight simulator.(24/160,161) This device was maintained for many years, and probably saved aircraft and lives by allowing student pilots to make mistakes while sitting still on the ground.

Some of the first pilots trained by the Wrights were the members of their ill-fated exhibition team. As previously mentioned, flying exhibitions were an extremely lucrative business by this time. The Wrights charged promoters $1,000 per day for each plane and pilot. So for a six-day show with three planes and pilots, the Wrights took in $18,000. At that time, that was over ten years pay for most people. Since they paid their pilots $20 a week with a bonus of $50 for each flying day, they paid out less than $1,000 to those at risk for such a show. Of course there were shipping, ground crew, mechanics, and other expenses. But still, these were miserly wages considering the risks taken. By contrast, at that time Curtiss was paying his pilots nearly half the gross take.(24/220)

Meanwhile, back in Europe things were already starting to go sour for the Wrights. In England the Short brothers were still building Wright Flyers under license and honoring the terms of their contract. Sopwith was also building them. But late in the year Orville took a trip to the continent and found that the company that was supposed to be building Flyers in France had gone defunct, and the company in Germany was cheating them out of royalties. (1/1003,1004) It appeared the Italian company was doing something similar. Orville was so disgusted by what he saw that at the end of November he wrote Wilbur recommending that they abandon all their European operations.(1/1004)

But during this trip Orville was discouraged by more than just the manufacturing operations. It became very apparent to him that they were rapidly falling behind in technology as compared to many of the designers and manufacturers in Europe. While they had been busy negotiating production deals, waging patent battles, and receiving honoraria, the Europeans had surged ahead technologically with aft elevators, hinged controls, tractor (front-mounted) propellers, more advanced propeller designs, much better engines, enclosed fuselages and cockpits, and even ideas for potential armaments. The competition was rapidly leaving the Wrights behind.

Even in America competition was rendering some of their most cherished ideas obsolete. Although they had their Dayton factory up and running, for the plane they were building, the Model B, they had to abandon their beloved canard elevator as well as their catapult and launch rail. In fact, the only feature included in their 1906 patent that they still used was wing warping, and that had been disconnected from the rudder long ago rather than connected as described in their patent. They would even abandon wing warping in a few years.

Since the Wrights had largely sewn up U.S. Army business, Glenn Curtiss went after the U.S. Navy. One of his pilots, Eugene Ely, successfully demonstrated a shipboard takeoff in November of 1910 and a shipboard landing the following January. These were stunning demonstrations of confidence and bravery, as well as capability.(33/243)

All through the year emerging technology pushed aviation records ahead at a dizzying pace. At an air meet in Compton, California in the summer of 1910 Louis Paulhan reached what was thought to be the incredible altitude of 4,165 feet. But by the end of the year the altitude record had been pushed up to nearly 10,000 feet. Speeds were reaching 70 miles per hour. A fellow in Chicago by the name of John Moissant had built the world's first delta-winged airplane.(19/77) In Germany Hugo Junkers was granted a patent for the World's first flying wing aircraft.(42/172) Considering all the worldwide developments in aviation by the end of 1910, and taking another look at the Wright Model B, one cannot help but have some sympathy for the two self-taught guys who were first and had been so sure that they would dominate aviation for the foreseeable future.

1911

By 1911 American aircraft were no longer competitive at air meets in Europe. They had been eclipsed in speed, altitude, distance, and duration. Long distance cross-country events were all the rage in Europe, and these usually came with substantial prize money, more than enough to make the efforts worthwhile. For example, $20,000 was offered for a long-distance cross-channel flight. A prize of $50,000 was offered for a flight that would circumnavigate England, a total distance of some 1,000 miles. A $55,000 prize was put up for the winner of a Paris to Madrid race, while $60,000 was offered for a Paris-Rome-Turin race. But the grandest prize of all was $100,000 for a 1,025 mile "Circuit-of-Europe".(20/212-234) (These events are covered in detail in Arch Whitehouse's book *The Early Birds.*) Obviously a great deal of enthusiasm existed all over Europe for the burgeoning field of aviation. However competing in such events entailed not only a substantial outlay of resources but also a high degree of risk. Three pilots were killed near the start of the Circuit-of-Europe event.(20/233)

On the other hand, such events did force designers and builders to push the envelope with their creations. They were already finding that, while in 1911 biplanes still had the edge as far as structural strength and maneuverability went, the efficiency losses due to having four wing tips and lower aspect ratios were a heavy price to pay on long-distance events. As a result, over two-thirds of the airplanes entered for the Paris-to-Madrid race were monoplanes. (20/215)

Pilots, too, had to develop new skills to conquer the challenges presented by these events. Map reading was no longer sufficient to guide an aviator over the vast stretches of open countryside involved. They needed some kind of predictive technique to guide them to objectives far ahead of where they were. So a French lieutenant named Conneau developed the navigation procedure called "dead reckoning," with which a pilot could plot a course on a map from waypoint to waypoint, thus determining what direction to fly to reach the next point. Conneau's real breakthrough was to devise ways to determine and compensate for winds and compass errors. Using this technique, Lt. Conneau won the Circuit-of-Europe.(20/223)

In America the Wrights' latest version of their Flyer, the Model B, was still in full production even though it was rapidly becoming one of the world's most antiquated designs. William Randolph Hearst presented one last opportunity for a Wright Flyer to excel. He put up a prize of $50,000 for the first person to accomplish a coast-to-coast flight of the United States.(24/259,279) There were two main restrictions. The flight had to be completed within a thirty-day stretch, and the prize would only be offered for one year. Still, it seemed that if ground support could be arranged, the feat was imminently doable. Robert Fowler, (not to be confused with Harlan Fowler, the inventor of the translating wing flap) set out to fly eastward, while Cal Rodgers set out in the opposite direction. (An entertaining account of their sagas is presented in Sherwood Harris' book *The First to Fly.*) Both suffered numerous mechanical failures and crashes, Rodgers essentially demolishing and rebuilding his Wright Flyer, named the "Gin Fiz," five times. In the end he was the only one who made the distance. He did so by flying along railroad tracks which were used by an accompanying supply train full of spares and mechanics. Unfortunately it took Rodgers about two months to make the trip so he did not win the $50,000, just a place in history.

Glenn Curtiss achieved success with a seaplane design in 1911.(24/234) He used a float with a stepped bottom that let air in under it to break the suction that would develop between the bottom of a float and the water. In this time of few airports and few suitable mowed fields, a plane that could take off and land on water was a pretty useful item.

The year 1911 also gave a glimpse of the coming dark and destructive side of the new flying machines. The Turks invaded the Balkans that year, and were being opposed by the Italians who employed nine airplanes. Bored with just observing, the Italians took to throwing large grenades down on the Turks.(19/100) History has decided that this was the first use of an airplane as a weapon in war, the first time they were actually used to deliver weapons onto a target. Notably, this occurred three years before the beginning of World War I.

1912–1914

Phenomenal progress was being made in aviation technology, but it was coming at a price, and not just a monetary one. Although the first fatality in a powered airplane was recorded in 1908, by the summer of 1912 at least 155 airmen had been killed.(19/96) Certainly, many of these had been killed by the inconsistent structural and aerodynamic integrity of these early planes. But many were also killed by taking a pretty good airplane and pushing the envelope, trying to do things that had never been done before, or at least hadn't been done with that airplane. A number met their death attempting the dreaded loop, a maneuver considered the holy grail of aerobatics at that time. Finally a Frenchman, Adolph Peglud, accomplished it and survived in 1913, in a single-winged Bleriot no less.(19/92) Within a year others had done it. In fact the American, Lincoln Beachey, considered by many to have been the greatest stunt flier of the era, went on to do more than a thousand loops over the next few years.

Another feat that some would say took more guts than the loop was the first parachute jump from an airplane. This was accomplished by Captain Albert Barry over Jefferson Barracks just south of St. Louis, Missouri.(19/97)

He jumped from a height of about 15,000 feet at a time when most people didn't even know airplanes could get that high.

International flying meets were becoming more and more intensely competitive during the years just before World War I. Faster planes and the desire for faster and tighter maneuverability were drastically increasing the bending loads on wings. As a result, the almost paper-thin wings characteristic of pre-1910 aircraft were giving way to thicker wing cross sections. In some cases, the maximum thickness was approaching 10 percent of the chord length (the distance from the front edge to the back edge of the wing). Not only was this allowing the use of a deep transverse beam or spar to resist wing bending, but designers were finding that these thicker sections actually had better lift-to-drag ratios and were capable of operating over a wider range of angles of attack. Eventually, storing fuel in these newfound spaces would reduce the flying stresses at the wing roots, although in this era designers of combat planes were reluctant to spread fuel tanks over such a wide area. But even though wings were getting thicker, throughout World War I most all aircraft still had slightly concave surfaces on the bottoms of their wings rather than the convex surfaces we are used to seeing in modern times.

Without doubt, the French Deperdussin racers built in 1912 and 1913 represent the pinnacle of the state of the art in aircraft design during this period. Although Armand Deperdussin owned the "Society de Production des Appareils Deperdussin," more commonly known as "SPAD", the aircraft was actually designed by Louis Bechereau.(35/128) The plane had a circular laminated wood fuselage that fully enclosed the cockpit and engine, and a large propeller spinner for streamlining.(24/280,281) It had fixed but cleanly designed landing gear, and highly swept vertical and horizontal tails. It was a monoplane with a fairly thin wing and a very clean installation requiring only two streamlined external bracing struts. Except for these two struts and the associated wires, it looks like it could have been a design from the early 1930s. The 1912 version was the first airplane to exceed 100 miles per hour, and the 1913 model won the Gordon Bennett speed trophy at 125 miles per hour. (35/129) Bechereau went on to design the famous "SPAD" combat airplane of World War I.(30/147)

A comparison of photos of the 1913 Deperdussin with its contemporary Wright Flyer, the Model E, strikingly illustrates the stunning slip of the Wright brothers' aircraft into aviation's antiquity. (Figure 58) The Deperdussin was certainly ahead of its time, but so were the Wrights' machines a scant five years earlier. Those interested in seeing more early 20th century aircraft would really enjoy the magnificent collection of photos in reference 18, *Aviation, The Pioneer Years* edited by Ben Mackwoth-Praed.

Figure 58A: The 1912/1913 Deperdussin

Figure 58B: The 1913 Wright Model E

By this time the creative steam had escaped from the Wrights' operation. Wilbur died of typhoid at the age of forty-five on May 30, 1912.(14/204) Thus developed an amazing irony between the Wright brothers' careers and typhoid. They claimed that the real start of their interest in manned flight was when Wilbur read of the exploits of various experimenters to Orville while Orville was recovering from a bout with typhoid in 1896. If so, typhoid was responsible for getting the Wrights started in aviation, and it was responsible for finally ending their productive association with it sixteen years later.

After Wilbur's death Orville struggled on for a few years with patent battles and production and royalty problems. But many said his heart wasn't in it, and that he believed stress resulting from the patent problems was largely what killed his brother. In reality, the Wrights had chosen, six or seven years earlier, to shut down their creative juices and to concentrate their efforts instead on stifling or capitalizing upon the creativity of others throughout the world. More than anything, it was probably the realization of what a bad decision that was that led to their stress and creative malaise—that, plus the fact that just those two, working in isolated secrecy, could not fully take advantage of the plethora and interplay of ideas that occurred among designers in Europe. Within a few years Orville bought back the outstanding stock of the Wright Company and then sold the company to a group of eastern industrialists.(1/1098)

From 1909 to 1914, the maximum speed of aircraft had grown from 48 to 127 miles per hour. Maximum range had been increased from 145 miles to 635 miles, and the maximum altitude from 1,486 feet to an amazing 20,079 feet.(15/71) Aircraft had matured from mere show or stunt devices to machines capable of performing useful and even vital functions. And, as has often been the case, the new technology found its first widespread application in warfare.

As mentioned in the previous section, the first recorded "bombing" missions were flown by the Italians against the Turks in the Balkans in 1911. The "bombs" were actually little more than large grenades. Then, in 1913 a new milestone was achieved. Two Americans, each flying for opposite factions in the Mexican Revolution, fired pistols at each other while in the air.(19/100) Thus began air-to-air combat. The following year World War I began in Europe. And so goes another common misunderstanding, that air combat originated after the start of World War I.

It seems just about impossible to establish with any degree of certainty the quantitative state of worldwide aviation in July of 1914 at the start of the war. One source says Germany had spent the equivalent of 20 million dollars on aviation by the start of the war, while another says 73 million. One source says the Germans had 2,000 aircraft, while another says 246. Similarly conflicting statements about national inventories and expenditures can be found regarding British, French, Italian, Russian, and even the United States.(13/66,

15/77, 20/256) One could spend months, if not years, trying to sort out the truth from these claims. From what I have seen, the figures given in Hildreth and Nalty's *1001 Questions Answered About Aviation History* represent a pretty tight group of statistics and are pretty close to reality. They claim that at the start of the war England had 179 airplanes, France 120, Russia 150, Germany 380, and Italy 9.(19/103) Other sources indicate that the French may have had twice as many as quoted here. The Smithsonian presents numbers that are three to four times these figures. But what is clear is that the U.S. Army had no more than a handful of airplanes, and none of these were fit for combat. It is true that the army did not feel the urgency to build forces that the European powers did. Still, these figures make it apparent that the Wrights had been fairly successful at stifling the efforts of other manufacturers in America. Yet no Wright aircraft had progressed to the level of practicality or usefulness for anything other than observation or sport flying.

What was perhaps even worse was the stifling effects the Wrights' patents and legal actions had on aerodynamic and aviation research in the United States. With little chance of practical application, few commercial organizations or academic institutions were willing to devote time and resources to aviation related research. This left the U.S. woefully behind in even understanding the proper design of aircraft.(41/295)

Regarding the basic layout of World War I combat airplanes, with only one or two exceptions, none used wing warping, none used canards, none used skids, launch rails, catapults, and, to my knowledge, none used coordinated controls or any other of the Wrights' "innovations". Although most were biplanes and all used cambered wings, those were not Wright inventions. Despite the German "Eindecker" with which Baron von Richthofen had so much success, monoplanes had generally not yet reached the level of structural rigidity required for combat maneuvering. (Much of von Richthofen's success with the Eindecker was due to it having one of the first centerline mounted fully synchronized machine guns along with his tactic of surprise.) In fact, at the beginning of the war, both England and France banned monoplanes as being "unsafe" for military use.(19/103) A couple of triplanes were tried, the German Folker version being produced in some numbers, but the efficiency losses associated with six wing tips and very low aspect ratios outweighed the structural and maneuvering advantages.

Although wood and fabric were to dominate aircraft construction for many years to come, Hugo Junkers built the first all-metal prototype combat aircraft in 1915.(42/173) It was not considered practical since he used iron for its construction. However four years later he built another airplane out of duralumin, an aluminum-magnesium alloy.(42/86) Although strong and much lighter, it was to be over a decade before even this metal was to attain widespread acceptance.

Not all uses for aircraft at this time were for combat and killing. On New Year's Day, seven months before the war broke out, the first scheduled airline was established. Curtiss seaplanes were used to fly 22 miles every day from St. Petersburg, Florida, to Tampa and back, crossing Tampa Bay in the process. (19/99) Looking at a map today this hardly seems worth it, the two cities being so close to each other. But there were no bridges across the bay back then. Storms were frequent and unpredictable, and the shallow water of the bay would whip up some pretty nasty seas for shallow draft ferries to navigate. A trip by land around the swamps at the northern end of the bay took at least all day at that time. So it would seem that the air service would have provided a useful function. Nonetheless, it was terminated after little more than a month.

One source claims that by the end of World War I Great Britain had built 55,000 airplanes, France 68,000, Germany 48,000, and the United States 15,000.(15/103) These numbers seem incredibly large, but then so do the confirmed numbers of aircraft produced during World War II. By the time of the Great War, Orville was a rich man, a millionaire over a century ago. Still, I wonder if sometimes when he laid to rest at the end of the day he ever wondered what his life would have been like if he had actually gotten a 10 percent royalty on even just the allied aircraft. But by then nobody paid any more attention to the Wright patents, which are the subject of the next chapter.

CHAPTER VI

Patents

I n the next few chapters we turn away from the technical aspects of early aviation and look at the legal, personal, and financial aspects of the Wright brothers' participation in it. We have just seen how the Wrights made a transition from the undisputed leaders in aviation technology to becoming, although still famous names, minor participants and essentially noncontributors to its progress. Similarly, in these chapters we will see the Wrights' transition from innocent, selfless, generous young experimenters eager to learn, into what some saw as selfish, greedy, vindictive men who were willing to stretch the truth in order to trample over the rights of those who preceded and followed them.

Most authors have chosen to ignore or at least downplay these aspects of the Wright brothers' characters and activities rather than tarnish the legend of their early work. Some do, however, discuss these facts briefly. A few, such as Seth Shulman in his very pro-Glenn Curtiss book *Unlocking the Sky*, give fairly extensive, somewhat anti-Wright accounts. I have tried to maintain objectivity by working largely from the Wrights' writings and material written to them, as well as from their patents. Although rather unappealing aspects of their characters and activities do surface, readers should keep two things in mind: The Wright brothers did have legitimate rights just like any other inventors, and they did do the work described in Chapter III. They did develop the world's first manned, powered, and, by the end of 1905, fully controlled airplane.

Genesis of the Patents

In the beginning there were just a couple of young guys in Dayton, Ohio, with a pile of articles about daring aviation experimenters in America and Europe. Many of these aviators were risking their lives, indeed some losing their lives, to experience the thrill of leaving the earth and soaring like birds. None of these men were making any money by struggling with flight. In fact, those like Maxim and Santos-Dumont among others, had pretty much demonstrated that the way to end up with a small fortune from aviation was to start with a big one. In 1896, when the Wrights began taking serious interest in the subject, it seemed to many that the day when the secrets of flight would all be discovered, perfected, and developed to the point of profitability was decades away. It certainly wasn't clear that a couple guys who made their money merely by fixing, building, and selling bicycles could even generate enough extra funds to accomplish any significant research in such a complex and perplexing subject. As they put it in 1908, "In the beginning we had no thought of recovering what we were expending, which was not great and was limited to what we could afford for recreation".(2/87)

They still felt the same way while they were building their first glider in 1900. In their introductory letter to Octave Chanute on May 13th Wilbur wrote, "I believe no financial profit will accrue to the inventor of the first flying machine and that only those who are willing to give as well as receive suggestions can hope to link their names with the honor of its discovery".(1/17) These certainly appear to be the words of two selfless guys who were generously willing to contribute what time and treasure they could afford, with no expectation of huge financial gain. They only hoped that by sharing what knowledge they could acquire with others, they might have earned a small place in the history of early aviation. I suggest you mark this paragraph for future reference as you read the rest of this and the following chapter. The metamorphosis is amazing.

It is hard to say exactly when the Wrights decided that they were in possession of valuable knowledge that no one else had. But just when they decided to begin preparations for making big money off of this knowledge is much clearer. One of the earliest indications that they felt they were in posses-sion of important secrets appears in a letter dated May 29, 1902. Chanute had just written Wilbur, asking permission to send drawings of their glider to a German colleague, Major Hermann Moedebeck, for publication in Germany. Wilbur replied, "I do not think that drawings will reveal very much....so our secrets are safe enough".(1/235) This was obviously not the first time they had thought about guarding their hard-won knowledge.

By late October of 1902 the brothers had perfected their glider design to the point that they could keep it flying fairly straight and level no matter what gusts or crosswinds they might encounter. They decided at that point that they were ready to progress to a powered machine. One of the first things they did upon returning to Dayton was to give a fairly detailed report on their suc-cess with the 1902 Kitty Hawk tests to Octave Chanute who hadn't been able to spend much time at the camp that year. Upon learning of their progress, Chanute wrote them back on December 9th. His letter included the sugges-tion "You had better patent your improvements".(1/290) This is the earliest reference I have found to patenting their work. But Chanute's reply is impor-tant for another reason. Note that he refers to their "improvements". Since seven years later he was testifying against the Wrights in patent litigations, many have suggested that Chanute was duplicitous, a turncoat. But it is clear that he was suggesting that they patent only what they had created that others before them had not. By this he would have been referring to their coordi-nated roll and rudder controls, not such things as wing warping or the rudder itself. Chanute was well aware that warping had been invented and patented long before the Wrights began. In fact, he was instrumental in getting a patent for Mouillard for just such a device.

The Wrights attempted to spread their patents over all forms of roll con-trol even though Chanute had been telling them for years that these also had all been done and patented before. Other aviators, also aware of these previ-ous patents, called on Chanute to testify in their defense when prosecuted by the Wrights. Of course, had he refused he could have been subpoenaed and put under oath anyway. It is clear that throughout all this Chanute was as open and honest as possible to all concerned from the very start.

Two days later, in their reply to Chanute's suggestion, Wilbur advised that they had their "patent specifications about complete and hoped to have them filed soon". (1/290) The U.S. Patent Office recorded the receipt of their first application on March 23, 1903. Unfortunately, their "homemade" patent application was denied for "lack of clarity." The Wrights then realized they had better get professional help. After extensive checking around for references, they ended up hiring Harry A. Toulmin, whose office was about 18 miles from Dayton in Springfield, Ohio.(1/414)

I have not determined just why they hired someone outside of Dayton, a much larger city. In any case, Toulmin produced an incredibly detailed and legalistic document that was granted as patent 821,393 on May 22, 1906. It consisted of ten pages, including three detailed drawings and 855 lines of text covering the final version of their 1902 glider, describing the vehicle in every way imaginable. Toulmin went on to serve the Wrights for many years, being involved in a number of their patent infringement cases.

One reason the Wrights felt a sense of urgency in getting their patent was a letter from Augustus Herring, the talented and successful experimenter who was a member of Chanute's group. He wrote the Wrights a week after their powered success in December 1903 claiming he had flown his powered plane twice in 1898 and that they were using his wing shape and design. Wilbur later admitted they were using his design in letters of 1909 and 1910, and Orville admitted the same in his deposition for the Mouillard case in 1920. (1/413,972,1006 & 2/12,13) However, at the time they made no such admission. Herring added that he was willing to settle the matter for a one-third share of their claims. On January 8th Wilbur wrote Chanute saying that they did not take Herring's claims seriously and they didn't think he would cause any trouble.(1/417) Nevertheless, their decision to hire Toulmin at that time indicates that they had some concern that, at the least, Herring could have complicated and prolonged their patent award process.

The Wrights went on to establish six more patents in the United States. Not long after submitting the first of these they started covering their bases in Europe. By 1910 they had been granted four patents in the United Kingdom, three in France, six in Italy, four in Spain, two in Austria, five in Belgium, three in Hungary, and one in Russia.(1/1228-1232) Within the following three years they were granted six in Germany, although these were subsequently decreed invalid since Major Moedebeck had previously published the information in them in 1902. As in their first U.S. patent, the complete description and functioning of their 1902 glider and more was covered in these countries. Judging from this, it would have seemed that the Wright brothers were in a position to become two of the richest men in the entire world—either that, or they were in a position to suppress the development of aviation worldwide for some time. Neither happened.

Contents of the Patents

The Wright brothers' first and most famous patent, number 821,393, covers all aspects of the construction and operation of the final version of their 1902 glider, although it twice mentions that the vehicle could be powered by gravity or mechanical means.(4/1) It includes thirteen specific claims covering every possible variation of describing it that they could think of. The second patent they submitted on February 10, 1908 was for Orville's autopilot system. It used pivoted air vanes and a pendulum for sensors, and it employed compressed air to actuate the flight control surfaces. Apparently the device never reached commercial application. However it did represent the recognition that their airplanes were at best tiring to fly, and at worse very difficult for many to fly consistently.

Their third and fourth patent applications were submitted on February 17, 1908. One of these covered the use of front and rear vertical rudders to counteract warp-induced yaw. From a legal standpoint, the other patent was more important. In addition to extending their coverage to discussing drag producing surfaces near the wing tips to counteract warp-induced yaw, it also attempted to extend their wing warping coverage to include all forms of roll-inducing adjustable surfaces near the wing extremities. The remaining three Wright patents cover a mechanism for actuating the horizontal pitch control, a version of the split wing flap, and a toy that Orville came up with in 1923. For the purposes of our discussion, only the first one and the one that read-dressed roll control, number 987,662, are relevant.

The first patent contained three drawings of the 1902 glider in fine detail, including the rigging scheme that allowed distortion of the vehicle's extremities resulting in warping the wings for roll control. The text, consisting of 855 lines, clearly describes a biplane glider with vertical spacing struts that have pivots on each end, wing warping as the sole means of roll control, a coordinated vertical aft rudder that moved only in conjunction with wing warping, and a forward elevator that could tilt up or down for pitch control. The document is obviously written in a legalistic manner and in a fashion consistent with other major technical patents.

Appearing on the first page of the text is, without doubt, the most surprising statement in the entire document. In fact, I find it to be the most amazing statement in any Wright document. It is their best and most accurate description of how their vehicle actually flies, what physical phenomenon causes it to leave the ground and sustain itself in the air. And it is absolutely wrong! Lines 37 to 43 state, "in flying machines of the character to which this invention relates, the apparatus is supported in the air by reason of the contact of the air and the *under surface* of one or more aeroplanes, the contact-surface being presented at a small angle of incidence to the air." (Italics mine) Of course, anyone today who is even remotely familiar with flight knows it is the lowered pressure over the top of the cambered wing that is primarily responsible for lift. It's true that theirs was a common misconception throughout the century preceding the Wrights. As we saw way back in Chapter I, that's how the "airplane" or "aeroplane" got its grammatically misleading name in the English language. However much more correct explanations of lift were given by Horatio Phillips and mentioned in at least three places in Chanute's book, and by Augustus Herring in his article in James Means 1897 annual, both of which the Wrights obtained in 1899.(8/157,166,169 & 39/56))

In addition to the statements mentioned above, the first couple of pages of the patent cover construction of the machine. A description of wing warping appears early on the third page, lines 15 through 21. Just a little farther, in lines 38 through 45, an important statement appears which says "We wish it to be understood, however, that our invention is not limited to this particular construction, since any construction whereby the angular relations of the lateral margins of the aeroplanes may be varied in opposite directions with respect to the normal planes of said aeroplanes comes within the scope of our invention." This is an extremely key statement regarding the various litigations the Wrights had with those who subsequently used hinged ailerons or separate winglets. The Wrights maintained that this statement covered these other devices. Others maintained that "lateral margins of the aeroplanes" clearly referred to the outer portions of the wings proper, and thus the statement merely refers to ways of actuating wing warping. The Wrights countered that "lateral margins" need not mean all the way from the leading edge of the wing to the trailing edge. But then their opponents could counter that, as used numerous times everywhere else in the document, that's exactly what it meant. We'll return to this point later.

On page three, lines 46 to 75, the patent states that it may be desirable to warp one side without warping the other, a clear infringement of Moulard's patent as well as others. Interestingly, on lines 113 to 115 of the third page, the Wrights state that their warping could be employed "in the same way" on a single-winged monoplane, but they gave no explanation of how.

At the beginning of page four is another important passage. It states, "the lateral shifting of the cradle serves to turn the rudder to one side or the other of the line of flight." The cradle referred to is the hip cradle that actuated wing warping. Thus the vertical rudder is stated to be always coordinated with the wing warping and actually deflected by the roll control. Lines 10 through 15 and 56 through 63 clarify exactly how the rudder moves to counteract the asymmetric drag created by wing warping. These passages are particularly interesting since this patent was granted a year after the Wrights had disconnected the rudder from wing warping and provided a separate control for it in order to make turns. The Wrights later claimed that the disconnect wouldn't have been necessary, but they certainly found it indispensable on their 1905 aircraft and all those that followed.

The latter portion of page four and the first part of page five discuss the construction and functioning of the flexible canard, or forward horizontal control surface. They stated their belief that bending the surface was better than just changing the angle of a flat surface. This was probably true since bending it would result in a cambered surface at the appropriate angle of attack rather than a flat one. Nevertheless, shortly after the patent was filed they made a permanent switch to rigid pivoted surfaces. They also pointed out that the canard was used to keep the aircraft from pitching out of "balance" and to keep it from diving into the earth after a stall.

The latter third of the fifth page and most of the sixth are taken up with alternate descriptions of their wing warping system. It is important to note that these are not descriptions of other roll control systems or even other methods of wing warping. They are actually different ways of describing the one system that they used in 1902. Also on page six are a couple descriptions of wing warping with the coordinated vertical rudder. The seventh and last page of text include descriptions of their canard, the whole control system (including warping, rudder, and canard), a description of the vertical rudder installation, and descriptions of the rope rigging which activates the wing warp and rudder.

As comprehensive as this first patent was in describing their 1902 glider, it wasn't the only one that addressed aircraft control. The other was the third patent they obtained which was applied for on February, 17th, 1908 and granted on March 21st, 1911. It is U.S. patent number 987,662 and was also drawn up with the assistance of H.A. Toulmin in Springfield, Ohio.

The first thing one notices in the 406-line text is that this patent is intended to cover improvements on the device addressed in their first patent, i.e., the 1902 glider. This is explicitly stated in lines 17 through 20. However earlier in the same sentence, on lines 15 through 17, the statement from their first patent claiming that the vehicle can be propelled "either by the application of mechanical power or by the utilization of the force of gravity" is repeated. Immediately following this is the first attempt to extend their roll control coverage to all forms by replacing the term "lateral margins" with "horizontal surfaces."

Also scattered throughout this patent is a different means of yaw control than that appearing in the first patent. Here they proposed a pair of vertical rudder-like vanes, each set between the pair of wing tips on either side of the biplane. The idea was to turn one out whenever the roll control was activated, and let the vertical vane on the other side float free to trim with the airflow. In this manner they would create an asymmetric drag on the aircraft to counteract the asymmetric drag created by the wing warp or whatever roll control was used. Interestingly, although such devices could theoretically have obviated the need for their aft-mounted vertical tail surfaces, such a modification is not mentioned. Not only that, there is no record of the Wrights ever having built or flown an aircraft with the yaw control scheme described in this patent. In fact, it is discussed nowhere else in any of their writings that survive.

The remainder of the first page and the first half of the second page is a description of a biplane with wing warping along with the cabling system needed to activate it. The system described is slightly different from that appearing in the first patent. The second half of the second page describes the vertical vanes between the wing tips and how they could be activated in coordination with wing warping.

Then, about a quarter of the way into the third page appears the second, and more explicit, attempt to claim propriety over all forms of roll control. It states, "It will likewise be understood that the words 'horizontal surfaces,' 'adjustable horizontal surfaces' and the like, as used in the specification and claims, refer to adjustable wings or lateral surfaces which effect lateral balance, irrespective of whether or not the adjustable surfaces are formed integral with the supporting surface." The "supporting surface" here is the main lifting wing(s). Thus, they were actually claiming the rights to any roll control, whether it was integral to the wing, such as warping or ailerons, or separate, such as winglets. They did this although they had only ever used wing warping, and although these methods of control had all been previously patented by others.

The rest of the third page and some of the fourth contain thirteen specific claims covering just about every way of describing roll control that the Wrights could think of. All of these claims covered the mysterious vertical drag vanes as well. Eleven of them were worded so as to possibly also cover ailerons, while three of them could be construed to include separate winglets.

Since the meanings of these various specific claims were argued over for years in numerous courtrooms, I should explain briefly how I arrived at the above interpretations. If the Wrights' term "helicoidal warp" or "helicoidal adjustment" were used, I interpreted these terms to mean wing warping only. If a term like "aeroplane comprising adjustable horizontal surfaces" was used, I allowed it to include both warping and ailerons, since by "aeroplane" they obviously meant a lifting wing. If the statements referred to a "flying machine" that had "adjustable horizontal surfaces," I allowed it to include wing warping, ailerons, and separate winglets. This is admittedly leaning toward the Wright brothers' interpretation of the wording. However, any other interpretation would render discussion of the various litigations unnecessary. And, since the Wrights did eventually obtain favorable judgments in many of these cases, these interpretations must have prevailed in some courts. Of course, these claims should have all failed on precedence as discussed in the next section.

In any case, the Wrights felt pretty secure with this patent. A few weeks after filing it they wrote Chanute that the patent will "cover broadly the idea of using horizontal surfaces." They also wrote, "We do not believe it will be found easy to construct machines....without palpable infringement of our claims".(1/858)

It's Been Done Before—and Patented

It certainly would appear that if the liberal interpretation I just used of the Wrights' wording prevailed, and if the patents were valid, the Wright brothers would have had the production and use of airplanes pretty well locked up. These were, in fact, the two major points of contention in the ensuing legal battles over these patents: Were the patents valid (unprecedented), and what did the words in them mean? It's logical to look at them first from the standpoint of validity. Were there any patents before them covering the same things?

The uses of roll control devices by early aviation experimenters that preceded the Wrights was mentioned in numerous places in Chapters I and II of this book, but it is useful here to make a concise listing of these events:

1857: LeBris introduces *wing warping* on his vehicle and *patents* it.

1868: M.P.W. Boulton *patents* opposing moveable wing flaps (*ailerons*) in England.

1870: Richard Hart draws schemes for *wing warping* and *ailerons* (envisioned mainly as yawing devices).

1871: Charles Renard uses separate *winglets* for roll control on unmanned gliders.

1880s: Francis Wenham presents an airplane design with triangular *winglets* for turning.

1880s: John Montgomery experiments with *ailerons* and a form of *wing warping* for roll control and turning.

1890: Clemet Ader employs *wing warping* on his patented airplane.

1896: Pierre Mouillard flies a manned glider with *warping* wing tips and obtains a *U.S. patent* on them in 1897.

1896: Otto Lilienthal uses *wing warping* on at least one of his gliders.

Here we have six instances, going back forty years before the Wrights, of the use of wing warping, and at least three of them were patented. Here also are three instances of the development of ailerons over thirty years before the Wrights flew, with at least one of them patented. And, for good measure, we also have two instances of the use of separate winglets for roll control. Although I could not confirm that the winglets were patented, it appears highly likely that was the case. This list certainly indicates that the Wrights' patents 821,393 and 987,662 were not unprecedented in regards to wing warping or any other known form of roll control. (Lift "spoilers", panels that flip up on the tops of wings to destroy lift and produce drag, had not yet been invented.)

The Wrights and their lawyers employed a number of tactics to avoid this problem. First, they of course left the burden of finding previous patents on their opponents' lawyers. Then they questioned the validity of them by questioning whether they had actually been used. But they had to be careful because they themselves had never used ailerons or winglets either. They also claimed that if there were any differences in the geometric shape or activating mechanisms of these schemes, then their patents were still valid. Finally, if the previous experimenters' explanations of the uses of their devices were different from the explanations of the Wrights, e.g. for yaw versus roll, then the Wrights would claim exclusivity. This was in spite of the fact that in almost every case the devices would cause both effects.

On numerous occasions Octave Chanute had advised the Wrights that their wing warping was not a new discovery. In fact he had actually provided a copy of Pierre Mouillard's 1897 wing warping patent to the Wrights on the 6th of December 1902.(1/287) Chanute, you'll recall, had been instrumental in getting the U.S. patent for Mouillard. In 1896 Mouillard had written Chanute stating "My moveable planes....at the wing tips....are indispensable. It is they which permit one to go to the left or right." Since they were that important, Chanute recommended that Mouillard patent them in the United States and offered his assistance in doing so.(1/941) Thus the patent was obtained on April 18, 1897.

In court cases their opponents claimed that others had used wing warping, and indeed ailerons and winglets, before. Therefore the Wrights' patent was not unprecedented. The Wrights then claimed that, whether or not this was true, predecessors generally did not use these devices in coordinated opposition, and they used them for yaw, not roll, control, i.e. not to maintain lateral balance as described in their patent. This was a rather specious argument because whether or not the warping was automatically opposable, the effect would have been the same on any of the aircraft in question, namely brief initial rising of the downward-warped wing, followed immediately by its drifting back and dropping, and the aircraft banking and turning *into* the downward warped wing. Mouillard used it like that to turn, as do modern parasailers. Mouillard's system only twisted the tips downward, and each side was controlled separately.(1/963,964) He stated that his warping was used for turning; he did not specifically mention "lateral balance."

This gets to the crux of the patent battles. The Wrights further claimed they were using their opposing wing warping in conjunction with an interconnected moveable rudder to maintain lateral balance, and no one had done that before. In other words, what they were really patenting was the combination of wing warping and an automatic simultaneously moveable vertical rudder to enable the aircraft to hold its heading so it could regain lateral balance. (43/34) But this argument gets into a really grey area. Other aircraft had wing warping and moveable rudders. So this argument goes beyond design of the vehicle and really concerns how it is operated. The question then becomes, *is method of operation really patentable?* Not only that, five years earlier the Wrights had disconnected their coordinated controls in order to successfully complete turns. So the method of using the controls was completely up to the operator in both theirs and others' vehicles. Could a pilot's thoughts and actions really amount to a patent violation?

There is evidence throughout the Wrights' writings of the word games they were playing. In May 1907 Wilbur was on his way from Dayton to New York to catch a cruise to Europe. On the sixteenth, while en route to New York, he was struck with a thought that he felt important enough to jot down and send back to Orville immediately.(1/759) In his letter he cautioned his brother to get to their lawyer quickly and have him include different wording in the new patent they were having drawn up. Wilbur instructed them "not to specify in the claims that the twistable surfaces are the 'wings' or 'supporting surfaces' but to merely call them 'horizontal surfaces.'" The intent here is obvious—to spread their patent coverage from the twistable wing segments (which they had actually used) to ailerons, winglets, or any other form of roll control (which others were using but they had never used). Wilbur's wording is, as we have seen, reflected in patent 987,662 which was finally granted in 1911.

The Wrights developed their skills at these legalistic word games to a fairly high level. When discussing their own patents, their interpretations of the words were the broadest imaginable. But when the debate turned to anyone else's patents, suddenly their interpretations were only the strictest possible. Thus in their patents "lateral margins" or "horizontal surfaces" to them meant portions of the wings, hinged ailerons, or separate winglets. On the other hand, "warping" in anyone else's previous patent had to include the entire activation scheme as well as the precise result and use intended, whether it be yawing, rolling, or both. Otherwise, they claimed it was something different from what they were doing. Similarly, they would argue predecessors' patents to be invalid since the devices hadn't been used as patented, while they, in fact, had never used hardly any of what they claimed in patent 987,662. Finally, they and their legal team would jump back and fourth between the design and operation arguments, depending on which the opposition seemed less adept at defending.

In 1909 one of Glenn Curtiss' lawyers, Mr. Emerson R. Newell, asked Chanute for a relevant statement. As always, Chanute was willing to state the truth as he saw it. As mentioned before, he actually had no choice since he could be subpoenaed and put under oath anyway. He issued a statement on October 14th of that year saying "The bare idea of warping and twisting the wings is old". He even mentioned a Count d'Esterno who wrote a lengthy article about it in France around 1860, and who, he believed, had taken out a patent on it in France.(1/967) He also recounted his role in getting the U.S. patent for Mouillard.

But perhaps Chanute made the most damaging statements to the Wrights' cause, and certainly to their friendship, in an interview for the January 1910 issue of the *New York World* magazine. In it he is quoted as stating "The fundamental principle underlying the warping of the tips for the purpose of balance was understood even before….d'Esterno's pamphlet fifty years ago…." and "Warping tips were actually used in flight by Pierre Mouillard in 1885….The idea is protected in a patent granted to him by the U.S. government in 1897." He went on,"There is no question that the fundamental principle underlying [wing warping] was well-known before the Wrights incorporated it in their machine".(1/980,981)

More than one person brought this article to the Wrights' attention, and they immediately fired off a complaint to Chanute on the 20th of January, 1910. Wilbur wrote "In our affidavits we said that when we invented this system we were not aware that such an idea had ever suggested itself to any other person, and that we were the first to make a machine embodying it, and also that we were the first to demonstrate its value to the world, and that the world owed the invention to us and to no one else".(1/979) Here again the Wrights played word games. Yes, in 1899 when they discovered wing warping, they may well have been unaware that anyone else before them had thought of it. But long before they patented it, even before they applied for a patent, they were made aware by Chanute himself of others who had used and documented it. Wilbur's other statements are irrelevant since, as he was well aware, one didn't have to entirely construct a device to patent it. Nor did one have to "demonstrate it….to the world". He and his brother certainly didn't do that with ailerons or winglets which they were claiming the rights to in 987,662.

Chanute immediately responded to this complaint stating that while the actuating mechanism they used may have been unique, wing warping most certainly was not. He also objected to Wilbur having said in a speech that he had "turned up" at their shop in Dayton in 1901 as if it were a surprise and somehow he was spying on them. Chanute pointed out that they had been inviting him to come for over a year. He added, "I am afraid, my friend, that your usually sound judgment had been warped by the desire for great wealth". (1/981) There is no indication that Chanute was aware of the irony of his having used the term "warped."

There is little point in further discussing the merits or faults of the Wrights' various claims or litigation arguments regarding their patents. These were argued ad infinitum by dozens of well-qualified and well-paid counselors and witnesses in courtrooms in many countries over many years. The records of these proceedings are enough material for a small library. Generally, the Wrights eventually prevailed, at least temporarily, in the majority of their domestic and foreign challenges, French courts finding for the Wrights against Farman, Bleriot, and in seven other infringement cases.(1/1024) The courts often overlooked the technical merits of arguments and leaned in the Wrights' favor merely because of their stature in aviation. An example of this is the case of the Wrights' claim against Glenn Curtiss' lateral controls. Here the United States Circuit Court of Appeals judge openly stated that he would allow a "liberal interpretation" in the Wrights' favor since they were the "pioneers in the art of flying".(43/197 & 254)

Their most significant defeat was in Germany. Shortly after the German patents were granted, all six were nullified because of prior disclosure, Chanute having released material on the Wrights' machines before the patents were filed.(1/1041) This same argument could not be used in France since the Wrights had filed two weeks before the material was released in that country.

In January of 1906, Wilbur had sent a letter to Chanute saying that they preferred to sell a patented item to governments in order to keep their business simple so they could concentrate on their aviation research. (1/626) In later years they lamented the fact that all the litigation battles had diverted them from the engineering that they loved, to fighting for what they believed to be their just rewards. In a letter to a European associate during January of 1912 Wilbur wrote "We had hoped in 1906 to sell our invention to governments for enough money to satisfy our needs and then devote our time to science, but the jealousy of certain persons blocked this plan, and compelled us to rely on our patents and commercial exploitation." He went on, "When we think what we might have accomplished if we had been able to devote this time to experiments, we feel very sad…."   (1/1035)

I would agree with Wilbur that it certainly was a shame that they got all tied up in litigations instead of the science of flight. But after all, the choice was certainly theirs. If they really thought they could have made so many more advancements to aviation, they should have gone ahead and done so. That in itself could have kept them at the pinnacle of aircraft development. And that would have insured them the financial success they so dearly sought. However, considering their limited resources, their penchant for working in isolation, and their open distain for the efforts of their contemporaries or predecessors in aviation, it seems doubtful that they could have had that much more to contribute to the science of aviation.

In spite of all this, one can sometimes sympathize with the Wrights, particularly when, as they rarely did, they showed a sense of humor about how things developed. On April 6th,1912 Wilbur penned one of the last letters he was to write before falling ill with his fatal bout of typhoid. It was to an old cohort, E.C. Huffaker, one of Chanute's associates who visited them a couple times during the Kitty Hawk tests. In it Wilbur mused about how, from the early years up through 1907, many, particularly in Europe, doubted that they had had the success they claimed, especially with power and maneuverability. Then, when the Wright brothers tried to enforce their patents, the plaintiffs claimed that they didn't get their ideas from the Wrights. Wilbur wrote, "It is rather amusing, after having been called fools and fakers for six or eight years, to find now that people knew exactly how to fly all the time".(1/1041)

That Darned Glenn Curtiss

Without doubt the greatest antagonist to, or victim of, the Wright brothers and their patents was right here in the United States in the form of Glenn Curtiss. They probably came to rue the day, September 7, 1906, when they allowed Curtiss into their shop and showed him some of their equipment and the progress they had made. That seems to have been the start of Curtiss' real interest in heavier-than-air flying machines. Although the main topic of discussion that day was propeller design, he was shown photos of some of their aircraft. Within two years Curtiss had built an aircraft with a basic design that some considered superior to anything the Wrights had yet flown. Not only that, he gave demonstrations to huge public audiences before the Wrights had, and produced and sold airplanes and even began a flying school before the Wrights did.

Curtiss designed and built his first aircraft, the June Bug, in late 1907 and early 1908 while a member of Alexander Bell's Aerial Experiment Association. When this group was getting started, another member, U.S. Army Lt. Tom Selfridge, wrote to the Wrights requesting any information they might be able to provide on the construction of airplanes. Wilbur wrote back referring the group to their first patent covering their 1902 glider. (1/997,998) The A.E.A. did obtain a copy of the document, and indeed some basic similarities can be seen between the group's early aircraft and the Wrights' machines. However, for roll control Curtiss used four separate triangular winglets that extended beyond the main wings. No parts of the wings were adjustable or bendable in any way. The other main difference between the June Bug and a Flyer was that although they both used forward elevators, the June Bug also had a horizontal stabilizer in the rear for pitch stability. Otherwise they were similar, both biplanes of comparable dimensions using pusher props.

Figure 59: Curtiss June Bug, 1908

On the fourth of July, 1908 Curtiss gave the first widely publicized demonstration of an airplane flight in America near his base of operations in
Hammondsport, New York, winning the Scientific American trophy for the
first officially witnessed airplane flight of over 1 kilometer in the United States.
(21/142) Two weeks later the Wrights fired off a letter notifying Curtiss that
he was in violation of their patent.(1/907) Keep in mind, however, that this
was three years before they were issued the patent that attempted to cover
such things as ailerons and winglets. All they had at that time was their first
patent which only contained references to warpable "lateral margins" of the
main wings. Although the Wrights asserted that claim 14 of the patent covered
Curtiss' winglets, clearly these words did not describe Curtiss' configuration.
(43/67) Nonetheless, the Wrights generously offered to license Curtiss for
exhibitions, generously that is for at least 10 percent of the gross take. Curtiss
and the other members of the A.E.A. promptly ignored the Wrights' letter
and proceeded on.

The following year, Curtiss introduced an improved version of the June
Bug called the Gold Bug. But his real pride and joy was a hot rod of a biplane
nicknamed the Rheims Racer. He constructed this stripped-down lightweight
speedster expressly to win the Gordon-Bennett trophy race to be held at the
international air meet at Rheims, France in August of 1909. The race was

to be two laps of a rectangular 10-kilometer track.(21/155) Most all of the noteworthy European aviators were there, but the odds-on favorite to win the big race was Louis Bleriot with his slick monoplane. Then, while everyone was preparing for the race, word came through from America that the Wright brothers had filed suit against the A.E.A., The Curtiss Airplane Company, and Glenn Curtiss himself.(21/160) The international aviation fraternity at Rheims was in shock. Curtiss, however, concentrated on the task at hand and continued to assemble and tune his aircraft. He ended up beating Bleriot's time by six seconds to win the event and the trophy.(21/164)

Back in America the publisher of *Aeronautics* magazine, Mr. E.L. Jones, had queried Octave Chanute as to what he thought of the Wright/Curtiss lawsuit. Chanute replied "I think the Wrights have made a blunder by bringing suit at this time. Not only will this antagonize very many persons, but it may disclose some prior patents which will invalidate their more important claims".(1/962) At that time Chanute was probably the most knowledgeable and unbiased judge of the validity of the Wright patent and the true extent of its coverage, and it was clear he had grave doubts about both.

In any case, the Wrights pressed ahead with their prosecutions, even filing for past damages and seeking court orders to have all of Curtiss' aircraft destroyed. Much of the case depended upon whether Curtiss' aircraft could be controlled in roll using winglets without using the vertical rudder. Some expert witnesses testified that it could, while others stated that they had seen Curtiss manually employ the rudder while using the winglets.(43/122-150) (Of course, using just the winglets in opposition would have cause rolling without any substantial drag imbalance or heading change, while using them in conjunction with the rudder would have entered the craft into a coordinated turn.) In January of 1910 Judge John R. Hazel of the New York Circuit Court decided in favor of the Wrights.(1/1087) But, by posting a bond and an appeal to the Federal Circuit Court of Appeals, Curtiss was able to continue his business and other activities as before without paying royalties to the Wrights. The appellate court eventually overturned the Circuit Court's ruling.(30/116)

John Hazel was more of a politician than a judge, and apparently a crooked one at that. He had been declared unfit for the bench by the New York Bar Association but was appointed through an underhanded political process. He of course had no technical awareness whatsoever.

Although it is the nature of such proceedings that both sides will stretch the truth toward their favor, a couple statements by the Wrights are noteworthy. In a rebuttal deposition submitted for the February–March 1910 hearings, Wilbur gave an interesting account of the problems they'd had while learning to turn their aircraft. You may recall from Chapter III that they recorded suffering numerous crashes in 1904 and 1905, some of them quite severe and requiring extensive reconstruction of the airframe, engine, and propellers. But describing this testing in the deposition Wilbur merely wrote, "On a few occasions the machine did not respond promptly and came to the ground in a somewhat tilted position".(1/469-472) He also gave testimony regarding how easily the aircraft could be turned with the coordinated, or interconnected, rudder. This statement was, at the least, quite creative since, as you recall from Chapter III, they had to disconnect the rudder from the warp control interconnect in order to hold and exit from turns in 1905.(1/471,2/46) And they had not used interconnected controls since.

While the case was under appeal Curtiss pressed ahead with aircraft development, production, demonstrations, and sales. By 1912 his company was selling aircraft to the U.S. Army and developing seaplanes for the U.S. Navy. (17/157) Finally, on February 21, 1913 Judge Hazel again found in favor of the Wrights, and this time, on January 13 1914, the U.S. Circuit Court of Appeals upheld Judge Hazel's decision.(14/204) (Amusingly, in the second paragraph of his 33-page decision Judge Hazel gave the Wrights' incorrect explanation of how their aircraft generated lift.)(43/193)

Curtiss lost these decisions in spite of the fact that Henry Ford, in sympathy with Curtiss, had thrown the weight of his legal staff behind Curtiss' effort.(21/70) At that point the only legal maneuver left to Curtiss would have been the U.S. Supreme Court. But it was extremely unlikely that the Supremes would hear a patent case. Curtiss tried to avoid paying royalties to the Wrights by leasing his aircraft rather than selling them.(13/62) However the Wrights demanded back payment of royalties on the aircraft he had already sold. Moreover, while the Wrights were claiming 10 percent royalties on other manufacturer's aircraft, they were by this time demanding 20 percent from the Curtiss firm.(21/184) Many aircraft manufacturers were lucky to be making 15 percent on their sales.

During this same period the Wrights, along with their financial backers, were suing for patent infringement in England, France, and Germany and they were busy trying to keep foreign aviators out of America. Some of the more notable examples were a suit filed in October of 1909 against Ralph Saulnier for selling Bleriots in the United States, and another filed in February of that year against Louis Paulhan for staging flying exhibitions of Bleriots and Farmans in the U.S. (14/196) They also filed against an Englishman, Claude Graham-White, for performing in the United States. It turned out that the Wrights got relatively little from these cases because very few of them ever reached settlement. The French cases were not resolved before the Wrights' patents expired in 1917, and as we saw, the German patents were invalidated due to prior disclosure.(14/196)

In 1916 the United States entered World War I with only a small handful of largely uncompetitive and unserviceable military aircraft. By then the warring countries each had thousands of vastly superior aircraft. So in 1917 the federal government forced the sale of all U.S. aviation patents to a pool which was accessible to all manufacturers.(14/196) The companies, in particular Wright and Curtiss, ended up sharing royalty proceeds fairly equitably, and none were to be charged on exhibitions. By this time, although the Wright Company was capitalized at over one million dollars, the Curtiss Company was substantially larger. This was due to Curtiss producing more modern competitive designs. In one last vindictive expression of hate, Orville took every opportunity to blame Glenn Curtiss for Wilbur's premature death. He claimed the stress brought on by the Curtiss lawsuits weakened Wilbur, making him more susceptible to the typhoid that killed him. Stress may well have been a factor. But if it was, it was just as likely brought on by the realization that by devoting themselves to legal battles, the Wrights and their products were becoming technically antiquated. It seems a shame that such a wonderful invention brought so much bitterness to its creators.

CHAPTER VII

Secrets, Spies, and Enemies

Secrets

There has always been a difference of opinion over just how secretive the Wright brothers were regarding their aviation developments. Those who claim they weren't secretive cite numerous examples of their openness in discussing their accomplishments, particularly the lengthy and comprehensive talks they gave to the Western Society of Engineers in Chicago in 1901 and 1903. They also cite the test sessions in the open Huffman Prairie near Dayton in 1904 and 1905. But those adhering to the secrecy theory can also cite many examples from the Wrights' own words. They note the isolation of the Kitty Hawk test site, the timing of the Huffman Prairie flights to avoid the trolleys, and they point to the numerous patents as ultimate proof of the Wrights' motivation for secrecy. I believe that while there is some truth to both theories, particularly early on, it wasn't long before their concern for secrecy dominated their actions.

The earliest indication of the Wrights' concern for secrecy appears in a letter from Wilbur to Octave Chanute not long after they made contact with him. On November 26,1900 Wilbur wrote, "for the present [we] would not wish any publication in detail of the methods of operation or construction of the machine".(1/45) Some have interpreted this as merely their concern for avoiding embarrassment in case drastic changes were found to be necessary. But within the next year and a half their true motivation became obvious.

During the 1890s, a German Army Major, Hermann Moedebeck, took a strong interest in Otto Lilienthal's gliding experiments as well as those of Pilcher in England and Chanute's group in America. He took it upon himself to publish a periodic handbook on the latest developments in aviation. This became the source of much of Chanute's information, and visa versa. Chanute asked the Wrights if he could provide Moedebeck with information and drawings of their 1901 glider. On the 29th of May, 1902 Wilbur replied, "I do not think that drawings will reveal very much of the principles of operation of our machines unless accompanied with somewhat extended explanations, so our secrets are safe enough".(1/235) At this point their "methods" of a year and a half previously had become "secrets". Not only that, but they must be kept "safe". Safe for what? Safe enough for them to be the first to come up with a powered airplane, or safe enough to allow them to obtain patents and financial control over the future of aviation?

In one more year the answers to these questions became obvious. In July of 1903 Chanute was in the midst of providing information on the Wrights' experiments to a French magazine, but he was unclear about how the Wrights' moveable vertical aft rudder was employed. Although the Wrights answered him, they cautioned that the explanation was "not for publication". They explained in a July 24th letter that "the laws of France and Germany provide that patents will be held invalid if the matter claimed has been publicly printed", and that they therefore preferred to "exercise reasonable caution about the details of [their] machine until the question of patents [was] settled".(1/346) By this time they had filed their first patent and had plans to financially lock up the production and use of airplanes worldwide if they were successful in developing their powered machine. No doubt they already had this in mind when they wrote the earlier statements about "methods" and "secrets". Before moving on, it is interesting to note the extent of their knowledge of foreign patent laws over six months before they signed the contract with the Flint company.

But even more interesting is that soon after this exchange of letters Wilbur denied having such concern for secrets. Chanute had quickly written them back, expressing surprise at their concern for foreign patents along with his willingness to respect their wishes. Wilbur immediately shot back, "The trouble was not that it gave away our secrets, but that it attributed to us ancient methods which we do not use".(1/349) Contradicting himself again in the next sentence, he wrote, "We could not propose a substitute without going into matters we think it safest to keep out of print for the present." Aside from the fact that they had no "ancient" methods, giving a wrong one to Chanute would have in no way jeopardized their chances to obtain patents for the right one.

One motivation for secrecy which the Wrights almost never mentioned was vanity. They had a great deal of pride and, like many of us, reacted poorly to ridicule. However they almost never admitted this trait. The closest to an admission I have seen is in a letter Wilbur wrote to George Spratt on the first of June, 1903. He asked Spratt not to mention the coming powered machine to anybody since "the newspapers would take great delight in following us in order to record our troubles." There was no mention in the letter of design or procedural secrets. They simply couldn't stand the idea of being the butt of jokes.

Although Chanute had been the source for most of the information the Wrights obtained on their predecessors' work, by 1903 they were becoming increasingly concerned with the reciprocal nature of Chanute's worldwide aviation information exchange. On August 27th Chanute notified the Wrights that he had sent about one hundred copies of Wilbur's Western Society of Engineers speech to his European subscribers.(1/351) This served to heighten the Wrights' concern that the two-way street of information between them and Chanute had, by that time, begun to largely run away from them. So, after the powered flights at Kitty Hawk the Wrights really clamped the lid down. Wilbur sent a telegram to Chanute on December, 28, 1903 saying in its entirety, "We are giving no pictures nor descriptions of machine or methods at present".(1/401)

For decades preceding the Wrights it had been typical practice for aviation experimenters to publish what test data they could develop that might be useful to other aviation researchers. Wenham, Phillips, Lilienthal, Maxim, Langley and many others had done this. It seemed to be the normal and honorable thing to do. However the Wrights never did publish their wind tunnel data even though they thought correctly that it was the most accurate and extensive set of design data yet created. Eventually, upon Orville's death in 1948, the notebooks were given to the Library of Congress and finally organized and published by Marvin McFarland in his "The Papers of Wilbur and Orville Wright" in 1953. It seemed neither Wilbur nor Orville could ever find the time to organize them for publication. Obviously, at least during the early years, they didn't want the competition to take advantage of what they felt was the secret to the design of efficient wings and propellers.

There has also been controversy over how secretive the Wrights meant to be about their 1904 and 1905 tests on the Huffman Prairie near Dayton. To briefly recap, at the start of their 1904 test series on May 26th they had invited about thirty-five area dignitaries and press to witness their first flight. (26/123) On this day the airplane went off the end of the track without lifting off. On the next day a few of the press and observers came back, but engine problems prevented a flight.(2/86) That was it for the press. They didn't come back. Most everyone concluded that the Wrights' machines were incapable of flight and not worth wasting time on.

So, were these failures to fly in front of observers truly unforeseen disappointments, or were they elaborate hoaxes? It was over three months later that they constructed their catapult which they proceeded to rely upon for take-offs for many years. Indeed, they found that the 1904 machine was incapable of taking off on its own without at least a 15- mile-per-hour headwind. And it is true that their early machines were notoriously finicky at starts. Moreover, they had refused to let the press take any photographs of their machine. Instead reporters were to rely on their own verbal accounts of the flights. So, if the demonstrations were planned failures, the amount of planning and premeditation would have been quite elaborate. Still, it has also been noted by many that even after they began flying, the flight schedule was timed to avoid passages of the Dayton-Springfield and Simms-Yellow Springs trolleys.

I would come down on the side of those first 1904 flights being chance failures, but for a couple reservations. Years later, while preparing for a demonstration flight in France, Wilbur wrote to Orville "No doubt an attempt will be made to spy upon us while we are making the trial flight. But we have already thought out a plan which we are certain will baffle such efforts as neatly as we fooled the newspapers during the two seasons we were experimenting at Simms".(21/52) So, unless Wilbur was taking credit for something they pulled off by accident (which is possible), the Wrights had indeed been making deliberate extended efforts to deceive the press.

There is additional correspondence that further clarifies the issue. Much of Wilbur's 1905 correspondence is peppered with references to keeping their vehicles and their progress secret and out of the newspapers.(1/500-530) One of the most direct passages appears in an October 5, 1905 letter Wilbur sent to Chanute. It says, "Up to the present we have been very fortunate in our relations with newspaper reporters, but intelligence of what we are doing is gradually spreading through the neighborhood and we are fearful that we will soon have to discontinue experiment….we have decided to keep our experiments strictly secret".(1/460) It doesn't get more direct than that.

So the preponderance of evidence indicates that the Wrights were making a substantial effort to severely restrict the amount of knowledge that was getting out regarding the design of their machines, their operation, and the amount of success they were having. I believe this constitutes a fairly high degree of secrecy. But there was another aspect to what they were doing. They seemed almost eager to let the word out that indeed their machines could fly and fly well. As long as any observers were not technically knowledgeable, the Wrights didn't seem too concerned. They were shrewd enough to know that if they were going to gain credibility with potential customers, a little publicity was a good thing. On the other hand, they weren't going to let anyone steal their designs, their secrets. They wouldn't even let official emissaries from foreign governments see the machines sitting on the ground without a preliminary signed contract.

In view of the significance of their developments, one could say that such precautions were prudent and understandable. But then, as they occasionally did, the Wrights tried to have it both ways. The June 25th, 1908 edition of *Scientific American* magazine contained an editorial stating "Curtiss….made public flights antedating the open flights of the Wrights". The magazine was referring to Curtiss' flights in New York which were viewed by thousands. Wilbur immediately fired off a letter complaining "In 1904 and 1905 we were flying every few days in a field alongside the main wagon road and electric trolley line from Dayton to Springfield, and hundreds of travelers and inhabitants saw the machine in flight. Anyone who wished could look. We merely did not advertise the flights in the newspapers".(1/998) Indeed.

The final but perhaps greatest act of secrecy by the Wrights took place after they were both dead. Orville had gone through the entire collection of correspondence that they had written and others had written to them. No doubt he also screened their notes, test records, photos, and such. One source claims he set aside a large quantity for destruction and so stipulated that in his will. All these documents were to be destroyed immediately upon his death.(29/All) On February the 19th,1948, about three weeks after his death, the boxes, supposedly unopened, were taken to the nearby National Cash Register incinerator by a lawyer and burned in their furnace. Some have generously suggested that Orville just didn't want personal or confusing information to become available. But it is also possible that he was aware that the documents to be destroyed contradicted legends that had built up, unrestrained by the Wrights themselves. These papers may also have contained some of their more questionable legal shenanigans which Orville did not want to tarnish their legacy. He may have even wanted to protect some of the embellishments he had added over the years concerning his role in their various achievements. Some of the statements he made to Fred Kelley for his biography on the brothers contradicted the remaining records of their work made at the time Wilbur recorded them. In any case, it appears there was a substantial amount of material that Orville wanted kept secret forever.

Spies

Lest you think I am merely trying to sensationalize this book by having such an exciting section title, let me say at the outset that the Wrights were both spied upon and mounted their own spy operation. By this I don't mean just overtly observing someone else's equipment or testing. I'm talking about covert observations and photography, false identities, the whole works. Actually, it turned out the Wrights had good reasons for their precautions. As they say, just because you're paranoid doesn't mean there isn't someone out to get you.

During the 1904 test session at Huffman Prairie the Wrights' aircraft did not have enough power to get out of ground effect as explained in Chapter IV. Since Wilbur and Orville were flying below 30 feet of altitude it was not possible for anyone on the trolley or highway to see much of anything. But by 1905, with more power, they were routinely flying well above the treetops. As a result, a number of people had gotten off at Simms Station and observed the flights. You'll recall that Simms Station was a trolley transfer point, so it was a legitimate place for people to be waiting around.

There are a few stories about who may have spied on the Wrights in 1905. But at least one attempt was uncovered and confirmed by the Wrights themselves. One day they noticed two men, who they assumed were hunters, wandering about the nearby fields. Although game was scarce in the area, they had seen men appearing to be hunters in the area before. The next day, evidently having accomplished all they could at a distance, the two men walked right up to the Wrights' facility. One of them had a camera, not a small item in 1905. The Wrights told them that they were welcome to visit but that they could take no pictures. The "visitors" examined the aircraft thoroughly while it was in the shed. Although one of them identified himself as a freelance writer, the Wrights' mechanic, Charlie Taylor, didn't buy it. Charlie said the guy knew the proper terms for all of the aircraft's parts, something no layman would possibly have known back then.(26/136,137) Neither man gave his real name.

Years later Orville saw a picture of one of the men in a New York newspaper. Later he actually met the man and found out that he was none other than Charles Manley, the chief engineer and intended test pilot for Professor Samuel Langley at the Smithsonian Institution. It was not determined whether the fellows had done the undercover job in 1905 for Professor Langley. However it's doubtful since by that time Langley had been washed up as far as aviation was concerned. Perhaps Manley had ideas of creating an airplane on his own.

We saw in the last section that the Wrights concluded testing at Huffman Prairie in October 1905 due to lack of security for their secrets. In January 1906 Wilbur wrote Chanute asking if he knew of any isolated yet satisfactory testing grounds.(1/681) Wilbur specifically mentioned the barrier islands off the southwest coast of Florida. He seemed particularly interested in St. James City, a fishing village at the southern tip of Pine Island that Chanute had suggested years earlier. With but one narrow bridge to the island and relatively few inhabitants, Wilbur thought they might be able to "control the activities of spies." Apparently Chanute had nothing more to contribute and the idea was dropped. But this exchange shows that the Wrights did want to continue testing and development if it could be done in a secure environment. Not finding such a place, they decided to quit. Even at this early date the Wrights had put secrecy and hiding their technology above achieving further progress.

It turns out that the Wrights were not just targets in early aviation's industrial espionage activities. They themselves mounted a covert operation against Glenn Curtiss' school and testing facility in Hammondsport, New York. To do so, they enlisted the aid of their relatively unknown brother Lorin. While he didn't do too badly for his first assignment, it seems Lorin was somewhat lacking in tradecraft.

In January of 1914 the Federal Court of Appeals had found in favor of the Wrights in their patent infringement suit against Curtiss. In an effort to find new evidence which would have allowed a motion for a new trial, the Curtiss team tried to attack the Wrights' claim of inventing the airplane by showing that they had not created the first plane *capable* of powered flight. The Smithsonian was willing to argue, in support of Curtiss, that Langley's Aerodrome tandem-winged airplane had indeed been capable of flight. You'll recall that was the airplane launched twice from the houseboat just before the Wrights flew in 1903. Both times it immediately fell into the Potomac River. Curtiss and the Smithsonian were willing to accept Langley's explanation that it was the launcher that snagged the wing supports and caused the vehicle's structural failures and resulting crashes. The Wrights' team argued that the Aerodrome was structurally unsound, and consequently it wasn't capable of flying, even if that point were somehow relevant.

Well, Curtiss' team thought it was relevant enough that it would be worth proving whether or not the Aerodrome could have flown. So Curtiss undertook to get the airplane out of the Smithsonian's storage facility, refurbish it, and attempt to fly it. However, assuming that Langley was right about the launcher snagging it, they decided not to launch the vehicle in that manner. Instead they chose to put floats on it and allow it to take off from the water under its own power. The attachment of floats required that a number of modifications to the structure be made which opened up a whole other bru-ha-ha. Did the modifications also fix whatever structural weaknesses might have made it unairworthy originally? The Wright team said yes; the Curtiss team said no. Fred Kelly's book *"The Wright Brothers, a Biography"* lists dozens of changes that the Curtiss team supposedly made to the "Aerodrome". (26/312,313)

Orville decided that they had better get some good intelligence on the vehicle and its tests. Being well known himself, he decided to enlist the aid of "special agent" Lorin Wright, his brother.(1/1087-1092) For some reason Lorin, with absolutely no experience, took to the task and arrived in the vicinity of Hammondsport, New York on the evening of June 3rd,1915. He actually stayed in Bath, a few miles to the south, rather than register at the hotel in Hammondsport, and he even registered under the pseudonym "W.L. Oren". (30/134) The next day, after identifying himself incorrectly, Lorin boldly entered the Curtiss facility, talked to a number of personnel, and entered the hangars. He discretely took pictures of all the machines he encountered and even had the nerve to climb onto them and work the controls, evidently without raising suspicion. That night he returned to Bath and wrote up an intelligence report.

The following morning, June 5th, he returned to the training and testing facility and saw that they were making ready to test the Langley machine, his primary target. They had actually flown it for a couple short test hops the previous year but found the long neglected engine lacking for power. So they had made some structural modifications and mounted a Curtiss engine of nearly twice the power as the original. One of the students Lorin had chatted with the day before had told him that they had already flown the machine with the new engine. He claimed it had gone about 1/4 mile at about 5 feet in altitude but they couldn't turn it. Turning was to be their goal on this day.

Lorin found an inconspicuous vantage point about 200 yards away and got out his trusty camera and field glasses and prepared for action. At about 10:00 a.m. the machine was fired up. After running about 1,000 feet along the water the rear wings folded up much like they did on Langley's second attempt in 1903. When they towed the wreckage ashore Lorin abandoned his hidden position and walked right up and began taking pictures of the wrecked craft. At that point a number of Curtiss' personnel cornered him and demanded that he relinquish his film. More and more people joined the crowd and it became evident to Lorin that giving up the film was the only way he was going to get out of there. So he complied. (Evidently Lorin hadn't practiced the art of palm-switching an unexposed roll for the one they wanted.) Lorin stuck around for a little while, feigning interest in other aircraft but trying to observe the dismantling of the Langley machine. Finally, under heavy surveillance, he decided to cut his losses and leave.(30/134)

Thus ended the career of "special agent" Lorin Wright. Although he'd lost his film he evidently never properly identified himself and therefore hadn't blown his cover. The information he gathered didn't turn out to be necessary since Curtiss' team mounted no serious challenge to the Federal Court decision. Nonetheless, the episode makes for an amusing story. It also illustrates the extent to which a guy whose brother had claimed "No financial profit will accrue to the inventor of the first flying machine" was willing to go fifteen years later in order to make money from it.

Enemies

Inevitably, enforcing their hard-won patents, which the Wrights were legally entitled to do, was going to make them some enemies. Unfortunately, they often did so in such belligerent and public ways and at such awkward times that they generated a great deal of animosity from others, even from many who weren't directly involved in these disputes. It sometimes seems as though they were after more than their just due. They also sought to punish their adversaries by publicly humiliating them. As a result, justified or not, by 1914 the Wrights had become scorned or despised by many, if not most, of those in aviation, as well as a substantial percentage of the general public in a number of countries.

Without a doubt one of the Wrights' earliest and biggest public relations disasters occurred in late August of 1909. A year earlier Wilbur had become the toast of Europe by giving his spectacular flying demonstrations at LeMans, France. He had elicited a great deal of admiration from both the world's aviation community and its public in general. But as we saw, while Glenn Curtiss and most of the world's prominent aviators were preparing for the great Rheims meet and air race, word came from America that the Wright brothers had filed suit against Curtiss' company, him personally, and Bell's A.E.A. group.(21/160) It was made clear that the suit was over Curtiss' use of a form of roll control. Not only that, it was one that the Wrights had never even used, winglets. The Wrights were insisting on substantial royalties from his manufacturing and sales activities as well as from the proceeds of all his exhibitions.

Except for the Wrights, who were aware that their aircraft wouldn't have been competitive, all the world's aviation community was at Rheims for the meet. The Voisins, Farman, Delagrange, Bleriot, Santos-Dumont, and over thirty other entrants were there.(24/144) And all were absolutely shocked by the news. The Wrights had patents working or granted in England, France, Belgium, Austria, Italy, and Germany. So if the Wrights were coming after Curtiss, a countryman, for having roll control, none of them were safe. This was viewed as the first shot in what could become a world war of aircraft patent battles. Curtiss, who was well-liked and respected, was showered with sympathy from fellow airmen and builders as well as from members of the European press who heard about it. Over 300,000 spectators had come from all over Europe to view the week-long event. No one had envisioned that the brotherhood of early aviators would be so viciously attacked by one of its own. As Marvin McFarland, the compiler of the Wright papers wrote, this incident "turned the hand of almost every man in aviation against them".(1/1092) As far as European opinion was concerned, in one week the Wrights had gone from being the toast of European aviation to just toast.

The following year another major incident occurred that further turned world opinion against the Wrights. In 1908 Wilbur had been warmly received when he came over to put on a series of hundreds of flight demonstrations. So in March of 1910, at the invitation of a group of American promoters, the famous French aviator Louis Paulhan put together a flight demonstration team to come to America. He assembled two Bleriots, two Farmans, four pilots, and the necessary mechanics and ground crews. Upon their arrival in New York they rented a large building at the Jamaica Race Track. They needed it to assemble and prepare their machines and to store and repair them between exhibitions. The Wrights immediately filed an injunction against Paulhan, demanding that he post a bond of $25,000 for every month that he was on tour in the United States.(30/115) He and his backers ignored the order and refused to pay.

One afternoon, about halfway through Paulhan's tour, Wilbur stormed into Paulhan's private New York facility with two of his lawyers in tow and proceeded to charge all around the building in a rage. According to Paulhan, Wilbur "threw himself on our machines, touching everything and shouting and yelling like a madman". Wilbur roared "We made the art of flying possible, and all the people in it have us to thank!"(30/115) Of course, word of this rampage made it back to France and the rest of Europe with Paulhan. That was enough to convince European aviators that anyone not already operating under license from the Wrights was fair game for a lawsuit from them.

This incident received publicity in the American press as well as in Europe. A fellow by the name of Ludlow wrote an article about it in *Aircraft* magazine. Wilbur immediately picked a fight with him too.(1/992,993) Ludlow had pointed out that Clemet Ader, the famous Frenchman who experimented with powered flight in the 1890s, supposedly made a significant flight well before the Wrights, thereby possibly invalidating their claims. (See Chapter II) Wilbur challenged Ludlow's assertion, saying that Ader had done no such thing. By this time Ader had become somewhat of an icon in French aviation even though many were aware that some of the accomplishments credited to him had been exaggerated. So Wilbur's allegation that Ader had been nothing but a fraud and failure was not taken kindly in France. Wilbur's days of flying in France were over. The Wrights became the subject of widespread ridicule and jokes. One of the most famous cartoons of the time in Europe showed the Wrights glaring up at airplanes and shaking their fists at them for using "their air". The following year, while on a business trip to Europe, Wilbur wrote back to Orville that in view of the public sentiment against them he doubted that any further patent decisions would go their way in France.(1/1022)

Still the belligerence of the Wrights toward foreign aviators was not diminished. Orville carried on the crusade after Wilbur's death. In January of 1914 he wrote to a Mr. Arnold Kruckman commenting about foreign aviators who intended to fly in the United States as part of an "around the world" demonstration. In his letter Orville declared "It is not our intention....to allow foreign aviators to come into America to make money out of flying". (1/1075) Evidently Orville Wright still had fantasies about monopolizing aviation, at least within the United States, just months before the outbreak of World War I.

Animosity toward the Wrights was by no means confined to Europe. Word of their actions against the French aviators had spread throughout the United States. But the big story in the United States was the legal action against Curtiss and Bell. Curtiss was a daring yet extremely capable young gentleman, just the type of character the press adores. The Wrights on the other hand, while having proved their aviation capabilities, had few other engaging qualities, certainly little that the press could use to develop characters of interest with which the general public could sympathize. Consequently, public opinion from 1910 on seemed to often favor their rivals.

Sentiment against the Wrights was also prevalent within industrial circles. Many of America's most successful and prominent industrialists knew they owed their success to the capitalistic free enterprise system. There were thousands of patent holders to be sure, but few aggressively attempted to lock up an entire industry and hold it hostage to impossible demands. The access these leaders had to the press allowed them to further fan public opinion against the Wrights.

Perhaps the most agitated of these formidable leaders of industry was Henry Ford. He had just concluded a tremendously expensive and well-publicized battle with George Selden who claimed he had invented the automobile and had obtained a patent on it on November 19, 1895. Selden had demanded royalties on all automobiles and Henry Ford chose to fight rather than pay.(30/128) Ford assembled a legal team and eventually, after lengthy litigation, he prevailed. But to do so he had to overturn a decision by a federal judge named John Hazel. That was no less than the same Judge Hazel who later twice found in favor of the Wrights against Glenn Curtiss. So deep were Ford's convictions on these matters, and animosity toward Hazel, that he personally offered Curtiss the services of his entire legal team for as long as it took, at Ford's expense.(21/175, 176, 211, 212) This may well also have been somewhat of a proxy battle for Ford since he had ideas about getting into aviation himself. Ford's lawyer, W. Benton Crisp, advised Curtiss to avoid the Wrights' patent by disconnecting his ailerons or winglets and controlling them separately.(30/128) Orville sued against this, which was incredibly duplicitous since this was precisely what the Wrights had claimed was the difference between theirs and Mouillard's patents when they were defending their patent. Yet again a great deal of publicity surrounded these proceedings since, in many ways, the future of aviation in America was at stake. And of course much of this publicity was not favorable to the Wright brothers. With Ford's help Curtiss was able to survive until the federal government took control of all U.S. aviation patents in 1917.

It seems ironic that although Henry Ford gave Curtiss such direct and valuable help in battling the Wrights, both their original Dayton family home as well as their bicycle/aircraft shop have ended up on display in Ford's Greenfield Village technology museum in Dearborn, Michigan. Ford bought them both and had them moved to Dearborn in 1936, twelve years before Orville's death.(14/17) (The story around Dayton is that the Wrights stipulated that the Wright home and shop must forever remain on Dayton soil. So Henry Ford had a foot or so scooped up, trucked to Dearborn, and spread out to set the Wrights' buildings on.) But then, it's also somewhat ironic that after decades of battling the Smithsonian over who had the exclusive right to claim the first powered manned airplane capable of flight, the Wrights' 1903 craft should end up in the Smithsonian's Air and Space Museum.

Actually, that didn't happen until 1948, and then only after the Smithsonian signed an agreement stating that "Neither the Smithsonian Institution or its successors, nor any museum or other agency, bureau, or facilities administered for the United States by the Smithsonian Institution or its successors shall publish or permit to be displayed a statement or label in connection with or in respect of any aircraft model or design of earlier date than the Wright aeroplane of 1903, claiming in effect that such aircraft was capable of carrying

a man under its own power in controlled flight". The Smithsonian still oper-
ates under this restriction and has since gone out of its way to mollify the
proponents of the Wright legend. Under the 1903 Flyer a plaque contains
the popular phrase that the Wrights "....discovered the principles of human
flight". This in spite of the fact that they did not discover the cambered wing
or how it works, and they were not the first to attempt control over all three
axes of motion.

Returning to our story, as mentioned in the last chapter, the situation
between the Wrights and Curtiss eventually degenerated to the point that
while the Wrights were generally asking for royalties of 10 percent from everyone else, they were demanding 20 percent from Curtiss and his company.
(21/184) At a time when manufacturers were not making that much in profit
on their sales, this was an obvious attempt to drive Curtiss out of business.

The viciousness of the Wrights' persecution of Curtiss even turned
their chief engineer at the Wright Airplane Company against them. Grover
Loening, who had been their engineering manager for over a year, became
disgusted with, as he put it, their consuming fight "for revenge and prestige"
against Glenn Curtiss.(21/179) He also was of the opinion that by pros-
ecuting Curtiss so aggressively the Wrights had "turned the hand of almost
every man in aviation against them".(21/46) He added that the Wrights
"openly despised" Curtiss and harbored a "vicious hatred and rivalry" toward him.(21/206) This rivalry got to the point that early in 1914 Orville
wrote the Secretaries of the U.S. Army and Navy demanding that they stop
payments to the Curtiss Aeroplane Company for aircraft they purchased
even before Judge Hazel's ruling in favor of the Wrights.(1/1075,1076)
What's more, he actually threatened to sue the U.S. military if they continued to purchase Curtiss aircraft. No matter how much sympathy one might
have for the claims of the Wrights, it is evident that by this time Orville had
lost all sense of reality concerning his ability to financially control the growing worldwide aircraft industry.

Grover Loening was not the only associate whose friendship the Wrights
lost because of their quest for financial riches. On the 29th of January, 1910
Wilbur wrote a lengthy letter to Octave Chanute laying out a whole litany of
gripes he and Orville had about his actions dating all the way back to 1902.
(1/982-986) These included denials that he had told them early on about roll
controls used by their predecessors or the existence of the Mouillard patent,
his statements about their desire for great wealth, and not correcting a French

article saying he had contributed money and key ideas to their early efforts. Of course the technical information was all in Chanute's book which he had sent them in 1900. Oddly enough, they didn't even mention what I would think should have been their biggest gripe, Chanute's distribution of Wilbur's 1901 and 1903 Western Society of Engineers speeches and illustrations to his contacts in Europe. This had cost the Wrights their German patents and greatly undermined their patents in France. Yet there is no mention of this in Wilbur's January 1910 letter.

It was during this exchange of accusations that Chanute sent the letter previously quoted, wherein he told Wilbur "Your usually sound judgment has been warped by the desire for great wealth".(1/982) Wilbur countered, "If holding a different view constitutes us almost criminals as some seem to think, we are not ashamed".(1/983) It was shortly after this that Chanute told Dr. Spratt that Wilbur's letters were becoming "violent" in nature and that the "prospects are that we will have a row." Chanute added, "He [Wilbur] had greatly changed his attitude within the last three years".(1/986,987)

As it turned out, the only thing that kept the Wright/Chanute disagreement from developing into an even more bitter conflict was Octave Chanute's death later in the year. It seems extremely unfortunate that such a close and productive friendship had to come to such a sad end. Undoubtedly there were times when Chanute must have seemed like more trouble than he was worth to the Wrights. Although he made some statements detrimental to the Wrights' cause, they were honest opinions and often made under threat of subpoenas. But let's don't forget, Chanute was largely responsible for giving them a running start with his own collection of data and translations of Lilienthal's book, as well as designs for the cambered trussed biplane wing, center of pressure locations, the wind tunnel, and the catapult. And he did his best to warn them of the coming competition.

When the Smithsonian awarded the Langley Medal to the Wrights on February 10, 1910, Chanute, who was the chairman of the award committee, did not even attend. But when Chanute died Wilbur was asked to deliver a eulogy. Having little choice, he rose to the occasion and delivered a quite gracious and generous remembrance. Little did he know he was to outlive Chanute by less than two years.

Wilbur and Orville didn't manage to confine their personal disagreements to those outside of the immediate family. In Chapter V we saw Wilbur's extreme irritation with Orville over the condition of the Flyer when he uncrated it in France in 1908. He wrote Orville accusing him of "idiocy" and saying that his conscience "ought to be pretty sore". But that was not the first time Wilbur had registered such complaints. On July 20th of the previous year he had written an extensive letter to his father complaining about Orville's judgment and inability to conduct business. He referred to Orville as being "in one of his peculiar spells".(1/803-805)

We should probably cut the brothers some slack regarding these outbursts. Working together constantly and trying to accomplish so much that had never been done before, under such difficult circumstances for many years, would have, at times, strained the best relationship. Charlie Taylor, their machinist from back in the bicycle shop, said that, although they often argued technical points heatedly, they never held a grudge with each other.(14/28)

But what seems absolutely unforgivable is how Orville turned on their sister Katherine. Not long after their mother died, Katherine, though only fifteen years old, dug in and took over the motherly duties of taking care of the household, her father, and her brothers. That responsibility plus school was far from an easy job in the nineteenth century. Upon her graduation from high school, her grateful father sent her off to fulfil her dream of getting a college degree.(14/26) In 1898 she graduated with a teaching degree and returned to Dayton to teach in the local high school. After teaching for some years she took a break in 1908 to assist Orville in his convalescence from the Ft. Meyers crash. But then she became more and more involved with Wilbur and Orville's aviation business, traveling to Europe and working for years as their secretary, assistant business manager, etc., and never returned to her teaching career.

Finally, after having devoted most of her life to her brothers, she decided it was time to have a little piece of her life for herself. At the age of fifty-two, on November 20,1926 Kate married an old college sweetheart.(21/56) Immediately upon hearing of her plans Orville became enraged at her "abandonment" of him. He was described as "furious" and "inconsolable" and he broke off all contact with her after her marriage. No one could convince him to see or talk with his sister until she was on her deathbed three years later. (40/363,364) I have seen a number of accounts of this episode, and none put it in any more favorable light than that described here.

However even turning against faithful Katherine was not the most grievous thing Orville did. That was taking the credit for the first successful powered flight away from his brother. Wilbur had written to Octave Chanute in 1907 stating that it was his and Orville's judgment that to be considered a successful controlled flight the distance covered would have to exceed 300 feet. Anything less was considered by them to have been just a lucky hop amounting to "nothing". So according to this criterion, neither Wilbur's flight on the 14th of December 1903, nor their first three on December 17th qualified. These were all less than 200 feet long. In fact, by their measurements, Orville's "first flight" on the 17th was only about than ten feet longer than Wilbur's hop on the 14th. Only Wilbur's last flight in 1903 qualified as a true flight according to their own criterion and measurement. This seems to have been Wilbur's position anyway.

Then, a year after Wilbur's death Orville wrote an article for *Flying* magazine titled "How We Made the First Flight".(1/395) In it he claimed the honor by stating that, since they had been flying into a strong headwind instead of calm air, he actually went the equivalent of 540 feet on the first flight of the 17th rather than the 120 feet actually measured. In this manner Orville convinced himself, and strove to convince others, that he, not his brother, had made the world's first manned, controlled, powered flight. This of course totally ignores the fact that without a 25-mile-per-hour headwind their 1903 aircraft couldn't even have taken off. Not only that, Augustus Herring's alleged 1898 flight of eight seconds and 75 feet into a 26 mile per hour headwind was equivalent to at least 350 feet in calm air. If verifiable, it could have qualified as the first manned, powered, "controlled" flight according to Orville's revised criterion.

On December 17, 1928 the first monument to the 1903 flights was dedicated at Kitty Hawk, North Carolina. The Library of Congress' photographic collection contains a photo of Orville standing next to the monument, his brother having by then been dead for over sixteen years. The plaque on the monument read, "The first successful flight of an airplane was made from this spot by Orville Wright on December 17, 1903....in a machine designed and built by Wilbur Wright and Orville Wright." Orville is standing there with a pleased and proud smile on his face. Perhaps, as Wilbur once told him, Orville's "conscience was pretty sore". In any case, when the permanent national monument was dedicated on November 14, 1932 the inscription read: "In Commemoration of the Conquest of the Air by the Brothers Wilbur and Orville Wright, Conceived by Genius, Achieved by Dauntless Resolution and Unconquerable Faith."

By 1914 the Wrights had engaged in three dozen lawsuits.(21/57) They had become widely disliked, if not hated, by many within the aircraft industry and aviation in general.(21/58) It seems like such a shame that two men capable of such deep understanding of things technical, and who gave birth to such a wonderful thing as manned powered flight, could not find a way to get their share of satisfaction and reward without becoming despised by so many. Maybe some of the animosity toward them was not deserved. But, as the examples given in this and the previous chapter indicate, a lot of it was.

CHAPTER VIII

Birth of the Aviation Industry

Marketing and Sales

A s with many of the Wrights' actions, there are a few aspects of their efforts to market their invention that seem surprising. The first is how early they tried to sell airplanes. Just a few weeks after the 1903 powered flights they wrote Dr. George Spratt claiming that they were "receiving daily offers" by investors willing to finance an airplane manufacturing business. They were suspicious of these offers and resolved to deal directly with national governments. Then they began these negotiations before they could even reliably turn their aircraft, in fact before they could even get out of ground effect. The second thing is that, contrary to some of their statements, they began trying to sell to foreign governments at the same time they first approached the United States government. And finally, it is surprising that they so grossly and completely misread the progress of their competition. In this section we'll examine these and other aspects of their efforts to market their invention.

As previously stated, the Wrights were still struggling to maintain and especially exit turns in 1904. They were suffering regular crashes and were in no position to demonstrate the capabilities of their machine. So it is no surprise that when a representative of the British Army, a Lt. Col. John Capper, came to witness a flight in October 1904 while they were testing, they declined to demonstrate their vehicle.(1/494,495) In addition, as we have seen, they were intensely interested in keeping their design secret from technically knowledgeable eyes at that time.

By the time they concluded their 1904 testing session in early December, they felt they had discovered the clues to successfully maneuvering their airplane. These were decoupling the rudder from wing warping, taking out anhedral, and adding more power. So, betting on the come, they began efforts to market their invention immediately after the New Year before any of these alterations could be tested. On January 3rd, 1905, less than a month after the conclusion of the 1904 testing, Wilbur met with the Dayton area U.S. Congressman, Representative Robert Nevin.(1/494,495) The purpose was to get Congressman Nevin's advice on the best way to approach the U.S. military regarding the sale of Wright Flyers. Congressman Nevin suggested Wilbur write a letter which he would forward through President Taft to the War Department. Wilbur did so on the 18th of January. But before that, on January 10th, he had also sent a query to Lt. Col. Capper of the British Army, the same officer who had been sent to visit them in Dayton a few months earlier.(1/495) So Wilbur initiated contact with the British representative over a week before he first contacted the United States Government. Thus, the often-stated myth that the Wrights didn't contact foreigners for sale of their aircraft until after they were turned down by the U.S. Army is exactly that, a myth.

In May of 1905 Wilbur wrote Octave Chanute that they were ready to build an aircraft for use in war.(1/493) One wonders what they were thinking. They had not yet been able to turn and return to level flight with any assurance that they wouldn't crash. And they had not yet flown above an altitude of 35 or 40 feet, or at a speed of over 35 miles per hour. Their aircraft could have been brought down with a rock thrown into the propeller—that is, if it didn't crash on its own first. They were obviously in a tremendous rush to begin manufacturing and selling airplanes. The cycle business was still in existence, so they shouldn't have been destitute. And they claimed to be positive that no one else was even close to inventing an airplane. Still, they must have been motivated by one or the other of these concerns, if not both. In spite of the bravado they evidenced on occasion, they were probably most concerned about potential competition. As it turned out, the Wrights never did come up with a design that was fit for combat.

The Wrights developed a negotiating tactic that, on the face of it, seemed reasonable. They wanted to present a preliminary conditional contract to the customer, at this time the U.S. and foreign militaries. This contract would specify a number of performance requirements that the Wrights and their machine would have to fulfil, such as carrying two people and flying at a minimum speed and altitude for a minimum time and distance. The preliminary contract would then specify that if these requirements were met or exceeded, the customer would be bound to enter into another contract to buy aircraft of a specified number and cost to be determined in the second contract. This is not unlike a lot of business done today. The Wrights were concerned that in the process of demonstrating their aircraft too much of its design and operation would be revealed. Technically qualified observers would have been able to, within a short time, duplicate their Flyers, negating the need to deal with the Wrights. No doubt this was a reasonable concern, particularly as regarded foreign governments not subject to United States courts.

The other key ingredient of their negotiations was price. They demanded about $100,000 or its foreign monetary equivalent for one aircraft and the training of a couple pilots to fly it.(1/729) This was an incredible price in 1905. One could buy an ocean-going ship for that price. In fact, you can buy a brand new small airplane *today*, over a century later, for that price. Again one wonders if maybe the Wrights were actually concerned about future competition and thought they'd better strike while the iron was hot. They certainly didn't need that much money that fast.

These conditions seemed no more than reasonably prudent to the Wrights. But, looking at them from the standpoint of potential customers, the Wrights were demanding a contract for six figures for something spectacular that no one had seen or heard of ever being done before, and they wanted a signed contract before they would even let anyone see the machine, much less see it work. These are pretty tough conditions to force on government officials charged with spending their constituents' tax money wisely. And don't forget, both the U.S. government (with Langley) and the French government (with Ader) had already been burned for substantial amounts of money for a similar invention with nothing to show for it. It's no wonder governments were reluctant for some time to deal with the Wrights on their terms.

The result was pretty much a standoff. By the summer of 1905, both the U.S. Army and the British Ministry of Defense had turned the initial Wright proposals down. However, the British were still interested in sending an officer to witness a flight before signing a contract.(1/495) In November the Wrights turned this proposal down. Wilbur wrote the French ambassador in November offering a similar deal of a demonstration after signing a preliminary contract, but they turned down the Wrights the following month. (1/529) Negotiations with the French were then reopened in January of 1906.(1/688) In October of 1905 they made a second proposal to the U.S. Army.(1/518) This one included a two-man machine capable of 100 mile flights, once again a feat they had never even approached. Again the army insisted on a non-obligating demonstration, and again the Wrights refused. The following spring the Wrights made another offer to the British War Office, and again it was refused.

By the fall of 1906 the Wrights had been trying to sell their airplane to the U.S. Army and foreign governments for nearly two years with no success. But by then the problem was not just their contract terms. It was becoming clear that others, particularly in France, were very close to solving the problems of manned flight. Perhaps soon the Wrights wouldn't be running the only game in town. During these two years Chanute had been busily monitoring foreign and domestic progress in developing flying machines, and he had been keeping the Wrights apprised of these developments. He tried to warn them that perhaps they should be more compromising in their negotiating positions while they still had substantial leverage, but the Wrights didn't see it that way. Their attitude is best revealed in the letter previously quoted in Chapter V, but worth repeating here. On October 10th,1906 they responded to Chanute's concerns, writing that they were holding to their terms. They wrote, "We are convinced that no one will be able to develop a practical flyer within five years. We do not believe there is a chance in one hundred that anyone will have a machine....within five years. It is many times five years."(1/729,730) They couldn't believe that anyone else could stumble across all the things they had grappled with and come up with all the solutions they had found in order to create an airplane. What the Wrights didn't realize was that the others didn't have to. These other pioneering aviators could come up with their own solutions avoiding many of the Wrights' problems, and thus create their own airplane designs which, in some ways, were superior to Wright Flyers.

Near the end of 1906 the Wrights began negotiating with an international trading company in New York represented by Mr. Charles R. Flint. This group had been successful at marketing cars, ships, and even submarines to foreign governments. Letters on hand at the Wright State University library reveal that on July 31st,1907 the Wrights asked Flint's group for $190,000 cash plus $350,000 in stock upon formation of the Wright Company. The following November they requested 20 percent royalties on all sales and proceeds outside of the United States and Great Britain. Although interim agreements were negotiated, the Wrights' final contract with Flint and Company, dated November 27, 1909 and amended on the first of January, 1912, provided the Wrights with 10 percent of sales, infringement awards, and other proceeds. They were also to receive $500,000 in cash and stock.(1/749,750) They would have to support the company with technical advice and oversight as well as demonstrations. In support of Flint's negotiations Wilbur put on spectacular flight demonstrations in France, and elsewhere in Europe.

After Glenn Curtiss gave his flight demonstrations in New York in 1908 the Wrights dropped their prices. The cost to the army went from $100,000 down to $25,000.(21/62) As a result of their flight demonstrations, price reductions, and the efforts of Flint's group, by 1910 Wright Flyers were in production in Dayton, England, France, and beginning in Germany. In fact, by the end of 1908 the French manufacturer had built approximately two dozen Flyers under license, this well before any had been built for sale in the United States.(14/172)

Production

Most accounts of the aircraft built by the Wrights end with the first powered Flyer of 1903. Those authors that continue on with aircraft development usually drop discussion of the Wright brothers after the 1908 Flyer models used by Orville at Ft. Meyer and Wilbur in France. This is probably because by 1910 Wright airplanes were no longer state-of-the-art aircraft designs and consequently they were seldom used for major demonstrations or record flights. Not only that, by 1910 their aircraft had acquired a reputation as difficult and dangerous due to their instabilities. However, the Wright Company did continue on to develop at least fifteen subsequent improved designs before Orville totally retired from an active role and sold the company.

During the period from 1907 to 1909 the Wrights built seven airplanes. (1/1193) These were actually built under the direct hand or supervision of Wilbur and Orville themselves. These designs were essentially updated versions of the 1905 plane. But 1909 was the breakthrough year for the Wrights in the United States business wise. By the end of that year they had successfully completed their acceptance tests for the U.S. Army, they had a final contract, and they were planning a manufacturing facility in Dayton, Ohio.(1/951) The Wright Company was financed by a group of eastern investors. The group included a number of men who were famous in the field of transportation, as well as such prominent names as Cornelius Vanderbilt and Robert J. Collier. They had put up a total of $200,000 cash along with $800,000 in other securities. Wilbur and Orville were to get cash, stock, and 10 percent royalties on all proceeds. Wilbur was named president of the company and Orville vice president. In practice Orville did most of the managing while Wilbur was involved with the legal team fighting patent battles.(26/271&14/195) Although the largest contract was with the U.S. Army, a number of civilian sales were also made, mostly to exhibition flyers. The first civil sale was to Collier, the major investor in the firm. The Dayton factory had begun none too soon. As a result of Orville's disappointing trip to Europe in 1910, and Wilbur's in 1911, the brothers decided to abandon European activities.(14/203) Their fortune would have to be made in the United States.

Early in 1910 the Wrights set up a flying school near Montgomery, Alabama to take advantage of the relatively mild winter weather there. (1/274) This location is now Maxwell Air Force Base. Later in the same year they began a flight school on their old test site at Huffman Prairie, now in the center of the Wright-Patterson Air Force Base complex. With manufacturing and sales, a number of busy exhibition teams, and two flight schools, business in the United States was booming for the Wrights by the end of 1910. And by then they had introduced the Model B Flyer. Within the next six years over a dozen new models of aircraft were developed. For the record we'll take a quick tour through these designs to see how they evolved.

The Model B was actually the first major design change for the Wrights since 1903. After a series of tests at Huffman Prairie, the catapult and launch rail were finally abandoned and wheels were incorporated into the design. Also, their beloved canard forward elevator was finally dropped in favor of a horizontal tail.(1/1197,1198) These changes had been long overdue. To give the aft-mounted control surfaces more effectiveness, the tail was greatly lengthened and small vertical "whisker" panels were located out in front of the main wings. These assisted the rudder in turning the aircraft by holding the nose in place as the tail swung out. (The forward fuselage performs this function on modern aircraft.) The Model B had two seats, weighed about

1250 pounds, and was sold for $5,000 , a far cry from the $100,000 they had tried to charge the U.S. Army just a couple years earlier.

In 1912 the Model C succeeded the B. This aircraft was faster and had a larger engine and slightly flatter wing camber.(1/1200,1201) It and the Model B were primarily what the U.S. Army bought. They also developed a fairly primitive floatplane version of the C. The next model, the D, was smaller, lighter, more powerful, and was built to the U.S. Army's requirement for a "speed scout." The Model D was capable of 67 miles per hour and cost about $6,000.(1/1203)

By May of 1912 Wilbur had become increasingly concerned about their competition. In spite of their introduction of new models, many other manufacturers in the United States and Europe were introducing even more advanced models and, in some cases, selling them for half the price of the Wrights' aircraft. But apparently Wilbur was willing to take the attitude of, if you can't beat 'em, skim off their profit. So on May 4th he wrote a member of their legal team urging them not to delay any of the patent cases any longer. (1/1042) That appears to have been the last letter Wilbur wrote before his death on May 30, 1912.

An absolutely stunning example of how far behind in aircraft design the Wrights were becoming is a comparison of the Model E with the French Deperdussin racer of the same year. (Remember Figures 58 A&B?) Both aircraft were intended as high-performance vehicles, and although they were contemporaries, they appear to be twenty years apart in design sophistication. The Model E, introduced in 1913, was basically a scaled down high-performance version of the C. Because it was primarily intended for use in air shows, it had high maneuverability and could be disassembled and reassembled quickly.(1/1203, 1204)

The Model F, delivered to the U.S. Army in 1914, was the first Wright airplane to have an enclosed fuselage.(1/1205) It was a much more modern looking design than the E. Although the fuselage looked very boat-like, it was not intended for water operation. The Model G, introduced in 1914, featured that capability.(1/1205) The Model G was actually designed by Grover Loening, the fellow who was soon to become a rival of Orville Wright. The fuselage or "hull" was only about 60 percent of the overall length of the airplane, and its bottom was stepped to allow easy release from the suction of the water at takeoff. The structure going aft to hold the tail surfaces was still of the open stick and wire truss design. Loening said much of the design was dictated by Orville's insistence that it look different from Curtiss' designs.(30/157)

The first Wright model with a fully enclosed continuous fuselage was the Model H of 1914.(1/1207) It could also be considered the first Wright cargo carrier as it had a useful load capacity of 1,000 pounds. No models "I" or "J" were produced.

The Model K heralded major departures in design for the Wright Company. Having just won their major patent battle with the Curtiss Aeroplane Company over lateral or roll control, they promptly abandoned their patented wing warping and adopted hinged ailerons in 1915. By then ailerons had become the universal form of roll control. One wonders how long that feature had been "waiting in the wings" so to speak, for the patent battles to be resolved. The Model K was a floatplane developed in an attempt to take over Curtiss' hard-won business with the U.S. Navy.(1/1208) The plane had a full-length, tapered, enclosed fuselage of square cross section and was the first Wright design to use a tractor (front-mounted) propeller, which was also a near universal feature by then.

Looking back at this evolution of designs, one cannot help but notice that the Wrights had gradually given up on essentially all of the features they were so proud of in their original designs. The Wrights' aircraft were still biplanes, a feature copied from Chanute, but they no longer used launch rails and catapults, pusher props, canards, wing warping, and of course they were no longer inherently unstable vehicles. The statement has often been made that every modern airplane owes its basic design to that of the 1903 Wright Flyer. But a far more accurate statement would be that within twelve years, no aircraft, including the Wrights', owed any of its design to the original Flyer. The only commonalities, cambered biplane wings with a vertical tail and cambered twisted propellers, had been established before the Wrights began.

Aside from the powered airplane designs developed by the Wright Company, there were a couple other developments worth mentioning. In 1911 Orville personally created a new glider taking advantage of the company's latest design and construction techniques. It was a biplane with horizontal and vertical tails and a fixed vertical vane in front. Orville took this machine to Kitty Hawk, and on the 24th of October 1911, set a new world gliding duration record of 9 minutes and 45 seconds, a record that stood for nearly ten years. Interestingly, he did this basically "soaring" over one spot with a strong wind, covering a distance of only about 40 yards.(14/107-111)

The other pet project of Orville's was his attempt to develop the world's first autopilot.(1/1039) He actually began this project in 1907 and it can be looked upon as an indicator of how difficult and tiring their airplanes were to fly. For sensors the system used trim vanes capable of measuring angles of attack and yaw, and a pendulum device to assist in measuring roll or tilt of the vehicle. The device released compressed air from a reservoir tank that, through a system of mechanical linkages, activated the flight control surfaces. I have seen nothing that indicates how effective the system became. The duration of its use would have been limited by the quantity of compressed air in the tank, so by March of 1912 Orville had eliminated the need for compressed air.(1/1039) Although Orville won the Collier Trophy in 1913 for this device, his years of tinkering with the system were eventually rendered moot when Lawrence Sperry of Sperry Gyroscope fame produced a far superior flight stability system in 1914.(30/125)

Even while vice president of the Wright Company Orville carried on as the company's chief test pilot. Some of this testing was not without risk since it involved the development of his autopilot, a complicated system capable of going haywire at any time. Tests were conducted as usual on Huffman Prairie, and it was always obvious when the "boss" was flying. All the other Wright pilots wore leather jackets, gloves, goggles, and even leather helmets, typical flight gear for the time. But Orville always worked and flew in an immaculate business suit with starched collar and tie.(26/275) While a source of humor (when he wasn't around), his dress also commanded respect, not just because of the impression of class and formality, but also for the bravado exhibited by his shunning protective clothing.

It is hard to say just how much money the Wrights eventually made from the aircraft business. One source states that by the end of 1909 they had about $250,000 in the bank, another $100,000 for the startup of their company in Dayton, and stock in their companies worth close to a third of a million dollars.(14/190,191) After Wilbur's death in 1912 Orville wrote his brother Reuchlin concerning Wilbur's will. In the letter Orville claimed that Wilbur wanted the company to stay together and for Orville to run it. Orville was to disburse $50,000 each to Reuchlin, Lorin, and Katherine. (1/1044) At this time Orville stated that between him and Wilbur they had about $300,000 in cash and Wilbur had $25,000 in company stock.(1/1049) Although a princely sum in 1912, it seems likely that with all the operations going on in the United States and Europe, including manufacturing and licensing royalties, flight schools, air shows, etc., Orville had substantially understated his and his brother's financial position. Expenses for the various legal battles had been coming out of company funds since 1908 in Europe and 1910 in the United States.

In 1914 Orville bought out the other stockholders in the Wright Company. (26/285) By the following year, when the company had been in business for six years, Orville estimated they had built only about one hundred airplanes, mostly "B" and "C" models.(14/191) They had sold only fourteen to the U.S. Army.(14/196) The rest had gone mostly to showmen. The Navy was still buying Curtiss aircraft. These figures were far lower than Orville had anticipated. So in 1915 Orville sold all the stock back to the original investors for a sum that Grover Loening claims was about one million dollars.(27/Chapter 3) The following year he sold the rights to all his patents to the company. This group had also bought out a California airplane manufacturer, Glen L. Martin, so in 1916 they merged the two into the Wright-Martin Company.(1/1112) The Wright-Martin group sold the four-thousand-square-foot Dayton plant to an automotive parts manufacturer the following year.(1/1113)

In 1917 Orville and a group of local Dayton investors formed a new aircraft manufacturing firm, the Dayton-Wright Company, at a new location in Dayton.(1/1116) Orville's official position was senior consulting engineer, but his real contribution was the market value of the Wright name. This company's primary business during World War I was building a foreign aircraft, the British deHavilland DH-4, under license. While the DH-4 was considered by many to be one of the best performing designs of the war, they were also considered fire traps due to the vulnerable location of the fuel tank and were nicknamed "flying coffins".(27/Chapter 3) Many were destroyed after the war without ever being flown. There was even a congressional investigation into the matter.

After that Orville drifted off into his own endeavors. His most time-consuming outside activity was serving for 28 years on the board of the National Advisory Committee for Aeronautics, the precursor to NASA, The rest of his time he tinkered away in his mansion or in his own well-equipped Dayton laboratory, occasionally interrupted by a ceremony, tribute, or honor. Orville was to live to see yet one more insult from the Curtiss name when the Curtiss-Wright Corporation was formed in 1929 (as opposed to the Wright-Curtiss Corporation). Although Orville's last flight was on Howard Hughes own Lockheed Constellation in April of 1944, he actually lived to see the flight of a jet-propelled airplane and supersonic flight. Orville died on the 30th of January, 1948 at the age of seventy-six. It's a shame that Wilbur couldn't have lived as long to see the evolution of their invention.

The Industry Explodes

With the last section concludes the saga of the Wright brothers' direct involvement with the start of aviation. But it is interesting to take a few pages to outline how the American aviation industry grew like a family tree from the roots laid down by the Wright brothers and the first American competitor they inspired, Glenn Curtiss.

We just saw in the last section that the original Wright Company merged with the Martin Company in 1916. The Martin Company was the result of young Glenn L. **Martin**'s obsession with aviation that began in early 1909 when a Curtiss biplane was forced down in Santa Anna, California not far from his home.(12/35) Martin climbed all over the aircraft making numerous sketches and notes. An auto mechanic and dealer, with a little research he could see a lot about how and why things worked. Martin immediately set about building an aircraft in his auto garage. He incorporated many of his own ideas and "improvements", completing the machine in a matter of months. Unfortunately he crashed on his very first takeoff run totally destroying it.

Not to be denied his dream of flight, Glen immediately started on his second airplane, but this time he stuck very closely to the design of the Curtiss machine he had examined in such detail the year before.(24/113) For help he conscripted what must have been his very understanding and handy mother as his primary assistant. Needing the garage for income, he built this second craft in a nearby abandoned church building. By 1910 Martin had completed the machine and had taught himself how to fly it without wrecking it. He then hit the exhibition circuit wearing fancy outfits and billing himself as "The Flying Dude."

Martin's big break came in 1914 when the U.S. Army grounded all Wright and Curtiss aircraft due to a spate of crashes.(30/160) By then he had earned enough from exhibitions to start his own manufacturing company. Still, he often had to return to the exhibition circuit to keep the company afloat while it was getting started. Eventually his company had enough business to warrant more engineering talent.(24/214) The first he hired was a bright M.I.T.

286 THE WRIGHT STORY

engineer by the name of Donald **Douglas**. The second was a young guy from back east named Lawrence D. **Bell**. Later Martin hired an excellent engineer by the name of "Dutch" Kindelberger. Over the years the Martin Company had some of the most talented designers in the country.

After a few years Don Douglas went off, as talented and ambitious young men do, and started his own aircraft manufacturing business. In 1920 he began working out of an attic over a large lumber mill.(13/64) Within twenty years his firm was the world's largest producer of commercial aircraft. Douglas' DC-3, designed in the 1930s, is the most prolific and famous commercial aircraft of all time. Some are still in service. Eventually "Dutch" Kindleberger also left Martin in 1934 and, after a stint with Don Douglas, he became the chief of another aircraft company, **North American** Aviation. Ten years later this company produced the world's best fighter airplane, the P-51, and 40 years later the B-1 swing-wing strategic bomber. A year after Dutch left Martin, Larry Bell, who had become Martin's general manager, started his own firm which, during the 1940s and 1950s, designed the world's fastest and highest-flying research planes. The firm continues to build excellent helicopters today.

An early customer of the Martin Company was a young self-made logging millionaire from Washington state. He had become hooked on flying in 1914 after getting rides in a Curtiss float plane. Soon he became more enamored with airplanes than with logs, and decided to build them himself. He went on to establish United Airlines, the first in the U.S., and ultimately became the most financially successful aircraft manufacturer in the world. His name was William E. **Boeing**. (24/214)

Around the time Glen Martin's company was struggling to become successful, some immigrant brothers came to California and, aware of Martin's successes, they all became intensely interested in aviation. One of them, Victor, had already built a powered tandem-winged airplane. Then Allan managed to buy a Curtiss biplane and went on the exhibition circuit. By 1912 he had earned enough money that he and his brother Malcolm had set up the Alco Hydro-Aeroplane Company which eventually failed. But in 1926 they started another airplane manufacturing company just over the hills from Hollywood. They found that Americans had a tough time properly pronouncing the guttural "gh" in their last name, the name of the company. So they decided to spell it like most people were pronouncing it anyway. They changed the name from Loughead to **Lockheed**. (24/211-213)

One of the first men they hired was a gifted engineer from Douglas Aircraft. Although they made him chief designer, he also went off on his own the following year and started his own aircraft company. It seems he had some unusual ideas about how an airplane could be designed. His name was John K., better known as "Jack", **Northrop.** (24/214) Although his early flying wing designs met with limited unsuccess, currently the world's most advanced bomber, the B-2, is one of his company's flying wing designs.

As we have seen, retaining good chief designers was a chronic problem in those days. The industry was growing so fast that there always seemed to be room for another manufacturer. But finally in 1933, Lockheed managed to hire a young engineer who stayed with them for nearly a half a century. He eventually became their chief designer and oversaw the creation of what has been, for over a half century, the fastest and highest-flying production airplane in the world, the SR-71. His name was **Kelly Johnson**, and he became the most famous airplane designer in the world being involved with the design of the P-38, Constellation airliner, P-80, F-94, F-104, U-2, as well as the SR-71.

Probably the most capable designer that the fledgling Wright Aircraft Company hired was Grover Loening. He designed the first Wright seaplane, the Model G. However he was not comfortable working for Orville Wright, and soon left to start his own company. Finally, after about fifteen years of limited success, he sold his company to the Keystone Aircraft Corporation in 1929. At that point three of Loening's best engineers struck out on their own, forming yet another company. This turned out to be another of the aerospace industries greatest successes and was named after one of the three original founders, Leroy **Grumman**.

Going back to Dayton again, Orville's second company, the Dayton-Wright Company, survived the wartime DH-4 debacle, but meeting with little success, it merged with the Gallaudet Aircraft Company to form the **Consolidated** Aircraft Corporation in 1923. Consolidated merged with **Vultee** Aircraft in 1943 and later changed the name to **Convair. General Dynamics** took over Convair in 1953, soon producing the world's first supersonic bomber, the B-58 Hustler and, in the 1960s, the F-111 swing wing fighter-bomber. Eventually GD was sold to McDonnell-Douglas, who soon dissolved it in 1996. Thus died the last aircraft company that could trace its lineage directly back to the Wright brothers.

Glen Martin was to provide the American aircraft industry with yet another giant. An employee hired by his company in 1933 was to prove that it was not too late to muscle out room for yet another major independent airplane producer. In 1939 he left Martin and started a company on the north side of St. Louis' famous Lambert Field. James Smith **McDonnell**'s company, under his leadership and that of his son "Sandy," was to provide the U.S. Navy with its top fighter planes during the 1960s and 1970s, and the Air Force with its front-line fighters from the 1960s through the 1990s. These aircraft, the F-4 and F-15, were each considered the most capable fighter planes in the world during their eras.

But there was one major U.S. manufacturer of military aircraft whose roots did not trace back to the Wrights or Glenn Curtiss. Alexander deSeversky, an aeronautical engineer and refugee from the Communist revolution in Russia, started an aircraft company in 1931, but the venture was financially unsuccessful. Evidently deSeversky was an excellent designer but not much of a corporate manager, so In 1939 he was ousted as president and the company was renamed the **Republic** Aviation Corporation. This reorganized company was to gain fame as the manufacturer of the powerful World War II P-47 Thunderbolt and the rugged F-105 Thunderchief or "Thud".

Long before many of these famous names got started, in fact while Wilbur and Orville were just getting their factory going, a young lad in the middle of Kansas was reading of the exploits of the Wrights, Curtis, Martin, and the Europeans and getting the bug himself. But being in the middle of nowhere aviation wise, and not having enough money to buy an airplane or flying lessons, he decided to build his own. He completed the first one in 1911. Learning to fly it on his own, he crashed so many times that he had to skip meals just to buy the materials with which to repair his crates.(24/210,211) But eventually he got better at flying, and his planes got better too. Finally, in 1924, he partnered with two more aviators to form an airplane manufacturing and sales company. This determined and very lucky guy was Clyde **Cessna**. Later his two partners became quite successful on their own. They were Lloyd **Stearman** and Walter Beech of **Beechcraft**. Cessna went on to become the most successful builder of private and general aviation aircraft in the world.

In 1927 the Taylor brothers started an aircraft manufacturing company, but within a few years, they went bankrupt. Although not in the aircraft business, a Pennsylvania oilman could not pass up the opportunity to buy the company in 1930 for $761. Bill, though not an airplane designer, had an eye for good people, and after a few years he had the company back on its feet under his name, the **Piper** Aircraft Corporation. Probably more Americans have learned to fly in Piper aircraft than in any other. Eventually, the Taylor brothers had some success with their **Taylorcraft** line.

Although these famous names of the American aircraft industry never used any of the design features that the Wrights brothers originated, they still had them to thank for initially inspiring an industry that set them all on a path to wealth and fame. In this sense, the Wright brothers did indeed give birth to aviation.

This amazing expansion of the U.S. aircraft industry took place during the first half-century of aviation. It was "Dutch" Kindleburger and Don Douglas, with the help of Bill Boeing, that organized the resources of the American auto industry and others to produce over a quarter of a million aircraft during the five years of World War Two. In fact, at peak production Ford's Willow Run plant was rolling out the Worlds largest four-engined bombers, the B-24, at the rate of one an hour! Soon Boeing was building an even bigger and much more complicated bomber, the B-29, at a rate of over 100 per month.

During the space age many of these aircraft companies transitioned into aerospace corporations. The first U.S. manned space vehicles, Mercury and Gemini, were made in St. Louis by the McDonnell corporation. In fact, Apollo 11 took off on the first moon landing mission in 1969 using a Boeing first stage, a North American second stage, a Douglas third or lunar injection stage, and a North American lunar command module.

Unfortunately, over the last half-century many of these famous names have disappeared. Others have been swallowed up or merged together. This has been an inevitable consequence of the increased capabilities of modern aircraft, as well as the tremendous increases in prices of these aircraft. We are now left with only a few major "aerospace" conglomerates such as Lockheed-Martin, Northrop-Grumman, and Boeing which absorbed McDonnell, who had previously merged with Douglas. It no doubt had to happen. But airplane guys of my generation remember all of those companies and lament the loss of some of those famous names from America's golden age of aviation.

CHAPTER IX

The Real Story

The previous chapters have covered a lot of ground concerning the Wright brothers' contributions to aviation. There were detailed examinations of the technical aspects of their designs and flight testing as well as overviews of their litigation and marketing activities. Much of this information, derived mostly from their own writings, is quite different from what is usually portrayed, so it will be worthwhile to summarize the results in a final chapter. But before beginning a general discussion we will return to the thirty points of "common knowledge" listed in the introduction. Scattered throughout this book are the detailed reasons, indeed the proofs, why all these statements are false. Now let's pull these reasons together and address each point specifically in light of what we have seen.

Common Knowledge

1. At the time the Wrights began their work the general consensus of knowledgeable experts was that manned flight was not possible.

By 1900, not only knowledgeable experts, but substantial portions of the educated public in general were well aware that manned flight had been accomplished thousands of times. The gliding exploits of Lilienthal, Pilcher, and Chanute's group were covered in newspapers and magazines throughout the world. A few were aware of even earlier successes going all the way back to Sir George Cayley a half century earlier. Anyone with a serious interest in the subject of aviation knew that it was just a matter of time, and not very much time, before someone successfully applied mechanical power to a flying machine and flew in it. This is evidenced by the numerous prizes offered, one even proposed in the U.S. Congress, for anyone creating such a machine.

2. The Wrights derived little of value from Professor Langley's experiments at the Smithsonian.

In fact Wilbur wrote that the success of Langley's powered models was what convinced them that the time for powered flight had arrived and they had better get started if they wanted to be the first to develop an airplane.

3. The Wrights were the first to make substantial tests with a wind tunnel that was totally of their own design.

Here is the first example of two incorrect statements for the price of one. Not only was their tunnel far from the first, it was, in at least one crucial way, not their original design. At least ten wind tunnels had been built and used before the Wrights built theirs, going back to the one Francis Wenham built in England in 1871. In a couple cases, for example the work done by Horatio Phillips in the 1880s, the testing was, in some ways, more sophisticated than that done by the Wrights.

A key feature of the Wrights' tunnel, the balance device for measuring lift-to-drag ratios, was suggested to them by Dr. George Spratt, an aviation experimenter and cohort of Octave Chanute. He laid out the concept while visiting their Kitty Hawk test site in 1901. It is likely Dr. Spratt got the design from someone else, but in any case, Orville acknowledged his contribution to their work in a sworn legal deposition written in 1920. Chanute showed the Wrights photos of others' tunnel components which also must have influenced, if not dictated, the Wrights' wind tunnel design.

I have found no mention of a wind tunnel by the Wrights before the summer of 1901. So it appears the whole idea was given to the Wrights by Chanute and his cohorts so that the Wrights could prove to themselves that the solution to their lift problem was to adopt a conventional wing shape.

4. *The Wrights were the first to study various wing camber shapes, wing planform shapes, and lift-to-drag ratios.*

These, and much more, were studied and documented by many of the Wrights' predecessors going all the way back to Cayley's work in 1804. Some used wind tunnels, some used models, and others used whirling arm devices. These were powered by a weight pulling a string running over a pulley and wrapped around a vertical axle with a horizontal arm attached that had a test section on its end.

5. *Octave Chanute gave the Wrights very little in the way of ideas or technical support.*

Octave Chanute, through his book, his associates, and over a hundred letters, gave the Wrights invaluable help including

- He told them the best gliding sites were the Carolina and Georgia coasts.
- Recommended they first test gliders unmanned with tethering lines.
- Recommended they first master control of gliders before adding power.
- The design of a light weight trussed biplane.
- Proper wing camber and aspect ratios (Which the Wrights didn't use).
- Through his associates, the proper movements of wing centers of lift.
- The design of wind tunnels and measuring equipment.
- The concept of a cambered twisted propeller in his book.
- The all-important catapult design that allowed them to fly anywhere, in any conditions, for seven years.

In fact, it is evident from the above that without Chanute's assistance the Wrights would not have had success as rapidly as they did, if at all.

6. *With their wind tunnel, the Wrights found major errors in Otto Lilienthal's data and then used their own results to solve their lifting problem caused by his data.*

In reality, the Wrights never found substantial errors in Lilienthal's data with their wind tunnel and said so. They had already adopted the correct wing area for their 1901 glider, so Lilienthal's only real error, recommending too high a value of Smeaton's coefficient, had been eliminated by the Wrights before they even built their tunnel. What they did find from their wind tunnel was that they had to abandon the unusual camber shapes and aspect ratios they had been using, and adopt those that had been used by Lilienthal and many others. They also admitted this in a letter to Octave Chanute.

7. The Wrights were the first to understand the principles of flight.

This is a broad, over generalized, but often made statement. The most basic principle of flight is how cambered wings create lift. In 1884 Horatio Phillips published a nearly correct explanation of lowered pressure being generated on the top surface of a cambered airfoil and this being primarily responsible for the generation of lift. A few years later Otto Lilienthal and Augustus Herring published even more correct explanations. The Wrights possessed this information from Phillips and Herring.

Another basic principle of flight is the ability to change direction. But the Wrights created the rudders of their 1902 and 1903 vehicles to allow the roll control to function properly while maintaining straight and level flight, not to turn. Those machines were not intended or used to turn. However, there were many models and gliders before the Wrights that had independently adjustable rudders and could turn.

8. The Wrights soon found out that airfoils produce lift by creating lowered air pressures above the wing.

This is the most stunning revelation of the research for this book. Essentially correct explanations of cambered wing lift had been documented up to two decades earlier by Phillips, Lilienthal, and Herring. The Wrights had at least two of these explanations in their reference material. Still, in all their writings they gave a widely accepted and totally incorrect explanation of the phenomenon of lift on a cambered surface. In their key patent, as well as numerous other documents and even speeches, they explained lift as the reaction of a wing to air particles impacting on its lower surface. They typically referred to a wing as functioning on the "principle of the inclined plane". It's true they used cambered wing sections, but they thought the function of the curvature was to allow some air particles to impact on the front of the upper surface thereby keeping the wing from flipping over backwards. The evidence indicates that the Wrights maintained this erroneous theory for years after their first powered flights.

9. The Wrights originated the concepts of first testing gliders with tethering lines from the ground and mastering balance and control before adding power.

Tethered testing was recommended by Octave Chanute in his book, and mastering balance and control was recommended in both Lilienthal's and Chanute's books. The Wrights had all this information before they started tests.

10. *The Wrights were the first to make over 1,000 glides.*
Many with only a cursory knowledge of aviation history have read about those I refer to as the "great gliders" and know that they made thousands of glides before the Wrights began. But it is still impressive to reflect on the fact that Lilienthal made in the neighborhood of 2,000 glides, Pilcher close to 1,000, and Chanute's group near Chicago was credited with at least 1,500 glides.

11. *From the very beginning the Wrights believed that an airplane would have to be inherently unstable and would require constant balancing by the pilot.*
Nearly all airplanes are in fact designed to be inherently stable and do not require constant balancing. This has been true since long before the Wrights began. In 1804 Sir George Cayley built stable gliders, as did many experimenters throughout the nineteenth century. The Wrights were well aware of this. Chanute constantly reminded them. They originally thought their canard configuration would be stable, but their understanding of how a cambered wing operated was backwards and their configuration turned out to be unstable.

Also, they did not like the effects that Kitty Hawk winds had on their machines and believed they could come up with a design that would be stable in normal flight, insensitive to these disturbances, and recoverable from stalls at low altitude. It turned out they couldn't, and their resulting machines, while barely flyable at Kitty Hawk, were also unusually difficult to fly anywhere else.

12. *The Wrights used the forward mounted pitch control, or canard, from the very start of their testing.*
They actually used a conventional aft horizontal stabilizer/elevator on their first test machine in 1899. In 1900 at Kitty Hawk, they flew their glider with the elevator both in front and behind. But by sometime in October of 1900, they decided to keep the elevator in front of the main wings. They occasionally still thought about putting their elevator in the back but that would have weakened their patent and the progress of their competition didn't allow them the time to develop a new configuration.

13. The Wrights retained the canard elevator for better control of level flight.

Actually, their canard gave extremely erratic control of level flight, making smooth steady flight by a Wright Flyer, particularly early ones, nearly impossible. The main reason they retained the canard, as they stated many times, was for trans- and post-stall pitch control. For safety reasons they did not want their planes to backslide or dive headlong into the ground after a stall. They felt that with the forward elevator, if they did stall, they could keep the craft fairly level, causing it to "pancake" in flat, thus allowing it to impact the ground at a much slower speed and with less damage to machine or the prone occupant. This no doubt worked on numerous occasions during the early years.

14. The Wrights were the first to control sideways tilt (or roll) of an aircraft.

An airplane's roll can be controlled passively as with dihedral, or actively as with aerodynamic controls such as wing warping, winglets, or ailerons. These had all been tried long before the Wrights began. Cayley is credited with inventing automatically stabilizing dihedral in 1809. During the nineteenth century others such as LeBris, Boulton, Montgomery, Ader, Hart, and Mouillard had all used various forms of the aerodynamic roll controls mentioned above. Lift "spoilers" that disrupted the airflow over the tops of wings were not invented until wings became thicker in later years.

15. The Wrights originated the concept of wing warping for lateral control, which greatly facilitated their success at flight control.

Wing warping had not only been used by a number of experimenters that preceded the Wrights, it had even been patented. LeBris, Mouillard, Ader, Hart, and even Lilienthal had tried forms of warping on their machines, and Mouillard was granted a U.S. patent for it in 1897. Octave Chanute repeatedly apprised the Wrights of this, but they ignored his warnings.

Of the three methods of active roll control known at the time, wing warping, ailerons, and separate winglets, warping was the worst choice the Wrights could have made. It caused appreciable asymmetric drag, and thus substantial yaw rates, which reversed its effect and caused slips, spins, and innumerable crashes. Its use forced a number of redesigns of their machines and ultimately contributed to their obsolescence. Ailerons would have decreased the problem significantly, and separate winglets would have avoided it completely. Spoilers actually create favorable drag and roll for turning, but these were not invented until much later.

16. *The Wrights devised the coordinated rudder in order to make turns.*

In fact, the Wrights devised the coordinated rudder in order to fly straight. When their early gliders became tilted toward one side and they employed wing warping to bring them back level, the drag differential because of warping induced a yaw rate that reversed the roll correction, making the original problem worse. The rudder was employed to combat the induced yaw, keep the aircraft pointed in the original direction, and thus allow the warping to work as intended. The rudder was integrated with warping because until 1905 they only used it with warping in order to stay straight, and the pilot workload was already high. The rudder actually had to be disconnected from warping in 1905 in order to make and exit turns.

17. *The Wrights could make controlled turns with their 1902 and 1903 aircraft.*

Not only could the Wrights not make intentional turns with these vehicles, they were not even trying to. Their entire effort until well into 1904 was directed toward being able to fly straight and level. They consistently stated this on numerous occasions, even in their patent. But the adverse conditions encountered at Kitty Hawk made this quite a struggle. They never seriously attempted to make controlled turns until the fall of 1904 at Huffman Prairie near Dayton, and they were not consistently successful at it until October of 1905 after they had disconnected the rudder from their roll control.

18. *The Wrights' engine was one of the most powerful for its weight at the time.*

Actually, the Wrights' first engine did not have a particularly impressive power-to-weight ratio for its time. The engine Charles Manley and the Balzer Company came up with for Langley's "Aerodrome," a direct contemporary of the Wrights, was four times as powerful as the Wrights' engine at the same weight. Moreover, due to overheating, the Wrights' 1903 engine was severely limited in running time to about 2 minutes. The Wrights probably chose to fabricate their own engines for cost savings as much as anything else.

19. *The Wrights were the first to recognize that propeller blades should be shaped like twisted airfoils.*

In 1885 Sidney Hollands demonstrated to the Aeronautical Society of Great Britain that a cambered and twisted propeller was more efficient than either a flat or flat, twisted one. This was reported on in Chanute's book which the Wrights obtained in 1899. Clemet Ader's 1890 aircraft appears to have had a cambered prop. At least three propeller designers were using cambered, twisted airfoil shapes in their air propeller theories before the Wrights tackled the problem. In fact, Sir George Cayley, in an 1810 magazine article, showed a helicopter-like device where the propeller blades were actually stiffened cambered bird feathers. Thus, although he had no satisfactory source of rotational power, Cayley seems to have recognized the advantage of propellers having cambered sections nearly a century before the Wrights tackled the problem.

20. They used two propellers to cancel out torque reactions.
Actually they decided they needed two propellers to reduce both their diameter and rotation speeds. Counter rotation was then just an obvious benefit.

21. The Wrights were the first to come up with a mathematical technique for propeller design.
At least three designers of ship's propellers, namely Lanchester, Drzweicke, and Prandtl, had developed mathematical techniques for the design of cambered twisted air propellers although these were not quite as complete as the Wrights' procedure. It appears the Wrights may have developed their procedure just before they became aware of these previous methods.

22. The Wrights were the first to take a manned powered aircraft off from level ground.
It seems fairly well documented that in 1890 a Frenchman, Clement Ader, made a hop of 165 feet (the entire length of his testing field) but only reached an altitude of a couple feet. Some discount this claim because of his later failures, yet this particular flight had a number of sworn witnesses, some from the French Aeronautical Society. There is no doubt that Hiram Maxim's 4-ton behemoth lifted off for a few hundred feet in 1894 before a broken restraining rail fouled a prop, ending the unintended "flight".

23. The 1903 Flyer was capable of taking off from level ground using only its own power.
The December 17, 1903 flights were from level ground and under the machine's own power, but they were done into at least a 25 mile-per-hour headwind representing 90% of the aircraft's necessary flying speed. In other words, the wind was blowing so hard that the airplane was almost flying sitting still. Their engine only added about 5 or 6 miles per hour to the over

25-mile-per-hour headwind. Subsequent Flyers typically took off with the aid of strong headwinds or powerful catapults. Wright aircraft couldn't take off unaided for another seven years.

24. The Wrights were eager to demonstrate their aircraft after their early flights.
The Wrights were eager to convince people, particularly the U.S. and foreign militaries, that they could fly, but they were loath to let anyone see their aircraft, either in the air or on the ground. Testing was done at times and locations that limited the possibility of knowledgeable observers being present and, according to them, they curtailed testing in 1905 due to developing interest in their activities. Since they were satisfied with their aircraft's performance, they refused to fly again for two and a half years. Then they would not demonstrate their aircraft unless they had a signed contingency contract beforehand.

25. The Wrights were not preoccupied with financial gain and were willing to share their knowledge with others.
Some have cited Wilbur's introductory letter to Octave Chanute as evidence that the Wrights did not seek great personal wealth or gain as a result of their aviation experiments and were more than willing to share any knowledge they might obtain with colleagues. Early on they did give a couple presentations to the Western Society of Engineers at Chanute's request. But it's clear that within a couple years, when they thought they had something of consequence, they slammed the lid down tight on any details of their machines or their operation. The discretion with which they conducted testing, and in particular negotiations for sales, cannot be denied. Also, contrary to normal practice, they did not publish their wind tunnel or other test results.

Soon patent litigations consumed their efforts and they did not keep up with the rapid pace of aviation development. They were, of course, entitled to substantial rewards for starting an industry that would change the world, but they were after at least 10 percent of all aviation-related incomes worldwide. Eventually even their oldest cohort and mentor, Octave Chanute, became disgusted with their having become "warped by the desire for great wealth".

26. The U.S. Army thought Wright Flyers were good airplanes but could see no practical uses for them.

Yet again we have two falsehoods for the price of one. The U.S. Army Signal Corps really wanted airplanes and appreciated their potential for reconnaissance if nothing else. They also didn't want to be at a disadvantage to European forces that were after aircraft. But the senior Army Staff had just spent $50,000 on Langley's fiasco and were unwilling to be made fools of again. They were also no doubt reluctant to accept the logistics headaches of an airplane that required the laying of launch rails and the erection of a huge catapult every time and place it was to take off. And they knew others were developing aircraft that didn't need these encumbrances.

The U.S. Army also knew how dangerous Wright Flyers were. After all, the first fatality in a powered airplane was an army officer, Lt. Tom Selfridge, who was killed in a Wright Flyer. Then, when the army finally gave in to the Wrights' domestic monopoly and bought Wright Flyers, most of the Wright trained army pilots were killed in them in a little over a year.

27. The Wrights only approached foreign governments for sales after having been turned down by the U.S. Army.

Actually, in January of 1905, the Wrights sent a proposal to their British Army contact a week before they sent their first one to the United States Government. Negotiations with the U.S. War Department had not been completely abandoned in November 1905 when they contacted the French ambassador offering their aircraft for sale. In any case, these solicitations represented an impressive degree of audacity considering that they weren't even able to reliably execute turns with their airplane until October of 1905.

28. Wright aircraft designs were copied for many years by builders worldwide.

Although the Wrights were sure that their way was the only way the rest of the world was going to learn to fly, and they took out their patents accordingly, in actuality the rest of the aviation world, including that in America, took little more than fleeting notice of their design. A few tried the canard, and after Wilbur's exciting demonstration in France in 1908, a number of builders adopted wing warping. However most builders quickly abandoned these designs in favor of ailerons and the horizontal tail. Nearly all were using trussed and cambered biplane wings, but these were features the Wrights had copied from their predecessors. By 1915 none of the design features that could be said to have been originated by the Wrights were used by any aircraft, including their own.

29. The Wrights led the development of aircraft for the first ten years of powered flight.
    In reality, by the time the Wrights sold their first airplanes in late 1909 there were other aircraft being sold in the United States and Europe that had superior features, in particular the ability to takeoff unaided and inherent stability. By 1910 Wright aircraft were no longer state-of-the-art designs and had developed a reputation for being very difficult and dangerous to fly. So, late that year the Wrights abandoned the canard, changing to the conventional horizontal tail. They also adopted the wheeled undercarriage, a universal feature of other designs. At most, Wright aircraft could be said to have led aviation development for only two to four years.

30. The Wright airplane manufacturing company was the first successful one.
    The Voisin brothers in France and Glenn Curtiss in the United States were selling aircraft before the Wrights formed the Wright Company, in fact, before the Wrights even gave their 1908 demonstrations. Despite introducing at least ten new models, the Wright Company sold only about one hundred planes during its six-year existence. In 1915 Orville sold out to a holding company that merged it with the Martin Company. He was asked to lead a new company, Dayton-Wright, in 1917. It survived by producing a flawed foreign design, the DH-4, under license. This company was sold off a few years after the war. So not only was the Wright Company not the first one, it would be a stretch to consider either of these companies much of a success.

    It really is amazing to see how erroneous all this conventional wisdom is. Even more surprising is how much of it is revealed by the Wrights' own words. As Wilbur once wrote to Dr. Spratt, "Isn't it astonishing that all these secrets have been preserved for so many years just so that we could discover them?" (1/313) I don't doubt that in another hundred years some of these same falsehoods will still be told. In fact, while this book was being written, a senior official of the National Air and Space Museum stated many of these same misconceptions in an interview on public television. My hope is that eventually others who have more stature in the aeronautical history fraternity than myself, and who have not committed their reputations to these falsehoods, will take advantage of the numerous references I have called out and will lend their impetus toward correcting the historical record.

So What Did Happen?

We've just listed what is not true about the Wright brothers. So then, what is true? What is the real story?

First, any idea that there wasn't much useful information for the Wrights to build upon in creating their flying machines is completely false. For over a century preceding them a tremendous amount of very good aviation research was conducted by dozens of qualified experimenters. Unfortunately it was mixed in with a lot of bad information too. Amazingly, some of the best material was compiled by Sir George Cayley one hundred years before the Wrights began. He built a whirling arm device to study airfoil camber shapes, wing planform shapes, aspect ratios, lift-to-drag ratios, as well as the effects of angles of attack, speed, and streamlining on lift and drag. He had even constructed and tested stable flying models with adjustable tail controls. Then a half century before the Wrights, Cayley constructed two full-scale gliders in which his assistants briefly flew.

Wenham and Browning constructed the first wind tunnels in England thirty years before the Wrights, and with these they tested the locations and travel patterns of centers of pressure in addition to the things Cayley had investigated. Fifteen years before the Wrights began their research, Phillips used his wind tunnel to develop amazingly modern looking airfoil shapes. Both he and Lilienthal determined that cambered wings produced lift because of a lowered pressure on their upper surface, something the Wrights didn't understand over twenty years later. Professor Montgomery in California developed a glider that was stable and controllable fifteen years before the Wrights started. Clemet Ader was said to have made short hops with his steam-powered aircraft in France ten years before the Wrights began.

About this same time Hiram Maxim, after doing wind tunnel research, built a huge steam-powered machine in England which tore through its restraints and was airborne for about ten seconds. Then, in the decade just preceding the Wrights' work, the "great gliders," Lilienthal, Pilcher, and Chanute's group, made thousands of unpowered stable glides. In fact, Pilcher had a powered machine nearly ready but he died in a demonstration glide shortly before he was to test his powered aircraft. Had Lilienthal not been killed he may well have flown a powered aircraft within a couple years, several years before the Wrights. One of Chanute's cohorts, Augustus Herring, is said to have made a couple brief hops in a powered craft in 1898 before a fire destroyed it.

Long before the Wrights began their studies, the manner by which wings produce lift and the shape they should have to do so were understood and the information was published. Such components as smoothly cambered wings, biplane construction, aft horizontal and vertical stabilizers and controls, and gasoline engines were recognized by experimenters as essential or desired features of a successful flying machine. Even roll controls and cambered twisted propellers had been devised. It would seem that by 1900 one could basically combine these features into a reasonable balanced machine to achieve success, that is after you sorted through all the bad information, not that all that would be easy.

To a limited extent, that is what the Wrights did. But they included major exceptions, and these exceptions led to most of the difficulties they encountered in developing their flying machines. Their misplaced fear of Lilienthal's and Pilcher's fate led them to adopt the forward elevator, or canard, which made their aircraft unstable and ultimately caused them far more trouble than it was worth. In fact, their fixation on the canard control and the inability of many to use it safely was a major contributor to the Wrights' failure to lead the aircraft industry. But we're getting ahead of our story.

An even bigger cause of their difficulties in developing an airplane was the use of wing warping. Unfortunately, this was the worst method of roll control they could have used. It induced a yaw rate and the resulting roll reversal which in turn led to slipping and spinning crashes. Their fix to the problem, a coordinated vertical tail, soon had to be abandoned in order to make turns. So then, instead of the remedy operating automatically, it had to be done manually, further complicating the operation of a Wright Flyer. Then, years later when wings became thicker and stronger and more aerodynamically efficient, the Wrights were stuck, largely because of patent battles, with their thin warpable wings. This was another major reason for the Wrights' limited success as aircraft manufacturers.

Their 1900 glider was undersized, evidently due to using Lilienthal's recommended too high value of Smeaton's coefficient, but this was corrected the following year. Another peculiar feature of early Wright designs that ultimately didn't impede their progress more than a couple years was the use of odd wing camber shapes and aspect ratios in their 1900 and 1901 gliders. This camber shape, having its maximum height just behind the leading edges of the wings with the remainder of the section flat or reflexed, was an attempt to achieve reasonable pitch stability with the canard and a result of their erroneous impact theory of how wings generate lift. Fortunately, although they still did not discover the error in their aerodynamic theory, their wind tunnel tests recommended by Chanute, Spratt, and Huffaker near the end of 1901 convinced them to adopt more traditional camber and aspect ratio shapes for the 1902 glider. This solved their lift problem and paved the way for their powered flights of 1903 and beyond.

Another decision that caused difficulties during the Wrights' gliding tests was adopting the seemingly prudent procedure of first testing their vehicles tethered to operators on the ground. Although this technique allowed them to make fairly precise measurements of their glider's lift and drag characteristics, it totally eliminated the possibility of vehicle yaw, and thus completely masked the wing warp-induced yaw and roll control reversal problems. Fortunately, the Wrights worked their way past this problem also. But one wonders, had they found the control reversal problem in 1899 or even 1900, might they have changed to a different, less troublesome form of roll control? Probably not.

One other significant contributor to the problems the Wrights experienced was the nature of the test site they adopted, Kitty Hawk and Kill Devil Hill, North Carolina. They wanted large soft hills and stiff breezes for good safe gliding and the coastal sand dunes near Kitty Hawk certainly provided those. But gliding along the sloping hill faces allowed the winds to get under the windward wing and tilt their machines into the hillsides. This caused the Wrights to abandon the wing dihedral that had been used so successfully by many before them, and to adopt the opposite, anhedral, for their machines. Anhedral did help alleviate the hillside crosswind problem, but it made their aircraft unstable in roll under all conditions. They struggled along with anhedral for over four years, finally abandoning it in 1905 in order to successfully make turns.

These problems, wing size and shape, the canard, adverse control reactions, and anhedral, all came together at the end of the 1901 test session to drive the brothers into the deepest period of frustration and despair that they experienced. Their vehicle didn't have enough lift, was unstable in pitch, unstable in roll, and it had no directional control or stability. Not only that, the pitch control was oversensitive and the roll control often worked backwards. The Wrights decided that the faults lay with the information they had used from their predecessors. So they resolved to ignore all work that had been done by others, and proceeded to use only their own reasoning and data. They had largely been doing this already, but by late in 1901 it became doctrine.

Upon returning to Dayton in August of 1901 they did an extensive analysis of their Kitty Hawk gliding data in preparation for a speech Chanute had talked them into giving to the Western society of Engineers which Wilbur gave that September. After that they commenced airfoil tests with a turntable balance mounted horizontally over the front wheel of a bicycle. These tests and analyses indicated that Langley's value of 0.0033 for Smeaton's coefficient was much more accurate than Lilienthal's 0.0055, thus justifying nearly doubling their wing area from the 1900 machine to the 1901 vehicle.

Seeing the need for a much more detailed set of design data, the Wrights constructed a wind tunnel incorporating design information they had gotten from Octave Chanute and George Spratt that past summer at Kitty Hawk. They commenced testing with the tunnel in November of 1901. This testing proved that Lilienthal's lift coefficient table was completely accurate but that they had applied it to a totally inappropriate wing shape. Using data obtained with their tunnel they designed a glider for 1902 that had a much improved more typical camber shape and Lilienthal's aspect ratio. This glider was their first to include twin fixed vertical stabilizers aft of the wings intended to keep the glider on course while correcting inadvertent tilting of the vehicle. Finding that fixed stabilizers didn't work, they converted them to a moveable rudder and connected it to their wing warping control. Finally the glider was capable of maintaining a straight and level course and flew excellently.

For 1903 this glider was upscaled and the new vehicle fitted with a gasoline engine and dual pusher propeller system, all of their own design and fabrication. At Kitty Hawk on December 17th of 1903, with strong headwinds providing over 80 percent of the necessary lift, this powered vehicle briefly flew to their satisfaction on their fourth attempt. But beyond the existence of an excellent photograph, the events of December,1903 are not really significant since the flights were of minimum distance, basically out of control, and ended in minor crashes. In fact, the first crash on the 14th, and the last on the 17th, were so bad that the aircraft couldn't be flown again without substantial repairs.

Unfortunately, by 1903 they had become so dependent upon the Kitty Hawk winds, which were sometimes capable of lifting a stationary aircraft, that they designed the first powered machine accordingly. It had enough power to maintain an airspeed of 30 miles per hour or so, but it couldn't get there unless the wind was already blowing at close to 25 miles per hour. There wasn't nearly enough power to accelerate it from rest to flying speed in calm air.

The following year they were flying at Huffman Prairie just east of Dayton. Prevailing winds there were nothing near what they had at Kitty Hawk, and although their new engine was slightly improved, their new aircraft was also heavier. So they still could not reliably take off unassisted. They decided to build a catapult of the type recommended to them by Chanute. It worked fine for 1904 and 1905 allowing them to conduct flight tests even in calm weather.

Over the two years of testing at Dayton they made major refinements to their aircraft, increasing the power of their engines, improving propellers, disconnecting the rudder to operate independently, switching their wing design from anhedral to dihedral, lengthening their vehicles, and relocating their centers of gravity. By the end of October, 1905, they had developed an airplane that, although still unstable, could climb out of ground effect, be turned and maneuvered, and do pretty much whatever they asked of it. And it was the first in the world with such capabilities.

But the problem was that they came to depend on the launching device in their subsequent designs. Consequently, their airplanes were the only ones burdened with a great deal of heavy, awkward, time and manpower-intensive support equipment in order to operate. This logistics burden greatly diminished the appeal of Wright Flyers to the U.S. Army and Navy as well as foreign militaries and other customers.

The Wrights didn't fly in 1906 and 1907, but in 1908 Wilbur in France, and Orville in America, gave flight demonstrations that set the skeptical world on its ear. By then others were flying, particularly in France. But no one could come close to the display of control and maneuverability that the Wrights demonstrated. However it was becoming clear that there were many ways to make a good airplane, and one need not copy the Wrights to do it. And many in Europe and America were doing just that. As a result, by the end of 1908 the Wrights had considerable competition. By 1909 there were a number of designs that were superior to Wright Flyers, and by 1910 the Wright design was obsolete. Other than being somewhat longer and having two upright seats, the airplane they were producing in early 1910 was nearly indistinguishable from the 1903 machine.

Later that year the Wrights had to give up on their beloved canard elevator and the catapult and rail launch system. They adopted the rear horizontal elevator and a wheeled undercarriage, but by then it was too late. Their aircraft had already gained a reputation as underperforming hard to fly killers. This was primarily due to their relatively low power, pitch instability, and tricky roll control. Technically they should have switched from wing warping to ailerons or winglets in 1902, and they could have safely gotten rid of the canard by 1905. But they became locked into them by their attitudes, the relentless pace of their competition, and by their patents. This extracted a heavy toll in both sales and pilots. Within a period of fifteen months eight of the first fourteen U.S. Army pilots, and five of the nine Wright exhibition team pilots, had been killed in Wright Flyers. In fact, by 1912 one fourth of all aviation deaths had happened in Wright Flyers even though they numbered only a tiny fraction of the world's aircraft.

Backing up a bit, by 1905 the Wrights had made some crucial decisions. As they saw it, because of the failure of all their predecessors and the intricate struggle they themselves had endured, they concluded that they had discovered the only way to make a successful, controlled, powered airplane. Therefore, the only way anyone else could do it was to copy theirs. They also believed that their sacrifices were so great, and their accomplishments so spectacular, that they were entitled to a tremendous amount of respect and wealth. So they embarked on a campaign to sell their aircraft in the United States and throughout Europe, and to freeze out all competition through the vigorous enforcement of all-inclusive patents. In lieu of this they would extract substantial royalties, at least 10 percent, from any who wished to profit from the aviation business in any way, again through the enforcement of their patents.

It almost seems that, as a result of their total fixation on this course of action, they were unaware of the tremendous strides being made in aircraft design by Glenn Curtiss in the United States and by many others in Europe. If they were aware, their response was to pursue the marketing and patent litigation courses even more urgently. But the litigations were not going well. Although they seemed to have some triumphs in the battles in France and the United States, appeals and various other dodging and delaying tactics by their opponents were meeting with success. In Germany all their patents were nullified because of previous disclosures of the technical features of their aircraft.

As a result of all this litigation and related tactics the Wrights made enemies throughout the aviation community worldwide. Even the sentiments of large portions of the interested press and general public were turning against them. Then, with Wilbur's death on the 30th of May, 1912 at the age of 45, any creative spark the Wrights may have had left was gone. By that time they had abandoned every feature of their patented designs except wing warping.

Over the next couple of years the aerodynamic and structural advantages of thicker wings became evident to many designers. But these thicker wing designs could not be twisted or warped. So finally in 1915 after some patent cases had been settled, Orville gave in and began the use of hinged ailerons for roll control. By then none of the design features actually originated by the Wrights were being used in any aircraft, including their own. Although they had won a few battles, their patents had largely become moot. Then, with the looming entry of the United States into World War I, the government forced a permanent settlement. All major aircraft patents were put into a pool from which all could draw, and relatively modest royalties were shared appropriately.

However the Wrights' intransigence had taken its toll on American aviation. At the start of the war the major European countries each had hundreds of aircraft while the U.S. Army had but a handful of unserviceable uncompetitive machines. This was in large part due to the Wrights' patent battles having stifled both academic aviation research and aircraft development in America. Orville had even attempted to sue the U.S. Army for buying some of Curtiss' aircraft.

Finally, in 1915 Orville bought up the majority of outstanding stock in the Wright Company and sold it to a New York holding corporation. A couple years later he and a group of local Dayton investors formed the Dayton Wright Company. However they did not create any significant designs and survived by building English DeHaviland DH-4's under license for the remainder of the war. After that Orville drifted off to tinker in his private Dayton laboratory and enjoy his mansion in southeast Dayton, as well as serving on the board at the NACA (NASA's precursor) for many years. He had amassed a multimillion-dollar fortune from aviation, but he profited mostly from selling the Wright name to companies that capitalized from using it. He died in 1948 after having flown in a four-engined pressurized airliner and witnessing the advent of the jet age.

This book has been written not to criticize the Wright brothers but to set the record straight concerning what they did and why they did it. They made some good decisions and some bad decisions, both in the technical area and in the business world. They adopted the idea that it was crucial to learn how to aerodynamically control an aircraft before adding the complication of power. This proved to be the right way to go, their best decision. They decided to stick close to one design and keep refining it, solving one problem after another rather than making basic changes. This was a questionable decision. They decided that it was worth it to have an airplane that was unstable and difficult to fly all the time in order to avoid occasionally unfavorable characteristics. The rest of the aviation world disagreed, rendering this a bad decision. They believed that through long hard work they had come up with a highly desirable product for which they should be richly rewarded. This was a fair decision. They also thought they had discovered the only way to make an airplane, and if they could keep everyone else from copying theirs, they could charge exorbitant prices for the foreseeable future, a wrong decision. Worst of all, they chose to put their efforts into their various legal wranglings rather than into improving their product until it was too late. This was their most costly decision.

Perhaps the most impressive accomplishment of the Wrights, at least from an engineering standpoint, was learning how to create a balanced and fully integrated design. Through lift-to-drag ratio measurements at Kitty Hawk and lift-to-drag and parasite drag measurements in their wind tunnel, they could accurately calculate the overall drag of their aircraft in level flight based upon the weight it had to lift. They then knew the thrust required from their spinning advancing propellers and could translate that into horsepower needed from an engine. Through rpm and cylinder pressure they could calculate the size engine that was required to propel their airplane. No one before them and none of their contemporaries, at least into 1906, had come close to this degree of understanding and design capability. In fact, I doubt that any other vehicle throughout history—car, boat, train, anything—was initially created with the degree of understanding the Wrights had of their machines. The development of this quantitative and integrated design capability at the birth of manned powered flight is what elevates the Wright brothers above their predecessors and contemporaries, and places them among history's greatest inventors.

But the real story of Wilbur and Orville's contribution to aviation has a strange twist. While their struggle was primarily a technical one, their actual contribution was not. None of the design features they themselves originated proved useful. Instead, whether they liked it or not, their real achievement was to show the world that the time for powered flight had come, man could do it, and those who were willing and able had better get busy. From a technology standpoint, it can be argued that many others deserve much of the credit for the creation of aviation. For instance, many believe that George Cayley contributed more new knowledge to aviation than the Wrights did. But history is partial to human involvement, and the Wrights were the first to put the human into the air, whenever he wanted, going wherever he wanted, for as long as his fuel held out. For this they rightfully deserve the honor.

We should also come away from this story realizing that there are often very fine lines between perseverance and stubbornness, confidence and arrogance, and the desire for compensation and greed. Often these lines delineate the difference between success and failure. Wilbur and Orville trod both sides of these lines, as have many others. As a result, like many others, they experienced both great success and disappointment.

As stated in the Preface some 300 pages earlier, we have no right to expect perfection from the Wrights, nor do we have any obligation to portray their work as such. But you don't have to be perfect to do great things. Their work, as it really stands, is worthy of deep respect and admiration. And the accomplishments of others need not be ignored in order to render the Wrights their due honor.

GLOSSARY
Aviation Terminology

The following aeronautical terms appear in the text. Although some are explained as they appear, it is useful to have them all defined in one location as a quick reference. This also avoids constantly bogging down the story with technical explanations that some readers may not care to endure.

AERODYNAMIC CENTER – The point about which the pitching moment of the airplane will stay constant with small changes in its angle of attack. (This simplifies stability calculations.)

AILERON – Moveable hinged panels on the aft outer portions of wings, which deflect opposite of each other to create or control roll, or sideways tilt, of an airplane.

ANGLE OF ATTACK – The angle between a line going straight back from the front edge to the aft edge of a wing, and the direction of flight (or the oncoming airflow).

ANHEDRAL – The angle at which a wing is bent down from straight across as viewed from ahead or behind. (The tips are lower than the middle of the wing in level flight).

ASPECT RATIO – The span of a wing from tip to tip, divided by the average distance from the front edge to the aft edge of the wing (the average chord). It is actually calculated by dividing the square of the wing span by the planform area of the wing.

BIPLANE – An aircraft with two main lifting wings, one above the other.

CAMBER – The curvature or arch of a wing surface from front to rear, as viewed from an end or tip. It's value is often measured as a percentage of the chord, positive up, at the maximum distance of the wing's mid-thickness line from the straight chord line.

CANARD – A horizontal surface placed in front of the main wing(s). When deflected it causes up or down movement (pitch) of the aircraft's nose.

CENTER OF PRESSURE – The point on an airfoil or wing through which the lift and drag can be considered acting without generating a rotating moment. (I.e., it's angle of attack balances there.)

CHORD – The straight line or distance from the front edge to the back or aft edge of a wing or control surface.

DIHEDRAL – The angle at which a wing is bent up from straight across as viewed from ahead or behind. (The tips are higher than the middle of the wing in level flight.)

DOWNWASH – The overall downward motion of air all around, and particularly behind, a lifting wing as it moves through the air.

ELEVATOR – A horizontal surface at the front or rear of an airplane that deflects up or down to point the aircraft's nose up or down (change pitch) in flight.

FLOW SEPARATION – The tendency for air, under some conditions, to not closely follow the shape of a wing or other body as it moves through the air.

GLIDE RATIO – The distance a gliding airplane moves forward divided by the distance it comes down in a given time.

LIFT-TO-DRAG RATIO – The amount of weight an airplane or wing can lift divided by the resistance force to its motion through the air.

MONOPLANE – An airplane with one main lifting wing.

NEUTRAL POINT – The point at which a flying aircraft could have its center of gravity located and it would not try to pitch up or down. It would be neutrally stable in pitch.

PITCH – The movement of an aircraft's nose (or tail) up or down.

PLANFORM – The shape of a wing when viewed from directly above or below.

PUSHER PROPELLERS – Propellers mounted behind the main lifting wing(s).

ROLL – Tilting of an aircraft to one side or the other.

RUDDER – A vertical surface, usually at the rear of an airplane, that can be deflected to the right or left to move the nose toward the right or left.

STABILIZER – A fixed surface that tends to keep an airplane flying straight and level.

STATIC MARGIN – The distance along the mean chord of a wing from the neutral point forward to the aircraft's center of gravity. (Can be negative if the center of gravity is behind the neutral point.) It is a measure of how stable an airplane is. Positive is stable, negative unstable. It is usually expressed as a decimal fraction or percentage of the chord length.

TANDEM WING – An airplane with two sets of wings, one behind the other.

TRACTOR PROPELLERS – Propellers located ahead of the main lifting wings.

WARPING – Twisting the extremities of a flexible wing in opposite directions to cause the airplane to roll toward one side, or to swing its nose left or right.

WINGLETS – Separate, small horizontal panels near the tips of wings, which move up or down opposite of each other to cause the airplane to roll toward one side.

WING LOADING – The weight a wing can or is lifting divided by its area.

WING SECTION – The total shape of the top and bottom surfaces on a wing, seen as if a vertical slice were taken from the front edge straight back to the aft edge.

YAW – The movement of an aircraft's nose or tail toward the right or left.

APPENDIX 1

Very Slow Flight

Many airplane people are aware that at supersonic flight speeds aircraft handle somewhat differently. But much less appreciated is that at extremely slow flight speeds aircraft also can behave much differently than one might normally expect. Depending upon the size and shape of the airplane, these slow speed effects begin well under 100 miles per hour and thus are seldom encountered. However early Wright Flyers and gliders flew at 20 to 35 miles per hour and consequently were well within the low speed region of concern. Indeed, this, and the choice of wing warping, were the causes of some of the Wrights' biggest problems.

When the Wrights tested their 1899 device and 1900 and 1901 gliders they usually flew them like kites with the wing tips tied or tethered to operators on the ground. So although the vehicles could roll from side to side and bob up and down in pitch somewhat, they could not yaw or change direction. Under this condition the wing warping roll control appeared to be working fine. But when glided free of constraints, as wing warping was applied to bring a tilted aircraft back level, although the wing getting more angle of attack initially increased its lift, it acquired an even larger increase in drag. Lift is directly proportional to angle of attack, but drag has a parabolic relationship to angle of attack. That is, drag increased more nearly as the square of the increase in angle of attack. An example of this situation is depicted in Figure 60.

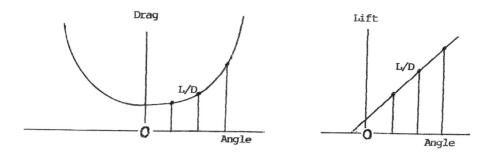

Figure 60: Drag and Lift Versus Angle of Attack (Typical)

An aircraft is typically operated at an angle of attack that will give it as much lift as possible without getting past the angle at which drag increases greatly. This is shown on both the lift and drag curves as the point L/D. That is the region where the Wrights typically would have flown their gliders. The other points show where the outer portions of the wings would be operating under warped conditions, one side at the higher points, and the other at the lower points. Looking at the lift curve, it appears that, in this example, while one end would lose about 30% in lift due to its reduced angle of attack, the other would gain another 30% in lift due to its increased angle, resulting in the outer portion of the higher angled side having about twice the lift of the other.

But looking at the drag curve, and remembering that the Wrights were trying to bring an already tilted aircraft back level, we see that while the drag on the higher wing with the lower angle has gone down a little, the drag on the other wing has nearly doubled. Early Wright gliders had no vertical stabilizers or rudders, and thus no directional stability or control. So this effect placed a strong turning moment on the Wrights' aircraft about their vertical axes, and they immediately began turning or yawing toward the lower, higher angled, higher drag wing at an accelerating rate. Very soon the higher angle of attack wing was flying substantially slower than the one with the lower angle. Since both lift and drag are also proportional to the square of flight speed, the lower and slower wing was then producing less lift than the other even though it was at a higher angle. (In some cases, early Wright gliders could end up with the downward warped wing essentially stopped and generating no lift at all.) Thus the airplane rolled further into the low wing and the effect of the Wrights' roll control was reversed. If continued, it would bank and turn further until the plane spun into the sand, what the Wrights called "well digging".

At modern flight speeds the difference in outer wing speeds because of yaw or turn rate is insignificant compared to the overall speed of the craft. But at the slow speeds the Wrights flew they are quite comparable. That is why the Wrights had to confront this problem while few modern airplanes would be affected by it.

Some actual numerical examples will illustrate the point. Although the mathematics in these examples are not presented in step-by-step detail, they can be verified easily enough. Consider an airplane with a moderate yaw rate of 30 degrees per second. You can see how slow this is by taking three full seconds to rotate your hand from pointing straight ahead to sideways. At this yaw rate, their 1901 glider, with a wingspan of over 22 feet and a flight speed of just over 20 miles per hour, would have one wing tip going nearly 50% faster than the other. Even at half the angle of attack, the faster tip would have 11 percent more lift than the slower one. So even though it is at twice the angle, the slower wing would drop farther.

Considering their 1902 glider with a 30-foot wingspan flying at about 25 miles per hour with the same slow yaw rate, the faster tip would be going nearly 55% faster than the slower one. Squaring this ratio, and allowing the faster wing only half the angle of attack, it would still be developing nearly 20% more lift than the one with the higher angle. Again the aircraft would roll farther into the lower wing even though it had a higher angle of attack. And don't forget, the anhedral in the Wright vehicles accelerated this adverse roll even more. As previously mentioned, with such a low flight speed and a substantial yaw rate, the receding high-angled wing tip could be nearly stopped.

To show how peculiar this effect is to low flight speed, consider the 1903 Flyer if it could have gone 100 miles per hour. With a 40-foot span, a 147 foot per second speed, and even a 45-degree-per-second yaw rate, one finds that this time, the faster wing develops only about 3/4 the lift of the slower wing, which has the higher angle of attack. So now the aircraft would roll toward the higher wing that is at a reduced angle, as intended.

This was a problem the Wrights grappled with for over two years, finally overcoming it with their coordinated rudder. But it seems a shame that they had to put so much effort into coping with a problem that could have been largely avoided with the use of ailerons, or totally avoided with the use of separate winglets. Ailerons generate much less drag asymmetry since only a small flap at the trailing edge is moved rather than the whole wing. And since winglets operate by turning one up and one down from a level or trimmed position, they can be set to generate no drag asymmetry whatsoever. Both these devices had been documented before the Wrights began.

The truly unfortunate aspect of this problem was that, for the Wrights, it never really went away until 1915. After disconnecting the rudder from wing warping in 1905 in order to be able to turn the aircraft, the rudder had to be deflected manually in order to cope with the warping reversal problem. This required extra vigilance and actions by pilots, contributing to the consensus that their planes were trickier to fly than others, and consequently less desirable.

Ironically, for the past 20 years aeronautical engineers have been reconsidering wing warping for high speed airplanes because of the possibility of weight, drag, and maintenance reductions. These schemes would bend flexible outer portions of wings near their trailing edges, possibly through the use of piezoelectric panels that bend when an electric current is applied. Some like to say that this research indicates that the Wrights had it right all along. However such a development, if it ever occurred, would be possible only because of today's automatic electronic controls and higher flight speeds, and would in no way validate the use of wing warping at the beginning of the twentieth century.

APPENDIX 2

Ground Effect

The ground effect is a phenomenon whereby airplanes flying extremely close to the ground experience a substantial reduction in drag. When a wing is producing lift in free flight with no boundaries such as the ground nearby, there is a very strong downwash of air behind the wing. In fact, from a reaction or momentum standpoint, it's a fair statement to say that airplanes fly by blowing air down. In subsonic flight, viscosity (the tendency of air to stick to, or pull on, itself) causes this downward motion of the air to feed forward creating an underlying downward motion to the air all around the wing. In free flight a wing must be set at an increased angle of attack that will generate the lift required to sustain the vehicle's weight with the wing immersed within this downward flowing air. The increased angle of attack creates more drag, essentially the *induced drag.*

But when a plane is very near the ground the air can't flow downward, and it remains, one might say, more solidly in place as the wing goes by. Consequently, the wing can then generate the required lift at a lesser angle of attack relative to the ground. At this lesser angle, the wing creates less drag. The two situations are depicted in Figure 61.

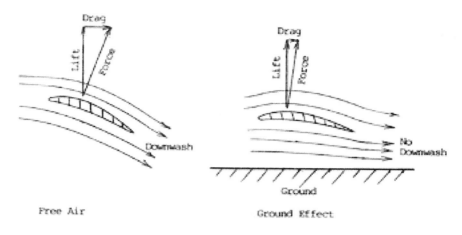

Figure 61: The Ground Effect

Many engineers and pilots like to picture the ground effect as a cushion of air that pushes up on the wings and gives them more lift. But that is a pointless concept since the airplane doesn't need more lift. So what pilots do is slow down when landing, or push the nose down to get rid of the extra lift. And when they do, they lower the angle of attack reducing the aircraft's drag as stated before. This is precisely what pelicans do when they glide for seemingly endless periods of time within inches of the water's surface. They know they can go twice as far without flapping by staying this low.

The Wrights had an unprecedented capability to accurately calculate the power their aircraft needed to overcome drag and fly. But they apparently had no awareness of the ground effect, so they didn't know they had done all their flying (until 1905) in this unusually low drag environment. Since they didn't account for this, or for the acceleration needed for takeoff, their 1903 and 1904 aircraft didn't have the power to climb out of ground effect.

How high can the ground effect be effective? Usually up to a height of from about three times the wing chord to roughly the span of the wing. It depends upon the size and aspect ratio of the wing more than anything else. So it is evident that the Wrights didn't get completely out of the ground effect until they were able to exceed about 40 feet of altitude, which was in 1905.

The Wright brothers were not the only airplane builders who had trouble getting out of the ground effect. There may well have been a more modern and quite famous example. Many engineers believe that the Hughes H-4 Hercules, better known as the "Spruce Goose," was at least a borderline example of such a craft. With a projected maximum takeoff weight of over 400,000 pounds and about 24,000 aggregate horsepower, there is no question that the vehicle was underpowered. Although its chief designer quoted a service ceiling of 20,000 feet, it was only taken to an altitude of about 30 feet off of the water on its single flight, which lasted less than a minute. Only Howard Hughes, the pilot, knew if it could have gotten higher.

Of course, modern-day 747s with more than three times the power and the same weight have no problem. But a more fair comparison would be a contemporary aircraft of about the same weight, namely the Convair B-36. With nearly 30 percent more power and much less drag, a loaded B-36 could only generate a speed in the vertical direction of about 18 miles per hour.

The Hercules was never flown again, Hughes claiming there was no point to it since, with the cessation of war, the government was no longer interested. But Howard seemed like the kind of guy who would have insisted on proving that his vision was correct, if at all possible. So there remain those who believe that the master showman had fooled the world into believing that the H-4 was a fully capable aircraft when in fact it couldn't have flown out of ground effect with any substantial load, if at all.

Sources for References

1. Marvin W. McFarland. 1953. *The Papers of Wilbur and Orville Wright.* New York: McGraw-Hill.
2. Fred C. Kelley, ed. 1953. *How We Invented the Airplane.* New York: Dover Publications. Includes: Orville Wright. 1920. *How We Invented the Airplane.* Legal Deposition. Orville Wright. 1919. *After the First Flights.* Legal Paper. Wilbur and Orville Wright. 1908. *The Wright Brothers' Aeroplane.* Washington, D.C.: The Century Magazine, Vol LXXVI, No. 5.
3. Howard S. Wolko, ed. 1967. *The Wright Flyer, An Engineering Perspective.* Washington, D.C.: Smithsonian Institution Press. Includes: John D. Anderson Jr. *Th e Wright Brothers: The First True Aeronautical Engineers.* F.E.C. Culick and Henry R. Jex. *Aerodynamics, Stability, and Control of the 1903 Wright Flyer.* Fredrick J. Hooven. *Longitudinal Dynamics of the Wright Brothers' Early Flyers.* Harvey H. Lippincott . *Propulsion Systems of the Wright Brothers.* Howard S. Wolko. *Structural Design of the 1903 Wright Flyer.*
4. Wright, Orville, and Wilbur Wright. 1904. United States Patent No. 821,393, Washington, D.C., 1906.
5. Wright, Orville, and Wilbur Wright. 1908. United States Patent No. 987,662, Washington, D.C., 1911.
6. Sir George Cayley. 1809. *On Aerial Navigation: Nicholson's Journal of Natural Philosophy, Chemistry, and the Arts,* November, 1809, February, 1810, and March, 1810.
7. Lawrence Pritchard. 1962. *Sir George Cayley – Inventor of the Airplane.* New York: Horizon Press.

8. Octave Chanute. 1894. *Progress in Flying Machines*; A compilation of articles from 1891 to 1894. Long Beach, California, 1976: Lorenz and Herweg.

9. Otto and Gustav Lilienthal.1889. *Birdflight as the Basis of Aviation*. Hummelstown, Pennsylvania, 2001: Markowski.

10. Philip Jarrett. 1987. *Another Icarus – Percy Pilcher and the Quest for Flight*. Washington, D.C.: Smithsonian Institution Press.

11. Smithsonian National Air and Space Museum. 1989. *Milestones of Aviation*. New York: Hugh Lanter Levin Associates.

12. Donald S. Lopez. 1995. *Smithsonian Guides – Aviation*. New York: Simon and Schuster.

13. Walter J. Boyne. 1996. *The Smithsonian Book of Flight*. Washington, D.C.: Smithsonian Institution Press.

14. Tom Crouch and Peter Jacob. 2003. *The Wright Brothers and the Invention of the Aerial Age*. Washington, D.C.: The National Geographic Society.

15. Christopher Chant. 1978. *Aviation – An Illustrated History*. London, England: Orbis Publishing.

16. Michel Taylor and David Mondey. 1983. *Milestones of Flight*. London, England: Janes.

17. The Editors of American Heritage. 1962. *The American Heritage History of Flight*. New York: Simon and Shuster.

18. Ben Mackworth-Praed. 1990. *Aviation – The Pioneer Years*. London, England: Studio Editions Ltd.

19. C.H. Hildreth and Bernard C. Nalty. 1969. *1001 Questions Answered About Aviation History*. New York: Dodd, Mead, and Company.

20. Arch Whitehouse.1965. *The Early Birds*. New York: Doubleday and Company.

21. Seth Shulman. 2002. *Unlocking the Sky*. New York: Harper-Collins.

22. John Blake. 1984. *Early Airplanes*. London, England: Camden House Books, Purnell and Sons.

23. Valerie Moolman. 1980. *The Road to Kitty Hawk*. Alexandria, Virginia: Time-Life Books.

24. Sherwood Harris. 1970. *The First to Fly*. New York: Simon and Schuster.

25. John Walsh. 1975. *One Day at Kitty Hawk*. New York: Thomas Y. Crowell and Company.

26. Fred C. Kelly. 1989. *The Wright Brothers, A Biography*. New York: Dover Publishing Inc.

27. Grover Loening. 1935. *Our Wings Grow Faster*. New York: Doubleday Publishing.
28. *Wings of Madness*. 2009. Documentary Film: PBS.ORG.
29. Joe Gertler. 2003. *Flight Journal*, December 2003. Wilton, Connecticut: Air Age Publishing.
30. Curtis Pendergast. 1981. *The First Aviators*. Alexandria, Virginia: Time-Life Books.
31. Dee Richard. 2007. *The Man who Discovered Flight: George Cayley and the First Airplane*. Toronto, Canada: McClelland and Stewart.
32. W.J. Jackman and Thomas H. Russell. 1910. *Flying Machines: Construction and Operation*. Chicago, Illinois: Charles C. Thompson.
33. Phil Scott, ed. 1995. *The Shoulders of Giants*. Reading, Massachusetts: Addison-Wesley Publications.
34. Peter L. Jakab. 1990. *Visions of a Flying Machine*. Washington, D.C.: Smithsonian Institution Press.
35. Tom D. Crouch. 2003. *Wings: A History of Aviation from Kites to the Space Age*. New York: W.W. Norton and Company.
36. 1909. *The Automobile* Magazine, September 30, 1909. New York: Class Journal Company.
37. James Means (ed). 1895. *The Aeronautical Annual*. Hummelstown, PA: Markowski International Publishers.
38. James Means (ed). 1896. *The Aeronautical Annual*. Hummelstown, PA: Markowski International Publishers.
39. James Means (ed). 1897. *The Aeronautical Annual*. Hummelstown, PA: Markowski International Publishers.
40. James Tobin. 2003. *To Conquer the Air*. New York, New York: Simon and Schuster, Free Press.
41. John D. Anderson Jr. 1997. *A History of Aerodynamics*. Cambridge, New York: Cambridge University Press.
42. John D. Anderson Jr. 2002. *The Airplane, A History of its Technology*. Reston, Virginia: American Institute of Aeronautics and Astronautics.
43. James Head. 2008 *Warped Wings*. Mustang, Oklahoma: Tate Publishing and Enterprises.

Made in the USA
Middletown, DE
22 June 2023

33238630R00195